The Tempting of Tavernake

E. Phillips Oppenheim

Table of Contents

BOOK ONE

CHAPTER I. DESPAIR AND INTEREST

They stood upon the roof of a London boarding-house in the neighborhood of Russell Square—one of those grim shelters, the refuge of Transatlantic curiosity and British penury. The girl —she represented the former race was leaning against the frail palisading, with gloomy expression and eyes set as though in fixed contemplation of the uninspiring panorama. The young man—unmistakably, uncompromisingly English—stood with his back to the chimney a few feet away, watching his companion. The silence between them was as yet unbroken, had lasted, indeed, since she had stolen away from the shabby drawing-room below, where a florid lady with a raucous voice had been shouting a music-hall ditty. Close upon her heels, but without speech of any sort, he had followed. They were almost strangers, except for the occasional word or two of greeting which the etiquette of the establishment demanded. Yet she had accepted his espionage without any protest of word or look. He had followed her with a very definite object. Had she surmised it, he wondered? She had not turned her head or vouchsafed even a single question or remark to him since he had pushed his way through the trap-door almost at her heels and stepped out on to the leads. Yet it seemed to him that she must guess.

Below them, what seemed to be the phantasm of a painted city, a wilderness of housetops, of smoke-wreathed spires and chimneys, stretched away to a murky, blood-red horizon. Even as they stood there, a deeper color stained the sky, an angry sun began to sink into the piled up masses of thick, vaporous clouds. The girl watched with an air of sullen yet absorbed interest. Her companion's eyes were still fixed wholly and critically upon her. Who was she, he wondered? Why had she left her own country to come to a city where she seemed to have no friends, no manner of interest? In that caravansary of the world's stricken ones she had been an almost unnoticed figure, silent, indisposed for conversation, not in any obvious manner attractive. Her clothes, notwithstanding their air of having come from a first-class dressmaker, were shabby and out of fashion, their extreme neatness in itself pathetic. She was thin, yet not without a certain buoyant lightness of movement always at variance with her tired eyes, her ceaseless air of dejection. And withal she was a rebel. It was written in her attitude, it was evident in her lowering, militant expression, the smouldering fire in her eyes proclaimed it. Her long, rather narrow face was gripped between her hands; her elbows rested upon the brick parapet. She gazed at that world of blood-red mists, of unshapely, grotesque buildings, of strange, tawdry colors; she listened to the medley of sounds— crude, shrill, insistent, something like the groaning of a world stripped naked—and she had all the time the air of one who hates the thing she looks upon.

Tavernake, whose curiosity concerning his companion remained unappeased, decided that the moment for speech had arrived. He took a step forward upon the soft, pulpy leads. Even then he hesitated before he finally committed himself. About his appearance little was remarkable save the general air of determination which gave character to his undistinguished features. He was something above the medium height, broad-set, and with rather more thick black hair than he knew how to arrange advantageously. He wore a shirt which was somewhat frayed, and an indifferent tie; his boots were heavy and clumsy; he wore also a suit of ready-made clothes with the air of one who knew that they were ready-made and was satisfied with them. People of a nervous or sensitive disposition would, without doubt, have found him irritating but for a certain nameless gift— an almost Napoleonic concentration upon the things of the passing moment, which was in itself impressive and which somehow disarmed criticism.

"About that bracelet!" he said at last.

She moved her head and looked at him. A young man of less assurance would have turned and fled. Not so Tavernake.

Once sure of his ground he was immovable. There was murder in her eyes but he was not even disturbed.

"I saw you take it from the little table by the piano, you know," he continued. "It was rather a rash thing to do. Mrs. Fitzgerald was looking for it before I reached the stairs. I expect she has called the police in by now."

Slowly her hand stole into the depths of her pocket and emerged. Something flashed for a moment high over her head. The young man caught her wrist just in time, caught it in a veritable grip of iron. Then, indeed, the evil fires flashed from her eyes, her teeth gleamed white, her bosom rose and fell in a storm of angry, unuttered sobs. She was dry-eyed and still speechless, but for all that she was a tigress. A strangely-cut silhouette they formed there upon the housetops, with a background of empty sky, their feet sinking in the warm leads.

"I think I had better take it," he said. "Let go."

Her fingers yielded the bracelet—a tawdry, ill-designed affair of rubies and diamonds. He looked at it disapprovingly.

"That's an ugly thing to go to prison for," he remarked, slipping it into his pocket. "It was a stupid thing to do, anyhow, you know. You couldn't have got away with it—unless," he added, looking over the parapet as though struck with a sudden idea, "unless you had a confederate below."

He heard the rush of her skirts and he was only just in time. Nothing, in fact, but a considerable amount of presence of mind and the full exercise of a strength which was continually providing surprises for his acquaintances, was sufficient to save her. Their struggles upon the very edge of the roof dislodged a brick from the palisading, which went hurtling down into the street. They both paused to watch it, his arms still gripping her and one foot pressed against an iron rod. It was immediately after they had seen it pitch harmlessly into the road that a new sensation came to this phlegmatic young man. For the first time in his life, he realized that it was possible to feel a certain pleasurable emotion in the close grasp of a being of the opposite sex. Consequently, although she had now ceased to struggle, he kept his arms locked around her, looking into her face with an interest intense enough, but more analytical than emotional, as though seeking to discover the meaning of this curious throbbing of his pulses. She herself, as though exhausted, remained quite passive, shivering a little in his grasp and breathing like a hunted animal whose last hour has come. Their eyes met; then she tore herself away.

"You are a hateful person," she said deliberately, "a hateful, interfering person. I detest you."

"I think that we will go down now," he replied.

He raised the trap-door and glanced at her significantly. She held her skirts closely together and passed through it without looking at him. She stepped lightly down the ladder and without hesitation descended also a flight of uncarpeted attic stairs. Here, however, upon the landing, she awaited him with obvious reluctance.

"Are you going to send for the police?" she asked without looking at him.

"No," he answered.

"Why not?"

"If I had meant to give you away I should have told Mrs. Fitzgerald at once that I had seen you take her bracelet, instead of following you out on to the roof."

"Do you mind telling me what you do propose to do, then?" she continued still without looking at him, still without the slightest note of appeal in her tone.

He withdrew the bracelet from his pocket and balanced it upon his finger.

"I am going to say that I took it for a joke," he declared.

She hesitated.

"Mrs. Fitzgerald's sense of humor is not elastic," she warned him.

"She will be very angry, of course," he assented, "but she will not believe that I meant to steal it."

The girl moved slowly a few steps away.

"I suppose that I ought to thank you," she said, still with averted face and sullen manner. "You have really been very decent. I am much obliged."

"Are you not coming down?" he asked.

"Not at present," she answered. "I am going to my room."

He looked around the landing on which they stood, at the miserable, uncarpeted floor, the ill-painted doors on which the long-forgotten varnish stood out in blisters, the jumble of dilapidated hot-water cans, a mop, and a medley of brooms and rags all thrown down together in a corner.

"But these are the servants' quarters, surely," he remarked.

"They are good enough for me; my room is here," she told him, turning the handle of one of the doors and disappearing. The prompt turning of the key sounded, he thought, a little ungracious.

With the bracelet in his hand, Tavernake descended three more flights of stairs and entered the drawing-room of the private hotel conducted by Mrs. Raithby Lawrence, whose husband, one learned from her frequent reiteration of the fact, had once occupied a distinguished post in the Merchant Service of his country. The disturbance following upon the disappearance of the bracelet was evidently at its height. There were at least a dozen people in the room, most of whom were standing up. The central figure of them all was Mrs. Fitzgerald, large and florid, whose yellow hair with its varied shades frankly admitted its indebtedness to peroxide; a lady of the dashing type, who had once made her mark in the music-halls, but was now happily married to a commercial traveler who was seldom visible. Mrs. Fitzgerald was talking.

"In respectable boarding-houses, Mrs. Lawrence," she declared with great emphasis, "thefts may sometimes take place, I will admit, in the servants' quarters, and with all their temptations, poor things, it's not so much to be wondered at. But no such thing as this has ever happened to me before—to have jewelry taken almost from my person in the drawing-room of what should be a well-conducted establishment. Not a servant in the room, remember, from the moment I took it off until I got up from the piano and found it missing. It's your guests you've got to look after, Mrs. Lawrence, sorry to say it though I am."

Mrs. Lawrence managed here, through sheer loss of breath on the part of her assailant, to interpose a tearful protest.

"I am quite sure," she protested feebly, "that there is not a person in this house who would dream of stealing anything, however valuable it was. I am most particular always about references."

"Valuable, indeed!" Mrs. Fitzgerald continued with increased volubility. "I'd have you understand that I am not one of those who wear trumpery jewelry. Thirty-five guineas that bracelet cost me if it cost a penny, and if my husband were only at home I could show you the receipt."

Then there came an interruption of almost tragical interest. Mrs. Fitzgerald, her mouth still open, her stream of eloquence suddenly arrested, stood with her artificially darkened eyes riveted upon the stolid, self-composed figure in the doorway. Every one else was gazing in the same direction. Tavernake was holding the bracelet in the palm of his hand.

"Thirty-five guineas!" he repeated. "If I had known that it was worth as much as that, I do not think that I should have dared to touch it."

"You—you took it!" Mrs. Fitzgerald gasped.

"I am afraid," he admitted, "that it was rather a clumsy joke. I apologize, Mrs. Fitzgerald. I hope you did not really imagine that it had been stolen."

One was conscious of the little thrill of emotion which marked the termination of the episode. Most of the people not directly concerned were disappointed; they were being robbed of their excitement, their hopes of a tragical denouement were frustrated. Mrs. Lawrence's worn face plainly showed her relief. The lady with the yellow hair, on the other hand, who had now succeeded in working herself up into a towering rage, snatched the bracelet from the young man's fingers and with a purple flush in her cheeks was obviously struggling with an intense desire to box his ears.

"That's not good enough for a tale!" she exclaimed harshly. "I tell you I don't believe a word of it. Took it for a joke, indeed! I only wish my husband were here; he'd know what to do."

"Your husband couldn't do much more than get your bracelet back, ma'am," Mrs. Lawrence replied with acerbity. "Such a fuss and calling every one thieves, too! I'd be ashamed to be so suspicious."

Mrs. Fitzgerald glared haughtily at her hostess.

"It's all very well for those that don't possess any jewelry and don't know the value of it, to talk," she declared, with her eyes fixed upon a black jet ornament which hung from the other woman's neck. "What I say is this, and you may just as well hear it from me now as later. I don't believe this cock-and-bull story of Mr. Tavernake's. Them as took my bracelet from that table meant keeping it, only they hadn't the courage. And I'm not referring to you, Mr. Tavernake," the lady continued vigorously, "because I don't believe you took it, for all your talk about a joke. And whom you may be shielding it wouldn't take me two guesses to name, and your motive must be clear to every one. The common hussy!"

"You are exciting yourself unnecessarily, Mrs. Fitzgerald," Tavernake remarked. "Let me assure you that it was I who took your bracelet from that table."

Mrs. Fitzgerald regarded him scornfully.

"Do you expect me to believe a tale like that?" she demanded.

"Why not?" Tavernake replied. "It is the truth. I am sorry that you have been so upset—"

"It is not the truth!"

More sensation! Another unexpected entrance! Once more interest in the affair was revived. After all, the lookers-on felt that they were not to be robbed of their tragedy. An old lady with yellow cheeks and jet black eyes leaned forward with her hand to her ear, anxious not to miss a syllable of what was coming. Tavernake bit his lip; it was the girl from the roof who had entered the room.

"I have no doubt," she continued in a cool, clear tone, "that Mrs. Fitzgerald's first guess would have been correct. I took the bracelet. I did not take it for a joke, I did not take it because I admire it—I think it is hideously ugly. I took it because I had no money."

She paused and looked around at them all, quietly, yet with something in her face from which they all shrank. She stood where the light fell full upon her shabby black gown and dejected-looking hat. The hollows in her pale cheeks, and the faint rims under her eyes, were clearly manifest; but notwithstanding her fragile appearance, she held herself with composure and even dignity. Twenty—thirty seconds must have passed whilst she stood there, slowly finishing the buttoning of her gloves. No one attempted to break the silence. She dominated them all—they felt that she had something more to say. Even Mrs. Fitzgerald felt a weight upon her tongue.

"It was a clumsy attempt," she went on. "I should have had no idea where to raise money upon the thing, but I apologize to you, nevertheless, Mrs. Fitzgerald, for the anxiety which my removal of your valuable property must have caused you," she added, turning to the owner of the bracelet, whose cheeks were once more hot with anger at the contempt in the girl's tone. "I suppose I ought to thank you, Mr. Tavernake, also, for your well-meant effort to preserve my character. In future, that shall be my sole charge. Has any one anything more to say to me before I go?"

Somehow or other, no one had. Mrs. Fitzgerald was irritated and fuming, but she contented herself with a snort. Her speech was ready enough as a rule, but there was a look in this girl's eyes from which she was glad enough to turn away. Mrs. Lawrence made a weak attempt at a farewell.

"I am sure," she began, "we are all sorry for what's occurred and that you must go—not that perhaps it isn't better, under the circumstances," she added hastily. "As regards—"

"There is nothing owing to you," the girl interrupted calmly. "You may congratulate yourself upon that, for if there were you would not get it. Nor have I stolen anything else."

"About your luggage?" Mrs. Lawrence asked.

"When I need it, I will send for it," the girl replied.

She turned her back upon them and before they realized it she was gone. She had, indeed, something of the grand manner. She had come to plead guilty to a theft and she had left them all feeling a little like snubbed children. Mrs. Fitzgerald, as soon as the spell of the girl's presence was removed, was one of the first to recover herself. She felt herself beginning to grow hot with renewed indignation.

"A thief!" she exclaimed looking around the room. "Just an ordinary self-convicted thief! That's what I call her, and nothing else. And here we all stood like a lot of ninnies. Why, if I'd done my duty I'd have locked the door and sent for a policeman."

"Too late now, anyway," Mrs. Lawrence declared. "She's gone for good, and no mistake. Walked right out of the house. I heard her slam the front door."

"And a good job, too," Mrs. Fitzgerald armed. "We don't

want any of her sort here—not those who've got things of value about them. I bet she didn't leave America for nothing."

A little gray-haired lady, who had not as yet spoken, and who very seldom took part in any discussion at all, looked up from her knitting. She was desperately poor but she had charitable instincts.

"I wonder what made her want to steal," she remarked quietly.

"A born thief," Mrs. Fitzgerald declared with conviction, —"a real bad lot. One of your sly-looking ones, I call her."

The little lady sighed.

"When I was better off," she continued, "I used to help at a soup kitchen in Poplar. I have never forgotten a certain look we used to see occasionally in the faces of some of the men and women. I found out what it meant—it was hunger. Once or twice lately I have passed the girl who has just gone out, upon the stairs, and she almost frightened me. She had just the same look in her eyes. I noticed it yesterday—it was just before dinner, too—but she never came down."

"She paid so much for her room and extra for meals," Mrs. Lawrence said thoughtfully. "She never would have a meal unless she paid for it at the time. To tell you the truth, I was feeling a bit uneasy about her. She hasn't been in the dining-room for two days, and from what they tell me there's no signs of her having eaten anything in her room. As for getting anything out, why should she? It would be cheaper for her here than anywhere, if she'd got any money at all."

There was an uncomfortable silence. The little old lady with the knitting looked down the street into the sultry darkness which had swallowed up the girl.

"I wonder whether Mr. Tavernake knows anything about her," some one suggested.

But Tavernake was not in the room.

CHAPTER II. A TETE-A-TETE SUPPER

Tavernake caught her up in New Oxford Street and fell at once into step with her. He wasted no time whatever upon preliminaries.

"I should be glad," he said, "if you would tell me your name."

Her first glance at him was fierce enough to have terrified a different sort of man. Upon Tavernake it had absolutely no effect.

"You need not unless you like, of course," he went on, "but I wish to talk to you for a few moments and I thought that it would be more convenient if I addressed you by name. I do not remember to have heard it mentioned at Blenheim House, and Mrs. Lawrence, as you know, does not introduce her guests."

By this time they had walked a score or so of paces together. The girl, after her first furious glance, had taken absolutely no notice of him except to quicken her pace a little. Tavernake remained by her side, however, showing not the slightest sense of embarrassment or annoyance. He seemed perfectly content to wait and he had not in the least the appearance of a man who could be easily shaken off. From a fit of furious anger she passed suddenly and without warning to a state of half hysterical amusement.

"You are a foolish, absurd person," she declared. "Please go away. I do not wish you to walk with me."

Tavernake remained imperturbable. She remembered suddenly his intervention on her behalf.

"If you insist upon knowing," she said, "my name at Blenheim House was Beatrice Burnay. I am much obliged to you for what you did for me there, but that is finished. I do not wish to have any conversation with you, and I absolutely object to your company. Please leave me at once."

"I am sorry," he answered, "but that is not possible."

"Not possible?" she repeated, wonderingly.

He shook his head.

"You have no money, you have eaten no dinner, and I do not believe that you have any idea where you are going," he declared, deliberately.

Her face was once more dark with anger.

"Even if that were the truth," she insisted, "tell me what concern it is of yours? Your reminding me of these facts is simply an impertinence."

"I am sorry that you look upon it in that light," he remarked, still without the least sign of discomposure. "We will, if you do not mind, waive the discussion for the moment. Do you prefer a small restaurant or a corner in a big one? There is music at Frascati's but there are not so many people in the smaller ones."

She turned half around upon the pavement and looked at him steadfastly. His personality was at last beginning to interest her. His square jaw and measured speech were indices of a character at least unusual. She recognized certain invincible qualities under an exterior absolutely commonplace.

"Are you as persistent about everything in life?" she asked him.

"Why not?" he replied. "I try always to be consistent."

"What is your name?"

"Leonard Tavernake," he answered, promptly.

"Are you well off—I mean moderately well off?"

"I have a quite sufficient income."

"Have you any one dependent upon you?"

"Not a soul," he declared. "I am my own master in every sense of the word."

She laughed in an odd sort of way.

"Then you shall pay for your persistence," she said,—"I mean that I may as well rob you of a sovereign as the restaurant people."

"You must tell me now where you would like to go to," he insisted. "It is getting late."

"I do not like these foreign places," she replied. "I should prefer to go to the grill-room of a good restaurant."

"We will take a taxicab," he announced. "You have no objection?"

She shrugged her shoulders.

"If you have the money and don't mind spending it," she said, "I will admit that I have had all the walking I want. Besides, the toe of my boot is worn through and I find it painful. Yesterday I tramped ten miles trying to find a man who was getting up a concert party for the provinces."

"And did you find him?" he asked, hailing a cab.

"Yes, I found him," she answered, indifferently. "We went through the usual programme. He heard me sing, tried to kiss me and promised to let me know. Nobody ever refuses anything in my profession, you see. They promise to let you know."

"Are you a singer, then, or an actress?"

"I am neither," she told him. "I said 'my profession' because it is the only one to which I have ever tried to belong. I have never succeeded in obtaining an engagement in this country. I do not suppose that even if I had persevered I should ever have had one."

"You have given up the idea, then," he remarked.

"I have given it up," she admitted, a little curtly. "Please do not think, because I am allowing you to be my companion for a short time, that you may ask me questions. How fast these taxies go!"

They drew up at their destination—a well-known restaurant in Regent Street. He paid the cabman and they descended a flight of stairs into the grill-room.

"I hope that this place will suit you," he said. "I have not much experience of restaurants."

She looked around and nodded.

"Yes," she replied, "I think that it will do."

She was very shabbily dressed, and he, although his appearance was by no means ordinary, was certainly not of the type which inspires immediate respect in even the grill-room of a fashionable restaurant. Nevertheless, they received prompt and almost officious service. Tavernake, as he watched his companion's air, her manner of seating herself and accepting the attentions of the head waiter, felt that nameless impulse which was responsible for his having followed her from Blenheim House and which he could only call curiosity, becoming stronger. An exceedingly matter-of-fact person, he was also by instinct and habit observant. He never doubted but that she belonged to a class of society from which the guests at the boarding-house where they had both lived were seldom recruited, and of which he himself knew little. He was not in the least a snob, this young man, but he found the fact interesting. Life with him was already very much the same as a ledger account—a matter of debits and credits, and he had never failed to include among the latter that curious gift of breeding for which he himself, denied it by heritage, had somehow substituted a complete and exceedingly rare naturalness.

"I should like," she announced, laying down the carte, "a fried sole, some cutlets, an ice, and black coffee."

The waiter bowed.

"And for Monsieur?"

Tavernake glanced at his watch; it was already ten o'clock.

"I will take the same," he declared.

"And to drink?"

She seemed indifferent.

"Any light wine," she answered, carelessly, "white or red."

Tavernake took up the wine list and ordered sauterne. They were left alone in their corner for a few minutes, almost the only occupants of the place.

"You are sure that you can afford this?" she asked, looking at him critically. "It may cost you a sovereign or thirty shillings."

He studied the prices on the menu.

"I can afford it quite well and I have plenty of money with me," he assured her, "but I do not think that it will cost more than eighteen shillings. While we are waiting for the sole, shall we talk? I can tell you, if you choose to hear, why I followed you from the boardinghouse."

"I don't mind listening to you," she told him, "or I will talk with you about anything you like. There is only one subject which I cannot discuss; that subject is myself and my own doings."

Tavernake was silent for a moment.

"That makes conversation a bit difficult," he remarked. She leaned back in her chair.

"After this evening," she said, "I go out of your life as completely and finally as though I had never existed. I have a fancy to take my poor secrets with me. If you wish to talk, tell me about yourself. You have gone out of your way to be kind to me. I wonder why. It doesn't seem to be your role."

He smiled slowly. His face was fashioned upon broad lines and the relaxing of his lips lightened it wonderfully. He had good teeth, clear gray eyes, and coarse black hair which he wore a trifle long; his forehead was too massive for good looks.

"No," he admitted, "I do not think that benevolence is one of my characteristics."

Her dark eyes were turned full upon him; her red lips, redder than ever they seemed against the pallor of her cheeks and her deep brown hair, curled slightly. There was something almost insolent in her tone.

"You understand, I hope," she continued, "that you have nothing whatever to look for from me in return for this sum which you propose to expend for my entertainment?"

"I understand that," he replied.

"Not even gratitude," she persisted. "I really do not feel grateful to you. You are probably doing this to gratify some selfish interest or curiosity. I warn you that I am quite incapable of any of the proper sentiments of life."

"Your gratitude would be of no value to me whatever," he assured her.

She was still not wholly satisfied. His complete stolidity frustrated every effort she made to penetrate beneath the surface.

"If I believed," she went on, "that you were one of those men—the world is full of them, you know—who will help a woman with a reasonable appearance so long as it does not seriously interfere with their own comfort—"

"Your sex has nothing whatever to do with it," he interrupted. "As to your appearance, I have not even considered it. I could not tell you whether you are beautiful or ugly—I am no judge of these matters. What I have done, I have done because it pleased me to do it."

"Do you always do what pleases you?" she asked.

"Nearly always."

She looked him over again attentively, with an interest obviously impersonal, a trifle supercilious.

"I suppose," she remarked, "you consider yourself one of the strong people of the world?"

"I do not know about that," he answered. "I do not often think about myself."

"I mean," she explained, "that you are one of those people who struggle hard to get just what they want in life."

His jaw suddenly tightened and she saw the likeness to Napoleon.

"I do more than struggle," he affirmed, "I succeed. If I make up my mind to do a thing, I do it; if I make up my mind to get a thing, I get it. It means hard work sometimes, but that is all."

For the first time, a really natural interest shone out of her eyes. The half sulky contempt with which she had received his advances passed away. She became at that moment a human being, self-forgetting, the heritage of her charms—for she really had a curious but very poignant attractiveness—suddenly evident. It was only a momentary lapse and it was entirely wasted. Not even one of the waiters happened to be looking that way, and Tavernake was thinking wholly of himself.

"It is a good deal to say—that," she remarked, reflectively.

"It is a good deal but it is not too much," he declared. "Every man who takes life seriously should say it."

Then she laughed—actually laughed—and he had a vision of flashing white teeth, of a mouth breaking into pleasant curves, of dark mirth-lit eyes, lustreless no longer, provocative, inspiring. A vague impression as of something pleasant warmed his blood. It was a rare thing for him to be so stirred, but even then it was not sufficient to disturb the focus of his thoughts.

"Tell me," she demanded, "what do you do? What is your profession or work?"

"I am with a firm of auctioneers and estate agents," he answered readily,—"Messrs. Dowling, Spence & Company the name is. Our offices are in Waterloo Place."

"You find it interesting?"

"Of course," he answered. "Interesting? Why not? I work at it."

"Are you a partner?"

"No," he admitted. "Six years ago I was a carpenter; then I became an errand boy in Mr. Dowling's office I had to learn the business, you see. To-day I am a sort of manager. In eighteen months' time—perhaps before that if they do not offer me a partnership—I shall start for myself."

Once more the subtlest of smiles flickered at the corners of her lips.

"Do they know yet?" she asked, with faint irony.

"Not yet," he replied, with absolute seriousness. "They might tell me to go, and I have a few things to learn yet. I would rather make experiments for some one else than for myself. I can use the results later; they will help me to make money."

She laughed softly and wiped the tears out of her eyes. They were really very beautiful eyes notwithstanding the dark rims encircling them.

"If only I had met you before!" she murmured.

"Why?" he asked.

She shook her head.

"Don't ask me," she begged. "It would not be good for your conceit, if you have any, to tell you."

"I have no conceit and I am not inquisitive," he said, "but I do not see why you laughed."

Their period of waiting came to an end at this point. The fish was brought and their conversation became disjointed. In the silence which followed, the old shadow crept over her face. Once only it lifted. It was while they were waiting for the cutlets. She leaned towards him, her elbows upon the tablecloth, her face supported by her fingers.

"I think that it is time we left these generalities," she insisted, "and you told me something rather more personal, something which I am very anxious to know. Tell me exactly why so self-centered a person as yourself should interest himself in a fellow-creature at all. It seems odd to me."

"It is odd," he admitted, frankly. "I will try to explain it to you but it will sound very bald, and I do not think that you will understand. I watched you a few nights ago out on the roof at Blenheim House. You were looking across the house-tops and you didn't seem to be seeing anything at all really, and yet all the time I knew that you were seeing things I couldn't, you were understanding and appreciating something which I knew nothing of, and it worried me. I tried to talk to you that evening, but you were rude."

"You really are a curious person," she remarked. "Are you always worried, then, if you find that some one else is seeing things or understanding things which are outside your comprehension?"

"Always," he replied promptly.

"You are too far-reaching," she affirmed. "You want to gather everything into your life. You cannot. You will only be unhappy if you try. No man can do it. You must learn your limitations or suffer all your days."

"Limitations!" He repeated the words with measureless scorn. "If I learn them at all," he declared, with unexpected force, "it will be with scars and bruises, for nothing else will content me."

"We are, I should say, almost the same age," she remarked slowly.

"I am twenty-five," he told her.

"I am twenty-two," she said. "It seems strange that two people whose ideas of life are as far apart as the Poles should have come together like this even for a moment. I do not understand it at all. Did you expect that I should tell you just what I saw in the clouds that night?"

"No," he answered, "not exactly. I have spoken of my first interest in you only. There are other things. I told a lie about the bracelet and I followed you out of the boarding-house and I brought you here, for some other for quite a different reason."

"Tell me what it was," she demanded.

"I do not know it myself," he declared solemnly. "I really and honestly do not know it. It is because I hoped that it might come to me while we were together, that I am here with you at this moment. I do not like impulses which I do not understand."

She laughed at him a little scornfully.

"After all," she said, "although it may not have dawned upon you yet, it is probably the same wretched reason. You are a man and you have the poison somewhere in your blood. I am really not bad-looking, you know."

He looked at her critically. She was a little over-slim, perhaps, but she was certainly wonderfully graceful. Even the poise of her head, the manner in which she leaned back in her chair, had its individuality. Her features, too, were good, though her mouth had grown a trifle hard. For the first time the dead pallor of her cheeks was relieved by a touch of color. Even Tavernake realized that there were great possibilities about her. Nevertheless, he shook his head.

"I do not agree with you in the least," he asserted firmly. "Your looks have nothing to do with it. I am sure that it is not that."

"Let me cross-examine you," she suggested. "Think carefully now. Does it give you no pleasure at all to be sitting here alone with me?"

He answered her deliberately; it was obvious that he was speaking the truth.

"I am not conscious that it does," he declared. "The only feeling I am aware of at the present moment in connection with you, is the curiosity of which I have already spoken."

She leaned a little towards him, extending her very shapely fingers. Once more the smile at her lips transformed her face.

"Look at my hand," she said. "Tell me—wouldn't you like to hold it just for a minute, if I gave it you?"

Her eyes challenged his, softly and yet imperiously. His whole attention, however, seemed to be absorbed by her finger-nails. It seemed strange to him that a girl in her straits should have devoted so much care to her hands.

"No," he answered deliberately, "I have no wish to hold your hand. Why should I?"

"Look at me," she insisted.

He did so without embarrassment or hesitation,—it was more than ever apparent that he was entirely truthful. She leaned back in her chair, laughing softly to herself.

"Oh, my friend Mr. Leonard Tavernake," she exclaimed, "if you were not so crudely, so adorably, so miraculously truthful, what a prig, prig, prig, you would be! The cutlets at last, thank goodness! Your cross-examination is over. I pronounce you 'Not Guilty!"'

During the progress of the rest of the meal, they talked very little. At its conclusion, Tavernake discharged the bill, having carefully checked each item and tipped the waiter the exact amount which the man had the right to expect. They ascended the stairs together to the street, the girl lingering a few steps behind. On the pavement her fingers touched his arm.

"I wonder, would you mind driving me down to the Embankment?" she asked almost humbly. "It was so close down there and I want some air."

This was an extravagance which he had scarcely contemplated, but he did not hesitate. He called a taxicab and seated himself by her side. Her manner seemed to have grown quieter and more subdued, her tone was no longer semi-belligerent.

"I will not keep you much longer," she promised. "I suppose I am not so strong as I used to be. I have had scarcely anything to eat for two days and conversation has become an unknown luxury. I think—it seems absurd—but I think that I am feeling a little faint."

"The air will soon revive you," he said. "As to our conversation, I am disappointed. I think that you are very foolish not to tell me more about yourself."

She closed her eyes, ignoring his remark. They turned presently into a narrower thoroughfare. She leaned towards him.

"You have been very good to me," she admitted almost timidly, "and I am afraid that I have not been very gracious. We shall not see one another again after this evening. I wonder— would you care to kiss me?"

He opened his lips and closed them again. He sat quite still, his eyes fixed upon the road ahead, until he had strangled something absolutely absurd, something unrecognizable.

"I would rather not," he decided quietly. "I know you mean to be kind but that sort of thing—well, I don't think I understand it. Besides," he added with a sudden naive relief, as he clutched at a fugitive but plausible thought, "if I did you would not believe the things which I have been telling you."

He had a curious idea that she was disappointed as she turned her head away, but she said nothing. Arrived at the Embankment, the cab came slowly to a standstill. The girl descended. There was something new in her manner; she looked away from him when she spoke.

"You had better leave me here," she said. "I am going to sit upon that seat."

Then came those few seconds' hesitation which were to count for a great deal in his life. The impulse which bade him stay with her was unaccountable but it conquered.

"If you do not object," he remarked with some stiffness, "I should like to sit here with you for a little time. There is certainly a breeze."

She made no comment but walked on. He paid the man and followed her to the empty seat. Opposite, some illuminated advertisements blazed their unsightly message across the murky sky. Between the two curving rows of yellow lights the river flowed—black, turgid, hopeless. Even here, though they had escaped from its absolute thrall, the far-away roar of the city beat upon their ears. She listened to it for a moment and then pressed her hands to the side of her head.

"Oh, how I hate it!" she moaned. "The voices, always the voices, calling, threatening, beating you away! Take my hands, Leonard Tavernake,—hold me."

He did as she bade him, clumsily, as yet without comprehension.

"You are not well," he muttered.

Her eyes opened and a flash of her old manner returned. She smiled at him, feebly but derisively.

"You foolish boy!" she cried. "Can't you see that I am dying? Hold my hands tightly and watch—watch! Here is one more thing you can see—that you cannot understand."

He saw the empty phial slip from her sleeve and fall on to the pavement. With a cry he sprang up and, carrying her in his arms, rushed out into the road.

CHAPTER III. AN UNPLEASANT MEETING

It was a quarter past eleven and the theatres were disgorging their usual nightly crowds. The most human thoroughfare in any of the world's great cities was at its best and brightest. Everywhere commissionaires were blowing their whistles, the streets were thronged with slowly-moving vehicles, the pavements were stirring with life. The little crowd which had gathered in front of the chemist's shop was swept away. After all, none of them knew exactly what they had been waiting for. There was a rumor that a woman had fainted or had met with an accident. Certainly she had been carried into the shop and into the inner room, the door of which was still closed. A few passers-by had gathered together and stared and waited for a few minutes, but had finally lost interest and melted away. A human thoroughfare, this, indeed, one of the pulses of the great city beating time night and day to the tragedies of life. The chemist's assistant, with impassive features, was serving a couple of casual customers from behind the counter. Only a few yards away, beyond the closed door, the chemist himself and a hastily summoned doctor fought with Death for the body of the girl who lay upon the floor, faint moans coming every now and then from her blue lips.

Tavernake, whose forced inaction during that terrible struggle had become a burden to him, slipped softly from the room as soon as the doctor had whispered that the acute crisis was over, and passed through the shop out into the street, a solemn, dazed figure among the light-hearted crowd. Even in those grim moments, the man's individualism spoke up to him. He was puzzled at his own action, He asked himself a question —not, indeed, with regret, but with something more than curiosity and actual selfprobing—as though, by concentrating his mind upon his recent course of action, he would be able to understand the motives which had influenced him. Why had he chosen to burden himself with the care of this desperate young woman? Supposing she lived, what was to become of her? He had acquired a certain definite responsibility with regard to her future, for whatever the doctor and his assistant might do, it was his own promptitude and presence of mind which had given her the first chance of life. Without a doubt, he had behaved foolishly. Why not vanish into the crowd and have done with it? What was it to him, after all, whether this girl lived or died? He had done his duty—more than his duty. Why not disappear now and let her take her chance? His common sense spoke to him loudly; such thoughts as these beat upon his brain.

Just for once in his life, however, his common sense exercised an altogether subordinate position. He knew very well, even while he listened to these voices, that he was only counting the minutes until he could return. Having absolutely decided that the only reasonable course left for him to pursue was to return home and leave the girl to her fate, he found himself back inside the shop within a quarter of an hour. The chemist had just come out from the inner room, and looked up at his entrance.

"She'll do now," he announced.

Tavernake nodded. He was amazed at his own sense of relief.

"I am glad," he declared.

The doctor joined them, his black bag in his hand, prepared for departure. He addressed himself to Tavernake as the responsible person.

"The young lady will be all right now," he said, "but she may be rather queer for a day or two. Fortunately, she made the usual mistake of people who are ignorant of medicine and its effects—she took enough poison to kill a whole household. You had better take care of her, young man," he added dryly. "She'll be getting into trouble if she tries this sort of thing again."

"Will she need any special attention during the next few days?" Tavernake asked. "The circumstances under which I brought her here are a little unusual, and I am not quite sure—"

"Take her home to bed," the doctor interrupted, "and you'll find she'll sleep it off. She seems to have a splendid constitution, although she has let herself run down. If you need any further advice and your own medical man is not available, I will come and see her if you send for me. Camden, my name is; telephone number 734 Gerrard."

"I should be glad to know the amount of your fee, if you please," Tavernake said.

"My fee is two guineas," the doctor answered.

Tavernake paid him and he went away. Already the shadow of the tragedy was passing. The chemist had joined his assistant and was busy dispensing drugs behind his counter.

"You can go in to the young lady, if you like," he remarked to Tavernake. "I dare say she'll feel better to have some one with her."

Tavernake passed slowly into the inner room, closing the door behind him. He was scarcely prepared for so piteous a sight. The girl's face was white and drawn as she lay upon the couch to which they had lifted her. The fighting spirit was dead; she was in a state of absolute and complete collapse. She opened her eyes at his coning, but closed them again almost immediately —less, it seemed, from any consciousness of his presence than from sheer exhaustion.

"I am glad that you are better," he whispered crossing the room to her side.

"Thank you," she murmured almost inaudibly.

Tavernake stood looking down upon her, and his sense of perplexity increased. Stretched on the hard horsehair couch she seemed, indeed, pitifully thin and younger than her years. The scowl, which had passed from her face, had served in some measure as a disguise.

"We shall have to leave here in a few minutes," he said, softly. "They will want to close the shop."

"I am so sorry," she faltered, "to have given you all this

trouble. You must send me to a hospital or the workhouse—anywhere."

"You are sure that there are no friends to whom I can send?" he asked.

"There is no one!"

She closed her eyes and Tavernake sat quite still on the end of her couch, his elbow upon his knee, his head resting upon his hand. Presently, the rush of customers having ceased, the chemist came in.

"I think, if I were you, I should take her home now," he remarked. "She'll probably drop off to sleep very soon and wake up much stronger. I have made up a prescription here in case of exhaustion."

Tavernake stared at the man. Take her home! His sense of humor was faint enough but he found himself trying to imagine the faces of Mrs. Lawrence or Mrs. Fitzgerald if he should return with her to the boardinghouse at such an hour.

"I suppose you know where she lives?" the chemist inquired curiously.

"Of course," Tavernake assented. "You are quite right. I dare say she is strong enough now to walk as far as the pavement."

He paid the bill for the medicines, and they lifted her from the couch. Between them she walked slowly into the outer shop. Then she began to drag on their arms and she looked up at the chemist a little piteously.

"May I sit down for a moment?" she begged. "I feel faint."

They placed her in one of the cane chairs facing the door. The chemist mixed her some sal volatile.

"I am sorry," she murmured, "so sorry. In a few minutes —I shall be better."

Outside, the throng of pedestrians had grown less, but from the great restaurant opposite a constant stream of motor-cars and carriages was slowly bringing away the supper guests. Tavernake stood at the door, watching them idly. The traffic was momentarily blocked and almost opposite to him a motor-car, the simple magnificence of which filled him with wonder, had come to a standstill. The chauffeur and footman both wore livery which was almost white. Inside a swinging vase of flowers was suspended from the roof. A man and a woman leaned back in luxurious easy-chairs. The man was dark and had the look of a foreigner. The woman was very fair. She wore a long ermine cloak and a tiara of pearls.

Tavernake, whose interest in the passing throngs was entirely superficial, found himself for some reason curiously attracted by this glimpse into a world of luxury of which he knew nothing; attracted, too, by the woman's delicate face with its uncommon type of beauty. Their eyes met as he stood there, stolid and motionless, framed in the doorway. Tavernake continued to stare, unmindful, perhaps unconscious, of the rudeness of his action. The woman, after a moment, glanced away at the shopwindow. A sudden thought seemed to strike her. She spoke through the tube at her side and turned to her companion. Meanwhile, the footman, leaning from his place, held out his arm in warning and the car was slowly backed to the side of the pavement. The lady felt for a moment in a bag of white satin which lay upon the round table in front of her, and handed a slip of paper through the open window to the servant who had already descended and was standing waiting. He came at once towards the shop, passing Tavernake, who remained in the door-way.

"Will you make this up at once, please?" he directed, handing the paper across to the chemist.

The chemist took it in his hand and turned away mechanically toward the dispensing room. Suddenly he paused, and, looking back, shook his head.

"For whom is this prescription required?" he asked.

"For my mistress," the man answered. "Her name is there."

"Where is she?"

"Outside; she is waiting for it."

"If she really wants this made up to-night," the chemist declared, "she must come in and sign the book."

The footman looked across the counter, for a moment, a little blankly.

"Am I to tell her that?" he inquired. "It's only a sleeping draught. Her regular chemist makes it up all right."

"That may be," the man behind the counter replied, "but, you see, I am not her regular chemist. You had better go and tell her so."

The footman departed upon his errand without a glance at the girl who was sitting within a few feet of him.

"I am very sorry, madam," he announced to his mistress, "that the chemist declines to make up the prescription unless you sign the book."

"Very well, then, I will come," she declared.

The woman, handed from the automobile by her servant, lifted her white satin skirts in both hands and stepped lightly across the pavement. Tavernake stood on one side to let her pass. She seemed to him to be, indeed, a creature of that other world of which he knew nothing. Her slow, graceful movements, the shimmer of her skirt, her silk stockings, the flashing of the diamond buckles upon her shoes, the faint perfume from her clothes, the soft touch of her ermine as she swept by—all these things were indeed strange to him. His eyes followed her with rapt interest as she approached the counter.

"You wish me to sign for my prescription?" she asked the chemist. "I will do so, with pleasure, if it is necessary, only you must not keep me waiting long."

Her voice was very low and very musical; the slight smile which had parted her tired lips, was almost pathetic. Even the chemist felt himself to be a human being. He turned at once to his shelves and began to prepare the drug.

"I am sorry, madam, that it should have been necessary to fetch you in," he said, apologetically. "My assistant will give you the book if you will kindly sign it."

The assistant dived beneath the counter, reappearing almost immediately with a black volume and a pen and ink. The chemist was engrossed upon his task; Tavernake's eyes were still riveted upon this woman, who seemed to him the most beautiful thing he had ever seen in life. No one was watching the girl. The chemist was the first to see her face, and that only in a looking glass. He stopped in the act of mixing his drug and turned slowly round. His expression was such that they all followed his eyes. The girl was sitting up in her chair, with a sudden spot of color burning in her cheeks, her fingers gripping the counter as though for support, her eyes dilated, unnatural, burning in their white setting with an unholy fire. The lady was the last to turn her head, and the bottle of eau-de-cologne which she had taken up from the counter, slipped with a crash to the floor. All expression seemed to pass from her face; the very life seemed drawn from it. Those who were watching her saw suddenly an old woman looking at something of which she was afraid.

The girl seemed to find an unnatural strength. She dragged herself up and turned wildly to Tavernake.

"Take me away," she cried, in a low voice. "Take me away at once."

The woman at the counter did not speak. Tavernake stepped quickly forward and then hesitated. The girl was on her feet now and she clutched at his arms. Her eyes besought him.

"You must take me away, please," she begged, hoarsely. "I am well now—quite well. I can walk."

Tavernake's lack of imagination stood him in good stead then. He simply did what he was told, did it in perfectly mechanical fashion, without asking any questions. With the girl leaning heavily upon his arm, he stepped into the street and almost immediately into a passing taxicab which he had hailed from the threshold of the shop. As he closed the door, he glanced behind him. The woman was standing there, half turned towards him, still with that strange, stony look upon her lifeless face. The chemist was bending across the counter towards her, wondering, perhaps, if another incident were to be drawn into his night's work. The eau-de-cologne was running in a little stream across the floor.

"Where to, sir?" the taxicab driver asked Tavernake.

"Where to?" Tavernake repeated.

The girl was clinging to his arm.

"Tell him to drive away from here," she whispered, "to drive anywhere, but away from here."

"Drive straight on," Tavernake directed, "along Fleet Street and up Holborn. I will give you the address later on."

The man changed his speed and their pace increased. Tavernake sat quite still, dumfounded by these amazing happenings. The girl by his side was clutching his arm, sobbing a little hysterically, holding him all the time as though in terror.

CHAPTER IV. BREAKFAST WITH BEATRICE

The girl, awakened, perhaps, by the passing of some heavy cart along the street below, or by the touch of the sunbeam which lay across her pillow, first opened her eyes and then, after a preliminary stare around, sat up in bed. The events of the previous night slowly shaped themselves in her mind. She remembered everything up to the commencement of that drive in the taxicab. Sometime after that she must have fainted. And now —what had become of her? Where was she?

She looked around her in ever-increasing surprise. Certainly it was the strangest room she had ever been in. The floor was dusty and innocent of any carpet; the window was bare and uncurtained. The walls were unpapered but covered here and there with strange-looking plans, one of them taking up nearly the whole side of the room—a very rough piece of work with little dabs of blue paint here and there, and shadings and diagrams which were absolutely unintelligible. She herself was lying upon a battered iron bedstead, and she was wearing a very coarse nightdress. Her own clothes were folded up and lay upon a piece of brown paper on the floor by the side of the bed. To all appearance, the room was entirely unfurnished, except that in the middle of it was a hideous papier mache screen.

After her first bewildered inspection of her surroundings, it was upon this screen that her attention was naturally directed. Obviously it must be there to conceal something. Very carefully she leaned out of bed until she was able to see around the corner of it. Then her heart gave a little jump and she was only just able to stifle an exclamation of fear. Some one was sitting there—a man—sitting on a battered cane chair, bending over a roll of papers which were stretched upon a rude deal table. She felt her cheeks grow hot. It must be Tavernake! Where had he brought her? What did his presence in the room mean?

The bed creaked heavily as she regained her former position. A voice came to her from behind the screen. She knew it at once. It was Tavernake's.

"Are you awake?" he asked.

"Yes," she answered,—"yes, I am awake. Is that Mr. Tavernake? Where am I, please?"

"First of all, are you better?" he inquired.

"I am better," she assured him, sitting up in bed and pulling the clothes to her chin. "I am quite well now. Tell me at once where I am and what you are doing over there."

"There is nothing to be terrified about," Tavernake answered. "To all effects and purposes, I am in another room. When I move to the door, as I shall do directly, I shall drag the screen with me. I can promise you—"

"Please explain everything," she begged, "quickly. I am most—uncomfortable."

"At half-past twelve this morning," Tavernake said, "I found myself alone in a taxicab with you, without any luggage or any idea where to go to. To make matters worse, you fainted. I tried two hotels but they refused to take you in; they were probably afraid that you were going to be ill. Then I thought of this room. I am employed, as you know, by a firm of estate agents. I do a great deal of work on my own account, however, which I prefer to do in secret, and unknown to any one. For that reason, I hired this room a year ago and I come here most evenings to work. Sometimes I stay late, so last month I bought a small bedstead and had it fixed up here. There is a woman who comes in to clean the room. I went to her house last night and persuaded her to come here. She undressed you and put you to bed. I am sorry that my presence here distresses you, but it is a large building and quite empty at night-time. I thought you might wake up and be frightened, so I borrowed this screen from the woman and have been sitting here."

"What, all night?" she gasped.

"Certainly," he answered. "The woman could not stop herself and this is not a residential building at all. All the lower floors are let for offices and warehouses, and there is no one else in the place until eight o'clock."

She put her hands to her head and sat quite still for a moment or two. It was really hard to take everything in.

"Aren't you very sleepy?" she asked, irrelevantly.

"Not very," he replied. "I dozed for an hour, a little time ago. Since then I have been looking through some plans which interest me very much."

"Can I get up?" she inquired, timidly.

"If you feel strong enough, please do," he answered, with manifest relief. "I shall move towards the door, dragging the screen in front of me. You will find a brush and comb and some hairpins on your clothes. I could not think of anything else to get for you, but, if you will dress, we will walk to London Bridge Station, which is just across the way, and while I order some breakfast you can go into the ladies' room and do your hair properly. I did my best to get hold of a looking-glass, but it was quite impossible."

The girl's sense of humor was suddenly awake. She had hard work not to scream. He had evidently thought out all these details in painstaking fashion, one by one.

"Thank you," she said. "I will get up immediately, if you will do as you say."

He clutched the screen from the inside and dragged it towards the door. On the threshold, he spoke to her once more.

"I shall sit upon the stairs just outside," he announced.

"I sha'n't be more than five minutes," she assured him.

She sprang out of bed and dressed quickly. There was nothing beyond where the screen had been except a table covered with plans, and a particularly hard cane chair which she dragged over for her own use. As she dressed, she began to realize how much this matter-of-fact, unimpressionable young man had done for her during the last few hours. The reflection affected her in a curious manner. She became afflicted with a shyness which she had not felt when he was in the room. When at last she had finished her toilette and opened the door, she was almost tongue-tied. He was sitting on the top step, with his back against the landing, and his eyes were closed. He opened them with a little start, however, as soon as he heard her approach.

"I am glad you have not been long," he remarked. "I want to be at my office at nine o'clock and I must go and have a bath somewhere. These stairs are rather steep. Please walk carefully."

She followed him in silence down three flights of stone steps. On each landing there were names upon the doors—two firms of hop merchants, a solicitor, and a commission agent. The ground floor was some sort of warehouse, from which came a strong smell of leather.

Tavernake opened the outside door with a small key and they passed into the street.

"London Bridge Station is just across the way," he said. "The refreshment room will be open and we can get some breakfast at once."

"What time is it?" she asked.

"About half-past seven."

She walked by his side quite meekly, and although there were many things which she was longing to say, she remained absolutely without the power of speech. Except that he was looking a little crumpled, there was nothing whatever in his appearance to indicate that he had been up all night. He looked exactly as he had done on the previous day, he seemed even quite unconscious that there was anything unusual in their relations. As soon as they arrived at the station, he pointed to the ladies' waiting-room.

"If you will go in and arrange your hair there," he said, "I will go and order breakfast and have a shave. I will be back here in about twenty minutes. You had better take this."

He offered her a shilling and she accepted it without hesitation. As soon as he had gone, however, she looked at the coin in her hand in blank wonder. She had accepted it from him with perfect naturalness and without even saying "Thank you!" With a queer little laugh, she pushed open the swinging doors and made her way into the waiting-room.

In hardly more than a quarter of an hour she emerged, to find Tavernake waiting for her. He had retied his tie, bought a fresh collar, had been shaved. She, too, had improved her appearance.

"Breakfast is waiting this way," he announced.

She followed him obediently and they sat down at a small table in the station refreshment-room.

"Mr. Tavernake," she asked, suddenly, "I must ask you something. Has anything like this ever happened to you before?"

"Nothing," he assured her, with some emphasis.

"You seem to take everything so much as a matter of course," she protested.

"Why not?"

"Oh, I don't know," she replied, a little feebly. "Only — "

She found relief in a sudden and perfectly natural laugh.

"Come," he said, "that is better. I am glad that you feel like laughing."

"As a matter of fact," she declared, "I feel much more like crying. Don't you know that you were very foolish last night? You ought to have left me alone. Why didn't you? You would have saved yourself a great deal of trouble."

He nodded, as though that point of view did, in some degree, commend itself to him.

"Yes," he admitted, "I suppose I should. I do not, even now, understand why I interfered. I can only remember that it didn't seem possible not to at the time. I suppose one must have impulses," he added, with a little frown.

"The reflection," she remarked, helping herself to another roll, "seems to annoy you."

"It does," he confessed. "I do not like to feel impelled to

do anything the reason for which is not apparent. I like to do just the things which seem likely to work out best for myself."

"How you must hate me!" she murmured.

"No, I do not hate you," he replied, "but, on the other hand, you have certainly been a trouble to me. First of all, I told a falsehood at the boarding-house, and I prefer always to tell the truth when I can. Then I followed you out of the house, which I disliked doing very much, and I seem to have spent a considerable portion of the time since, in your company, under somewhat extraordinary circumstances. I do not understand why I have done this."

"I suppose it is because you are a very good-hearted person," she remarked.

"But I am not," he assured her, calmly. "I am nothing of the sort. I have very little sympathy with good-hearted people. I think the world goes very much better when every one looks after himself, and the people who are not competent to do so go to the wall."

"It sounds a trifle selfish," she murmured.

"Perhaps it is. I have an idea that if I could phrase it differently it would become philosophy."

"Perhaps," she suggested, smiling across the table at him, "you have really done all this because you like me."

"I am quite sure that it is not that," he declared. "I feel an interest in you for which I cannot account, but it does not seem to me to be a personal one. Last night," he continued, "when I was sitting there waiting, I tried to puzzle it all out. I came to the conclusion that it was because you represent something which I do not understand. I am very curious and it always interests me to learn. I believe that must be the secret of my interest in you."

"You are very complimentary," she told him, mockingly. "I wonder what there is in the world which I could teach so superior a person as Mr. Tavernake?"

He took her question quite seriously.

"I wonder what there is myself," he answered. "And yet, in a way, I think I know."

"Your imagination should come to the rescue," she remarked.

"I have no imagination," he declared, gloomily.

They were silent for several minutes; she was still studying him.

"I wonder you don't ask me any questions about myself," she said, abruptly.

"There is only one thing," he answered, "concerning which I am in the least curious. Last night in the chemist's shop —"

"Don't!" she begged him, with suddenly whitening face. "Don't speak of that!"

"Very well," he replied, indifferently. "I thought that you were rather inviting my questions. You need not be afraid of any more. I really am not curious about personal matters; I find that my own life absorbs all my interests."

They had finished breakfast and he paid the bill. She began to put on her gloves.

"Whatever happens to me," she said, "I shall never forget that you have been very kind."

She hesitated for a moment and then she seemed to realize more completely how really kind he had been. There had been a certain crude delicacy about his actions which she had under-appreciated. She leaned towards him. There was nothing left this morning of that disfiguring sullenness. Her mouth was soft; her eyes were bright, almost appealing. If Tavernake had been a judge of woman's looks, he must certainly have found her attractive.

"I am very, very grateful to you," she continued, holding out her hand. "I shall always remember how kind you were. Good-bye!"

"You are not going?" he asked.

She laughed.

"Why, you didn't imagine that you had taken the care of me upon your shoulders for the rest of your life?" she demanded.

"No, I didn't imagine that," he answered. "At the same time, what plans have you made? Where are you going?"

"Oh! I shall think of something," she declared, indifferently.

He caught the gleam in her eyes, the sudden hopelessness which fell like a cloud upon her face. He spoke promptly and with decision.

"As a matter of fact," he remarked, "you do not know yourself. You are just going to drift out of this place and very likely find your way to a seat on the Embankment again."

Her lips quivered. She had tried to be brave but it was hard.

"Not necessarily," she replied. "Something may turn up."

He leaned a little across the table towards her.

"Listen," he said, deliberately, "I will make a proposition to you. It has come to me during the last few minutes. I am tired of the boarding-house and I wish to leave it. The work which I do at night is becoming more and more important. I should like to take two rooms somewhere. If I take a third, would you care to call yourself what I called you to the charwoman last night— my sister? I should expect you to look after the meals and my clothes, and help me in certain other ways. I cannot give you much of a salary," he continued, "but you would have an opportunity during the daytime of looking out for some work, if that is what you want, and you would at least have a roof and plenty to eat and drink."

She looked at him in blank amazement. It was obvious that his proposition was entirely honest.

"But, Mr. Tavernake," she protested, "you forget that I am not really your sister."

"Does that matter?" he asked, without flinching. "I think you understand the sort of person I am. You would have nothing to fear from any admiration on my part—or anything of that sort," he added, with some show of clumsiness. "Those things do not come in my life. I am ambitious to get on, to succeed and become wealthy. Other things I do not even think about."

She was speechless. After a short pause, he went on.

"I am proposing this arrangement as much for my own sake as for yours. I am very well read and I know most of what there is to be known in my profession. But there are other things concerning which I am ignorant. Some of these things I believe you could teach me."

Still speechless, she sat and looked at him for several moments. Outside, the station now was filled with a hurrying throng on their way to the day's work. Engines were shrieking, bells ringing, the press of footsteps was unceasing. In the dark, ill-ventilated room itself there was the rattle of crockery, the yawning of discontented-looking young women behind the bar, young women with their hair still in curl-papers, as yet unprepared for their weak little assaults upon the good-nature or susceptibility of their customers. A queer corner of life it seemed. She looked at her companion and realized how fragmentary was her knowledge of him. There was nothing to be gathered from his face. He seemed to have no expression. He was simply waiting for her reply, with his thoughts already half engrossed upon the business of the day.

"Really," she began, "I—"

He came back from his momentary wandering and looked at her. She suddenly altered the manner of her speech. It was a strange proposition, perhaps, but this was one of the strangest of men.

"I am quite willing to try it," she decided. "Will you tell me where I can meet you later on?"

"I have an hour and a half for luncheon at one o'clock,"

he said. "Meet me exactly at the southeast corner of Trafalgar Square. Would you like a little money?" he added, rising.

"I have plenty, thank you," she answered.

He laid half-a-crown upon the table and made an entry in a small memorandum book which he drew from his pocket.

"You had better keep this," he said, "in case you want it. I am going to leave you alone here. You can find your way anywhere, I am sure, and I am in a hurry. At one o'clock, remember. I hope you will still be feeling better."

He put on his hat and went away without a backward glance. Beatrice sat in her chair and watched him out of sight.

CHAPTER V. INTRODUCING Mrs. WENHAM GARDNER

A very distinguished client was engaging the attention of Mr. Dowling, Senior, of Messrs. Dowling, Spence & Company, auctioneers and estate agents, whose offices were situated in Waterloo Place, Pall Mall. Mr. Dowling was a fussy little man of between fifty and sixty years, who spent most of his time playing golf, and who, although he studiously contrived to ignore the fact, had long since lost touch with the details of his business. Consequently, in the absence of Mr. Dowling, Junior, who had developed a marked partiality for a certain bar in the locality, Tavernake was hastily summoned to the rescue from another part of the building, by a small boy violently out of breath.

"Never see the governor in such a fuss," the latter declared, confidentially, "She's asking no end of questions and he don't know a thing."

"Who is the lady?" Tavernake asked, on the way downstairs.

"Didn't hear her name," the boy replied. "She's all right, though, I can tell you—a regular slap-up beauty. Such a motor-car, too! Flowers and tables and all sorts of things inside. By Jove, won't the governor tear his hair if she goes before you get there!"

Tavernake quickened his steps and in a few moments knocked at the door of the private office and entered.

His chief welcomed him with a gesture of relief. The distinguished client of the firm, whose attention he was endeavoring to engage, had glanced toward the newcomer, at his first appearance, with an air of somewhat bored unconcern. Her eyes, however, did not immediately leave his face. On the contrary, from the moment of his entrance she watched him steadfastly. Tavernake, stolid, unruffled, at that time without comprehension, approached the desk.

"This is—er—Mr. Tavernake, our manager," Mr. Dowling announced, obsequiously. "In the absence of my son, he is in charge of the letting department. I have no doubt that he will be able to suggest something suitable. Tavernake," he continued, "this lady,"—he glanced at a card in front of him—"Mrs. Wenham Gardner of New York, is looking for a town house, and has been kind enough to favor us with an inquiry."

Tavernake made no immediate reply. Mr. Dowling was shortsighted, and in any case it would never have occurred to him to associate nervousness, or any form of emotion, with his responsible manager. The beautiful lady leaned back in her chair. Her lips were parted in a slight but very curious smile, her fingers supported her cheek, her eyelids were contracted as she looked into his face. Tavernake felt that their recognition was mutual. Once more he was back again in the tragic atmosphere of that chemist's shop, with Beatrice, half fainting, in his arms, the beautiful lady turned to stone. It was an odd tableau, that, so vividly imprinted upon his memory that it was there before him at this very moment. There was mystery in this woman's eyes, mystery and something else.

"I don't seem to have come across anything down here which—er—particularly attracts Mrs.—Mrs. Wenham Gardner," Mr. Dowling went on, taking up a little sheaf of papers from the desk. "I thought, perhaps, that the Bryanston Square house might have suited, but it seems that it is too small, far too small. Mrs. Gardner is used to entertaining, and has explained to me that she has a great many friends always coming and going from the other side of the water. She requires, apparently, twelve bedrooms, besides servants' quarters."

"Your list is scarcely up to date, sir," Tavernake reminded him. "If the rent is of no particular object, there is Grantham House."

Mr. Dowling's face was suddenly illuminated.

"Grantham House!" he exclaimed. "Precisely! Now I declare that it had absolutely slipped my memory for the moment—only for the moment, mind—that we have just had placed upon our books one of the most desirable mansions in the west end of London. A most valued client, too, one whom we are most anxious to oblige. Dear, dear me! It is very fortunate—very fortunate indeed that I happened to think of it, especially as it seems that no one had had the sense to place it upon my list. Tavernake, get the plans at once and show them to—er—to Mrs. Gardner."

Tavernake crossed the room in silence, opened a drawer, and returned with a stiff roll of papers, which he spread carefully out in front of this unexpected client. She spoke then for the first time since he had entered the room. Her voice was low and marvelously sweet. There was very little of the American accent about it, but something in the intonation, especially toward the end of her sentences, was just a trifle un-English.

"Where is this Grantham House?" she inquired.

"Within a stone's throw of Grosvenor Square," Tavernake answered, briskly. "It is really one of the most central spots in the west end. If you will allow me!"

For the next few minutes he was very fluent indeed. With pencil in hand, he explained the plans, dwelt on the advantages of the location, and from the very reserve of his praise created an impression that the house he was describing was the one absolutely perfect domicile in the whole of London.

"Can I look over the place?" she asked, when he had finished.

"By all means," Mr. Dowling declared, "by all means. I was on the point of suggesting it. It will be by far the most satisfactory proceeding. You will not be disappointed, my dear madam, I can assure you."

"I should like to do so, if I may, without delay," she said.

"There is no opportunity like the present," Mr. Dowling replied. "If you will permit me," he added, rising, "it will give me the greatest pleasure to escort you personally. My engagements for the rest of the day happen to be unimportant. Tavernake, let me have the keys of the rooms that are locked up. The caretaker, of course, is there in possession."

The beautiful visitor rose to her feet, and even that slight movement was accomplished with a grace unlike anything which Tavernake had ever seen before.

"I could not think of troubling you so far, Mr. Dowling," she protested. "It is not in the least necessary for you to come yourself. Your manager can, perhaps, spare me a few minutes. He seems to be so thoroughly posted in all the details," she added, apologetically, as she noticed the cloud on Mr. Dowling's brow.

"Just as you like, of course," he declared. "Mr. Tavernake can go, by all means. Now I come to think of it, it certainly would be inconvenient for me to be away from the office for more than a few minutes. Mr. Tavernake has all the details at his fingers' ends, and I only hope, Mrs. Gardner, that he will be able to persuade you to take the house. Our client," he added, with a bow, "would, I am sure, be delighted to hear that we had secured for him so distinguished a tenant."

She smiled at him, a delightful mixture of graciousness and condescension.

"You are very good," she answered. "The house sounds rather large for me but it depends so much upon circumstances. If you are ready, Mr. — "

"Tavernake," he told her.

"Mr. Tavernake," she continued, "my car is waiting outside and we might go on at once."

He bowed and held open the door for her, an office which he performed a little awkwardly. Mr. Dowling himself escorted her out on to the pavement. Tavernake stopped behind to get his hat, and passing out a moment afterwards, would have seated himself in front beside the chauffeur but that she held the door of the car open and beckoned to him.

"Will you come inside, please?" she insisted. "There are one or two questions which I might ask you as we go along.

Please direct the chauffeur."

He obeyed without a word; the car glided off. As they swung round the first corner, she leaned forward from among the cushions of her seat and looked at him. Then Tavernake was conscious of new things. As though by inspiration, he knew that her visit to the office of Messrs. Dowling, Spence & Company had been no chance one.

She remembered him, remembered him as the companion of Beatrice during that strange, brief meeting. It was an incomprehensible world, this, into which he had wandered. The woman's face had lost her languid, gracious expression. There was something there almost akin to tragedy. Her fingers fell upon his arm and her touch was no light one. She was gripping him almost fiercely.

"Mr. Tavernake," she said, "I have a memory for faces which seldom fails me. I have seen you before quite lately. You remember where, of course. Tell me the truth quickly, please."

The words seemed to leap from her lips. Beautiful and young though she undoubtedly was, her intense seriousness had suddenly aged her face. Tavernake was bewildered. He, too, was conscious of a curious emotional disturbance.

"The truth? What truth do you mean?" he demanded.

"It was you whom I saw with Beatrice!"

"You saw me one night about three weeks ago," he admitted slowly. "I was in a chemist's shop in the Strand. You were signing his book for a sleeping draught, I think."

She shivered all over.

"Yes, yes!" she cried. "Of course, I remember all about it. The young lady who was with you—what was she doing there? Where is she now?"

"The young lady was my sister," Tavernake answered stiffly.

Mrs. Wenham Gardner looked, for a moment, as though she would have struck him.

"You need not lie to me!" she exclaimed. "It is not worth while. Tell me where you met her, why you were with her at all in that intimate fashion, and where she is now!"

Tavernake realized at once that so far as this woman was concerned, the fable of his relationship with Beatrice was hopeless. She knew!

"Madam," he replied, "I made the acquaintance of the young lady with whom I was that evening, at the boarding-house where we both lived."

"What were you doing in the chemist's shop?" she demanded.

"The young lady had been ill," he proceeded deliberately, wondering how much to tell. "She had been taken very ill indeed. She was just recovering when you entered."

"Where is she now?" the woman asked eagerly. "Is she still at that boarding-house of which you spoke?"

"No," he answered.

Her fingers gripped his arm once more.

"Why do you answer me always in monosyllables? Don't you understand that you must tell me everything that you know about her. You must tell me where I can find her, at once."

Tavernake remained silent. The woman's voice had still that note of wonderful sweetness, but she had altogether lost her air of complete and aristocratic indifference. She was a very altered person now from the distinguished client who had first enlisted his services. For some reason or other, he knew that she was suffering from a terrible anxiety.

"I am not sure," he said at last, "whether I can do as you ask."

"What do you mean?" she exclaimed sharply.

"The young lady," he continued, "seemed, on the occasion to which you have referred, to be particularly anxious to avoid recognition. She hurried out of the place without speaking to you, and she has avoided the subject ever since. I do not know what her motives may have been, but I think that I should like to ask her first before I tell you where she is to be found."

Mrs. Wenham Gardner leaned towards him. It was certainly the first time that a woman in her apparent rank of life had looked upon Tavernake in such a manner. Her forehead was a little wrinkled, her lips were parted, her eyes were pathetically, delightfully eloquent.

"Mr. Tavernake, you must not—you must not refuse me," she pleaded. "If you only knew the importance of it, you would not hesitate for a moment. This is no idle curiosity on my part. I have reasons, very serious reasons indeed, for wishing to discover that poor girl's whereabouts at once. There is a possible danger of which she must be warned. No one can do it except myself."

"Are you her friend or her enemy?" Tavernake asked.

"Why do you ask such a question?" she demanded.

"I am only going by her expression when she saw you come into the chemist's shop," Tavernake persisted doggedly.

"It is a cruel suggestion, that," the woman cried. "I wish to be her friend, I am her friend. If I could only tell you everything, you would understand at once what a terrible situation, what a hideous quandary I am in."

Once more Tavernake paused for a few moments. He was never a quick thinker and the situation was certainly an embarrassing one for him.

"Madam," he replied at length, "I beg that you will tell me nothing. The young lady of whom you have spoken permits me to call myself her friend, and what she has not told me herself I do not wish to learn from others. I will tell her of this meeting with you, and if it is her desire, I will bring you her address myself within a few hours. I cannot do more than that."

Her face was suddenly cold and hard.

"You mean that you will not!" she exclaimed angrily.

"You are obstinate. I do not know how you dare to refuse what I ask."

The car had come to a standstill. He stepped out on to the pavement.

"This is Grantham House, madam," he announced. "Will you descend?"

He heard her draw a quick breath between her teeth and he caught a gleam in her eyes which made him feel vaguely uneasy. She was very angry indeed.

"I do not think that it is necessary for me to do so," she said frigidly. "I do not like the look of the house at all. I do not believe that it will suit me."

"At least, now that you are here," he protested, "you will, if you please, go over it. I should like you to see the ballroom. The decorations are supposed to be quite exceptional."

She hesitated for a moment and then, with a slight shrug of the shoulders, she yielded. There was a note in his tone not exactly insistent, and yet dominant, a note which she obeyed although secretly she wondered at herself for doing so. They passed inside the house and she followed him from room to room, leaving him to do all the talking. She seemed very little interested but every now and then she asked a languid question.

"I do not think that it is in the least likely to suit me," she decided at last. "It is all very magnificent, of course, but I consider that the rent is exorbitant."

Tavernake regarded her thoughtfully.

"I believe," he said, "that our client might be disposed to consider some reduction, in the event of your seriously entertaining taking the house. If you like, I will see him on the subject. I feel sure that the amount I have mentioned could be reduced, if the other conditions were satisfactory."

"There would be no harm in your doing so," she assented. "How soon can you come and let me know?"

"I might be able to ring you up this evening; certainly to-morrow morning," he answered.

She shook her head.

"I will not speak upon the telephone," she declared. "I only allow it in my rooms under protest. You must come and tell me what your client says. When can you see him?"

"It is doubtful whether I shall be able to find him this evening," he replied. "It would probably be to-morrow morning."

"You might go and try at once," she suggested.

He was a little surprised.

"You are really interested in the matter, then?" he inquired.

"Yes, yes," she told him, "of course I am interested. I want you to come and see me directly you have heard. It is important. Supposing you are able to find your client to-night, shall you have seen the young lady before then?"

"I am afraid not," he answered.

"You must try," she begged, laying her fingers upon his shoulder. "Mr. Tavernake, do please try. You can't realize what all this anxiety means to me. I am not at all well and I am seriously worried about—about that young lady. I tell you that I must have an interview with her. It is not for my sake so much as hers. She must be warned."

"Warned?" Tavernake repeated. "I really don't understand."

"Of course you don't!" she exclaimed impatiently. "Why should you understand? I don't want to offend you, Mr. Tavernake," she went on hurriedly. "I would like to treat you quite frankly. It really isn't your place to make difficulties like this. What is this young lady to you that you should presume to consider yourself her guardian?"

"She is a boarding-house acquaintance," Tavernake confessed, "nothing more."

"Then why did you tell me, only a moment ago, that she

was your sister?" Mrs. Gardner demanded.

Tavernake threw open the door before which they had been standing.

"This," he said, "is the famous dancing gallery. Lord Clumber is quite willing to allow the pictures to remain, and I may tell you that they are insured for over sixty thousand pounds. There is no finer dancing room than this in all London."

Her eyes swept around it carelessly.

"I have no doubt," she admitted coldly, "that it is very beautiful. I prefer to continue our discussion."

"The dining-room," he went on, "is almost as large. Lord Clumber tells us that he has frequently entertained eighty guests for dinner. The system of ventilation in this room is, as you see, entirely modern."

She took him by the arm and led him to a seat at the further end of the apartment.

"Mr. Tavernake," she said, making an obvious attempt to control her temper, "you seem like a very sensible young man, if you will allow me to say so, and I want to convince you that it is your duty to answer my questions. In the first place—don't be offended, will you?—but I cannot possibly see what interest you and that young lady can have in one another. You belong, to put it baldly, to altogether different social stations, and it is not easy to imagine what you could have in common."

She paused, but Tavernake had nothing to say. His gift of silence amounted sometimes almost to genius. She leaned so close to him while she waited in vain for his reply, that the ermine about her neck brushed his cheek. The perfume of her clothes and hair, the pleading of her deep violet-blue eyes, all helped to keep him tongue-tied. Nothing of this sort had ever happened to him before. He did not in the least understand what it could possibly mean.

"I am speaking to you now, Mr. Tavernake," she continued earnestly, "for your own good. When you tell the young lady, as you have promised to this evening, that you have seen me, and that I am very, very anxious to find out where she is, she will very likely go down on her knees and beg you to give me no information whatever about her. She will do her best to make you promise to keep us apart. And yet that is all because she does not understand. Believe me, it is better that you should tell me the truth. You cannot know her very well, Mr. Tavernake, but she is not very wise, that young lady. She is very obstinate, and she has some strange ideas. It is not well for her that she should be left in the world alone. You must see that for yourself, Mr. Tavernake."

"She seems a very sensible young lady," he declared slowly. "I should have thought that she would have been old enough to know for herself what she wanted and what was best for her."

The woman at his side wrung her hands with a little gesture of despair.

"Oh, why can't I make you understand!" she exclaimed, the emotion once more quivering in her tone. "How can I—how can I possibly make you believe me? Listen. Something has happened of which she does not know—something terrible. It is absolutely necessary, in her own interests as well as mine, that I see her, and that very shortly."

"I shall tell her exactly what you say," Tavernake answered apparently unmoved. "Perhaps it would be as well now if we went on to view the sleeping apartments."

"Never mind about the sleeping apartments!" she cried quickly. "You must do more than tell her. You can't believe that I want to bring harm upon any one. Do I look like it? Have I the appearance of a person of evil disposition? You can be that young lady's best friend, Mr. Tavernake, if you will. Take me to her now, this minute. Believe me, if you do that, you will never regret it as long as you live."

Tavernake studied the pattern of the parquet floor for

several moments. It was a difficult problem, this. Putting his own extraordinary sensations into the background, he was face to face with something which he did not comprehend, and he disliked the position intensely. After all, delay seemed safest.

"Madam," he protested, "a few hours more or less can make but little difference."

"That is for me to judge!" she exclaimed. "You say that because you do not understand. A few hours may make all the difference in the world."

He shook his head.

"I will tell you exactly what is in my mind," he said, deliberately. "The young lady was terrified when she saw you that night accidentally in the chemist's shop. She almost dragged me away, and although she was almost fainting when we reached the taxicab, her greatest and chief anxiety was that we should get away before you could follow us. I cannot forget this. Until I have received her permission, therefore, to disclose her whereabouts, we will, if you please, speak of something else."

He rose to his feet and glancing around was just in time to see the change in the face of his companion. That eloquently pleading smile had died away from her lips, her teeth were clenched. She looked like a woman struggling hard to control some overwhelming passion. Without the smile her lips seemed hard, even cruel. There were evil things shining out of her eyes. Tavernake felt chilled, almost afraid.

"We will see the rest of the house," she declared coldly.

They went on from room to room. Tavernake, recovering himself rapidly, master of his subject, was fluent and practical. The woman listened, with only a terse remark here and there. Once more they stood in the hall.

"Is there anything else you would like to see?" he asked.

"Nothing," she replied, "but there is one thing more I have to say."

He waited in stolid silence.

"Only a week ago," she went on, looking him in the face, "I told a man who is what you call, I think, an inquiry agent, that I would give a hundred pounds if he could discover that young woman for me within twenty-four hours."

Tavernake started, and the smile came back to the lips of Mrs. Wenham Gardner. After all, perhaps she had found the way!

"A hundred pounds is a great deal of money," he said thoughtfully.

She shrugged her shoulders.

"Not so very much," she replied. "About a fortnight's rent of this house, Mr. Tavernake."

"Is the offer still open?" he asked.

She looked into his eyes, and her face had once more the beautiful ingenuousness of a child.

"Mr. Tavernake," she said, "the offer is still open. Get into the car with me and drive back to my rooms at the Milan Court, and I will give you a cheque for a hundred pounds at once. It will be very easily earned and you may just as well take it, for now I know where you are employed, I could have you followed day by day until I discover for myself what you are so foolishly concealing. Be reasonable, Mr. Tavernake."

Tavernake stood quite still. His arms were folded, he was looking out of the hall window at the smoky vista of roofs and chimneys. From the soles of his ready-made boots to his ill-brushed hair, he was a commonplace young man. A hundred pounds was to him a vast sum of money. It represented a year's strenuous savings, perhaps more. The woman who watched him imagined that he was hesitating. Tavernake, however, had no such thought in his mind. He stood there instead, wondering what strange thing had come to him that the mention of a hundred pounds, delightful sum though it was, never tempted him for a single second. What this woman had said might be true. She would probably be able to discover the address easily enough without his help. Yet no such reflection seemed to make the least difference. From the days of his earliest boyhood, from the time when he had flung himself into the struggle, money had always meant much to him, money not for its own sake but as the key to those things which he coveted in life. Yet at that moment something stronger seemed to have asserted itself.

"You will come?" she whispered, passing her arm through his. "We will be there in less than five minutes, and I will write you the cheque before you tell me anything."

He moved towards the door indeed, but he drew a little away from her.

"Madam," he said, "I am sorry to seem so obstinate, but I thought I had made you understand some time ago. I do not feel at liberty to tell you anything without that young lady's permission."

"You refuse?" she cried, incredulously. "You refuse a hundred pounds?"

He opened the door of the car. He seemed scarcely to have heard her.

"At about eleven o'clock to-morrow morning," he announced, "I shall have the pleasure of calling upon you. I trust that you will have decided to take the house."

CHAPTER VI. QUESTIONS AND ANSWERS

Tavernake sat a few hours later at his evening meal in the tiny sitting-room of an apartment house in Chelsea. He wore a black tie, and although he had not yet aspired to a dinner coat, the details of his person and toilet showed signs of a new attention. Opposite to him was Beatrice.

"Tell me," she asked, as soon as the small maid-servant who brought in their first dish had disappeared, "what have you been doing all day? Have you been letting houses or surveying land or book-keeping, or have you been out to Marston Rise?"

It was her customary question, this. She really took an interest in his work.

"I have been attending a rich American client," he announced, "a compatriot of your own. I went with her to Grantham House in her own motor-car. I believe she thinks of taking it."

"American!" Beatrice remarked. "What was her name?"

Tavernake looked up from his plate across the little table, across the bowl of simple flowers which was its sole decoration.

"She called herself Mrs. Wenham Garner!"

Away like a flash went the new-found peace in the girl's face. She caught at her breath, her fingers gripped the table in front of her. Once more she was as he had known her first—pale, with great terrified eyes shining out of a haggard face.

"She has been to you," Beatrice gasped, "for a house? You are sure?"

"I am quite sure," Tavernake declared, calmly.

"You recognized her?"

He assented gravely.

"It was the woman who stood in the chemist's shop that night, signing her name in a book," he said.

He did not apologize in any way for the shock he had given her. He had done it deliberately. From that very first morning, when they had breakfasted together at London Bridge, he had felt that he deserved her confidence, and in a sense it was a grievance with him that she had withheld it.

"Did she recognize you?"

"Yes," he admitted. "I was sent for into the office and found her there with the chief. I felt sure that she recognized me from the first, and when she agreed to look at Grantham House, she insisted upon it that I should accompany her. While we were in the motor-car, she asked me about you. She wished for your address."

"Did you give it to her?" the girl cried, breathlessly.

"No; I said that I must consult you first."

She drew a little sigh of relief. Nevertheless, she was looking white and shaken.

"Did she say what she wanted me for?"

"She was very mysterious," Tavernake answered. "She spoke of some danger of which you knew nothing. Before I came away, she offered me a hundred pounds to let her know where you were."

Beatrice laughed softly.

"That is just like Elizabeth," she declared. "You must have made her very angry. When she wants anything, she wants it very badly indeed, and she will never believe that every person has not his price. Money means everything to her. If she had it, she would buy, buy, buy all the time."

"On the face of it," Tavernake remarked, soberly, "her offer seemed rather an absurd one. If she is in earnest, if she is really so anxious to discover your whereabouts, she will certainly be able to do so without my help."

"I am not so sure," Beatrice replied. "London is a great hiding place."

"A private detective," he began,—

Beatrice shook her head.

"I do not think," she said, "that Elizabeth will care to employ a private detective. Tell me, have you to see her upon this business again?"

"I am going to her flat at the Milan Court to-morrow morning at eleven o'clock."

Beatrice leaned back in her chair. Presently she recommenced her dinner. She had the air of one to whom a respite has been granted. Tavernake, in a way, began to resent this continued silence of hers. He had certainly hoped that she would at least have gone so far as to explain her anxiety to keep her whereabouts secret.

"You must remember," he went on, after a short pause, "that I am in a somewhat peculiar position with regard to you, Beatrice. I know so little that I do not even know how to answer in your interests such questions as Mrs. Wenham Gardner asked me. I am not complaining, but is this state of absolute ignorance necessary?"

A new thought seemed to come to Beatrice. She looked at her companion curiously.

"Tell me," she asked, "what did you think of Mrs. Wenham Gardner?"

Tavernake answered deliberately, and after a moment's reflection.

"I thought her," he said, "one of the most beautiful women I have ever seen in my life. That is not saying very much, perhaps, but to me it meant a good deal. She was exceedingly gracious and her interest in you seemed quite real and even affectionate. I do not understand why you should wish to hide from such a woman."

"You found her attractive?" Beatrice persisted.

"I found her very attractive indeed," Tavernake admitted, without hesitation. "She had an air with her. She was quite different from all the women I have ever met at the boarding-house or anywhere else. She has a face which reminded me somehow of the Madonnas you took me to see in the National Gallery the other day."

Beatrice shivered slightly. For some reason, his remark seemed to have distressed her.

"I am very, very sorry," she declared, "that Elizabeth ever came to your office. I want you to promise me, Leonard, that you will be careful whenever you are with her."

Tavernake laughed.

"Careful!" he repeated. "She isn't likely to be even civil to me tomorrow when I tell her that I have seen you and I refuse to give her your address. Careful, indeed! What has a poor clerk in a house-agent's office to fear from such a personage?"

The servant had reappeared with their second and last course. For a few moments they spoke of casual subjects. Afterwards, however, Tavernake asked a question.

"By the way," he said, "we are hoping to let Grantham House to Mrs. Wenham Gardner. I suppose she must be very wealthy?"

Beatrice looked at him curiously.

"Why do you come to me for information?" she demanded. "I suppose that she brought you references?"

"We haven't quite got to that stage yet," he answered. "Somehow or other, from her manner of talking and general appearance, I do not think that either Mr. Dowling or I doubted her financial position."

"I should never have thought you so credulous a person," remarked Beatrice, with a smile.

Tavernake was genuinely disturbed. His business instincts were aroused.

"Do you really mean that this Mrs. Wenham Gardner is not a person of substance?" he inquired.

Beatrice shrugged her shoulders.

"She is the wife of a man who had the reputation of being very wealthy," she replied. "She has no money of her own, I am sure."

"She still lives with her husband, I suppose?" Tavernake

asked.

Beatrice closed her eyes.

"I know very little about her," she declared. "Last time I heard, he had disappeared, gone away, or something of the sort."

"And she has no money," Tavernake persisted, "except what she gets from him? No settlement, even, or anything of that sort?"

"Nothing at all," Beatrice answered.

"This is very bad news," Tavernake remarked, thinking gloomily of his wasted day. "It will be a great disappointment to Mr. Dowling. Why, her motor-car was magnificent, and she talked as though money were no object at all. I suppose you are quite sure of what you are saying?"

Beatrice shrugged her shoulders.

"I ought to know," she answered, grimly, "for she is my sister."

Tavernake remained quite motionless for a minute, without speech; it was his way of showing surprise. When he was sure that he had grasped the import of her words, he spoke again.

"Your sister!" he repeated. "There is a likeness, of course. You are dark and she is fair, but there is a likeness. That would account," he continued, "for her anxiety to find you."

"It also accounts," Beatrice replied, with a little break of the lips, "for my anxiety that she should not find me. Leonard," she added, touching his hand for a moment with hers, "I wish that I could tell you everything, but there are things behind, things so terrible, that even to you, my dear brother, I could not speak of them."

Tavernake rose to his feet and lit a cigarette—a new habit with him, while Beatrice busied herself with a small coffee-making machine. He sat in an easy-chair and smoked slowly. He was still wearing his ready-made clothes, but his collar was of the fashionable shape, his tie well chosen and neatly adjusted. He seemed somehow to have developed.

"Beatrice," he asked, "what am I to tell your sister to-morrow?"

She shivered as she set his coffee-cup down by his side.

"Tell her, if you will, that I am well and not in want," she answered. "Tell her, too, that I refuse to send my address. Tell her that the one aim of my life is to keep the knowledge of my whereabouts a secret from her."

Tavernake relapsed into silence. He was thinking. Mysteries had no attraction for him—he loathed them. Against this one especially he felt a distinct grudge. Nevertheless, some instinct forbade his questioning the girl.

"Apart from more personal matters, then," he asked after some time, "you would not advise me to enter into any business negotiations with this lady?"

"You must not think of it," Beatrice replied, firmly. "So far as money is concerned, Elizabeth has no conscience whatever. The things she wants in life she will have somehow, but it is all the time at other people's expense. Some day she will have to pay for it."

Tavernake sighed.

"It is very unfortunate," he declared. "The commission on the letting of Grantham House would have been worth having."

"After all, it is only your firm's loss," she reminded him.

"It does not appeal to me like that," he continued. "So long as I am manager for Dowling & Spence, I feel these things personally. However, that does not matter. I am afraid it is a disagreeable subject for you, and we will not talk about it any longer."

She lit a cigarette with a little gesture of relief. She came once more to his side.

"Leonard," she said, "I know that I am treating you badly in telling you nothing, but it is simply because I do not want to descend to half truths. I should like to tell you all or nothing. At present I cannot tell you all."

"Very well," he replied, "I am quite content to leave it with you to do as you think best."

"Leonard," she continued, "of course you think me unreasonable. I can't help it. There are things between my sister and myself the knowledge of which is a constant nightmare to me. During the last few months of my life it has grown to be a perfect terror. It sent me into hiding at Blenheim House, it reconciled me even to the decision I came to that night on the Embankment. I had decided that sooner than go back, sooner than ask help from her or any one connected with her, I would do what I tried to do the time when you saved my life."

Tavernake looked at her wonderingly. She was, indeed, under the spell of some deep emotion. Her memory seemed to have carried her back into another world, somewhere far away from this dingy little sitting-room which they two were sharing together, back into a world where life and death were matters of small moment, where the great passions were unchained, and men and women moved among the naked things of life. Almost he felt the thrill of it. It was something new to him, the touch of a magic finger upon his eyelids. Then the moment passed and he was himself again, matter-of-fact, prosaic.

"Let us dismiss the subject finally," he said. "I must see your sister on business to-morrow, but it shall be for the last time."

"I think," she murmured, "that you will be wise."

He crossed the room and returned with a newspaper.

"I saw your music in the hall as I came in," he remarked. "Are you singing to-night?"

The question was entirely in his ordinary tone. It brought her back to the world of every-day things as nothing else could have done.

"Yes; isn't it luck?" she told him. "Three in one week. I only heard an hour ago."

"A city dinner?" he inquired.

"Something of the sort," she replied. "I am to be at the Whitehall Rooms at ten o'clock. If you are tired, Leonard, please let me go alone. I really do not mind. I can get a 'bus to the door, there and back again."

"I am not tired," he declared. "To tell you the truth, I scarcely know what it is to be tired. I shall go with you, of course."

She looked at him with a momentary admiration of his powerful frame, his strong, forceful face.

"It seems too bad," she remarked, "after a long day's work to drag you out again."

He smiled.

"I really like to come," he assured her. "Besides," he added, after a moment's pause, "I like to hear you sing."

"I wonder if you mean that?" she asked, looking at him curiously. "I have watched you once or twice when I have been singing to you. Do you really care for it?"

"Certainly I do. How can you doubt it? I do not," he continued, slowly, "understand music, or anything of that sort, of course, any more than I do the pictures you take me to see, and some of the books you talk about. There are lots of things I can't get the hang of entirely, but they all leave a sort of pleasure behind. One feels it even if one only half appreciates."

She came over to his chair.

"I am glad," she said, a little wistfully, "that there is one thing I do which you like."

He looked at her reprovingly.

"My dear Beatrice," he said, "I often wish I could make you understand how extraordinarily helpful and useful to me you have been."

"Tell me in what way?" she begged.

"You have given me," he assured her, "an insight into many things in life which I had found most perplexing. You see, you have traveled and I haven't. You have mixed with all classes of people, and I have gone steadily on in one groove. You have told me many things which I shall find very useful indeed later on."

"Dear me," she laughed, "you are making me quite conceited!"

"Anyhow," he replied, "I don't want you to look upon me, Beatrice, in any way as a benefactor. I am much more comfortable here than at the boarding-house and it is costing no more money, especially since you began to get those singing engagements. By the way, hadn't you better go and get ready?"

She smothered a sigh as she turned away and went slowly upstairs. To all appearance, no person who ever breathed was more ordinary than this strong-featured, self-centered young man who had put out his arm and snatched her from the Maelstrom. Yet it seemed to her that there was something almost unnatural about his unapproachability. She was convinced that he was entirely honest, not only with regard to his actual relations toward her, but with regard to all his purposes. Her sex did not even seem to exist for him. The fact that she was good-looking, and with her renewed health daily becoming more so, seemed to be of no account to him whatever. He showed interest in her appearance sometimes, but it was interest of an entirely impersonal sort. He simply expressed himself as satisfied or dissatisfied, as a matter of taste. It came to her at that moment that she had never seen him really relax. Only when he sat opposite to that great map which hung now in the further room, and wandered about from section to section with a pencil in one hand and a piece of rubber in another, did he show anything which in any way approached enthusiasm, and even then it was always the unmistakable enthusiasm born of dead things. Suddenly she laughed at herself in the little mirror, laughed softly but heartily. This was the guardian whom Fate had sent for her! If Elizabeth had only understood!

CHAPTER VII. Mr. PRITCHARD OF NEW YORK

Later in the evening, Beatrice and Tavernake traveled together in a motor omnibus from their rooms at Chelsea to Northumberland Avenue. Tavernake was getting quite used to the programme by now. They sat in a dimly-lit waiting-room until the time came for Beatrice to sing. Every now and then an excitable little person who was the secretary to some institution or other would run in and offer them refreshments, and tell them in what order they were to appear. To-night there was no departure from the ordinary course of things, except that there was slightly more stir. The dinner was a larger one than usual. It came to Beatrice's turn very soon after their arrival, and Tavernake, squeezing his way a few steps into the dining-room, stood with the waiters against the wall. He looked with curious eyes upon a scene with which he had no manner of sympathy.

A hundred or so of men had dined together in the cause of some charity. The odor of their dinner, mingled with the more aromatic perfume of the tobacco smoke which was already ascending in little blue clouds from the various tables, hung about the over-heated room, seeming, indeed, the fitting atmosphere for the long rows of guests. The majority of them were in a state of expansiveness. Their faces were redder than when they had sat down; a certain stiffness had departed from their shirt-fronts and their manners; their faces were flushed, their eyes watery. There were a few exceptions—paler-faced men who sat there with the air of endeavoring to bring themselves into accord with surroundings in which they had no real concern. Two of these looked up with interest at the first note of Beatrice's song. The one was sitting within a few places of the chairman, and he was too far away for his little start to be noticed by either Tavernake or Beatrice. The nearer one, however, Tavernake happened to be watching, and he saw the change in his expression. The man was, in his way, ugly. His face was certainly not a good one, although he did not appear to share the immediate weaknesses of his neighbors. To every note of the song he listened intently. When it was over, he rose and came toward Tavernake.

"I beg your pardon," he said, "but did I not see you come in with the young lady who has just been singing?"

"You may have," Tavernake answered. "I certainly did come with her."

"May I ask if you are related to her?"

Tavernake had got over his hesitation in replying to such questions, by now. He answered promptly.

"I am her brother," he declared.

The man produced a card.

"Please introduce me to her," he begged, laconically.

"Why should I?" Tavernake asked. "I have no reason to suppose that she desires to know you."

The man stared at him for a moment, and then laughed.

"Well," he said, "you had better show your sister my card. She is, I presume, a professional, as she is singing here. My desire to make her acquaintance is purely actuated by business motives."

Tavernake moved away toward the waiting-room.

The man, who according to his card was Mr. Sidney Grier, would have followed him in, but Tavernake stopped him.

"If you will wait here," he suggested, "I will see whether my sister desires to meet you."

Once more Mr. Sidney Grier looked surprised, but after a second glance at Tavernake he accepted his suggestion and remained outside. Tavernake took the card to Beatrice.

"Beatrice," he announced, "there is a man outside who has heard you sing and who wants to be introduced."

She took the card and her eyes opened wide.

"Do you know who he is?" Tavernake asked.

"Of course," she answered. "He is a great producer of musical comedies. Let me think."

She stood with the card in her hand. Some one else was singing now—an ordinary modern ballad of love and roses, rapture and despair. They heard the rising and falling of the woman's voice; the clatter of the dinner had ceased. Beatrice stood still thinking, her fingers clinching the card of Mr. Sidney Grier.

"You must bring him in," she said to Tavernake finally.

Tavernake went outside.

"My sister will see you," he remarked, with the air of one who brings good news.

Mr. Sidney Grier grunted. He was not used to being kept waiting, even for a second. Tavernake ushered him into the retiring room, and the other two musicians who were there stared at him as at a god.

"This is the gentleman whose card you have, Beatrice," Tavernake announced. "Mr. Sidney Grier—Miss Tavernake!"

The man smiled.

"Your brother seems to be suspicious of me," he declared. "I found it quite difficult to persuade him that you might find it interesting to talk to me for a few minutes."

"He does not quite understand," Beatrice answered. "He has not much experience of musical affairs or the stage, and your name would not have any significance for him."

Tavernake went outside and listened idly to the song which was proceeding. It was a class of music which secretly he preferred to the stranger and more haunting notes of Beatrice's melodies. Apparently the audience was of his opinion, for they received it with a vociferous encore, to which the young lady generously replied with a music-hall song about "A French lady from over the water." Towards the close of the applause which marked the conclusion of this effort, Tavernake felt himself touched lightly upon the arm. He turned round. By his side was standing the other dinner guest who had shown some interest in Beatrice. He was a man apparently of about forty years of age, tall and broad-shouldered, with black moustache, and dark, piercing eyes. Unlike most of the guests, he wore a short dinner-coat and black tie, from which, and his slight accent, Tavernake concluded that he was probably an American.

"Say, you'll forgive my speaking to you," he said, touching Tavernake on the arm. "My name is Pritchard. I saw you come in with the young lady who was singing a few minutes ago, and if you won't consider it a liberty, I'll be very glad indeed if you'll answer me one question."

Tavernake stiffened insensibly.

"It depends upon the question," he replied, shortly.

"Well, it's about the young lady, and that's a fact," Mr. Pritchard admitted. "I see that her name upon the programme is given as Miss Tavernake. I was seated at the other end of the room but she seemed to me remarkably like a young lady from the other side of the Atlantic, whom I am very anxious to meet."

"Perhaps you will kindly put your question in plain words," Tavernake said.

"Why, that's easy," Mr. Pritchard declared. "Is Miss Tavernake really her name, or an assumed one? I expect it's the same over here as in my country—a singer very often sings under another name than her own, you know," he added, noting Tavernake's gathering frown.

"The young lady in question is my sister, and I do not care to discuss her with strangers," Tavernake announced.

Mr. Pritchard nodded pleasantly.

"Why, of course, that ends the matter," he remarked. "Sorry to have troubled you, anyway."

He strolled off back to his seat and Tavernake returned thoughtfully to the dressing-room. He found Beatrice alone and waiting for him.

"You've got rid of that fellow, then?" he inquired.

Beatrice assented.

"Yes; he didn't stay very long," she replied.

"Who was he?" Tavernake asked, curiously.

"From a musical comedy point of view," she said, "he was the most important person in London. He is the emperor of stage-land. He can make the fortune of any girl in London who is reasonably good-looking and who can sing and dance ever so little."

"What did he want with you?" Tavernake demanded, suspiciously.

"He asked me whether I would like to go upon the stage. What do you think about it, Leonard?"

Tavernake, for some reason or other, was displeased.

"Would you earn much more money than by singing at these dinners?" he asked.

"Very, very much more," she assured him.

"And you would like the life?"

She laughed softly.

"Why not? It isn't so bad. I was on the stage in New York for some time under much worse conditions."

He remained silent for a few minutes. They had made their way into the street now and were waiting for an omnibus.

"What did you tell him?" he asked, abruptly.

She was looking down toward the Embankment, her eyes filled once more with the things which he could not understand.

"I have told him nothing yet," she murmured.

"You would like to accept?"

She nodded.

"I am not sure," she replied. "If only—I dared!"

CHAPTER VIII. WOMAN'S WILES

At eleven o'clock the next morning, Tavernake presented himself at the Milan Court and inquired for Mrs. Wenham Gardner. He was sent at once to her apartments in charge of a page. She was lying upon a sofa piled up with cushions, wrapped in a wonderful blue garment which seemed somehow to deepen the color of her eyes. By her side was a small table on which was some chocolate, a bowl of roses, and a roll of newspapers. She held out her hand toward Tavernake, but did not rise. There was something almost spiritual about her pallor, the delicate outline of her figure, so imperfectly concealed by the thin silk dressing-gown, the faint, tired smile with which she welcomed him.

"You will forgive my receiving you like this, Mr. Tavernake?" she begged. "To-day I have a headache. I have been anxious for your coming. You must sit by my side, please, and tell me at once whether you have seen Beatrice."

Tavernake did exactly as he was bidden. The chair toward which she had pointed was quite close to the sofa, but there was no other unoccupied in the room. She raised herself a little on the couch and turned towards him. Her eyes were fixed anxiously upon his, her forehead slightly wrinkled, her voice tremulous with eagerness.

"You have seen her?"

"I have," he admitted, looking steadily into the lining of his hat.

"She has been cruel," Elizabeth declared. "I can tell it from your face. You have bad news for me."

"I do not know," Tavernake replied, "whether she has been cruel or not. She refuses to allow me to tell you her address. She begged me, indeed, to keep away from you altogether."

"Why? Did she tell you why?"

"She says that you are her sister, that you have no money of your own and that your husband has left you," Tavernake answered, deliberately.

"Is that all?"

"No, it is not all," he continued. "As to the rest, she told me nothing definite. It is quite clear, however, that she is very anxious to keep away from you."

"But her reason?" Elizabeth persisted. "Did she give you no reason?"

Tavernake looked her in the face.

"She gave me no reason," he said.

"Do you believe that she is justified in treating me like this?" Elizabeth asked, playing nervously with a pendant which hung from her smooth, bare neck.

"Of course I do," he replied. "I am quite sure that she would not feel as she does unless you had been guilty of something very terrible indeed."

The woman on the couch winced as though some one had struck her. A more susceptible man than Tavernake must have felt a little remorseful at the tears which dimmed for a moment her beautiful eyes. Tavernake, however, although he felt a moment's uneasiness, although he felt himself assailed all the time by a curious new emotion which he utterly failed to understand, was nevertheless still immune. The things which were to happen to him had not yet, arrived.

"Of course," he continued, "I was very much disappointed to hear this, because I had hoped that we might have been able to let Grantham House to you. We cannot consider the matter at all now unless you pay for everything in advance."

She uncovered her eyes and looked at him. People so direct of speech as this had come very seldom into her life. She was conscious of a thrill of interest. The study of men was a passion with her. Here was indeed a new type!

"So you think that I am an adventuress," she murmured.

He reflected for a moment.

"I suppose," he admitted, "that it comes to that. I should

not have returned at all if I had not promised. If there is any message which you wish me to give your sister, I will take it, but I cannot tell you her address."

She laid her hand suddenly upon his, and raising herself a little on the couch, leaned towards him. Her eyes and her lips both pleaded with him.

"Mr. Tavernake," she said slowly, "Beatrice is such a dear, obstinate creature, but she does not quite appreciate my position. Do me a favor, please. If you have promised not to give me her address let me at least know some way or some place in which I could come across her. I am sure she will be glad afterwards, and I—I shall be very grateful."

Tavernake felt that he was enveloped by something which he did not understand, but his lack of experience was so great that he did not even wonder at his insensibility.

"I shall keep my word to your sister," he announced, "in the spirit as well as the letter. It is quite useless to ask me to do otherwise."

Elizabeth was at first amazed, then angry, how angry she scarcely knew even herself. She had been a spoilt child, she had grown into a spoilt woman. Men, at least, had been ready enough to do her bidding all her life. Her beauty was of that peculiar kind, half seductive, half pathetic, wholly irresistible. And now there had come this strange, almost impossible person, against the armor of whose indifference she had spent herself in vain. Her eyes filled with tears once more as she looked at him, and Tavernake became uneasy. He glanced at the clock and again toward the door.

"I think, if you will excuse me," he began,—

"Mr. Tavernake," she interrupted, "you are very unkind to me, very unkind indeed."

"I cannot help it," he answered.

"If you knew everything," she continued, "you would not be so obstinate. If Beatrice herself were here, if I could whisper something in her ear, she would be only too thankful that I had found her out. Beatrice has always misunderstood me, Mr. Tavernake. It is a little hard upon me, for we are both so far away from home, from our friends."

"You can send her any message you like by me," Tavernake declared. "If you like, I will wait while you write a letter. If you really have anything to say to her which might change her opinion, you can write it, can't you?"

She looked down at her hands—very beautiful and well-kept hands—and sighed. This young man, with his unusual imperturbability and hateful common sense, was getting on her nerves.

"It is so hard to write things, Mr. Tavernake," she said, "but, of course, it is something to know that if the worst happens I can send her a letter. I shall think about that for a short time. Meanwhile, there is so much about her I would love to have you tell me. She has no money, has she? How does she support herself?"

"She sings occasionally at concerts," Tavernake replied after a moment's pause. "I suppose there is no harm in telling you that."

Elizabeth leaned towards him. She was very loth indeed to acknowledge defeat. Once more her voice was deliciously soft, her forehead delicately wrinkled, her blue eyes filled with alluring light.

"Mr. Tavernake," she murmured, "do you know that you are not in the least kind to me? Beatrice and I are sisters, after all. Even she has admitted that. She left me most unkindly at a critical time in my life; she misunderstood things; if I were to see her, I could explain everything. I feel it very much that she is living apart from me in this city where we are both strangers. I am anxious about her, Mr. Tavernake. Does she want money? If so, will you take her some from me? Can't you suggest any way in which I could help her? Do be my friend, please, and advise me."

Life was certainly opening out for Tavernake. The atmosphere by which he was surrounded, which she was deliberately creating around him, was the atmosphere of an unknown world. It was a position, this, entirely novel to him. Nevertheless, he did his best to cope with it intelligently. He reflected carefully before he made any reply, he refused absolutely to listen to the strange voices singing in his ears, and he delivered his decision with his usual air of finality.

"I am afraid," he said, "that since Beatrice refuses even to let you know her whereabouts, she would not wish to accept anything from you. It seems a pity," he went on, the instincts of the money-saver stirring within him; "she is certainly none too well off."

The lady on the couch sighed.

"Beatrice has at least a friend," she murmured. "It is a great deal to have a friend. It is more than I have. We are both so far from home here. Often I am sorry that we ever left America. England is not a hospitable country, Mr. Tavernake."

Again this painfully literal young man spoke out what was in his mind.

"There was a gentleman in the motor-car with you the other night," he reminded her.

She bit her lip.

"He was just an acquaintance," she answered, "a man whom I used to know in New York, passing through London. He called on me and asked me to go to the theatre and supper. Why not? I have had a terrible time during the last few months, Mr. Tavernake, and I am very lonely—lonelier than ever since my sister deserted me."

Tavernake began to feel, ridiculous though it seemed, that in some subtle and inexplicable fashion he was in danger. At any rate, he was hopelessly bewildered. He did not understand why this very beautiful lady should look at him as though they were old friends, why her eyes should appeal to him so often for sympathy, why her fingers, which a moment ago were resting lightly upon his hand, and which she had drawn away with reluctance, should have burned him like pin-pricks of fire. The woman who wishes to allure may be as subtle as possible in her methods, but a sense of her purpose, however vague it may be, is generally communicated to her would be victim. Tavernake was becoming distinctly uneasy. He had no vanity. He knew from the first that this beautiful creature belonged to a world far removed from any of which he had any knowledge. The only solution of the situation which presented itself to him was that she might be thinking of borrowing money from him!

"There was never a time in my life," she continued softly, "when I felt that I needed a friend more. I am afraid that my sister has prejudiced you against me, Mr. Tavernake. Beatrice is very young, and the young are not always sympathetic, you know. They do not make allowances, they do not understand."

"Why did you tell Mr. Dowling things which were not true?" he asked bluntly.

She sighed, and looked down at the handkerchief with which she had been toying.

"It was a very silly piece of conceit," she admitted, "but, you see, I had to tell him something."

"Why did you come to the office at all?" he continued.

"Do you really want to know that?" she whispered softly.

"Well,—"

"I will tell you," she went on suddenly. "It sounds foolish, in a way, and yet it wasn't really, because, you see,"—she smiled at him—"I was anxious about Beatrice. I saw you come out of the office that morning, and I recognized you at once. I knew that it was you who had been with Beatrice. I made an excuse about the house to come and see whether I could find you out."

Tavernake, in whom the vanity was not yet born, missed

wholly the significance of her smile, her trifling hesitation.

"All that," he declared, "is no reason why you should have told Mr. Dowling that your husband was a millionaire and had given you carte blanche about taking a house."

"Did I mention—my husband?"

"Distinctly," he assured her.

For the first time she had faltered in her speech. Tavernake felt that she herself was shaken by some emotion. Her eyes for a moment were strangely-lit; something had come into her face which he did not understand. Then it passed. The delightful smile, half deprecating, half appealing, once more parted her lips; the gleam of horror no longer shone in her blue eyes.

"I am always so foolish about money," she declared, "so ignorant that I never know how I stand, but really I think that I have plenty, and a hundred or two more or less for rent didn't seem to matter much."

It was a point of view, this, which Tavernake utterly failed to comprehend. He looked at her in surprise.

"I suppose," he protested, "you know how much a year you have to live on?"

She shook her head.

"It seems to vary all the time," she sighed. "There are so many complications."

He looked at her in amazement.

"After all," he admitted, "you don't look as though you had much of a head for figures."

"If only I had some one to help me!" she murmured.

Tavernake moved uneasily in his chair. His sense of danger was growing.

"If you will excuse me now," he said, "I think that I must be getting back. I am an employee at Dowling, Spence & Company's, you know, and my time is not quite my own. I only came because I promised to."

"Mr. Tavernake," she begged, looking at him full out of those wonderful blue eyes, "please do me a great favor."

"What is it?" he asked with clumsy ungraciousness.

"Come and see me, every now and then, and let me know how my sister is. Perhaps you may be able to suggest some way in which I can help her."

Tavernake considered the question for a moment. He was angry with himself for the unaccountable sense of pleasure which her suggestion had given him.

"I am not quite sure," he said, "whether I had better come. Beatrice seemed quite anxious that I should not talk about her to you at all. She did not like my coming to-day."

"You seem to know a great deal about my sister," Elizabeth declared reflectively. "You call her by her Christian name and you appear to see her frequently. Perhaps, even, you are fond of her."

Tavernake met his questioner's inquiring gaze blankly. He was almost indignant.

"Fond of her!" he exclaimed. "I have never been fond of any one in my life, or anything—except my work," he added.

She looked at him a little bewildered at first.

"Oh, you strange person!" she cried, her lips breaking into a delightful smile. "Don't you know that you haven't begun to live at all yet? You don't even know anything about life, and at the back of it all you have capacity. Yes," she went on, "I think that you have the capacity for living."

Her hand fell upon his with a little gesture which was half a caress. He looked around him as though seeking for escape. He was on his feet now and he clutched at his hat.

"I must go," he insisted almost roughly.

"Am I keeping you?" she asked innocently. "Well, you shall go as soon as you please, only you must promise me one thing. You must come back, say within a week, and let me know how my sister is. I am not half so brutal as you think. I really am anxious about her. Please!"

"I will promise that," he answered.

"Wait one moment, then," she begged, turning to the letters by her side. "There is just something I want to ask you. Don't be impatient—it is entirely a matter of business."

All the time he was acutely conscious of that restless desire to get out of the room. The woman's white arms, from which the sleeves of her blue gown had fallen back, were stretched towards him as she lazily turned over her pile of correspondence. They were very beautiful arms and Tavernake, although he had had no experience, was dimly aware of the fact. Her eyes, too, seemed always to be trying to reach some part of him which was dead, or as yet unborn. He could feel her striving to get there, beating against the walls of his indifference. Why should a woman wear blue stockings because she had a blue gown, he wondered idly. She was not like Beatrice, this alluring, beautiful woman, who lay there talking to him in a manner whose meaning came to him only in strange, bewildering flashes. He could be with Beatrice and feel the truth of what he had once told her—that her sex was a thing which need not even be taken into account between them. With this woman it was different; he felt that she wished it to be different.

"Perhaps you had better tell me about that matter of business next time I am here," he suggested, with an abruptness which was almost brusque. "I must go now. I do not know why I have stayed so long."

She held out her fingers.

"You are a very sudden person," she declared, smiling at his discomfiture. "If you must go!"

He scarcely touched her hand, anxious only to get away. And then the door opened and a man of somewhat remarkable appearance entered the room with the air of a privileged person. He was oddly dressed, with little regard to the fashion of the moment. His black coat was cut after the mode of a past generation, his collar was of the type affected by Gladstone and his fellow-statesmen, his black bow was arranged with studied negligence and he showed more frilled white shirt-front than is usual in the daytime. His silk hat was glossy but broad-brimmed; his masses of gray hair, brushed back from a high, broad forehead, gave him almost a patriarchal aspect. His features were large and fairly well-shaped, but his mouth was weak and his cheeks lacked the color of a healthy life. Tavernake stared at him open-mouthed. He, for his part, looked at Tavernake as he might have looked at some strange wild animal.

"A thousand apologies, dear Elizabeth!" he exclaimed. "I knocked, but I imagine that you did not hear me. Knowing your habits, it did not occur to me that you might be engaged at this hour of the morning."

"It is a young man from the house agent's," she announced indifferently, "come to see me about a flat."

"In that case," he suggested amiably, "I am, perhaps, not in the way."

Elizabeth turned her head slightly and looked at him; he backed precipitately toward the door.

"In a few minutes," he said. "I will return in a few minutes."

Tavernake attempted to follow his example.

"There is no occasion for your friend to leave," he protested. "If you have any instructions for us, a note to the office will always bring some one here to see you."

She sat up on the couch and smiled at him. His obvious embarrassment amused her. It was a new sort of game, this, altogether.

"Come, Mr. Tavernake," she said, "three minutes more won't matter, will it? I will not keep you longer than that, I promise."

He came reluctantly a few steps back.

"I am sorry," he explained, "but we really are busy this

morning."

"This is business," she declared, still smiling at him pleasantly. "My sister has filled you with suspicions about me. Some of them may be justifiable, some are not. I am not so rich as I should like some people to believe. It is so much easier to live well, you know, when people believe that you are rolling in money. Still, I am by no means a pauper. I cannot afford to take Grantham House, but neither can I afford to go on living here. I have decided to make a change, to try and economize, to try and live within my means. Now will you bring me a list of small houses or flats, something at not more than say two or three hundred a year? It shall be strictly a business proceeding. I will pay you for your time, if that is necessary, and your commission in advance. There, you can't refuse my offer on those terms, can you?"

Tavernake remained silent. He was conscious that his lack of response seemed both sullen and awkward, but he was for the moment tongue-tied. His habit of inopportune self-analysis had once more asserted itself. He could not understand the curious nature of his mistrust of this woman, nor could he understand the pleasure which her suggestion gave him. He wanted to refuse, and yet he was glad to be able to tell himself that he was, after all, but an employee of his firm and not in a position to decline business on their behalf.

She leaned a little towards him; her tone was almost beseeching.

"You are not going to be unkind? You will not refuse me?" she pleaded.

"I will bring you a list," he answered heavily, "on the terms you suggest."

"To-morrow morning?" she begged.

"As soon as I am able," he promised.

Then he escaped. Outside in the corridor, the man who had interrupted his interview was walking backwards and forwards. Tavernake passed him without responding to his bland greeting. He forgot all about the lift and descended five flights of stairs....

A few minutes later, he presented himself at the office and reported that Mrs. Wenham Gardner had decided unfavorably about Grantham House, and that she was not disposed, indeed, to take premises of anything like such a rental. Mr. Dowling was disappointed, and inclined to think that his employee had mismanaged the affair.

"I wish that I had gone myself," he declared. "She obviously wished me to, but it happened to be inconvenient. By-the-bye, Tavernake, close the door, will you? There is another matter concerning which I should like to speak to you."

Tavernake did as he was bidden at once, without any disquietude. His own services to the firm were of such a nature that he had no misgiving whatever as to his employer's desire for a private interview.

"It is about the Marston Rise estate," Mr. Dowling explained, arranging his pince nez. "I believe that the time is coming when some sort of overtures should be made. You know what has been in my mind for a very considerable time."

Tavernake nodded.

"Yes," he admitted, "I know quite well."

"I did hear a rumor," Mr. Dowling continued, "that some one had bought one small plot on the outskirts of the estate. I dare say it is not true, and in any case it is not worth while troubling about, but it shows that the public is beginning to nibble. I am of opinion that the time is almost—yes, almost ripe for a move."

"Do you wish me to do anything in the matter, sir?" Tavernake asked.

"In the first place," Mr. Dowling declared, "I should like you to try to find out whether any of the plots have really been sold, and, if so, to whom, and what would be their price. Can you do this during the week?"

"I think so," Tavernake answered.

"Say Monday morning," Mr. Dowling suggested, taking down his hat. "I shall be playing golf to-morrow and Friday, and of course Saturday. Monday morning you might let me have a report."

Tavernake went back to his office. After all, then, things were to come to a crisis a little earlier than he had thought. He knew quite well that that report, if he made it honestly, and no other idea was likely to occur to him, would effectually sever his connection with Messrs. Dowling, Spence & Company.

CHAPTER IX. THE PLOT THICKENS

The man whom Tavernake had left walking up and down the corridor lost no time in presenting himself once more at the apartments of Mrs. Wenham Gardner. He entered the suite without ceremony, carefully closing both doors behind him. It became obvious then that his deportment on the occasion of his previous appearance had been in the nature of a bluff. The air with which he looked across the room at the woman who watched him was furtive; the hand which laid his hat upon the table was shaking; there was a gleam almost of terror in his eyes. The woman remained impassive, inscrutable, simply watching him. After a moment or two, however, she spoke—a single monosyllable.

"Well?"

The man broke down.

"Elizabeth," he exclaimed, "you are too—too ghastly! I can't stand it. You are unnatural."

She stretched herself upon the couch and turned towards him.

"Unnatural, am I?" she remarked. "And what are you?"

He sank into a chair. He had become very flabby indeed.

"What you are always calling me, I suppose," he muttered,—"a coward. You have so little consideration, Elizabeth. My health isn't what it was."

His eyes had wandered longingly toward the cupboard at the further end of the apartment. The woman upon the couch smiled.

"You may help yourself," she directed carelessly. "Perhaps then you will be able to tell me why you have come in such a state."

He crossed the room in a few hasty steps, his head and shoulders disappeared inside the cupboard. There was the sound of the withdrawal of a cork, the fizz of a sodawater syphon. He returned to his place a different man.

"You must remember my age, Elizabeth dear," he said, apologetically. "I haven't your nerve—it isn't likely that I should have. When I was twenty-five, there was nothing in the world of which I was afraid."

She looked him over critically.

"Perhaps I am not so absolutely courageous as you think," she remarked. "To tell you the truth, there are a good many things of which I am afraid when you come to me in such a state. I am afraid of you, of what you will do or say."

"You need not be," he assured her hastily. "When I am away from you, I am dumb. What I suffer no one knows. I keep it to myself."

She nodded, a little contemptuously.

"I suppose you do your best," she declared. "Tell me, now, what is this fresh thing which has disturbed you?"

Her visitor stared at her.

"Does there need to be any fresh thing?" he muttered.

"I suppose it is something about Wenham?" she asked.

The man shivered. He opened his lips and closed them again. The woman's tone, if possible, grew colder.

"I hope you are not going to tell me that you have disobeyed my orders," she said.

"No," he protested, "no! I was there yesterday. I came back by the mail from Penzance. I had to motor thirty miles to catch it."

"Something has happened, of course," she went on, "something which you are afraid to tell 'me. Sit up like a man, my dear father, and let me have the truth."

"Nothing fresh has happened at all," he assured her. "It is simply that the memory of the day I spent at that place and that the sight of him has got on my nerves till I can't sleep or think of anything else."

"What rubbish!" she exclaimed.

"You have only seen the place in fine weather," he

continued, dropping his voice a little. "Elizabeth, you have no idea what it is really like. Yesterday morning I got out of the train at Bodmin and I motored through to the village of Clawes. After that there were five miles to walk. There's no road, only a sort of broken track, and for the whole of that five miles there isn't even a farm building to be seen and I didn't meet a human soul. There was a sort of pall of white-gray mists everywhere over the moor, sometimes so dense that I couldn't see my way, and you could stop and listen and there wasn't a thing to be heard, not even a sheep bell."

She laughed softly..

"My dear, foolish father," she murmured, "you don't understand what a rest cure is. This is quite all right, quite as it should be. Poor Wenham has been seeing too many people all his life—that is why we have to keep him quiet for a time. You can skip the scenery. I suppose you got to the house at last?"

"Yes, I got there," continued her father. "You know what a bleak-looking place it is, right on the side of a bare hill—a square, gray stone place just the color of the hillside. Well, I got there and walked in. There was Ted Mathers, half dressed, no collar, with a bottle of whiskey on the table, playing some wretched game of cards by himself. Elizabeth, what a brute that man is!"

She shook her head.

"Go on," she said. "What about Wenham?"

"He was there in a corner, gazing out of the window. When I came he sprang up, but when he saw who it was, he—he tried to hide. He was afraid of me."

"Why?" she asked.

"He said that I—I reminded him of you."

"Absurd!" she murmured. "Tell me, how did he look?"

"Ill, wretched, paler and thinner than ever, and wilder looking."

"What did Mathers say about him?" she demanded.

"What could he? He told me that he cried all day and begged to be taken back to America."

"No one goes near the place, I suppose?" she asked.

"Not a soul. A man comes from the village to sell things once a week. Mathers knows when to expect him and takes care that Wenham is not around. They are out of the world there—no road, no paths, nothing to bring even a tourist. I could have imagined such a spot in Arizona, Elizabeth, but in England—no!"

"Has he any amusements at all?" she inquired.

The man's hands were shaking; once more his eyes went longingly toward the cupboard.

"He has made—a doll," he said, "carved it out of a piece of wood and dressed it in oddments from his ties. Mathers showed it to me as a joke. Elizabeth, it was wonderful—horrible!"

"Why?" she asked him.

"It is you," he continued, moistening his lips with his tongue, "you, in a blue gown—your favorite shade. He has even made blue stockings and strange little shoes. He has got some hair from somewhere and parted it just like yours."

"It sounds very touching," she remarked.

The man was shivering again.

"Elizabeth," he said, "I do not think that he means it kindly. Mathers took me up into his room. He has made something there which looks like a scaffold. The doll was hanging by a piece of string from the gallows. Elizabeth!—my God, but it was like you!" he cried, suddenly dropping his head upon his arms.

For a moment, a reflection of the terror which had seized him flashed in her own face. It passed quickly away. She laughed mockingly.

"My dear father," she protested, "you are certainly not yourself this morning."

"I saw you swinging," he muttered, "swinging by that piece of cord! There was a great black pin through your heart. Elizabeth, if he should get away sometime! If some one should come over from America and discover where he was! If he should find us out! Oh, my God, if he should find us out!"

Elizabeth had risen to her feet. She was standing now before the fire, her left elbow resting upon the mantelpiece, a trifle of silver gleaming in her right hand.

"Father," she said, "there is no danger in life for those who know no fear. Look at me."

His eyes sought hers, fascinated.

"If he should find me out," she continued, "it would be no such terrible thing, after all. It would be the end."

Her fingers disclosed the little ornament she was carrying —a tiny pistol. She slipped it back into her pocket. The man was wondering how such a thing as this came to be his daughter.

"You have courage, Elizabeth," he whispered.

"I have courage," she assented, "because I have brains. I never allow myself to be in a position where I should be likely to get the worst of it. Ever since the day when he turned so suddenly against me, I have been careful."

Her father leaned towards her.

"Elizabeth," he said, "I never really understood. What was it that came over him so suddenly? One day he was your slave, the next I think he would have murdered you if he could."

She shrugged her shoulders.

"Honestly," she replied, "I felt it impossible to keep up the sham any longer. I married Wenham Gardner in New York because he was supposed to be a millionaire and because it seemed to be the best thing to do, but as to living with him, I never meant that. You know how ridiculous his behavior was on the boat. He never let me out of his sight, but swore that he was going to give up smoking and drinking and lead a new life for my sake. I really believe he meant it, too."

"Wouldn't it have been better, dear," her father suggested, timidly, "to have encouraged him?"

She shook her head.

"He was absolutely hopeless," she declared. "You say that I have no nerves; that is because I do not allow myself to suffer. If I had gone on living with Wenham, it would have driven me mad. His habits, his manner of life, everything disgusted me. Until I came to see so much of him, I never understood what the term 'decadent' really can mean. The very touch of him grew to be hateful. No woman could live with such a man. By the way, he signed the draft, I suppose?"

Her father handed her a slip of paper, which she looked at and locked in her drawer.

"Did he make any trouble about it?" she asked.

The professor shivered.

"He refused to sign it," he said, in a low tone, "swore he would never sign it. Mathers sent me out for a few minutes, made me go into another room. When I came back, he gave me the draft. I heard him calling out."

"Mathers certainly earns his money," she remarked, drily.

He gazed at her with grudging admiration. This was his daughter, his own flesh and blood. Back through the years, for a moment, he seemed to see her, a child with hair down her back, sitting on his knee, listening to his stories, wondering at the little arts and tricks by which he had wrested their pennies and sixpennies from a credulous public. Phrenologist, hypnotist, conjurer—all these things the great Professor Franklin had called himself. Often, from the rude stage where he had given his performance, he had terrified to death the women and children of his audience. It flashed upon him at that moment that never, even in the days of her childhood, had he seen fear in Elizabeth's face.

"You should have been a man, Elizabeth," he muttered.

She shook her head, smiling as though not ill-pleased at

the compliment.

"The power of a man is so limited," she declared. "A woman has more weapons."

"More weapons indeed," the professor agreed, as his eyes traveled over the slim yet wonderful perfection of her form, lingered for a moment at the little knot of lace at her throat, wrestled with the delicate sweetness of her features, struggling hard to think from whom among his ancestors could have come a creature so physically attractive.

"More weapons, indeed," he repeated. "Elizabeth, what a gift—what a gift!"

"You speak," she replied, "as though it were an evil one."

"I was only thinking," he said, "that it seems a pity. You are so wonderful, we might have found an easier and a less dangerous way to fortune."

She smiled.

"The Bohemian blood in me, I suppose," she remarked. "The crooked ways attract, you know, when one has been brought up as I was."

"Your poor mother had no love for them," he reminded her.

"Beatrice has inherited everything that belonged to my mother. I am your own daughter, father. You ought to be proud of me. But there, I gave you another commission. Is it true that Jerry is really here?"

"He arrived in England on Wednesday on the Lusitania. He has been in town all the time since."

A distinct frown darkened her face.

"He must have had my letter, then," she murmured, half to herself.

"Without a doubt," her father admitted. "Elizabeth, why do you take chances about seeing this man? He was fond of you in New York, I know, but then he was fond of his brother, too. He may not believe your story. It may be dangerous."

She smiled.

"I think I can convince Jerry Gardner of anything I choose to tell him," she said. "Besides, it is absolutely necessary that I have some information about Wenham's affairs. He must have a great deal more money somewhere and I must find out how we are to get at it."

The professor shook his head.

"I don't like it," he muttered. "Supposing he finds Beatrice!"

Elizabeth shrugged her shoulders.

"Beatrice is made of silent stuff," she declared. "I should never be afraid of her. All the same, I wish I could find out just where she is. It would look better if we were living together."

The professor shook his head sadly.

"She left us of her own free will," he said, "and I don't believe, Elizabeth, that she would ever come back again. She knew very well what she was doing. She knew that our views of life were not hers. She didn't know half but she knew enough. You were quite right in what you said just now; Beatrice was more like her mother, and her mother was a good woman."

"Really!" Elizabeth remarked, insolently.

"Don't answer like that," he blustered, striking the table. "She was your mother, too."

The woman's face was inscrutable, hard, and flawless behind the little cloud of tobacco smoke. The man began to tremble once more. Every time he ventured to assert himself, a single look from her was sufficient to quell him.

"Elizabeth," he muttered, "you haven't a heart, you haven't a soul, you haven't a conscience. I wonder—what sort of a woman you are!"

"I am your daughter," she reminded him, pleasantly.

"I was never quite so bad as that," he went on, taking a large silk handkerchief from his pocket and dabbing his forehead. "I had to live and times were hard. I have cheated the public, perhaps. I haven't been above playing at cards a little cleverly, or making something where I could out of the weaker men. But, Elizabeth, I am afraid of you."

"Men are generally afraid of the big stakes," she remarked, flicking the ash from her cigarette. "They will cheat and lie for halfpennies, but they are bad gamblers when life or death—the big things are in the balance. Bah!" she went on. "Father, I want Jerry Gardner to come and see me."

"If you can't make him come, my dear," the professor said, "I am sure it will be of no use my trying."

"He has had my letter," she continued, half to herself; "he has had my letter and he does not come."

"There is nothing to be done but wait," her father decided.

"And meanwhile," she went on, "supposing he were to discover Beatrice, supposing they two were to come together; supposing he were to tell her what he knows and she were to tell him what she guessed!"

The professor buried his face in his hands. Elizabeth threw her cigarette away with an impatient gesture.

"What an idiot I am!" she declared. "What is the use of wasting time like this?"

There was a knock at the door. A trim-looking French maid presented herself. She addressed her mistress in voluble French. A coiffeur and a manicurist were waiting in the next apartment; it was time that Madame habited herself. The professor listened to these announcements with an air of half-admiring wonder.

"I suppose I must be going," he said, rising to his feet. "There is just one thing I should like to ask you, Elizabeth, if I may, before I go."

"Well?"

"Who was the young man whom I met here just now?"

"Why do you ask that?" she demanded.

"I really do not know," her father replied, thoughtfully, "except that his appearance seemed a little singular. In some respects he appeared so commonplace. His clothes and bearing, in fact, were so ordinary that I was surprised to find him here with you. And, on the other hand, his face—you must remember, my dear, that this is entirely a professional instinct; I am still interested in faces—"

"Quite so," she admitted. "Go on. The young man rather puzzles me myself. I should like to hear what you make of him. What did you think of his face?"

"There was something powerful about it," he declared, "something dogged, splendid, narrow, impossible,—the sort of face which belongs to a man who achieves great things because he is too stupid to recognize failure, even when it has him in its arms and its fingers are upon his throat. That young man has qualities, my dear, I am sure. Mind you, at present they are dormant, but he has qualities."

She led him to the door.

"My dear father," she said, "sometimes I really respect you. If you should come across that young man again, keep your eye upon him. He knows one thing at least which I wish he would tell us—he knows where Beatrice is."

Her father looked at her in amazement.

"He knows where Beatrice is and he has not told you?"

She nodded.

"You tried to have him tell you and he refused?" the professor persisted.

"Exactly," she admitted.

Her father put on his hat.

"I knew that young man was something out of the common."

CHAPTER X. THE JOY OF BATTLE

They sat on the trunk of a fallen tree, in the topmost corner of the field. In the hedge, close at hand, was a commotion of birds. In the elm tree, a little further away, a thrush was singing. A soft west wind blew in their faces; the air immediately around them was filled with sunlight. Yet almost to their feet stretched one of those great arms of the city—a suburb, with its miles of villas, its clanging of electric cars, its waste plots, its rows of struggling shops. And only a little further away still, the body itself—the huge city, throbbing beneath its pall of smoke and cloud. The girl, who had been gazing steadily downwards for several moments, turned at last to her companion.

"Do you know," she said, "that this makes me think of the first night you spoke to me? You remember it—up on the roof at Blenheim House?"

Tavernake did not answer for a moment. He was looking through a queerly-shaped instrument that he had brought with him at half-a-dozen stakes that he had laboriously driven into the ground some distance away. He was absolutely absorbed in his task.

"The main avenue," he muttered softly to himself. "Yes, it must be a trifle more to the left. Then we get all the offshoots parallel and the better houses have their southern aspect. I beg your pardon, Beatrice, did you say anything?" he broke off suddenly.

She smiled.

"Nothing worth mentioning. I was just thinking that it reminded me a little up here of the first time you and I ever talked together."

He glanced down at the panorama below, with its odd jumble of hideous buildings, softened here and there with wreaths of sunstained smoke, its great blots of ugliness irredeemable, insistent.

"It's different, of course," she went on. "I remember, even

now, the view from the house-top that night. In a sense, it was finer than this; everything was more lurid and yet more chaotic; one simply felt that underneath all those mysterious places was some great being, toiling and struggling—Life itself, groaning through space with human cogwheels. Up here one sees too much. Oh, my dear Leonard," she continued, "to think that you, too, should be one of the devastators!"

He fitted his instrument into its case and replaced it in his pocket.

"Come," he said, "you mustn't call me hard names. I shall remind you of the man whose works you are making me read. You know what he says—'The aesthete is, after all, only a dallier. The world lives and progresses by reason of its utilitarians.' This hill represents to me most of the things that are worth having in life."

She laughed shortly.

"You will cut down those hedges and drive away the birds to find a fresh home; you will plough up the green grass, cut out a street and lay down granite stones. Then I see your ugly little houses coming up like mushrooms all over the place. You are a vandal, my dear Leonard."

"I am simply obeying the law," he answered. "After all, even from your own point of view, I do not think that it is so bad. Look closer, and you will find that the hedges are blackened here and there with smuts. The birds will find a better dwelling place further away. See how the smoke from those factory chimneys is sending its smuts across these fields. They are no longer country; they are better gathered in."

She shivered.

"There is something about life," she said, sadly, "which terrifies me. Every force that counts seems to be destructive."

Up the steep hill behind them came the puffing and groaning of a small motor-car. They both turned their heads to watch it come into view. It was an insignificant affair of an almost extinct pattern, a single cylinder machine with a round tonneau back. The engine was knocking badly as the driver brought it to a standstill a few yards away from them. Involuntarily Tavernake stiffened as he saw the two men who descended from it, and who were already passing through the gate close to where they were. One was Mr. Dowling, the other the manager of the bank where they kept their account. Mr. Dowling recognized his manager with surprise but much cordiality.

"Dear me!" he exclaimed. "Dear me, this is most fortunate! You know Mr. Tavernake, of course, Belton? My manager, Mr. Tavernake—Mr. Belton, of the London & Westminster Bank. I have brought Mr. Belton up here, Tavernake, to have a look round, so that he may know what we mean to do with all the money we shall have to come and borrow, eh?"

The bank manager smiled.

"It is a very fine situation," he remarked.

The eyes of the two men fell upon Beatrice, who had drawn a little to one side.

"May we have the pleasure, Tavernake?" Mr. Dowling said, graciously. "You are not married, I believe?"

"No, this is my sister," Tavernake answered, slowly, —"Mr. Belton and Mr. Dowling."

The two men acknowledged the salute with some slight surprise. Beatrice, although her clothes were simple, had always the air of belonging to a different world.

"Your brother, my dear Miss Tavernake," Mr. Dowling declared, "is a perfect genius at discovering these desirable sites. This one I honestly consider to be the find of our lifetime. We have now," he proceeded, turning to Mr. Belton, "certain information that the cars will run to whatever point we desire in this vicinity, and the Metropolitan Railway has also arranged for an extension of its system. To-morrow I propose," Mr. Dowling continued, holding the sides of his coat and assuming a somewhat pompous manner, "to make an offer for the whole of this site. It will involve a very large sum of money indeed, but I am convinced that it will be a remunerative speculation."

Tavernake remained grimly silent. This was scarcely the time or the place which he would have selected for an explanation with his employer. There were signs, however, that the thing was to be forced upon him.

"I am very pleased indeed to meet you here, Tavernake," Mr. Dowling went on, "pleased both for personal reasons and because it shows, if I may be allowed to say so, the interest which you take in the firm's business, that you should devote your holiday to coming and—er—surveying the scene of our exploits, so to speak. Perhaps now that you are here you would be able to explain to Mr. Belton better than I should, just what it is that we propose."

Tavernake hesitated for a moment. Finally, however, he proceeded to make clear a very elaborate and carefully thought out building scheme, to which both men listened with much attention. When he had finished, however, he turned round to Mr. Dowling, facing him squarely.

"You will understand, sir," he concluded, "that a scheme such as I have pointed out could only be carried through if the whole of the property were in one person's hands. I may say that the information to which you referred a few days ago was perfectly correct. A considerable portion of the south side of the hill has already been purchased, besides certain other plots which would interfere considerably with any comprehensive scheme of building."

Mr. Dowling's face fell at once; his tone was one of annoyance mingled with irritation.

"Come, come," he declared, "this sounds very bad, Mr. Tavernake, very neglectful, very careless as to the interests of the firm. Why did we not keep our eye upon it? Why did we not forestall this other purchaser, eh? It appears to me that we have been slack, very slack indeed."

Tavernake took a small book from his pocket.

"You will remember, sir," he said, "that it was on the eleventh of May last year when I first spoke to you of this site."

"Well, well," Mr. Dowling exclaimed, sharply, "what of it?"

"You were starting out for a fortnight's golf somewhere," Tavernake continued, "and you promised to look into the affair when you returned. I spoke to you again but you declared that you were far too busy to go into the matter at all for the present, you didn't care about this side of London, you considered that we had enough on hand—in fact, you threw cold water upon the idea."

"I may not have been very enthusiastic at first," Mr. Dowling admitted, grudgingly. "Latterly, however, I have come round to your views."

"There have been several articles in various newspapers, and a good deal of talk," Tavernake remarked, "which have been more effectual, I think, in bringing you round, than my advice. However, what I wish to say to you is this, sir, that when I found myself unable to interest you in this scheme, I went into it myself to some extent."

"Went into it yourself?" Mr. Dowling repeated, incredulously. "What do you mean, Tavernake? What do you mean, sir?"

"I mean that I have invested my savings in the purchase of several plots of land upon this hillside," Tavernake explained.

"On your own account?" Mr. Dowling demanded. "Your savings, indeed!"

"Certainly," Tavernake answered. "Why not?"

"But it's the firm's business, sir—the firm's, not yours!"

"The firm had the opportunity," Tavernake pointed out, "and were not inclined to avail themselves of it. If I had not bought the land when I did, some one else would have bought the whole of it long ago."

Mr. Dowling was obviously in a furious temper.

"Do you mean to tell me, sir," he exclaimed, "that you dared to enter into private speculations while still an employee of the firm? It is a most unheard-of thing, unwarranted, ridiculous. I shall require you, sir, to at once make over the plots of land to us—to the firm, you understand. We shall give you your price, of course, although I expect you paid much more for it than we should have done. Still, we must give you what you paid, and four per cent interest for your money."

"I am sorry," Tavernake replied, "but I am afraid that I should require better terms than that. In fact," he continued, "I do not wish to sell. I have given a great deal of thought and time to this matter, and I intend to carry it out as a personal speculation."

"Then you will carry it out, sir, from some other place than from within the walls of my office," Mr. Dowling declared, furiously. "You understand that, Tavernake?"

"Perfectly," Tavernake answered. "You wish me to leave you. It is very unwise of you to suggest it, but I am quite prepared to go."

"You will either resell me those plots at cost price, or you shall not set foot within the office again," Mr. Dowling insisted. "It is a gross breach of faith, this. I never heard of such a thing in all my life. Most unprofessional, impossible behavior!"

Tavernake showed no signs of anger—he simply turned a little away.

"I shall not sell you my land, Mr. Dowling," he said, "and it will suit me very well to leave your employ. You appear," he continued, "to expect some one else to do the whole of the work for you while you reap the entire profits. Those days have gone by. My business in the world is to make a fortune for myself, and not for you!"

"How dare you, sir!" Mr. Dowling cried. "I never heard such impertinence in my life."

"You haven't done a stroke of work for five years," Tavernake went on, unmoved, "and my efforts have supplied you with a fairly good income. In future, those efforts will be directed towards my own advancement."

Mr. Dowling turned back toward the car.

"Young man," he said, "you can brazen it out as much as you like, but you have been guilty of a gross breach of faith. I shall take care that the exact situation is made known in all responsible quarters. You'll get no situation with any firm with whom I am acquainted—I can promise you that. If you have anything more to say to Dowling, Spence & Company, let it be in writing."

They parted company there and then. Tavernake and Beatrice went down the hill in silence.

"Does this bother you at all?" she inquired presently.

"Nothing to speak of," Tavernake answered. "It had to come. I wasn't quite ready but that doesn't matter."

"What shall you do now?" she asked.

"Borrow enough to buy the whole of the hill," he replied.

She looked back.

"Won't that mean a great deal of money?"

He nodded.

"It will be a big thing, of course," he admitted. "Never mind, I dare say I shall be able to interest some one in it. In any case, I never meant Mr. Dowling to make a fortune out of this."

They walked on in silence a little further. Then she spoke again, with some hesitation.

"I suppose that what you have done is quite fair, Leonard?"

He answered her promptly, without any sign of offence at her question.

"As a matter of fact," he confessed, "it is an unusual thing for any one in the employ of a firm of estate agents to make speculations on their own account in land. In this case, however, I consider that I was justified. I have opened up three building speculations for the firm, on each one of which they have made a great deal of money, and I have not even had my salary increased, or any recognition whatever offered me. There is a debt, of course, which an employee owes to his employer. There is also a debt, however, which the employer owes to his employee. In my case I have never been treated with the slightest consideration of any sort. What I have done I shall stick to. After all, I am more interested in making money for myself than for other people."

They had reached the corner of the field now, and turning into the lane commenced the steep descent. It was Sunday evening, and from all the little conventicles and tin churches below, the bells began their unmusical summons. From further away in the distance came the more melodious chiming from the Cathedral and the city churches. The shriller and nearer note, however, prevailed. The whole medley of sound was a discord. As they descended, they could see the black-coated throngs slowly moving towards the different places of worship. There was something uninspiring about it all. She shuddered.

"Leonard," she said, "I wonder why you are so anxious to get on in the world. Why do you want to be rich?"

He was glancing back toward the hill, the light of calculations in his eyes. Once more he was measuring out those plots of land, calculating rent, deducting interest.

"We all seek different things," he replied tolerantly, —"some fame, some pleasure. Mr. Dowling, for instance, has no other ambition than to muddle round the golf links a few strokes better than his partner."

"And you?" she asked.

"It is success I seek," he answered. "Women, as a rule, do not understand. You, for instance, Beatrice, are too sentimental. I am very practical. It is money that I want. I want money because money means success."

"And afterwards?" she whispered.

He was attending to her no longer. They were turning now into the broad thoroughfare at the bottom of the lane, at the end of which a tram-car was waiting. He scribbled a few, final notes into his pocket-book.

"To-morrow," he exclaimed, with the joy of battle in his tone, "to-morrow the fight begins in earnest!"

Beatrice passed her hand through his arm.

"Not only for you, dear friend, but for me," she said. "For you? What do you mean?" he asked quickly.

"I have been trying to tell you all day," she continued, "but you have been too engrossed. Yesterday afternoon I went to see Mr. Grier at the Atlas Theatre. I had my voice tried, and to-morrow night I am going to take a small part in the new musical comedy."

Tavernake stared at her in something like consternation. His ideas as to the stage and all that belonged to it were of a primitive order. Mrs. Fitzgerald was perhaps as near as possible to his idea of the type. He glanced incredulously at Beatrice— slim, quietly dressed, yet with the unmistakable, to him mysterious, distinction of breeding.

"You an actress!" he exclaimed.

She laughed softly.

"Dear Leonard," she said, "this is going to be a part of your education. To-morrow night you shall come to the theatre and wait for me at the stage-door."

CHAPTER XI. A BEWILDERING OFFER

Elizabeth stood with her hands behind her back, leaning slightly against the writing-table. The professor, with his broad-brimmed hat clinched in his fingers, walked restlessly up and down the little room. The discussion had not been altogether a pleasant one. Elizabeth was composed but serious, her father nervous and excited.

"You are mad, Elizabeth!" he declared. "Is it that you do not understand, or will not? I tell you that we must go."

She shrugged her shoulders.

"Where would you drag me to?" she asked. "We certainly can't go back to New York."

He turned fiercely upon her.

"Whose fault is it that we can't?" he demanded. "If it weren't for you and your confounded schemes, I could be walking down Broadway next week. God's own city it is, too!" he muttered. "I wish we'd never seen those two young men."

"It was a pity, perhaps," she admitted, "yet we had to do something. We were absolutely stonybroke, as they say over here."

"Anyway, we've got to get out of this," the professor declared.

"My dear father," she replied, "I will agree that if a new city or a new world could arise from the bottom of the sea, where Professor Franklin was unknown, and his beautiful daughter Elizabeth had neyer been heard of, it might perhaps be advisable for us to go there. As it is--"

"There is Rome," he exclaimed, "or some of the smaller places! We have money for a time. We could get another draft, perhaps, from Wenham."

She shook her head. "We are just as safe here as anywhere on the Continent," she remarked.

Once more he struck the table. Then he threw out his hands above his head with the melodramatic instinct which had always been strong in his blood.

"Do you think that I am a fool?" he cried. "Do you think I do not know that if there were not something moving in your brain you would think no more of that clerk, that bourgeois estate agent, than of the door-mat beneath your feet? It is what I always complain about. You make use of me as a tool. There are always things which I do not understand. He comes here, this young man, under a pretext, whether he knows it or not. You talk to him for an hour at a time. There should be nothing in your life which I do not know of, Elizabeth," he continued, his voice suddenly hoarse as he leaned towards her. "Can't you see that there is danger in friendships for you and for me, there is danger in intimacies of any sort? I share the danger; I have a right to share the knowledge. This young man has no money of his own, I take it. Of what use is he to us?"

"You are too hasty, my dear father," she replied. "Let me assure you that there is nothing at all mysterious about Mr. Tavernake. The simple truth is that the young man rather attracts me."

The professor gazed at her incredulously.

"Attracts you! He!"

"You have never perfectly understood me, my dear parent," she murmured. "You have never appreciated that trait in my character, that strange preference, if you like, for the absolutely original. Now in all my life I never met such a young man as this. He wears the clothes and he has the features and speech of just such a person as you have described, but there is a difference."

"A difference, indeed!" the professor interrupted roughly. "What difference, I should like to know?"

She shrugged her shoulders lightly.

"He is stolid without being stupid," she explained. "He is entirely self-centered. I smile at him, and he waits patiently until I have finished to get on with our business. I have said quite nice things to him and he has stared at me without change of expression, absolutely without pleasure or emotion of any sort."

"You are too vain, Elizabeth," her father declared. "You have been spoilt. There are a few people in the world whom even you might fail to charm. No doubt this young man is one of them."

She sighed gently.

"It really does seem," she admitted, "as though you were right, but we shall see. By-the-bye, hadn't you better go? The five minutes are nearly up."

He came over to her side, his hat and gloves in his hand, prepared for departure.

"Will you tell me, upon your honor, Elizabeth," he begged, "that there is no other reason for your interest? That you are not engaged in any fresh schemes of which I know nothing? Things are bad enough as they are. I cannot sleep, I cannot rest, for thinking of our position. If I thought that you had any fresh plans on hand—"

She flicked the ash from her cigarette and checked him with a little gesture.

"He knows where Beatrice is," she remarked thoughtfully, "and I can't get him to tell me. There is nothing beyond—absolutely nothing."...

When Tavernake was announced, Elizabeth was still smoking, sitting in an easy-chair and looking into the fire. Something in her attitude, the droop of her head as it rested upon her fingers, reminded him suddenly of Beatrice. He showed no other emotion than a sudden pause in his walk across the room. Even that, however, in a person whose machinelike attitude towards her provoked her resentment, was noticeable.

"Good morning, my friend!" she said pleasantly. "You have brought me the fresh list?"

"Unfortunately, no, madam," Tavernake answered. "I have called simply to announce that I am not able to be of any further assistance to you in the matter."

She looked at him for a moment without remark.

"Are you serious, Mr. Tavernake?" she asked.

"Yes," he replied. "The fact is I am not in a position to help you. I have left the employ of Messrs. Dowling, Spence & Company."

"Of your own accord?" she inquired quietly.

"No, I was dismissed," he confessed. "I should have been compelled to leave in a very short time, but Mr. Dowling forestalled me."

"Won't you sit down and tell me about it?" she invited.

He looked her in the eyes, square and unflinching. He was still able to do that!

"It could not possibly interest you," he said.

"And—my sister? You have seen her?"

"I have seen your sister," Tavernake answered, without hesitation.

"You have a message for me?"

"None," he declared.

"She refuses—to be reconciled, then?"

"I am afraid she has no friendly feelings towards you."

"She gave you no reason?"

"No direct reason," he admitted, "but her attitude is—quite uncompromising."

She rose and swept across the floor towards him. With firm but gentle fingers she took his worn bowler hat and mended gloves from his hand. Her gesture guided him towards a sofa.

"Beatrice has prejudiced you against me," she murmured. "It is not fair. Please come and sit down—for five minutes," she pleaded. "I want you to tell me why you have quarrelled with that funny little man, Mr. Dowling."

"But, madam,—" he protested.

"If you refuse, I shall think that my sister has been telling you stories about me," she declared, watching him closely.

Tavernake drew a little away from her but seated himself on the sofa which she had indicated. He took up as much room as possible, and to his relief she did not persist in her first intention, which was obviously to seat herself beside him.

"Your sister has told me nothing about you whatsoever," he said deliberately. "At the same time, she asked me not to give you her address."

"We will talk about that presently," she interrupted. "In the first place, tell me why you have left your place."

"Mr. Dowling discovered," he told her, in a matter-of-fact tone, "that I had been doing some business on my own account. He was quite right to disapprove. I have not been back to the office since he found it out."

"What sort of business?" she asked.

"The business of the firm is to buy property in undeveloped districts and sell it for building estate," he explained. "I have been very successful hitherto in finding sites for their operations. A short time ago, I discovered one so good that I invested all my own savings in buying certain lots, and have an option upon the whole. Mr. Dowling found it out and dismissed me."

"But it seems most unfair," she declared.

"Not at all," he answered. "In Mr. Dowling's place I should have done the same thing. Every one with his way in life to make must look out for himself. Strictly speaking, what I did was wrong. I wish, however, that I had done it before. One must think of one's self first."

"And now?" she inquired. "What are you going to do now?"

"I am going to find a capitalist or float a company to buy the rest of the site," he announced. "After that, we must see about building. There is no hurry about that, though. The first thing is to secure the site."

"How much money does it require?"

"About twelve thousand pounds," he told her.

"It seems very little," she murmured.

"The need for money comes afterwards," he explained. "We want to drain and plan and build without mortgages. As soon as we are sure of the site, one can think of that. My option only extends for a week or so."

"Do you really think that it is a good speculation?" she asked.

"I do not think about such matters," he answered, drily. "I know."

She leaned back in her chair, watching him for several seconds—admiring him, as a matter of fact. The profound conviction of his words was almost inspiring. In her presence, and she knew that she was a very beautiful woman, he appeared, notwithstanding his absence of any knowledge of her sex and his lack of social status, unmoved, wholly undisturbed. He sat there in perfect naturalness. It did not seem to him even unaccountable that she should be interested in his concerns. He was not conceited or aggressive in any way. His complete self-confidence lacked any militant impulse. He was—himself, impervious to surroundings, however unusual.

"Why should I not be your capitalist?" she inquired slowly.

"Have you as much as twelve thousand pounds that you want to invest?" he asked, incredulously.

She rose to her feet and moved across to her desk. He sat quite still, watching her without any apparent curiosity. She unlocked a drawer and returned to him with a bankbook in her hand.

"Add that up," she directed, "and tell me how much I have."

He drew a lead pencil from his pocket and quickly added up the total.

"If you have not given any cheques since this was made

up," he said calmly, "you have a credit balance of thirteen thousand, one hundred and eighteen pounds, nine shillings and fourpence. It is very foolish of you to keep so much money on current account. You are absolutely losing about eight pounds a week."

She smiled.

"It is foolish of me, I suppose," she admitted, "but I have no one to advise me just now. My father knows no more about money than a child, and I have just had quite a large amount paid to me in cash. I only wish we could get Beatrice to share some of this, Mr. Tavernake."

He made no remark. To all appearance, he had never heard of her sister. She came and sat down by his side again.

"Will you have me for a partner, Mr. Tavernake?" she whispered.

Then, indeed, for a moment, the impassivity of his features relaxed. He was frankly amazed.

"You cannot mean this," he declared. "You know nothing about the value of the property, nothing about the affair at all. It is quite impossible."

"I know what you have told me," she said. "Is not that enough? You are sure that it will make money and you have just told me how foolish I am to keep so much money in my bank. Very well, then, I give it to you to invest. You must pay me quite a good deal of interest."

"But you know nothing about me," he protested, "nothing about the property."

"One must trust somebody," she replied. "Why shouldn't I trust you?"

He was nonplussed. This woman seemed to have an answer for everything. Besides, when once he had got over the unexpectedness of the thing, it was, of course, a wonderful stroke of fortune for him. Then came a whole rush of thoughts, a glow which he thrust back sternly. It would mean seeing her often; it would mean coming here to her rooms; it would mean, perhaps, that she might come to look upon him as a friend. He set his teeth hard. This was folly!

"Have you any idea about terms?" he inquired.

She laughed softly.

"My dear friend," she said, "why do you ask me such a question? You know quite well that I am not competent to discuss terms with you. Listen. You are engaged in a speculation to carry out which you want the loan of twelve thousand pounds. Draw up a paper in which you state what my share will be of the profits, what interest I shall get for my money, and give particulars of the property. Then I will take it to my solicitor, if you insist upon it, although I am willing to accept what you think is fair."

"You must take it to a solicitor, of course," he answered, thoughtfully. "I may as well tell you at once, however, that he will probably advise you against investing it in such a way."

"That will make no difference at all," she declared. "Solicitors hate all investments, I know, except their horrid mortgages. There are only two conditions that I shall make."

"What are they?" he asked.

"The first is that you must not say a word of this to my sister."

Tavernake frowned.

"That is a little difficult," he remarked. "It happens that your sister knows something about the estate and my plans."

"There is no need to tell her the name of your partner," Elizabeth said. "I want this to be our secret entirely, yours and mine."

Her hand fell upon his; he gripped the sides of his chair. Again he was conscious of this bewildering, incomprehensible sensation.

"And the other condition?" he demanded, hoarsely.

"That you come sometimes and tell me how things are

going on."

"Come here?" he repeated.

She nodded.

"Please! I am very lonely. I shall look forward to your visits."

Tavernake rose slowly to his feet. He held out his hand—she knew better than to attempt to keep him. He made a speech which was for him gallant, but while he made it he looked into her eyes with a directness to which she was indeed unaccustomed.

"I shall come," he said. "I should have wanted to come, anyhow."

Then he turned abruptly away and left the room. It was the first speech of its sort which he had ever made in his life.

CHAPTER XII. TAVERNAKE BLUNDERS

Tavernake felt that he had indeed wandered into an alien world as he took his place the following evening among the little crowd of people who were waiting outside the stage-door of the Atlas Theatre. These were surroundings to which he was totally unaccustomed. Two very handsome motor-cars were drawn up against the curb, and behind them a string of electric broughams and taxicabs, proving conclusively that the young ladies of the Atlas Theatre were popular in other than purely theatrical circles.

The handful of young men by whom Tavernake was surrounded were of a genus unknown to him. They were all dressed exactly alike, they all seemed to breathe the same atmosphere, to exhibit the same indifference towards the other loungers. One or two more privileged passed in through the stage-door and disappeared. Tavernake contented himself with standing on the edge of the curbstone, his hands thrust into the pockets of his dark overcoat, his bowler hat, which was not quite the correct shape, slightly on the back of his head; his serious, stolid face illuminated by the gleam from a neighboring gas lamp.

Presently, people began to emerge from the door. First of all, the musicians and a little stream of stage hands.

Then a girl's hat appeared in the doorway, and the first of the Atlas young ladies came out, to be claimed at once by her escort. Very soon afterwards, Beatrice arrived. She recognized Tavernake at once and crossed over to him.

"Well?" she asked.

"You looked very nice," he said, slowly, as he led the way down the street. "Of course, I knew about your singing, but everything else—seemed such a surprise."

"For instance?"

"Why, I mean your dancing," he went on, "and somehow or other you looked different on the stage."

She shook her head.

"'Different' won't do for me," she persisted. "I must have

something more specific."

"Well, then, you looked much prettier than I thought you were," Tavernake declared, solemnly. "You looked exceedingly nice."

"You really thought so?" she asked, a little doubtfully.

"I really thought so. I thought you looked much nicer than any of the others."

She squeezed his arm affectionately.

"Dear Leonard," she said, "it's so nice to have you think so. Do you know, Mr. Grier actually asked me out to supper."

"What impertinence!" Tavernake muttered.

Beatrice threw her head back and laughed.

"My dear brother," she protested, "it was a tremendous compliment. You must remember that it was entirely through him, too, that I got the engagement. Four pounds a week I am going to have. Just think of it!"

"Four pounds a week is all very well," Tavernake admitted. "It seems a great deal of money to earn like that. But I don't think you ought to go out to supper with any one whom you know so slightly."

"Dear prig! You know, you are a shocking prig, Leonard."

"Am I?" he answered, without offence, and with the air of one seriously considering the subject.

"Of course you are. How could you help it, living the sort of life you've led all your days? Never mind, I like you for it. I don't know whether I want to go out to supper with anybody—I really haven't decided yet—but if I did, it would certainly be better for me to go with Mr. Grier, because he can do me no end of good at the theatre, if he likes."

Tavernake was silent for several moments. He was conscious of feeling something which he did not altogether understand. He only knew that it involved a strong and unreasonable dislike to Mr. Grier. Then he remembered that he was her brother, that he had the right to speak with authority.

"I hope that you will not go out to supper with any one," he said.

She began to laugh but checked herself.

"Well," she remarked, "that sounds very terrible. Shall we take a 'bus? To tell you the truth, I am dying of hunger. We rehearsed for two hours before the performance, and I ate nothing but a sandwich—I was so excited."

Tavernake hesitated a moment—he certainly was not himself this evening!

"Would you like to have some supper at a restaurant," he asked, "before we go home?"

"I should love it," she declared, taking his arm as they passed through a stream of people. "To tell you the truth, I was so hoping that you would propose it."

"I think," Tavernake said, deliberately, "that there is a place a little way along here."

They pushed their way down the Strand and entered a restaurant which Tavernake knew only by name. A small table was found for them and Beatrice looked about with delight.

"Isn't this jolly!" she exclaimed, taking off her gloves. "Why, there are five or six of the girls from the theatre here already. There are two, see, at the corner table, and the fair-haired girl—she is just behind me in the chorus."

Tavernake glanced around. The young women whom she pointed out were all escorted by men who were scrupulously attired in evening dress. She seemed to read his thoughts as she laughed at him.

"You stupid boy," she said. "You don't suppose that I want to be like them, do you? There are lots of things it's delightful to look on at, and that's all. Isn't this fish good? I love this place."

Tavernake looked around him with an interest which he took no pains to conceal. Certainly the little groups of people by whom they were surrounded on every side had the air of finding some zest in life which up to the present, at any rate, had escaped him. They came streaming in, finding friends everywhere, laughing and talking, insisting upon tables in impossible places, calling out greetings to acquaintances across the room, chaffing the maitre d'hotel who was hastening from table to table. The gathering babel of voices was mingled every now and then with the popping of corks, and behind it all were the soft strains of a very seductive little band, perched up in the balcony. Tavernake felt the color mounting into his cheeks. It was true: there was something here which was new to him!

"Beatrice," he asked her suddenly, "have you ever drunk champagne?"

She laughed at him.

"Often, my dear brother," she answered. "Why?"

"I never have," he confessed. "We are going to have some now."

She would have checked him but he had summoned a waiter imperiously and given his order.

"My dear Leonard," she protested, "this is shocking extravagance."

"Is it?" he replied. "I don't care. Tell me about the theatre. Were they kind to you there? Will you be able to keep your place?"

"The girls were all much nicer than I expected," she told him, "and the musical director said that my voice was much too good for the chorus. Oh, I do hope that they will keep me!"

"They would be idiots if they didn't," he declared, vigorously. "You sing better and you dance more gracefully and to me you seemed much prettier than any one else there."

She laughed into his eyes.

"My dear brother," she exclaimed, "your education is progressing indeed! It is positively the first evening I have ever heard you attempt to make pretty speeches, and you are quite an adept already."

"I don't know about that," he protested. "I suppose it never occurred to me before that you were good-looking," he added, examining her critically, "or I dare say I should have told you so. You see, one doesn't notice these things in an ordinary way. Lots of other people must have told you so, though."

"I was never spoilt with compliments," she said. "You see, I had a beautiful sister."

The words seemed to have escaped her unconsciously. Almost as they passed her lips, her expression changed. She shivered, as though reminded of something unpleasant. Tavernake, however, noticed nothing. For the greater part of the day he had been sedulously fighting against a new and unaccustomed state of mind. He had found his thoughts slipping away, time after time, until he had had to set his teeth and use all his will power to keep his attention concentrated upon his work. And now once more they had escaped, again he felt the strange stir in his blood. The slight flush on his cheek grew suddenly deeper. He looked past the girl opposite to him, out of the restaurant, across the street, into that little sitting-room in the Milan Court. It was Elizabeth who was there in front of him. Again he heard her voice, saw the turn of her head, the slow, delightful curve of the lips, the eyes that looked into his and spoke to him the first strange whispers of a new language. His heart gave a quick throb. He was for the moment transformed, a prisoner no longer, a different person, indeed, from the stolid, well-behaved young man who found himself for the first time in his life in these unaccustomed surroundings. Then Beatrice leaned towards him, her voice brought him back to the present—not, alas, the voice which at that moment he would have given so much to have heard.

"To-night," she murmured, "I feel as though we were at the beginning of new things. We must drink a toast."

Tavernake filled her glass and his own.

"Luck to you in your new profession!" he said.

"And here is one after your own heart, you most curious of men!" she exclaimed, a few seconds later. "To the undiscovered in life!"

He drained his glass and set it down empty.

"The undiscovered," he muttered, looking around. "It is a very good toast, Beatrice. There are many things of which one might remain ignorant all one's life if one relied wholly upon one's own perceptions."

"I believe," she agreed, "that if I had not appeared you were in great danger of becoming narrow."

"I am sure of it," he answered, "but you see you came."

She was thoughtful for a moment.

"This reminds me just a little of that first dreary feast of ours," she said. "You knew what it was like then to feed a genuinely starving girl. And I was miserable, Leonard. It didn't seem to me that there was any other end save one."

"You've got over all that nonsense?" he asked anxiously.

"Yes, I suppose so," she answered. "You see, I've started life again and one gets stronger. But there are times even now," she added, "when I am afraid."

The mirth had suddenly died from her face. She looked older, tired, and careworn. The shadows were back under her eyes; she glanced around almost timorously. He filled her glass.

"That is foolishness," he said. "Nothing nor anybody can harm you now."

Some note in his voice attracted her attention. Strong and square, with hard, forceful face, he sat wholly at his ease among these unfamiliar surroundings, a very tower of refuge, she felt, to the weak. His face was not strikingly intellectual—she was not sure now about his mouth—but one seemed to feel that dogged nature, the tireless pains by which he would pursue any aim dear to him. The shadows passed away from her mind. What was dead was gone! It was not reasonable that she should be haunted all her days by the ghosts of other people's sins. The atmosphere of the place, the atmosphere of the last few hours, found its way again into her blood. After all, she was young, the music was sweet, her pulses were throbbing to the tune of this new life. She drank her wine and laughed, her head beating time to the music.

"We have been sad long enough," she declared. "You and I, my dear serious brother, will embark in earnest now upon the paths of frivolity. Tell me, how did things go to-day?"

It flashed into his mind that he had great news, but that it was not for her. About that matter there was still doubt in his mind, but he could not speak of it.

"I have had an offer," he said guardedly. "I cannot say much about it at present, for nothing is certain, but I am sure that I shall be able to raise the money somehow."

His tone was calm and confident. There was no self-assurance or bluster about it, and yet it was convincing. She looked at him curiously.

"You are a very positive person, Leonard," she remarked. "You must have great faith in yourself, I think."

He considered the question for a moment.

"Perhaps I have," he admitted. "I do not think that there is any other way to succeed."

The atmosphere of the place was becoming now almost languorous. The band had ceased to play; little parties of men and women were standing about, bidding one another goodnight. The lamps had been lowered, and in the gloom the voices and laughter seemed to have become lower and more insinuating; the lights in the eyes of the women, as they passed down the room on their way out, softer and more irresistible.

"I suppose we must go," she said reluctantly.

Tavernake paid his bill and they turned into the street. She took his arm and they turned westward. Even out here, the atmosphere of the restaurant appeared to have found its way. The soberness of life, its harder and more practical side, was for the moment obscured. It was not the daytime crowd, this, whose footsteps pressed the pavements. The careworn faces of the money-seekers had vanished. The men and women to whom life was something of a struggle had sought their homes—resting, perhaps, before they took up their labors again. Every moment taxicabs and motor-cars whirled by, flashing upon the night a momentary impression of men in evening dress, of women in soft garments with jewels in their hair. The spirit of pleasure seemed to have crept into the atmosphere. Even the poorer people whom they passed in the street, were laughing or singing.

Tavernake stopped short.

"To-night," he declared, "is not the night for omnibuses. We are going to have a taxicab. I know that you are tired."

"I should love it," she admitted.

They hailed one and drove off. Beatrice leaned back among the cushions and closed her eyes, her ungloved hand rested almost caressingly upon his. He leaned forward. There were new things in the world—he was sure of it now, sure though they were coming to him through the mists, coming to him so vaguely that even while he obeyed he did not understand. Her full, soft lips were slightly parted; her heavily-fringed eyelids closed; her deep brown hair, which had escaped bounds a little, drooping over her ear. His fingers suddenly clasped hers tightly.

"Beatrice!" he whispered.

She sat up with a start, her eyes questioning his, the breath coming quickly through her parted lips.

"Once you asked me to kiss you, Beatrice," he said. "To-night—I am going to."

She made no attempt to repulse him. He took her in his arms and kissed her. Even in that moment he knew that he had made a mistake. Nevertheless, he kissed her again and again, crushing her lips against his.

"Please let me go, Leonard," she begged at last.

He obeyed at once. He understood quite well that some strange thing had happened. It seemed to him during those next few minutes that everything which had passed that night was a dream, that this vivid picture of a life more intense, making larger demands upon the senses than anything he had yet experienced, was a mirage, a thing which would live only in his memory, a life in which he could never take any part. He had blundered; he had come into a new world and he had blundered. A sense of guilt was upon him. He had a sudden wild desire to cry out that it was Elizabeth whom he had kissed. Beatrice was sitting upright in her place, her head turned a little away from him. He felt that she was expecting him to speak—that there were inevitable words which he should say. His silence was a confession. He would have lied but the seal was upon his lips. So the moment passed, and Tavernake had taken another step forward towards his destiny! ...

As he helped her out of the cab, her fingers tightened for a moment upon his hand. She patted it gently as she passed out before him into the house, leaving the door open. When he had paid the cabman and followed, she had disappeared. He looked into the sitting-room; it was empty. Overhead, he could hear her footsteps as she ascended to her room.

CHAPTER XIII. AN EVENING CALL

In the morning, when he left for the city, she was not down. When he came home in the evening, she was gone. Without removing his hat or overcoat, he took the letter which he found propped up on the mantelpiece and addressed to him to the window and read it.

DEAR BROTHER LEONARD,—It wasn't your fault and I don't think it was mine. If either of us is to blame, it is certainly I, for though you are such a clever and ambitious young person, you really know very little indeed of the world,—not so much, I think, as I do. I am going to stay for a few nights, at any rate, with one of the girls at the theatre, who I know wants some one to share her tiny flat with her. Afterwards, I shall see.

Don't throw this letter in the fire and don't think me ungrateful. I shall never forget what you did for me. How could I?

I will send you my address as soon as I am sure of it, or you can always write me to the theatre.

Good-bye, dear Leonard,

YOUR SISTER BEATRICE.

Tavernake looked from the sheet of notepaper out across the gray square. He knew that he was very angry, angry though he deliberately folded the letter up and placed it in his pocket, angry though he took off his overcoat and hung it up with his usual care; but his anger was with himself. He had blundered badly. This episode of his life was one which he had better forget. It was absolutely out of harmony with all his ideas. He told himself that he was glad Beatrice was gone. Housekeeping with an imaginary sister in this practical world was an absurdity. Sooner or later it must have come to an end. Better now, before it had gone too far—better now, much better! All the same, he knew that he was going to be very lonely.

He rang the bell for the woman who waited upon them, and whom he seldom saw, for Beatrice herself had supplied their immediate wants. He found some dinner ready, which he ate with absolute unconsciousness. Then he threw himself fiercely into his work. It was all very well for the first hour or so, but as ten o'clock grew near he began to find a curious difficulty in keeping his attention fixed upon those calculations. The matter of average rentals, percentage upon capital—things which but yesterday he had found fascinating—seemed suddenly irksome. He could fix his attention upon nothing. At last he pushed his papers away, put on his hat and coat, and walked into the street.

At the Milan Court, the hall-porter received his inquiry for Elizabeth with an air of faint but well-bred surprise. Tavernake, in those days, was a person exceedingly difficult to place. His clothes so obviously denoted the station in life which he really occupied, while the slight imperiousness of his manner, his absolute freedom from any sort of nervousness or awkwardness, seemed to bespeak a consideration which those who had to deal with him as a stranger found sometimes a little puzzling.

"Mrs. Wenham Gardner is in her rooms, I believe, sir," the man said. "If you will wait for a moment, I will inquire."

He disappeared into his office, thrusting his head out, a moment or two later, with the telephone receiver still in his hand.

"Mrs. Gardner would like the name again, sir, please," he remarked.

Tavernake repeated it firmly.

"You might say," he added, "that I shall not detain her for more than a few minutes."

The man disappeared once more. When he returned, he indicated the lift to Tavernake.

"If you will go up to the fifth floor, sir," he said, "Mrs. Gardner will see you."

Tavernake found his courage almost leaving him as he knocked at the door of her rooms. Her French maid ushered him into the little sitting-room, where, to his dismay, he found three men, one sitting on the table, the other two in easy-chairs. Elizabeth, in a dress of pale blue satin, was standing before the mirror. She turned round as Tavernake entered.

"Mr. Tavernake shall decide!" she exclaimed, waving her hand to him. "Mr. Tavernake, there is a difference of opinion about my earrings. Major Post here,"—she indicated a distinguished-looking elderly gentleman, with carefully trimmed beard and moustache, and an eyeglass attached to a thin band of black ribbon—"Major Post wants me to wear turquoises. I prefer my pearls. Mr. Crease half agrees with me, but as he never agrees with any one, on principle, he hates to say so. Mr. Faulkes is wavering. You shall decide; you, I know, are one of those people who never waver."

"I should wear the pearls," Tavernake said.

Elizabeth made them a little courtesy.

"You see, my dear friends," she declared, "you have to come to England, after all, to find a man who knows his own mind and speaks it without fear. The pearls it shall be."

"It may be decision," Crease drawled, speaking with a slight American accent, "or it may be gallantry. Mr. Tavernake knew your own choice."

"The last word, as usual," she sighed. "Now, if you good people will kindly go on downstairs, I will join you in a few minutes. Mr. Tavernake is my man of business and I am sure he has something to say to me."

She dismissed them all pleasantly. As soon as the door was closed she turned to Tavernake. Her manner seemed to become a shade less gracious.

"Well?"

"I don't know why I came," Tavernake confessed bluntly. "I was restless and I wanted to see you."

She looked at him for a moment and then she laughed. Tavernake felt a sense of relief; at least she was not angry.

"Oh, you strangest of mortals!" she exclaimed, holding

out her hands. "Well, you see me—in one of my most becoming gowns, too. What do you think of the fit?"

She swept round and faced him again with an expectant look. Tavernake, who knew nothing of women's fashions, still realized the superbness of that one unbroken line.

"I can't think how you can move a step in it," he said, "but you look—"

He paused. It was as though he had lost his breath. Then he set his teeth and finished.

"You look beautiful," he declared. "I suppose you know that. I suppose they've all been telling you so."

She shook her head.

"They haven't all your courage, dear Briton," she remarked, "and if they did tell me so, I am not sure that I should be convinced. You see, most of my friends have lived so long and lived so quickly that they have learned to play with words until one never knows whether the things they speak come from their hearts. With you it is different."

"Yes," Tavernake admitted, "with me it is different!"

She glanced at the clock.

"Well," she said, "you have seen me and I am glad to have seen you, and you may kiss my fingers if you like, and then you must run away. I am engaged to have supper with my friends downstairs."

He raised her fingers clumsily enough to his lips and kept them there for a moment. When he let them go, she wrung them as though in pain, and looked at him. She turned abruptly away. In a sense she was disappointed. After all, he was an easy victim!

"Elise," she called out, "my cloak."

Her maid came hurrying from the next room. Elizabeth turned towards her, holding out her shoulders. She nodded to Tavernake.

"You know the way down, Mr. Tavernake? I shall see you again soon, sha'n't I? Good-night!"

She scarcely glanced at him as she sent him away, yet
Tavernake walked on air.

CHAPTER XIV. A WARNING FROM Mr. PRITCHARD

Tavernake hesitated for a moment under the portico of the Milan Court, looking out at the rain which had suddenly commenced to descend. He scarcely noticed that he had a companion until the man who was standing by his side addressed him.

"Say, your name is Tavernake, isn't it?"

Tavernake, who had been on the point of striding away, turned sharply around. The man who had spoken to him was wearing morning clothes of dark gray tweed and a soft Homburg hat. His complexion was a little sallow and he was clean-shaven except for a slight black moustache. He was smoking a black cigar and his accent was transatlantic. Something about his appearance struck Tavernake as being vaguely familiar, but he could not at first recall where he had seen him before.

"That is my name, certainly," Tavernake admitted.

"I am going to ask you a somewhat impertinent question," his neighbor remarked.

"I suppose you can ask it," Tavernake rejoined. "I am not obliged to answer, am I?"

The man smiled.

"Come," he said, "that's honest, at any rate. Are you in a hurry for a few minutes?"

"I am in no particular hurry," Tavernake answered. "What do you want?"

"A few nights ago," the stranger continued, lowering his voice a little, "I met you with a young lady whose appearance, for some reason which we needn't go into, interested me. To-night I happened to overhear you inquiring, only a few minutes ago, for the sister of the same young lady."

"What you heard doesn't concern me in the least," Tavernake retorted. "I should say that you had no business to listen."

His companion smiled.

"Well," he declared, "I have always heard a good deal about British frankness, and it seems to me that I'm getting some. Anyway, I'll tell you where I come in. I am interested in Mrs. Wenham Gardner. I am interested, also, in her sister, whom I think you know—Miss Beatrice Franklin, not Miss Tavernake!"

Tavernake made no immediate reply. The man was an American, without a doubt. Perhaps he knew something of Beatrice. Perhaps this was one of the friends of that former life concerning which she had told him nothing.

"You are not, by any chance, proposing," Tavernake said at last, "to discuss either of these ladies with me? I do not know you or what your business may be. In any case, I am going now."

The other laid his hand on Tavernake's shoulder.

"You'll be soaked to the skin," he protested. "I want you to come into the smoking-room here with me for a few minutes. We will have a drink together and a little conversation, if you don't mind."

"But I do mind," Tavernake declared. "I don't know who you are and I don't want to know you, and I am not going to talk about Mrs. Gardner, or any other lady of my acquaintance, with strangers. Good-night!"

"One moment, please, Mr. Tavernake."

Tavernake hesitated. There was something curiously compelling in the other's smooth, distinct voice.

"I'd like you to take this card," he said. "I told you my name before but I expect you've forgotten it,—Pritchard—Sam Pritchard. Ever heard of me before?"

"Never!"

"Not to have heard of me in the United States," the other continued, with a grim smile, "would be a tribute to your respectability. Most of the crooks who find their way over here know of Sam Pritchard. I am a detective and I come from New York."

Tavernake turned and looked the man over. There was

something convincing about his tone and appearance. It did not occur to him to doubt for a moment a word of this stranger's story.

"You haven't anything against her—against either of them?" he asked, quickly.

"Nothing directly," the detective answered. "All the same, you have been calling upon Mrs. Wenham Gardner this evening, and if you are a friend of hers I think that you had better come along with me and have that talk."

"I will come," Tavernake agreed, "but I come as a listener. Remember that I have nothing to tell you. So far as you are concerned, I do not know either of those ladies."

Pritchard smiled.

"Well," he said, "I guess we'll let it go at that. All the same, if you don't mind, we'll talk. Come this way and we'll get to the smoking-room through the hotel. It's under cover."

Tavernake moved restlessly in his chair.

"What the devil is all this talk about crooks!" he exclaimed impatiently. "I didn't come here to listen to this sort of thing. I am not sure that I believe a word of what you say."

"Why should you," Pritchard remarked, "without proof? Look here."

He drew a leather case from his pocket and spread it out. There were a dozen photographs there of men in prison attire. The detective pointed to one, and with a little shiver Tavernake recognized the face of the man who had been sitting at the right hand of Elizabeth.

"You don't mean to say," he faltered, "that Mrs. Gardner —"

The detective folded up his case and replaced it in his pocket.

"No," he said, "we haven't any photographs of your lady friend there, nor of her sister. And yet, it may not be so far off."

"If you are trying to fasten anything upon those ladies,

—" Tavernake began, threateningly.

The detective laughed and patted him on the shoulder.

"It isn't my business to try and fasten things upon any one," he interrupted. "At the same time, you seem to be a friend of Mrs. Wenham Gardner, and it is just as well that some one should warn her."

"Warn her of what?" Tavernake asked.

The detective looked at his cigar meditatively.

"Make her understand that there is trouble ahead," he replied.

Tavernake sipped his whiskey and soda and lit a cigarette. Then he turned in his chair and looked thoughtfully at his companion. Pritchard was a striking-looking man, with hard, clean-cut features—a man of determination.

"Mr. Pritchard, I am a clerk in an estate office. My people were work-people and I am trying to better myself in the world. I haven't learned how to beat about a subject, but I have learned a little of the world, and I know that people such as you are not in the habit of doing things without a reason. Why the devil have you brought me in here to talk about Mrs. Gardner and her sister? If you've anything to say, why don't you go to Mrs. Gardner herself and say it? Why do you come and talk to strangers about their affairs? I am here listening to you, but I tell you straight I don't like it."

Pritchard nodded.

"Say, I am not sure that I don't like that sort of talk," he declared. "I know all about you, young man. You're in Dowling & Spence's office and you've got to quit. You've got an estate you want financing. Miss Beatrice Franklin was living under your roof—as your sister, I understand—until yesterday, and Mrs. Gardner, for some reason of her own, seems to be doing her best to add you to the list of her admirers. I am not sure what it all means but I could make a pretty good guess. Here's my point, though. You're right. I didn't bring you here for your health. I brought you here because you can do me a service and yourself one at the same time, and you'll be doing no one any harm, nobody you care about, anyway. I have no grudge against Miss Beatrice. I'd just as soon she kept out of the trouble that's coming."

"What is this service?" Tavernake asked.

Pritchard for the moment evaded the point.

"I dare say you can understand, Mr. Tavernake," he said, "that in my profession one has to sometimes go a long way round to get a man or a woman just where you want them. Now we merely glanced at that table as we came in, and I can tell you this for gospel truth—there isn't one of that crowd that I couldn't, if I liked, haul back to New York on some charge or another. You wonder why I don't do it. I'll tell you. It's because I am waiting—waiting until I can bring home something more serious, something that will keep them out of the way for just as long as possible. Do you follow me, Mr. Tavernake?"

"I suppose I do," Tavernake answered, doubtfully. "You are only talking of the men, of course?"

Pritchard smiled.

"My young friend," he agreed, "I am only talking of the men. At the same time, I guess I'm not betraying any confidence, or telling you anything that Mrs. Wenham Gardner doesn't know herself, when I say that she's doing her best to qualify for a similar position."

"You mean that she is doing something against the law!" Tavernake exclaimed, indignantly. "I don't believe it for a moment. If she is associating with these people, it's because she doesn't know who they are."

Pritchard flicked the ash from his cigar.

"Well," he said, "every man has a right to his own opinions, and for my part I like to hear any one stick up for his friends. It makes no odds to me. However, here are a few facts I am going to bring before you. Four months ago, one of the turns at a vaudeville show down Broadway consisted of a performance by a Professor Franklin and his two daughters, Elizabeth and Beatrice. The professor hypnotized, told fortunes, felt heads, and the usual rigmarole. Beatrice sang, Elizabeth danced. People came to see the show, not because it was any good but because the girls, even in New York, were beautiful."

"A music-hall in New York!" Tavernake muttered.

The detective nodded.

"Among the young bloods of the city," he continued, "were two brothers, as much alike as twins, although they aren't twins, whose names were Wenham and Jerry Gardner. There's nothing in fast life which those young men haven't tried. Between them, I should say they represented everything that was known of debauchery and dissipation. The eldest can't be more than twenty-seven to-day, but if you were to see them in the morning, either of them, before they had been massaged and galvanized into life, you'd think they were little old men, with just strength enough left to crawl about. Well, to cut a long story short, both of them fell in love with Elizabeth."

"Brutes!" Tavernake interjected.

"I guess they found Miss Elizabeth a pretty tough nut to crack," the detective went on. "Anyhow, you know what her price was from her name, which is hers right enough. Wenham, who was a year younger than his brother, was the first to bid it. Three months ago, Mr. and Mrs. Wenham Gardner, Miss Beatrice, and the devoted father left New York in the Lusitania and came to London."

"Where is this Wenham Gardner, then?" Tavernake demanded.

Pritchard took his cigar case from his pocket and selected another cigar.

"Say, that's where you strike the nail right on the head," he remarked. "Where is this Wenham Gardner?"

"I don't mind telling you, Mr. Tavernake, that to discover

his whereabouts is exactly what I am over on this side for. I have a commission from the family to find out, and a blank cheque to do it with."

"Do you mean that he has disappeared, then?" asked Tavernake.

"Off the face of the earth, sir," Pritchard replied. "Something like two months ago, the young married couple, with Miss Beatrice, started for a holiday tour somewhere down in the west of England. A few days after they started, Miss Beatrice comes back to London alone. She goes to a boarding-house, is practically penniless, but she has shaken her sister—has, I believe, never spoken with her since. A little later, Elizabeth alone turns up in London. She has plenty of money, more money than she has ever had the control of before in her life, but no husband."

"So far, I don't see anything remarkable about that," Tavernake interposed.

"That may or may not be," Pritchard answered, drily. "This creature, Wenham Gardner—I hate to call him a man—was her abject slave—up till the time they reached London, at any rate. He would never have quit of his own accord. He stopped quite suddenly communicating with all his friends. None of their cables, even, were answered."

"Why don't you go and ask Mrs. Gardner where he is?" Tavernake demanded bluntly.

"I have already," Pritchard declared, "taken that liberty. With tears in her eyes, she assured me that after some slight quarrel, in which she admits that she was the one to blame, her husband walked out of the house where they were staying, and she has not seen him since. She was quite ready with all the particulars, and even implored me to help find him."

"I cannot imagine," Tavernake said, "why any one should disbelieve her."

The detective smiled.

"There are a few little outside circumstances," he remarked, looking at the ash of his cigar. "In the first place, how do you suppose that this young Wenham Gardner spent the last week of his stay in New York?"

"How should I know?" Tavernake replied, impatiently.

"By realizing every cent of his property on which he could lay his hands," the detective continued. "It isn't at any time an easy business, and the Gardner interest is spread out in many directions, but he must have sailed with something like forty thousand pounds in hard cash. A suspicious person might presume that that forty thousand pounds has found its way to the stronger of the combination."

"Anything else?" Tavernake asked.

"I won't worry you much more," the detective answered. "There are a few other circumstances which seem to need explanation, but they can wait. There is one serious one, however, and that is where you come in."

"Indeed!" Tavernake remarked. "I was hoping you would come to that soon."

"The two sisters, Beatrice and Elizabeth, have been together ever since we can learn anything of their history. Those people who don't understand the disappearance of Wenham Gardner would like to know why they quarreled and parted, why Beatrice is keeping away from her sister in this strange manner. I personally, too, should like to know from Miss Beatrice when she last saw Wenham Gardner alive."

"You want me to ask Miss Beatrice these things?" Tavernake demanded.

"It might come better from you," Pritchard admitted. "I have written her to the theatre but naturally she has not replied."

Tavernake looked curiously at his companion.

"Do you really suppose," he asked, "that, even granted there were any unusual circumstances in connection with that quarrel—do you seriously suppose that Beatrice would give her sister away?"

The detective sighed.

"No doubt, Mr. Tavernake," he said, "these young ladies are friends of yours, and perhaps for that reason you are a little prejudiced in their favor. Their whole bringing-up and associations, however, have certainly not been of a strict order. I cannot help thinking that persuasion might be brought to bear upon Miss Beatrice, that it might be pointed out to her that a true story is the safest."

"Well, if you've finished," Tavernake declared, "I'd like to tell you what I think of your story. I think it's all d—d silly nonsense! This Wenham Gardner, by your own saying, was half mad. There was a quarrel and he's gone off to Paris or somewhere. As to your suggestions about Mrs. Gardner, I think they're infamous."

Pritchard was unmoved by his companion's warmth.

"Why, that's all right, Mr. Tavernake," he affirmed. "I can quite understand your feeling like that just at first. You see, I've been among crime and criminals all my days, and I learn to look for a certain set of motives when a thing of this sort happens. You've been brought up among honest folk, who go the straightforward way about life, and naturally you look at the same matter from a different point of view. But you and I have got to talk this out. I want you to understand that those very charming young ladies are not quite the class of young women whom you know anything about. Mind you, I haven't a word to say against Miss Beatrice. I dare say she's as straight as they make 'em. But—you must take another whiskey and soda, Mr. Tavernake. Now, I insist upon it. Tim, come right over here."

Mr. Pritchard seemed to have forgotten what he was talking about. The room had been suddenly invaded. The whole of the little supper party, whose individual members he had pointed out to his companion, came trooping into the room. They were all apparently on the best of terms with themselves, and they all seemed to make a point of absolutely ignoring Pritchard's presence. Elizabeth was the one exception. She was carrying a tiny Chinese spaniel under one arm; with the fingers of her other hand she held a tortoise-shell mounted monocle to her eye, and stared directly at the two men. Presently she came languidly across the room to them.

"Dear me," she said, "I had no idea that even your wide circle of acquaintances, Mr. Pritchard, included my friend, Mr. Tavernake."

The two men rose to their feet. Tavernake felt confused and angry. It was as though he had been playing the traitor in listening, even for a moment, to these stories.

"Mr. Pritchard introduced himself to me only a few minutes ago," he declared. "He brought me in here and I have been listening to a lot of rubbish from him of which I don't believe a single word."

She flashed a wonderful smile upon him.

"Mr. Pritchard is so very censorious," she murmured. "He takes such a very low view of human nature. After all, though, I suppose we must not blame him. I think that as men and women we do not exist to him. We are simply the pegs by means of which he can climb a little higher in the esteem of his employers."

Pritchard took up his soft hat and stick.

"Mrs. Gardner," he said, "I will confess that I have been wasting my time with this young man. You are a trifle severe upon me. You may find, and before long, that I am your best friend."

She laughed delightfully.

"Dear Mr. Pritchard," she exclaimed, "it is a strange thought, that! If only I dared hope that some day it might come true!"

"More unlikely things, madam, are happening every hour," the detective remarked. "The world—our little corner of it, at any rate—is full of anomalies. There might even come a time to any one of us three when liberty was more dangerous than the prison cell itself."

He nodded carelessly to Tavernake, and with a bow to Elizabeth turned and left the room. Elizabeth remained as though turned to stone, looking after him as he descended the stairs.

"The man is a fool!" Tavernake cried, roughly.

Elizabeth shook her head and sighed.

"He is something far more ineffective," she said. "He is just a little too clever."

CHAPTER, XV. GENERAL DISCONTENT

Elizabeth did not at once rejoin her friends. Instead, she sank on to the low settee close to where she had been standing, and drew Tavernake down to her side. She waved her hand across at the others, who were calling for her.

"In a moment, dear people," she said.

Then she leaned back among the cushions and laughed at her companion.

"Tell me, Mr. Tavernake," she asked, "don't you feel that you have stepped into a sort of modern Arabian Nights?"

"Why?"

"Oh, I know Mr. Pritchard's weakness," she continued. "He loves to throw a glamour around everything he says or does. Because he honors me by interesting himself in my concerns, he has probably told you all sorts of wonderful things about me and my friends. A very ingenious romancer, Mr. Pritchard, you know. Confess, now, didn't he tell you some stories about us?"

She might have spared herself the trouble of beating about the bush. There was no hesitation about Tavernake.

"He said that your friends were every one of them criminals," Tavernake declared, "and he admitted that he was working hard at the present moment to discover that you were one, too."

She laughed softly but heartily.

"I wonder what was his object," she remarked, "in taking you into his confidence."

"He happened to know," Tavernake explained, "that I was intimate with your sister. He wanted me to ask Beatrice a certain question."

Elizabeth laughed no more. She looked steadfastly into his eyes.

"And that question?"

"He wanted me to ask Beatrice why she left you and hid

herself in London."

She tried to smile but not very successfully.

"According to his story," Tavernake continued, "you and Beatrice and your husband were away together somewhere in the country. Something happened there, something which resulted in the disappearance of your husband. Beatrice came back alone and has not been near you since. Soon afterwards, you, too, came back alone. Mr. Gardner has not been seen or heard of."

Elizabeth was bending over her dog, but even Tavernake, unobservant though he was, could see that she was shaken.

"Pritchard is a clever man, generally," she remarked, "diabolically clever. Why has he told you all this, I wonder? He must have known that you would probably repeat it to me. Why does he want to show me his hand?"

"I have no idea," Tavernake replied. "These matters are all beyond me. They do not concern me in any way. I am not keeping you from your friends? Please send me away when you like."

"Don't go just yet," she begged. "Sit with me for a moment. Can't you see," she added, whispering, "that I have had a shock? Sit with me. I can't go back to those others just yet."

Tavernake did as he was bidden. The woman at his side was still caressing the little animal she carried. Watching her, however, Tavernake could see that her bosom was rising and falling quickly. There was an unnatural pallor in her cheeks, a terrified gleam in her eyes. Nevertheless, these things passed. In a very few seconds she was herself again.

"Come," she said, "it is not often that I give way. The only time I am ever afraid is when there is something which I do not understand. I do not understand Mr. Pritchard to-night. I know that he is my enemy. I cannot imagine why he should talk to you. He must have known that you would repeat all he said. It is not like him. Tell me, Mr. Tavernake, you have heard all sorts of things about me. Do you believe them? Do you believe

—it's rather a horrible thing to ask, isn't it?" she went on hurriedly,—"do you believe that I made away with my husband?"

"You surely do not need to ask me that question," Tavernake answered, fervently. "I should believe your word, whatever you told me. I should not believe that you could do anything wrong."

Her hand touched his for a moment and he was repaid.

"Don't think too well of me," she begged. "I don't want to disappoint you."

Some one pushed open the swing doors and she started nervously. It was only a waiter who passed through into the bar.

"What I think of you," Tavernake said slowly, "nothing could alter, but because I am stupid, I suppose, there is quite a good deal that I cannot understand. I cannot understand, for instance, why they should suspect you of having anything to do with your husband's disappearance. You can prove where you were when he left you?"

"Quite easily," she answered, "only, unfortunately, no one seems to have seen him go. He timed his departure so cunningly that he apparently vanished into thin air. Even then," she continued, "but for one thing I don't suppose that any one would have had suspicions. I dare say Mr. Pritchard told you that before we left New York my husband sold out some of his property and brought it over to Europe with him in cash. We had both determined that we would live abroad and have nothing more to do with America. It was not I who persuaded him to do this. It made no difference to me. If he had run away and left me, the courts would have given me money. If he had died and I had been a widow, he would have left me his property. But simply because there was all this money in our hands, and because he disappeared, his people and this man Pritchard suspect me."

"It is wicked," he muttered.

She turned slowly towards him.

"Mr. Tavernake," she said, "do you know that you can help me very much indeed?"

"I only wish I could," he replied. "Try me."

"Can't you see," she went on, "that the great thing against me is that Beatrice left me suddenly when we were on that wretched expedition, and came back alone? She is in London, I know, quite close to me, and still she hides. Pritchard asks himself why. Mr. Tavernake, go and tell her what people are saying, go and tell her everything that has happened, let her understand that her keeping away is doing me a terrible injury, beg her to come and let people see that we are reconciled, and warn her, too, against Pritchard. Will you do this for me?"

"Of course I will," Tavernake answered. "I will see her to-morrow."

Elizabeth drew a little sigh of relief.

"And you'll let me know what she says?" she asked, rising.

"I shall be only too glad to," Tavernake assured her.

"Good-night!"

She looked up into his face with a smile which had turned the heads of hardened stagers in New York. No wonder that Tavernake felt his heart beat against his ribs! He took her hands and held them for a moment. Then he turned abruptly away.

"Good-night!" he said.

He disappeared through the swing doors. She strolled across the room to where her friends were sitting in a circle, laughing and talking. Her father, who had just come in and joined them, gripped her by the arm as she sat down.

"What does it mean?" he demanded, with shaking voice. "Did you see that he was there with Pritchard—your young man —that wretched estate agent's clerk? I tell you that Pritchard was pumping him for all he was worth."

"My dear father," she whispered, coldly, "don't be

melodramatic. You give yourself away the whole time. Go to bed if you can't behave like a man."

The lights had been turned low, there was no one else in the room. The little old gentleman with the eyeglass leaned forward.

"Have you any notion, my dear Elizabeth," he asked, "why our friend Pritchard is so much in evidence just at present?"

"Not on account of you, Jimmy," she answered, "nor of any one else here, in fact. The truth is he has conceived a violent admiration for me—an admiration so pronounced, indeed, that he hates to let me out of his sight."

They all laughed uproariously. Then Walter Crease, the journalist, leaned forward,—a man with a long, narrow face, yellow-stained fingers, and hollow cheekbones. He glanced around the room before he spoke, and his voice sounded like a hoarse whisper.

"See here," he said, "seems to me Pritchard is getting mighty awkward. He hasn't got his posse around him in this country, anyway."

There was a dead silence for several seconds. Then the little old gentleman nodded solemnly.

"I am a trifle tired of Pritchard myself," he admitted, "and he certainly knows too much. He carries too much in his head to go around safely."

The eyes of Elizabeth were bright.

"He treats us like children," she declared. "To-night he has told the whole of my affairs to a perfect stranger. It is intolerable!"

The little party broke up soon after. Only Walter Crease and the man called Jimmy Post were left talking, and they retired into the window-seat, whispering together.

Tavernake, with his hands thrust deep in his overcoat pockets, left the hotel and strode along the Strand. Some fancy seized him before he had gone many paces, and turning abruptly to the left he descended to the Embankment. He made his way to the very seat upon which he had sat once before with Beatrice. With folded arms he leaned back in the corner, looking out across the river, at the curving line of lights, at the black, turgid waters, the slowly-moving hulk of a barge on its way down the stream. It was a new thing, this, for him to have to accuse himself of folly, of weakness. For the last few days he had moved in a mist of uncertainty, setting his heel upon all reflection, avoiding every issue. To-night he could escape those accusing thoughts no longer; to-night he was more than ever bitter with himself. What folly was this which had sprung up in his life—folly colossal, unimaginable, as unexpected as though it had fallen a thunderbolt from the skies! What had happened to change him so completely!

His thought traveled back to the boarding-house. It was there that the thing had begun. Before that night upon the roof, the finger-posts which he had set up with such care and deliberation along the road which led towards his coveted goal, had seemed to him to point with unfaltering directness towards everything in life worthy of consideration. To-night they were only dreary phantasms, marking time across a miserable plain. Perhaps, after all, there had been something in his nature, some rebel thing, intolerable yet to be reckoned with, which had been first born of that fateful curiosity of his. It had leapt up so suddenly, sprung with such scanty notice into strenuous and insistent life. Yet what place had it there? He must fight against it, root it out with both hands. What was this world of intrigue, this criminal, undesirable world, to him? His common sense forbade him altogether to dissociate Elizabeth from her friends, from her surroundings. She was the secret of the pain which was tearing at his heartstrings, of all the excitement, the joy, the passion which had swept like a full flood across the level way of his life, which had set him drifting among the unknown seas. Yet it was Beatrice who had brought this upon him. If she had never left, if he had not tasted the horrors of this new loneliness, he might have been able to struggle on. He missed her, missed her diabolically. The other things, marvelous though they were, had been more or less like a mirage. This world of new emotions had spread like a silken mesh over all his thoughts, over all his desires. Beatrice had been a tangible person, restful, delightful, a real companion, his one resource against this madness. And now she was gone, and he was powerless to get her back. He turned his head, he looked up the road along which he had torn that night with his arms around her. She owed him her life and she had gone! With all a man's inconsequence, it seemed to him as he rose heavily to his feet and started homeward, that she had repaid him with a certain amount of ingratitude, that she had left him at the one moment in his life when he needed her most.

CHAPTER XVI. AN OFFER OF MARRIAGE

The next afternoon, at half-past four, Tavernake was having tea with Beatrice in the tiny flat which she was sharing with another girl, off Kingsway. She opened the door to him herself, and though she chattered ceaselessly, it seemed to him that she was by no means at her ease. She installed him in the only available chair, an absurd little wicker thing many sizes too small for him, and seated herself upon the hearth-rug a few feet away.

"You have soon managed to find me out, Leonard," she remarked.

"Yes," he answered. "I had to go to the stage doorkeeper for your address."

"He hadn't the slightest right to give it you," she declared.

Tavernake shrugged his shoulders.

"I had to have it," he said simply.

"The power of the purse again!" she laughed. "Now that you are here, I don't believe that you are a bit glad to see me. Are you?"

He did not answer for a moment. He was thinking of that vigil upon the Embankment, of the long walk home, of the battle with himself, the continual striving to tear from his heart this new thing, for which, with a curious and most masculine inconsistency, he persisted in holding her responsible.

"You know, Leonard," she continued, getting up abruptly and beginning to make the tea, "I believe that you are angry with me. If you are, all I can say is that you are a very foolish person. I had to come away. Can't you see that?"

"I cannot," he answered stolidly.

She sighed.

"You are not a reasonable person," she declared. "I suppose it is because you have led such a queer life, and had no womenfolk to look after you. You don't understand. It was absurd, in a way, that I should ever have called myself your sister, that we should even have attempted such a ridiculous experiment. But after—after the other night—"

"Can't we forget that?" he interrupted.

She raised her eyes and looked at him.

"Can you?" she asked.

There was a curious, almost a pleading earnestness in her tone. Her eyes had something new to say, something which, though it failed to stir his blood, made him vaguely uncomfortable. Nevertheless, he answered her without hesitation.

"Yes," he replied, "I could forget it. I will promise to forget it."

It was unaccountable, but he almost fancied that he saw this new thing pass from her face, leaving her pale and tremulous. She looked away again and busied herself with the tea-caddy, but the fingers which held the spoon were shaking a little.

"Oh, I suppose I could forget," she said, "but it would be very difficult for either of us to behave as though it had never happened. Besides, it really was an impossible situation, you know," she went on, looking down into the tea-caddy. "It is much better for me to be here with Annie. You can come and see me now and then and we can still be very good friends."

Tavernake was annoyed. He said nothing, and Beatrice, glancing up, laughed at his gloomy expression.

"You certainly are," she declared, "the most impossible, the most primitive person I ever met. London isn't Arcadia, you know, and you are not my brother. Besides, you were such an autocrat. You didn't even like my going out to supper with Mr. Grier."

"I hate the fellow!" Tavernake admitted. "Are you seeing much of him?"

"He took us all out to supper last night," she replied. "I thought it was very kind of him to ask me."

"Kind, indeed! Does he want to marry you?" Tavernake demanded.

She set down the teapot and again she laughed softly. In her plain black gown, very simple, adorned only by the little white bow at her neck, quakerlike and spotless, with the added color in her cheeks, too, which seemed to have come there during the last few moments, she was a very alluring person.

"He can't," she declared. "He is married already."

Then there came to Tavernake an inspiration, an inspiration so wonderful that he gripped the sides of his chair and sat up. Here, after all, was the way out for him, the way out from his garden of madness, the way to escape from that mysterious, paralyzing yoke whose burden was already heavy upon his shoulders. In that swift, vivid moment he saw something of the truth. He saw himself losing all his virility, the tool and plaything of this woman who had bewitched him, a poor, fond creature living only for the kind words and glances she might throw him at her pleasure. In those few seconds he knew the true from the false. Without hesitation, he gripped with all the colossal selfishness of his unthinking sex at the rope which was thrown to him.

"Well, then, I do," he said firmly. "Will you marry me, Beatrice?"

She threw her head back and laughed, laughed long and softly, and Tavernake, simple and unversed in the ways of women, believed that she was indeed amused.

"Neither you nor any one else, dear Leonard!" she exclaimed.

"But I want you to," he persisted. "I think that you will."

There was coquetry now in the tantalizing look she flashed him.

"Am I, too, then, one of these things to be attained in your life?" she asked. "Dear Leonard, you mustn't say it like that. I don't like the look of your jaw. It frightens me."

"There is nothing to be afraid of in marrying me," he answered. "I should make you a very good husband. Some day you would be rich, very rich indeed. I am quite sure that I shall succeed, if not at once, very soon. There is plenty of money to be made in the world if one perseveres."

She had the air of trying to take him seriously.

"You sound quite convincing," she admitted, "but I do wish that you would put all these thoughts out of your mind, Leonard. It doesn't sound like you in the least. Remember what you told me that first night; you assured me that women had not the slightest part in your life."

"I have changed," he confessed. "I did not expect anything of the sort to happen, but it has. It would be foolish of me to deny it. I have been all my life learning, Beatrice," he continued, with a sudden curious softness in his tone, "and yet, somehow or other, it seems to me that I never knew anything at all until lately. There was no one to direct me, no one to show me just what is worth while in life. You have taught me a great deal, you have taught me how little I know. And there are things," he went on, solemnly, "of which I am afraid, things which I do not begin even to understand. Can't you see how it is with me? I am really very ignorant. I want some one who understands; I want you, Beatrice, very badly."

She patted the back of his hand caressingly.

"You mustn't talk like that, Leonard," she said. "I shouldn't make you a good wife. I am not going to marry any one."

"And why?" he asked.

She shook her head.

"That is my secret," she told him, looking into the fire.

"You mean to say that, you will never marry?" he persisted.

"Oh, I suppose I shall change, like other women," she answered. "Just at present, I feel like that."

"Is it because your sister's marriage—"

She caught hold of both his hands; her eyes were suddenly full of terror.

"You mustn't talk about Elizabeth," she begged, "you please mustn't talk about her. Promise that you won't."

"But I came here to talk about her," he replied.

Beatrice, for a moment, said nothing. Then she threw down his hands and laughed once more. As she flung herself back in her place, it seemed to Tavernake that he saw once more the girl who had stood upon the roof of the boarding-house.

"You came to talk about Elizabeth!" she exclaimed. "I forgot. Well, go on, what is it?"

"Your sister is in trouble!"

"Are you her confidant?" Beatrice asked.

"I am not exactly that," he admitted, "but she has asked me to come and see you."

Beatrice had suddenly grown hard, her lips were set together, even her attitude was uncompromising.

"Say exactly what you have to say," she told him. "I will not interrupt."

"It sounds foolish," Tavernake declared, "because I know so little, but it seems that your sister is being annoyed by a man named Pritchard, an American detective. She tells me that he suspects her of being concerned in some way with the disappearance of her husband. One of his reasons is that you left her abruptly and went into hiding, that you will not see or speak to her. She wishes you to be reconciled."

"Is that all?" Beatrice asked.

"It is all," he replied, "so long as you understand its significance. If you go to see your sister, or let her come to see you, this man Pritchard will have one of his causes for suspicion removed."

"So you came as Elizabeth's ambassador," Beatrice said, half as though to herself. "Well, here is my answer. I will not go to Elizabeth. If she finds out my whereabouts and comes here, then I shall go away again and hide. I shall never willingly exchange another word with her as long as I live."

Tavernake looked at her doubtfully.

"But she is your sister!" he explained.

"She is my sister," Beatrice repeated, "and yet what I have said to you I mean."

There was a short silence. Tavernake felt unaccountably ill at ease. Something had sprung up between them which he did not understand. He was swift to recognize, however, the note of absolute finality in her tone.

"I have given my message," he declared. "I shall tell her what you say. Perhaps I had better go now."

He half rose to his feet. Suddenly she lost control of herself.

"Leonard, Leonard," she cried, "don't you see that you are being very foolish indeed? You have been good to me. Let me try and repay it a little. Elizabeth is my sister, but listen! What I say to you now I say in deadly earnest. Elizabeth has no heart, she has no thought for other people, she makes use of them and they count for no more to her than the figures that pass through one's dreams. She has some sort of hateful gift," Beatrice continued, and her voice shook and her eyes flashed, "some hateful gift of attracting people to her and making them do her bidding, of spoiling their lives and throwing them away when they have ceased to be useful. Leonard, you must not let her do this with you."

He rose to his feet awkwardly. Very likely it was all true, and yet, what difference did it make?

"Thank you," he said.

They stood, for a moment, hand in hand. Then they heard the sound of a key in the lock.

"Here's Annie coming back!" Beatrice exclaimed.

Tavernake was introduced to Miss Annie Legarde, who

thought he was a very strange person indeed because he did not fit in with any of the types of men, young or old, of whom she knew anything. And as for Tavernake, he considered that Miss Annie Legarde would have looked at least as well in a hat half the size, and much better without the powder upon her face. Her clothes were obviously more expensive than Beatrice's, but they were put on with less care and taste.

Beatrice came out on to the landing with him.

"So you won't marry me, Beatrice?" he said, as she held out her hand.

She looked at him for a moment and then turned away with a faint sob, without even a word of farewell. He watched her disappear and heard the door shut. Slowly he began to descend the stone steps. There was something to him a little fateful about the closed door above, the long yet easy descent into the street.

CHAPTER XVII. THE BALCONY AT IMANO'S

At six o'clock that evening, Tavernake rang up the Milan Court and inquired for Elizabeth. There was a moment or two's delay and then he heard her reply. Even over the telephone wires, even though he stood, cramped and uncomfortable, in that stuffy little telephone booth, he felt the quick start of pleasure, the thrill of something different in life, which came to him always at the sound of her voice, at the slightest suggestion of her presence.

"Well, my friend, what fortune?" she asked him.

"None," he answered. "I have done my best. Beatrice will not listen to me."

"She will not come and see me?"

"She will not."

Elizabeth was silent for a moment. When she spoke again, there was a change in her tone.

"You have failed, then."

"I did everything that could be done," Tavernake insisted eagerly. "I am quite sure that nothing anybody could say would move Beatrice. She is very decided indeed."

"I have another idea," Elizabeth remarked, after a brief pause. "She will not come to me; very well, I must go to her. You must take me there."

"I cannot do that," Tavernake answered.

"Why not?"

"Beatrice has refused absolutely to permit me to tell you or any one else of her whereabouts," he declared. "Without her permission I cannot do it."

"Do you mean that?" she asked.

"Of course," he answered uncomfortably.

There was another silence. When she spoke again, her voice had changed for the second time. Tavernake felt his heart sink as he listened.

"Very well," she said. "I thought that you were my friend, that you wished to help me."

"I do," he replied, "but you would not have me break my word?"

"You are breaking your word with me," she told him.

"It is a different thing," he insisted.

"You will not take me there?" she said once more.

"I cannot," Tavernake answered.

"Very well, good-bye!"

"Don't go," he begged. "Can't I see you somewhere for a few minutes this evening?"

"I am afraid not," Elizabeth replied coolly.

"Are you going out?" he persisted.

"I am going to the Duke of York's Theatre with some friends," she answered. "I am sorry. You have disappointed me."

She rang off and he turned away from the telephone booth into the street. It seemed to him, as he walked down the crowded thoroughfare, that some reflection of his own self-contempt was visible in the countenances of the men and women who were hurrying past him. Wherever he looked, he was acutely conscious of it. In his heart he felt the bitter sense of shame of a man who wilfully succumbs to weakness. Yet that night he made his efforts.

For four hours he sat in his lonely rooms and worked. Then the unequal struggle was ended. With a groan he caught up his hat and coat and left the house. Half an hour later, he was among the little crowd of loiterers and footmen standing outside the doors of the Duke of York's Theatre.

It was still some time before the termination of the performance. As the slow minutes dragged by, he grew to hate himself, to hate this new thing in his life which had torn down his everyday standards, which had carried him off his feet in this strange and detestable fashion. It was a dormant sense, without a doubt, which Elizabeth had stirred into life—the sense of sex, quiescent in him so long, chiefly through his perfect physical sanity; perhaps, too, in some measure, from his half-starved imagination. It was significant, though, that once aroused it burned with surprising and unwavering fidelity. The whole world of women now were different creatures to him, but they left him as utterly unmoved as in his unawakened days. It was Elizabeth only he wanted, craved for fiercely, with all this late-born passion of mingled sentiment and desire. He felt himself, as he hung round there upon the pavement, rubbing shoulders with the liveried servants, the loafers, and the passers-by, a thing to be despised. He was like a whipped dog fawning back to his master. Yet if only he could persuade her to come with him, if it were but for an hour! If only she would sit opposite him in that wonderful little restaurant, where the lights and the music, the laughter and the wine, were all outward symbols of this new life from before which her fingers seemed to have torn aside the curtains! His heart beat with a fierce impatience. He watched the thin stream of people who left before the play was over, suburbanites mostly, in a hurry for their trains. Very soon the whole audience followed, commissionaires were busy with their whistles, the servants eagerly looking right and left for their masters. And then Elizabeth! She came out in the midst of half-a-dozen others, brilliant in a wonderful cloak and dress of turquoise blue, laughing with her friends, to all appearance the gayest of the party. Tavernake stepped quickly forward, but at that moment there was a crush and he could not advance. She passed within a yard of him, escorted by a couple of men, and for a moment their eyes met. She raised her eyebrows, as though in surprise, and her recognition was of the slightest. She passed on and entered a waiting motorcar, accompanied by the two men. Tavernake stood and looked after it. She did not even glance round. Except for that little gesture of cold surprise, she had ignored him. Tavernake, scarcely knowing what he did, turned slowly towards the Strand.

He was face to face now with a crisis before which he seemed powerless. Men were there in the world to be bullied, cajoled, or swept out of the way. What did one do with a woman who was kind one moment and insolent the next, who raised her eyebrows and passed on when he wanted her, when he was there longing for her? Those old solid dreams of his—wealth, power, his name on great prospectuses, a position in the world—these things now appeared like the day fancies of a child. He had seen his way towards them. Already he had felt his feet upon the rungs of the ladder which leads to material success. This was something different, something greater. Then a sense of despair chilled his heart. He felt how ignorant, how helpless he was. He had not even studied the first text-book of life. Those very qualities which had served him so well before were hopeless here. Persistence, Beatrice had told him once, only annoys a woman.

He came to a standstill outside the entrance to the Milan Court, and retraced his steps. The thought of Beatrice had brought something soothing with it. He felt that he must see her, see her at once. He walked back along the Strand and entered the restaurant where Beatrice and he had had their memorable supper. From the vestibule he could just see Grier's back as he stood talking to a waiter by the side of a round table in the middle of the room. Tavernake slowly withdrew and made his way upstairs. There were one or two little tables there in the balcony, hidden from the lower part of the room. He seated himself at one, handing his coat and hat mechanically to the waiter who came hurrying up.

"But, Monsieur," the man explained, with a deprecating gesture, "these tables are all taken."

Tavernake, who kept an account book in which he registered even his car fares, put five shillings in the man's hand.

"This one I will have," he said, firmly, and sat down.

The man looked at him and turned aside to speak to the head waiter. They conversed together in whispers. Tavernake took no notice. His jaw was set. Himself unseen, he was gazing steadfastly at that table below. The head waiter shrugged his shoulders and departed; his other clients must be mollified. There was a finality which was unanswerable about Tavernake's methods.

Tavernake ate and drank what they brought to him, ate and drank and suffered. Everything was as it had been that other night—the popping of corks, the soft music, the laughter of women, the pleasant, luxurious sense of warmth and gayety pervading the whole place.

It was all just the same, but this time he sat outside and looked on. Beatrice was seated next Grier, and on her other side was a young man of the type which Tavernake detested, partly because it inspired him with a reluctant but insistent sense of inferiority. The young man was handsome, tall, and thin. His evening clothes fitted him perfectly, his studs and links were of the latest mode, his white tie arranged as though by the fingers of an artist. And yet he was no tailor's model. A gentleman, beyond a doubt, Tavernake decided, watching grudgingly the courteous movement of his head, listening sometimes to his well-bred but rather languid voice. Beatrice laughed often into his face. She admired him, of course. How could she help it! Grier sat at her other side. He, too, talked to her whenever he had the chance. It was a new fever which Tavernake was tasting, a new fever burning in his blood. He was jealous; he hated the whole party below. In imagination he saw Elizabeth with her friends, supping most likely in that other, more resplendent restaurant, only a few yards away. He imagined her the centre of every attention. Without a doubt, she was looking at her neighbor as she had looked at him. Tavernake bit his lip, frowning. If he had had it in his power, in those black moments, to have thrown a thunderbolt from his place, he would have wrecked every table in the room, he would have watched with joy the white, startled faces of the revelers as they fled away into the night. It was a new torture, indescribable, bitter. Indeed, this curiosity of his, of which he had spoken to Beatrice as they had walked together down Oxford Street on that first evening, was being satisfied with a vengeance! He was learning of those other things of life. He had sipped at the sweetness; he was drinking the bitters!

An altercation by his side distracted him. Again there was the head waiter and a protesting guest. Tavernake looked up and recognized Professor Franklin. With his broad-brimmed hat in his hand, the professor, in fluent phraseology and a strong American accent, was making himself decidedly disagreeable.

"You had better send for your manager right away, young man," he declared. "On Tuesday night he brought me here himself and I engaged this table for the week. No, I tell you I won't have any other! I guess my order was good enough. You send for Luigi right here. You know who I am? Professor Franklin's my name, from New York, and if I say I mean to have a thing, I expect to get it."

For the first time he recognized Tavernake, and paused for a moment in his speech.

"Have I got your table, Professor?" Tavernake asked, slowly.

"You have, sir," the professor answered. "I did not recognize you when I came in or I would have addressed you personally. I have particular reasons for occupying a front table here every night this week."

The thoughts began to crowd in upon Tavernake's brain. He hesitated.

"Why not sit down with me?" he suggested.

The professor acquiesced without a word. The head waiter, with a sigh of relief, took his hat and overcoat and accepted his order. Tavernake leaned across the table.

"Professor," he said, "why do you insist upon sitting up here?"

The professor moved his head slowly downwards.

"My young friend, I speak to you in confidence?"

"In confidence," Tavernake repeated.

"I come here secretly," the professor continued, "because it is the only chance I have of seeing a very dear relative of mine. I am obliged to keep away from her just now, but from here I can watch, I can see that she is well."

"You mean your daughter Beatrice," Tavernake said, calmly.

The professor trembled all over.

"You know!" he muttered.

"Yes, I know," Tavernake answered. "I have been able to be of some slight assistance to your daughter Beatrice."

The professor grasped his hand.

"Yes, yes," he said, "Elizabeth is very angry with you because you will not tell her where to find the little girl. You are right, Mr. Tavernake. You must never tell her."

"I don't intend it," Tavernake declared.

"Say, this is a great evening for me!" the professor went on, eagerly. "I found out by accident myself. I was at the bar and I saw her come in with a lot of others."

"Why don't you go and speak to her?" Tavernake asked.

The professor shivered.

"There has been a disagreement," he explained. "Beatrice and Elizabeth have quarreled. Mind you, Beatrice was right."

"Then why don't you go to her instead of staying with Elizabeth?" Tavernake demanded, bluntly.

The professor temporarily collapsed. He drank heavily of the whiskey and soda by his side, and answered gloomily.

"My young friend," he said, "Beatrice, when she left us, was penniless. Mind you, Elizabeth is the one with brains. It is Elizabeth who has the money. She has a strong will, too. She keeps me there whether I will or not, she makes me do many things—many things, surely—which I hate. But Elizabeth has her way. If I had gone with Beatrice, if I were to go to her now, I should be only a burden upon her."

"You have no money, then?" Tavernake remarked.

The professor shook his head sadly.

"Speculations, my young friend," he replied, "speculations undertaken solely with the object of making a fortune for my children. I have had money and lost it."

"Can't you earn any?" Tavernake asked. "Beatrice doesn't seem extravagant."

The professor regarded this outspoken young man with an air of hurt dignity.

"If you will forgive me," he said. "I think that we will choose another subject of conversation."

"At any rate," Tavernake declared, "you must be fond of your daughter or you would not come here night after night just to look at her."

The professor shook out a handkerchief from his pocket and dabbed his eyes.

"Beatrice was always my favorite," he announced solemnly, "but Elizabeth—well, you can't get away from Elizabeth," he added, leaning across the table. "To tell you the truth, Mr. Tavernake, Elizabeth terrifies me sometimes, she is so bold. I am afraid where her scheming may land us. I would be happier with Beatrice if only she had the means to satisfy my trifling wants."

He turned to the waiter and ordered a pint of champagne.

"Veuve Clicquot '99," he instructed the man. "At my age," he remarked, with a sigh, "one has to be careful about these little matters. The wrong brand of champagne means a sleepless night."

Tavernake looked at him in a puzzled way. The professor was a riddle to him. He represented no type which had come within the orbit of his experience. With the arrival of the champagne, the professor became almost eloquent. He leaned forward, gazing stealthily down at the round table.

"If I could tell you of that girl's mother, Mr. Tavernake,"

he said, "if I could tell you what her history, our history, has been, it would seem to you so strange that you would probably regard me as a romancer. No, we have to carry our secrets with us."

"By-the-bye," Tavernake asked, "what are you a professor of?"

"Of the hidden sciences, sir," was the immediate reply. "Phrenology was my earliest love. Since then I have studied in the East; I have spent many years in a monastery in China. I have gratified in every way my natural love of the occult. I represent today those people of advanced thought who have traveled, even in spirit, for ever such a little distance across the line which divides the Seen from the Unseen, the Known from the Infinite."

He took a long draught of champagne. Tavernake gazed at him in blank amazement.

"I don't know much about science," he said. "It is only lately that I have begun to realize how ignorant I really am. Your daughter has helped to teach me."

The professor sighed heavily.

"A young woman of attainments, sir," he remarked, "of character, too. Look at the way she carries her head. That was a trick of her mother's."

"Don't you mean to speak to her at all, then?" Tavernake asked.

"I dare not," the professor replied. "I am naturally of a truthful disposition, and if Elizabeth were to ask me if I had spoken to her sister, I should give myself away at once. No, I look on and that is all."

Tavernake drummed with his fingers upon the tablecloth. Something in the merriment of that little party downstairs had filled him with a very bitter feeling.

"You ought to go and claim her, professor," he declared. "Look down at them now. Is that the best life for a girl? The men are almost strangers to her, and the girls are not fit for her to associate with. She has no friends, no relatives. Your daughter Elizabeth can do without you very well. She is strong enough to take care of herself."

"But my dear sir," the professor objected, "Beatrice could not support me."

Tavernake paid his bill without another word. Downstairs the lights had been lowered, the party at the round table were already upon their feet.

"Good-night, professor!" he said. "I am going to see the last of Beatrice from the top of the stairs."

The professor followed him—they stood there and watched her depart with Annie Legarde. The two girls got into a taxicab together, and Tavernake breathed a sigh of relief, a relief for which he was wholly unable to account, when he saw that Grier made no effort to follow them. As soon as the taxi had rolled away, they descended and passed into the street. Then the professor suddenly changed his tone.

"Mr. Tavernake," he said, "I know what you are thinking about me: I am a weak old man who drinks too much and who wasn't born altogether honest. I can't give up anything. I'd be happier, really happier, on a crust with Beatrice, but I daren't, I simply daren't try it. I prefer the flesh pots with Elizabeth, and you despise me for it. I don't blame you, Mr. Tavernake, but listen."

"Well?" Tavernake interjected.

The professor's fingers gripped his arm.

"You've known Beatrice longer—you don't know Elizabeth very well, but let me tell you this. Elizabeth is a very wonderful person. I know something about character, I know something about those hidden powers which men and women possess—strange powers which no one can understand, powers which drag a man to a woman's feet, or which make him shiver when he passes another even in a crowd. You see, these things are a science with me, Mr. Tavernake, but I don't pretend to understand everything. All I know is that Elizabeth is one of those people who can just do what she likes with men. I am her father and I am her slave. I tell myself that I would rather be with Beatrice, and I am as powerless to go as though I were bound with chains. You are a young ignorant man, Mr. Tavernake, you know nothing of life, and I will give you a word of warning. It is better for you that you keep away from over there."

He raised one hand and pointed across the street towards the Milan Court; with the other he once more gripped Tavernake's arm.

"Why she should take the trouble even to speak with you for a moment, I do not know," the professor continued, "but she does. It has pleased her to talk with you—why I can't imagine—only if I were you I would get away while there is yet time. She is my daughter but she has no heart, no pity. I saw her smile at you. I am sorry always for the man she smiles upon like that. Goodnight, Mr. Tavernake!"

The professor crossed the street. Tavernake watched him until he was out of sight. Then he felt an arm thrust through his.

"Why, this is what I call luck!" a familiar voice exclaimed. "Mr. Tavernake, you're the very man I was looking for!"

CHAPTER XVIII. A MIDNIGHT ADVENTURE

Tavernake was not sociably inclined and took no pains to conceal the fact. Mr. Pritchard, however, was not easily to be shaken off.

"So you've been palling up to the old man, eh?" he remarked, in friendly fashion.

"I came across the professor unexpectedly," Tavernake answered, coldly. "What do you want with me, please? I am on my way home."

Pritchard laughed softly to himself.

"Say, there's something about you Britishers I can't help admiring!" he declared. "You are downright, aren't you?"

"I suppose you think we are too clumsy to be anything else," Tavernake replied. "This is my 'bus coming. Good-night!"

Pritchard's hand, however, tightened upon his companion's arm.

"Look here, young man," he said, "don't you be foolish. I'm a valuable acquaintance for you, if you only realized it. Come along across the street with me. My club is on the Terrace, just below. Stroll along there with me and I'll tell you something about the professor, if you like."

"Thank you," Tavernake answered, "I don't think I care about hearing gossip. Besides, I think I know all there is to be known about him."

"Did you give Miss Beatrice my message?" Pritchard asked suddenly.

"If I did," Tavernake replied, "I have no answer for you."

"Will you tell her this," Pritchard began,—

"No, I will tell her nothing!" Tavernake interrupted. "You can look after your own affairs. I have no interest in them and I don't want to have. Good-night!"

Pritchard laughed again but he did not relax his grasp upon the other's arm.

"Now, Mr. Tavernake," he said, "it won't do for you to

quarrel with me. I shouldn't be surprised if you discovered that I am one of the most useful acquaintances you ever met in your life. You needn't come into the club unless you like, but walk as far as there with me. When we get on to the Terrace, with closed houses on one side and a palisade upon the other, I am going to say something to you."

"Very well," Tavernake decided, reluctantly. "I don't know what there is you can have to tell me, but I'll come as far as there, at any rate."

They crossed the Strand and turned into Adam Street. As they neared the further corner, Pritchard stepped from the pavement into the middle of the street, and looked searchingly around.

"Say, you'll excuse my being a little careful," he remarked. "This is rather a lonely part for the middle of London, and I have been followed for the last two days by people whose company I am not over keen about."

"Followed? What for?" Tavernake demanded.

"Oh, the usual thing!" answered the detective, with a shrug of the shoulders. "That company of crooks I showed you last night don't fancy having me around. They've a good many grudges up against Sam Pritchard. I am not quite so safe over here as I should be in New York. Most of them are off to Paris tomorrow, thank Heavens!"

"And you?" Tavernake asked. "Are you going, too?"

Pritchard shook his head.

"If only those fools would believe it, I'm not over here on their business at all. I came over on a special commission this time, as you know. I have a word of warning for you, Mr. Tavernake. I guess you won't like to hear it, but you've got to."

Tavernake stopped short.

"I don't want your warnings!" he said angrily. "I don't want you interfering in my affairs!"

The detective smiled quietly. Then a new expression

suddenly tightened his lips.

"Never mind about that just now!" he exclaimed. "See here, take this police whistle from my left hand, quick, and blow it for all that you are worth!"

It was characteristic of Tavernake that he was prepared to obey without a second's hesitation. The opportunity, however, was denied him. The events which followed came and passed like a thought. A blow on his left wrist and the whistle fell into the road. A dark figure had sprung up, apparently from space; a long arm was twined around Pritchard's neck, bending him backwards; there was a gleam of steel within a few inches of his throat. And then Tavernake saw a wonderful thing. With a turn of his wrist, Pritchard suddenly seemed to lift the form of his assailant into the air. Tavernake caught a swift impression of a man's white face, the head pointing to the street, the legs twitching convulsively. Head over heels Pritchard seemed to throw him, while the knife clattered harmlessly into the roadway. The man lay crumpled up and moaning before the door of one of the houses. Pritchard sprang after him. The door had been cautiously opened and the man crawled through; Pritchard followed; then the door closed and Tavernake beat upon it in vain.

For several seconds—it seemed to Tavernake much longer —he stood gazing at the door, breathing heavily, absolutely unable to collect his thoughts. The whole affair had happened with such amazing celerity! He could not bring himself to realize it, to believe that it was Pritchard who had been with him only a few seconds ago, who in danger of his life had performed that marvelous trick of jiu-jutsu, had followed his unknown assailant into that dark, mysterious house, from no single window of which was a single gleam of light visible. Tavernake had led an uneventful life. Of the passions which breed murder and the desire to kill he knew nothing. He was dazed with the suddenness of it all. How could such a thing happen in the midst of London, in a thoroughfare only momentarily deserted, at the further end of which, indeed, were many signs of life! Then the thought of that knife made him shiver—blue glittering steel cutting the air like whipcord. He remembered the look in the assassin's face—horrible, an epitome of the passions, which seemed to reveal to him in that moment the existence of some other, some unknown world, about which he had neither read nor dreamed.

The sound of footsteps came as an immense relief. A man came round the corner, smoking a cigarette and humming softly to himself. The presence of another human being seemed suddenly to bring Tavernake's feet back upon the earth. He moved toward the pavement and addressed the newcomer.

"Can you tell me how to get inside that house?" he asked quickly.

The man removed the cigarette from his mouth and stared at his questioner.

"I should ring the bell," he replied, "but surely it's unoccupied? What do you want to get in there for?"

"Less than a minute ago," Tavernake told him, "I was walking here with a friend. A man came up behind us and tried deliberately to stab him. He bolted afterwards through that door, my friend followed him, the door was closed in my face."

The newcomer was a youngish man, a musician, who had just come from a concert and was on his way to the club at the end of the street. Probably, had he been a journalist, his curiosity would have been greater than his incredulity. As it was, however, he gazed at Tavernake, for a moment, blankly.

"Look here," he said, "this doesn't sound a very likely story of yours, you know."

"I don't care whether it's likely or not," Tavernake answered hotly; "it's true! The knife's somewhere in the road there—it fell up against the railings."

They crossed the road together and searched. There were

no signs of the weapon. Tavernake peered over the railings.

"When my friend struck the other man and twisted him over," he explained, "the knife seemed to fly up into the air; it might even have reached the gardens."

His companion turned slowly away.

"Well, it's no use looking down there for it," he remarked. "We might try the door, if you like."

They leaned their weight against it, hammered at the panels, and waited. The door was fast closed and no reply came. The musician shrugged his shoulders and prepared to depart, after one more glance at Tavernake, half suspicious, half questioning.

"If you think it worth while," he said, "you had better fetch the police, perhaps. If you take my advice, though, I think I should go home and forget all about it."

He passed on, leaving Tavernake speechless. The idea that people might not believe his story had never seriously occurred to him. Yet all of a sudden he began to doubt it himself. He stepped back into the road and looked up at the windows of the house—dark, uncurtained, revealing no sign of life or habitation. Had he really taken that walk with Pritchard, stood on this spot with him only a minute or two ago? Then he picked up the police whistle and he had no longer any doubts. The whole scene was before him again, more vividly than ever. Even at this moment, Pritchard might be in need of help!

He turned and walked sharply to the corner of the Terrace, finding himself almost immediately face to face with a policeman.

"You must come into this house with me at once!" Tavernake exclaimed, pointing backwards. "A friend of mine was attacked here just now; a man tried to stab him. They are both in that house. The man ran away and my friend followed him. The door is closed and no one answers."

The constable looked at Tavernake very much as the

musician had done.

"Do either of them live there, sir?" he asked.

"How should I know!" Tavernake answered. "The man sprang upon my friend from behind. He had a knife in his hand —I saw it. My friend threw him over and he escaped into that house. They are both there now.

"Which house is it, sir?" the policeman inquired.

They were standing almost in front of it. The gate was open and Tavernake beat against the panels with the flat of his hand. Then, with a cry of triumph, he stooped down and picked something up from a crack in the flagged stones.

"The key!" he cried. "Come on, quick!"

He thrust it into the lock and turned it; the door swung smoothly open. The policeman laid his hand upon Tavernake's shoulder.

"Look here," he said, "let's have that story of yours again, a little more clearly. Who is it that's in this house?"

"Five minutes ago," Tavernake began, speaking rapidly, "I met a man in the Strand whom I know slightly—Pritchard, an American detective. He said that he had something to say to me and he asked me to walk round with him to a club in this Terrace. We were in the middle of the road there, talking, when a man sprang at him; he must have come up behind quite noiselessly. The man had a knife in his hand. My friend threw him head over heels—it was some trick of jiu-jutsu; I have seen it done at the Polytechnic. He fell in front of this door which must either have been ajar or else some one who was waiting must have let him in. He crawled through and my friend followed him. The door was slammed in my face."

"How long ago was this?" the policeman asked.

"Not much more than five minutes," Tavernake answered.

The policeman coughed.

"It's a very queer story, sir."

"It's true!" Tavernake declared, fiercely. "You and I have got to search this house."

The policeman nodded.

"There's no harm in that, sir, anyway."

He flashed his lantern around the hall—unfurnished, with paper hanging from the walls. Then they began to enter the rooms, one by one. Nowhere was there any sign of occupation. From floor to floor they passed, in grim silence. In the front chamber of the attic was a camp bedstead, two or three humble articles of furniture, and a small stove.

"Caretaker's kit," the policeman muttered. "Nothing seems to have been used for some time."

They descended the stairs again.

"You say you saw the two men enter this house, sir?" the policeman remarked doubtfully.

"I did," Tavernake declared. "There is no doubt about it."

"The back entrances are all properly locked," the policeman pointed out. "None of the windows by which any one could escape have been opened. We've been into every room. There's no one in the house now, sir, is there?"

"There doesn't seem to be," Tavernake admitted.

The policeman looked him over once more; Tavernake certainly had not the appearance of one attempting a hoax.

"I am afraid there is nothing more we can do, sir," the man said civilly. "You had better give me your name and address."

"Can't we go over the place once more?" Tavernake suggested. "I tell you I saw them come in."

"I have my beat outside to look after, sir," the constable answered. "If it wasn't that you seem respectable, I should begin to think that you wanted me out of the way for a bit. Name and address, please."

Tavernake gave them readily. They passed out together into the street.

"I shall report this matter," the man said, closing his book. "Perhaps the sergeant will have the house searched again. If you take my advice, sir," he added, "you'll go home."

"I saw them both pass through that door," Tavernake repeated, half to himself, still standing upon the pavement and staring at the unlit windows.

The constable made no reply but moved off. Soon he reached the corner of the Terrace and disappeared. Tavernake slowly crossed the road and with his back to the railings looked steadfastly at the dark front of gray stone houses. Big Ben struck one o'clock, several people passed backwards and forwards. Men were coming out from the club, and separating for the night; the roar of the city was growing fainter. Yet Tavernake felt indisposed to move. The look in that man's drawn white face and black eyes haunted him, There was tragedy there, the shadow of terrible things, fear, and the murderous desire to kill! Through that door they had passed, the two men, one in flight, the other in pursuit. Where were they now? Perhaps it had been a trap. Pritchard had spoken seriously enough of his enemies.

Then, as he stood there, he saw for the first time a thin line of light through the closely-drawn curtains of a room on the ground floor of the adjoining house. Without a moment's hesitation, he crossed the road and rang the bell. The door was opened, after a trifling delay, by a man in plain clothes, who might, however, have been a servant in mufti. He looked at Tavernake suspiciously.

"I am sorry to have disturbed you," Tavernake explained, "but I saw some one go in the house next to you, a little time ago. Can you tell me if you have heard any noises or voices during the last half-hour?"

The man shook his head.

"We have heard nothing, sir," he said.

"Who lives here?" Tavernake asked.

"Did you call me up at one o'clock in the morning to ask

silly questions?" the man replied insolently. "Every one's in bed here and I was just going."

"There's a light in your ground floor room," Tavernake remarked. "There's some one talking there now—I can hear voices."

The man closed the door in his face. For some time Tavernake wandered restlessly about, starting at last reluctantly homewards. He had reached the Strand and was crossing Trafalgar Square when a sudden thought held him. He stood still for a moment in the middle of the street. Then he turned abruptly round. In less than five minutes he was once more on the Terrace.

CHAPTER XIX. TAVERNAKE INTERVENES

Tavernake had the feelings of a man suddenly sobered as he turned once more into the Adelphi Terrace. Waiting until no one was in sight, he opened the door of the empty house with the Yale key which he had kept, and carefully closed it. He struck a match and listened for several minutes intently; not a sound from anywhere. He moved a few yards further to the bottom of the stairs, and listened again; still silence. He turned the handle of the ground floor apartment and commenced a fresh search. Room by room he examined by the light of his rapidly dwindling matches. This time he meant to leave behind him no possibility of any mistake. He even measured the depths of the walls for any secret hiding place. From room to room he passed, leisurely, always on the alert, always listening. Once, as he opened a door on the third floor there was a soft scurrying as though of a skirt across the floor. He struck a match quickly, to find a great rat sitting up and looking at him with black, beady eyes. It was the only sign of life he found in the whole building.

When he had finished his search, he came down to the ground floor and entered the room corresponding with the one from which he had heard voices in the adjoining house. He crouched here upon the dusty boards for some time, listening. Now and then he fancied that he could still hear voices on the other side of the wall, but he was never absolutely certain.

At last he rose to stretch himself, and almost as he did so a fresh sound from outside attracted his notice. A motor-car had turned into the Terrace. He walked to the uncurtained window and stood there, sure of being himself unseen. Then his heart gave a great leap. Unemotional though he was, this was a happening which might well have excited a more phlegmatic individual. A motor-car which he remembered very well, although it was driven now by a man in dark livery, had stopped at the next house. A woman and two men had descended. Tavernake never glanced at the latter; his eyes were fastened upon their companion. She was wrapped in a long cloak, but she lifted her skirts as she crossed the pavement, and he saw the flash of her silver buckles. Her carriage, her figure, were unmistakable. It was Elizabeth who was paying this early morning visit next door! Already the little party had disappeared. They did not even ring the bell. The door must have been opened silently at their coming. The motor-car glided off. Once more the Terrace was deserted.

Tavernake felt sure that he knew now the solution,—there was a way from this house into the next one. He struck another match and, standing back a few yards, looked critically at the dividing wall. In ancient days this had evidently been a dwelling-house of importance, elaborately decorated, as the fresco work upon the ceiling still indicated. The wall had been divided into three panels, with a high wainscoting. Inch by inch he examined it from one end to the other; he started from the back and came toward the front. About three-quarters of the way there, he paused. It was very simple, after all. The solid wall for a couple of feet suddenly ceased, and the design was continued with an expanse of stretched canvas, which yielded easily to his finger. He leaned his ear against it; he could hear now distinctly the sound of voices—he heard even the woman's laughter. For the height of about four feet the wall had been bodily removed. He made a small hole in the canvas—there was still darkness. He enlarged the hole until he could thrust his hand through—there was nothing but canvas the other side. He knew now where he was. There was only that single thickness of canvas between him and the room. He had but to make the smallest hole in it and he would be able to see through. Even now, with the removal of the barrier on his side, the voices were more distinct. A complete section of the wall had evidently been taken out and replaced by a detachable framework of wood covered with stretched canvas. He stood back for a moment and felt with his finger; he could almost trace the spot where the woodwork fitted upon hinges.

Then he went on his hands and knees again, and with his penknife in his hand he paused to listen. He could hear the man Crease talking—a slow, nasal drawl. Then he heard Pritchard's voice, followed by what seemed to be a groan. There was a silence, then Elizabeth seemed to ask a question. He heard her low laugh and some note in it sent a shiver through his body. Pritchard was speaking fiercely now. Then, in the middle of his sentence, there was silence once more, followed by another groan. He could almost feel the people in that room holding their breaths.

Tavernake was rapidly forgetting all caution. The point of his knife was through the canvas. Slowly he worked it round until a small piece, the size of a half-crown, was partially cut through. With infinite pains he got his head and shoulders into the small recess and for the first time looked into the room. Pritchard was sitting almost in the middle of the apartment; his arms seemed to be bound to the chair and his legs were tied together. A few yards away, Elizabeth, her fur coat laid aside, was lounging back in an easy-chair, her dress all glittering with sequins, a curious light in her eyes, a cruel smile parting her lips. By her side—sitting, in fact, on the arm of her chair—was Crease, his long, worn face paler, even, than usual; his lips curled in a smile of cynical amusement. Major Post was there, carefully dressed as though he had been attending some social gathering, standing upon the hearth-rug with his coat-tails under his arms. The professor, in whose face seemed written the most abject terror, was talking. Tavernake now could hear every word distinctly.

"My dear Elizabeth! My dear Crease! You are both too precipitate! I tell you that I protest—I protest most strongly. Mr. Pritchard, I am sure, with a little persuasion, will listen to reason. I will not be a party to any such proceeding as—as this. You understand, Crease? We have gone quite far enough as it is. I will not have it."

Elizabeth laughed softly.

"My dear father," she said, "you will really have to take something for your nerves. Nothing need happen to Mr. Pritchard at all unless he asks for it. He has his chance—. no one should expect more."

"You are right, my dear Elizabeth," declared Crease, speaking very slowly and with his usual drawl. "This question of his health for the future—at any rate, for the immediate future—is entirely in Pritchard's own hands. There is no one who has received so many warnings as he. Bramley was cautioned twice; Mallison was warned three times and burned to death; Forsith had word from us only once, and he was shot in a drunken brawl. This man Pritchard has been warned a dozen times, he has escaped death twice. The time has come to show him that we are in earnest. Threats are useless; the time has come for deeds. I say that if Pritchard refuses this trifling request of ours, let us see that he leaves this house in such a state that he will not be able to do us any harm for some time at least."

"But he will give his word!" the professor cried excitedly. "I am quite sure that if you allow me to talk to him reasonably, he will pledge his word to go back to the States and interfere no longer with your affairs."

Pritchard turned his head slightly. He was a little pale, and the blood was dropping slowly on to the floor from a wound in his temple, but his tone was contemptuous.

"I will give you my word, Professor, and you, Elizabeth Gardner, and you, Jim Post, and you, Walter Crease, that crippled, or straight, in evil or good health, from the very jaws of death I will hang on to life until you have paid your just debts. You understand that, all of you? I don't know what sort of a show this is. You may be in earnest, or you may be trying a rag. In any case, let me assure you of this. You won't get me to beg for mercy. If you force me to drink that stuff you are talking about, I'll find the antidote, and as sure as there's a prison in

America, so surely I'll make you suffer for it! If you take my advice," he went on slowly, "and I know what I'm talking about, you'll cut these ropes and set open your front door. You 'll live longer, all of you."

"An idiot," Elizabeth remarked pleasantly, "can do but little harm in the world. The word of a person of weak intellect is not to be relied upon. For my part, I am very tired of our friend, Mr. Pritchard. If you others had been disposed to go to much greater lengths, if you had said 'Hang him from the ceiling,' I should have been well pleased."

Pritchard made a slight movement in his chair—it was certainly not a movement of fear.

"Madam," he said, "I admire your candor. Let me return it. I don't believe there's one of you here has the pluck to attempt to do me any serious injury. If there is, get on with it. You hear, Mr. Walter Crease? Bring out that bottle of yours."

Crease removed his cigar from his lips and rose slowly to his feet. From his waistcoat pocket he produced a small phial, from which he drew the cork.

"Seems to me it's up to us to do the trick," he remarked languidly. "Catch hold of his forehead, Jimmy."

The man known as Major Post threw away his cigarette, and coming round behind Pritchard's chair, suddenly bent the man's head backward. Crease advanced, phial in hand. Then all Hell seemed to be let loose in Tavernake. He stepped back in his place and marked the extent of that wooden partition. Then, setting his teeth, he sprang at it, throwing the great weight of his massive shoulder against the framework door. Scratched and bleeding, but still upon his feet, he burst into the room, with the noise of bricks falling behind,—an apparition so unexpected that the little company gathered there seemed turned into some waxwork group from the Chamber of Horrors—motionless, without even the power of movement.

Tavernake, in those few moments, was like a giant among

a company of degenerates. He was strong, his muscles were like whipcord, and his condition was perfect. Walter Crease went over like a log before his fist; Major Post felt the revolver at which he had snatched struck from his hand, and he himself remembered nothing more till he came to his senses some time afterwards. A slash and a cut and Pritchard was free. The professor stood wringing his hands. Elizabeth had risen to her feet. She was pale, but she was still more nearly composed than any other person in the room. Tavernake and Pritchard were masters of the situation. Pritchard leaned toward the mirror and straightened his tie.

"I am afraid," he said looking down at Walter Crease's groaning figure, "that our hosts are scarcely in fit condition to take leave of us. Never mind, Mrs. Gardner, we excuse ourselves to you. I cannot pretend to be sorry that my friend's somewhat impetuous entrance has disturbed your plans for the evening, but I do hope that you will realize now the fatuousness of such methods in these days. Good-night! It is time we finished our stroll together, Tavernake."

They moved towards the door—there was no one to stop them. Only the professor tried to say a few words.

"My dear Mr. Pritchard—my dear Pritchard, if you will allow me to call you so," he exclaimed, "let me beg of you, before you leave us, not to take this trifling adventure too seriously! I can assure you that it was simply an attempt to coerce you, not in the least an affair to be taken seriously!"

Pritchard smiled.

"Professor," he said, "and you, Walter Crease, and you, Jimmy Post, if you're able to listen, listen to me. You have played the part of children to-night. So surely as men and women exist who live as you do, so surely must the law wait upon their heels. You cannot cheat justice. It is as inexorable as Time itself. When you try these little tricks, you simply give another turn to the wheel, add another danger to life. You had better learn to look upon me as necessary, all of you, for I am certainly inevitable."

They passed backwards through the door, then they went down the silent hall and out into the street. Even as they did so, the clock struck a quarter to two.

"My friend Tavernake," Pritchard declared, lighting a cigarette with steady fingers, "you are a man. Come into the club with me while I bathe my forehead. After all, we'll have that drink together before we say goodnight."

CHAPTER XX. A PLEASANT REUNION

Tavernake awoke some hours later with a puzzled sense of having lost his own identity, of having taken up another man's life, stepped into another man's shoes. From the day of his first arrival in London, a raw country youth, till the night when he had spoken to Beatrice on the roof of Blenheim House, nothing that could properly be called an adventure had ever happened to him. He had never for a moment felt the want of it; he had not even indulged in the reading of books of romance. The thing which had happened last night, as in the cold morning sunlight he sat up in his bed, seemed to him a thing grotesque, inconceivable. It was not really possible that those people—those well-bred, well-looking people—had seriously contemplated an enormity which seemed to belong to the back pages of history, or that he, Tavernake, had burst through a wall with no weapons in his hand, and had dominated the situation! He sat there steadily thinking. It was incredible, but it was true! There existed still in his mind some faint doubt as to whether they would really have proceeded to extremities. Pritchard himself had made light of the whole affair, afterwards had treated it, indeed, as a huge practical joke. Tavernake, remembering that little group as he had first seen it, remained doubtful.

By degrees, his own personal characteristics began to assert themselves. He began to wonder how his action would affect his commercial interests. He had probably made an enemy of this wonderful sister of Beatrice's, the woman who had so completely filled his thoughts during the last few days, the woman, too, who was to have found the money by means of which he was to set his feet upon the first rung of the ladder. This was a thing, he decided, which must be settled at once. He must see her and know exactly what terms they were on, whether or not she meant to be off with her bargain. The thought of action of any sort was stimulating. He rose and dressed, had his breakfast, and set out on his pilgrimage.

Soon after eleven o'clock, he presented himself at the Milan Court and asked for Mrs. Wenham Gardner. For several minutes he waited about in nervous anticipation, then he was told that she was not at home. More than a little disappointed, he pressed for news of her. The hall porter thought that she had gone down into the country, and if so it was doubtful when she would be back. Tavernake was now seriously disconcerted.

"I want particularly to wire to her," he insisted. "Please find out from her maid how I shall direct a telegram."

The hall porter, who was a most superior person, regarded him blandly.

"We do not give addresses, sir," he explained, "unless at the expressed wish of our clients. If you leave a telegram here, I will send it up to Mrs. Gardner's rooms to be forwarded."

Tavernake scribbled one out, begging for news of her return, added his address and left the place. Then he wandered aimlessly about the streets. There seemed something flat about the morning, some aftermath of the excitement of the previous night was still stirring in his blood. Nevertheless, he pulled himself together with an effort, called for a young surveyor whom he had engaged to assist him, and spent the rest of the day out upon the hill. Religiously he kept his thoughts turned upon his work until the twilight came. Then he hurried home to meet the disappointment which he had more than half anticipated. There was no telegram for him! He ate his dinner and sat with folded arms, looking out into the street. Still no telegram! The restlessness came back once more. Soon after ten o'clock it became unbearable. He found himself longing for company, the loneliness of his little room since the departure of Beatrice had never seemed so real a thing. He stood it as long as he could and then, catching up his hat and stick, he set his face eastwards, walking vigorously, and with frequent glances at the clocks he passed.

A few minutes past eleven o'clock, he found himself once

more in that dark thoroughfare at the back of the theatre. The lamp over the stage-door was flickering in the same uncertain manner, the same motor-cars were there, the same crowd of young men, except that each night they seemed to grow larger. This time he had a few minutes only to wait. Beatrice came out among the earliest. At the sight of her he was suddenly conscious that he had, after all, no excuse for coming, that she would probably cross-examine him about Elizabeth, would probably guess the secret of his torments. He shrank back, but he was a moment too late for she had seen him. With a few words of excuse to the others with whom she was talking, she picked up her skirts and came swiftly across the muddy street. Tavernake had no time to escape. He remained there until she came, but his cheeks were hot, and he had an uncomfortable feeling that his presence, that their meeting like this, was an embarrassment to both of them.

"My dear Leonard," she exclaimed, "why do you hide over there?"

"I don't know," he answered simply.

She laughed.

"It looks as though you didn't want to see me," she remarked. "If you didn't, why are you here?"

"I suppose I did want to see you," he replied. "Anyhow, I was lonely. I wanted to talk to some one. I walked all the way up here from Chelsea."

"You have something to tell me?" she suggested.

"There was something," he admitted. "I thought perhaps you ought to know. I had supper with your father last night. We talked about you."

She started as though he had struck her; her face was suddenly pale and anxious.

"Are you serious, Leonard?" she asked. "My father?"

He nodded.

"I am sorry," he said. "I ought not to have blundered it

out like that. I forgot that you—you were not seeing anything of him.”

“How did you meet him?”

“By accident,” he answered. “I was sitting alone up in the balcony at Imano's, and he wanted my table because he could see you from there, so we shared it, and then we began talking. I knew who he was, of course; I had seen him in your sister's room. He told me that he had engaged the table for every night this week.”

She looked across the road.

“I can't go out with those people now,” she declared. “Wait here for me.”

She went back to her friends and talked to them for a moment or two. Tavernake could hear Grier's protesting voice and Beatrice's light laugh. Evidently they were trying uselessly to persuade her to change her mind. Soon she came back to him.

“I am sorry,” he said reluctantly. “I am afraid that I have spoiled your evening.”

“Don't be foolish, please,” she replied taking his arm. “Do you believe that my father will be up in the balcony at Imano's to-night?”

Tavernake nodded.

“He told me so.”

“We will go and sit up there,” she decided. “He knows where I am to be found now so it doesn't matter. I should like to see him.”

They walked off together. Though she was evidently absent and distressed, Tavernake felt once more that sense of pleasant companionship which her near presence always brought him.

“There is something else I must ask you,” she began presently. “I want to know if you have seen Pritchard lately.”

“I was with him last night,” Tavernake answered.

She shivered.

"He was asking questions?"

"Not about you," Tavernake assured her quickly. "It is your sister in whom he is interested."

Beatrice nodded, but she seemed very little relieved. Tavernake could see that the old look of fear was back in her face.

"I am sorry, Beatrice," he said, regretfully. "I seem just now to be always bringing you reminiscences of the people whom it terrifies you to hear about."

She shook her head.

"It isn't your fault, Leonard," she declared, "only it is rather strange that you should be mixed up with them in any way, isn't it? I suppose some day you'll find out everything about me. Perhaps you'll be sorry then that you ever even called yourself my brother."

"Don't be foolish," he answered, brusquely.

She patted his hand.

"Is the speculation going all right?" she asked.

"I am hoping to get the money together this week," he replied. "If I get it, I shall be well off in a year, rich in five years."

"There is just a doubt about your getting it, then?" she inquired.

"Just a doubt," he admitted. "I have a solicitor who is doing his best to raise a loan, but I have not heard from him for two days. Then I have also a friend who has promised it to me, a friend upon whom I am not quite sure if I can rely."

They turned into the Strand.

"Tell me about my father, Leonard," she begged.

He hesitated; it was hard to know exactly how to speak of the professor.

"Perhaps if you have talked with him at all," she went on, "it will help you to understand one of the difficulties I had to face in life."

"He is, I should imagine, a little weak," Tavernake

suggested, hesitatingly.

"Very," she answered. "My mother left him in my charge, but I cannot keep him."

"Your sister—" he began.

She nodded.

"My sister has more influence than I. She makes life easier for him."

They reached the restaurant and made their way upstairs. Tavernake appropriated the same table and once more the head waiter protested.

"If the gentleman comes again to-night," Tavernake said, "you will find that he will be only too glad to have supper with us."

Then the professor came. He made his usual somewhat theatrical entrance, carrying his broad-brimmed hat in his hand, brandishing his silver-topped cane. When he saw Tavernake and Beatrice, he stopped short. Then he held out both hands, which Beatrice immediately seized. There were tears in his eyes, tears running down his cheeks. He sat down heavily in the chair which Tavernake was holding for him.

"Beatrice," he exclaimed, "why, this is most affecting! You have come here to have supper with your old father. You trust me, then?"

"Absolutely," she replied, still clasping his hands. "If you give me away to Elizabeth, it will be the end. The next time I shall never be found."

"For some days," he assured her, "I have known exactly where you were to be found. I have never spoken of it. You are safe. My meals up here," he added, with a little sigh, "have been sad feasts. To-night we will be cheerful. Some quails, I think, quails and some Clicquot for you, my dear. You need it. Ah, this is a happiness indeed!"

"You know Mr. Tavernake, father," she remarked, after he had given a somewhat lengthy order to the waiter.

"I met and talked with Mr. Tavernake here the other night," the professor admitted, with condescension.

"Mr. Tavernake was very good to me at a time when I needed help," Beatrice told him.

The professor grasped Tavernake's hands.

"You were good to my child," he said, "you were good to me. Waiter, three cocktails immediately," he ordered, turning round. "I must drink your health, Mr. Tavernake—I must drink your health at once."

Tavernake leaned forward towards Beatrice.

"I wonder," he suggested, "whether you would not rather be alone with your father."

She shook her head.

"You know so much," she replied, "and it really doesn't seem to matter. Tell me, father, how do you spend your time?"

"I must confess, dear," the professor said, "that I have little to do. Your sister Elizabeth is quite generous."

Beatrice sat back in her chair as though she had been struck.

"Father," she exclaimed, "listen! You are living on that money! Doesn't it seem terrible to you? Oh, how can you do it!"

The professor looked at his daughter with an expression of pained surprise.

"My dear," he explained, "your sister Elizabeth has always been the moneyed one of the family. She has brains and I trust her. It is not for me to inquire as to the source of the comforts she provides for me. I feel myself entitled to receive them, and so I accept."

"But, father," she went on, "can't you see—don't you know that it's his money—Wenham's?"

"It is not a matter, this, my child," the professor observed, sharply, "which we can discuss before strangers. Some day we will speak of it, you and I."

"Has he—been heard of?" she asked, in a whisper.

The professor frowned.

"A hot-tempered young man, my dear," he declared uneasily, "a hot tempered young man, indeed. Elizabeth gives me to understand that it was just an ordinary quarrel and away he went."

Beatrice was white to the lips.

"An ordinary quarrel!" she muttered.

She sat quite still. Tavernake unconsciously found himself watching her. There were things in her eyes which frightened him. It seemed as though she were looking out of the gay little restaurant, with its lights and music and air of comfort, out into some distant quarter of the world, some other and very different place. She was living through something which chilled her heart, something terrifying. Tavernake saw those things in her face and his eyes spelt them out mercilessly.

"Father," she whispered, leaning towards him, "do you believe what you have just been saying to me?"

It was the professor's turn to be disturbed. He concealed his discomfiture, however, with a gesture of annoyance.

"That is scarcely a proper question, Beatrice," he answered sharply. "Ah," he added, with more geniality, "the cocktails! My young friend Tavernake, I drink to our better acquaintance! You are English, as I can see, a real Britisher. Some day you must come out to our own great country—my daughter, of course, has told you that we are Americans. A great country, sir,—the greatest I have ever lived in—room to breathe, room to grow, room for a young man like you to plant his ambitions and watch them blossom. To our better acquaintance, Mr. Tavernake, and may we meet some day in the United States!"

Tavernake drank the first cocktail in his life and wiped the tears from his eyes. The professor found safety in conversation.

"You know," he went on, "that I am a man of science. Physiognomy delights me. Men and women as I meet them represent to me varying types of humanity, all interesting, all appealing to my peculiar love of the science of psychology. You, my dear Mr. Tavernake, if I may venture to be so personal, represent to me, as you sit there, the exact prototype of the young working Englishman. You are, I should judge, thorough, dogmatic, narrow, persistent, industrious, and bound to be successful according to the scope and nature of your ambitions. In this country you will never develop. In my country, sir, we should make a colossus of you. We should teach you not to be content with small things; we should raise your hand which you yourself kept to your side, and we should point your finger to the skies. Waiter," he added, turning abruptly round, "if the quails are not yet ready I will take another of these excellent cocktails."

Tavernake was embarrassed. He saw that Beatrice was anxious to talk to her father; he saw, also, that her father was determined not to talk to her. With a little sigh, however, she resigned herself to the inevitable.

"I have lectured, sir," the professor continued, "in most of the cities of the United States, upon the human race. The tendencies of every unit of the human race are my peculiar study. When I speak to you of phrenology, sir, you smile, and you think, perhaps, of a man who sits in a back room and takes your shilling for feeling the bumps of your head. I am not of this order of scientific men, sir. I have diplomas from every university worth mentioning. I blend the sciences which treat with the human race. I know something of all of them. Character reading to me is at once a passion and a science. Leave me alone with a man or a woman for five minutes, paint me a map of Life, and I will set the signposts along which that person will travel, and I shall not miss one."

"You are doing no work over here, father, are you?" Beatrice asked.

"None, my dear," he answered, with a faint note of regret in his tone. "Your sister Elizabeth seemed scarcely to desire it.

Her movements are very uncertain and she likes to have me constantly at hand. My daughter Elizabeth," he continued, turning to Tavernake, "is a very beautiful young woman, left in my charge under peculiar circumstances. I feel it my duty, therefore, to be constantly at hand."

Again there was a flash of that strange look in the girl's face. She leaned forward, but her father declined to meet her gaze.

"May I ask one or two personal questions?" she faltered. "Remember, I have not seen or heard anything from either of you for seven months."

"By all means, my dear," the professor declared. "Your sister, I am glad to say, is well. I myself am as you see me. We have had a pleasant time and we have met some dear old friends from the other side. Our greatest trouble is that you are temporarily lost to us."

"Elizabeth doesn't guess—"

"My child," the professor interrupted, "I have been loyal to you. If Elizabeth knew that I could tell her at any moment your exact whereabouts, I think that she would be more angry with me than ever she has been in her life, and, my dear," he added, "you know, when Elizabeth is angry, things are apt to be unpleasant. But I have been dumb. I have not spoken, nor shall I. Yet," the professor went on, "you must not think, Beatrice, that because I yield to your whim in this matter I recognize any sufficient cause why you should voluntarily estrange yourself from those whose right and privilege it is to look after you. You are able, I am glad to see, to make your way in the world. I have attended the Atlas Theatre, and I am glad to see that you have lost none of your old skill in the song and dance. You are deservedly popular there. Soon, I have no doubt, you will aspire to more important parts. Still, my dear child," the professor continued, disposing of his second cocktail, "I see no reason why your very laudable desire to remain independent should be

194

incompatible with a life under your sister's roof and my protection. Mr. Tavernake here, with his British instincts, will, I am sure, agree with me that it is not well for a young lady—my own daughter, sir, but I may say it—of considerable personal attractions, to live alone or under the chaperonage merely of these other young ladies of the theatre."

"I think,", Tavernake said, "that your daughter must have very strong reasons for preferring to live alone."

"Imaginary ones, my dear sir," the professor assured him, —"altogether imaginary. The quails at last! And the Clicquot! Now this is really a delightful little meeting. I drink to its repetition. This is indeed a treat for me. Beatrice, my love to you! Mr. Tavernake, my best respects! The only vintage, sir," he concluded, setting down his empty glass appreciatively.

"To go back to what you were saying just now," Tavernake remarked, "I quite agree with you about Beatrice's living alone. I am very anxious for her to marry me."

The professor set down his knife and fork. His appearance was one of ponderous theatricality.

"Sir," he declared, "this is indeed a most momentous statement. Am I to take it as a serious offer for my daughter's hand?"

Beatrice leaned over and laid her fingers upon his.

"Father," she said, "it doesn't matter please. I am not willing to marry Mr. Tavernake."

The professor looked from one to the other and coughed.

"Are Mr. Tavernake's means," he asked, "of sufficient importance to warrant his entering into matrimony?"

"I have no money at all to speak of," Tavernake answered. "That really isn't important. I shall very soon make all that your daughter can spend."

"I agree with my daughter, sir," the professor declared. "The subject might well be left until such time as you have improved your position. We will dismiss it, therefore,—dismiss it at once. We will talk—"

"Father," Beatrice interrupted, "let us talk about yourself. Don't you think you would be more contented, happier, if you were to try to arrange for a few—a few demonstrations or lectures over here, as you at first intended? I know that you must find having nothing to do such a strain upon you," she added.

It was perhaps by accident that her eyes were fixed upon the glass which the professor was carrying to his lips. He set it down at once.

"My child," he said, in a low tone, "I understand you."

"No, no," she insisted, "I didn't mean that, but you are always better when you are working. A man like you," she went on, a little wistfully, "should not waste his talents."

He sighed.

"You are perhaps right, my child," he admitted. "I will go and see my agents to-morrow. Up till now," he went on, "I have refused all offers. I have felt that Elizabeth, the care of Elizabeth in her peculiar position, demanded my whole attention. Perhaps you are right. Perhaps I have over-estimated the necessity of being constantly at her right hand. She is a very clever woman Elizabeth," he concluded, "very clever indeed."

"Where is she now, father?" Beatrice asked.

"She motored into the country early this morning with some friends," the professor said. "They went to a party last night with Walter Crease, London correspondent to the New York Gazette," he explained, turning a little away from Tavernake. "They were all home very late, I understand, and Elizabeth complained of a headache this morning. Personally, I regret to say that I was not up when they left."

Beatrice leaned quite close to her father.

"Do you see anything of the man Pritchard?" she inquired.

The professor was suddenly flabby. He set down his glass, spilling half its contents. He stole a quick glance at Tavernake.

"My child," he exclaimed, "you ought to consider my nerves! You know very well that the sudden mention of any one whom I dislike so intensely is bad for me. I am surprised at you, Beatrice. You show a culpable lack of consideration for my infirmities."

"I am sorry, father," she whispered, "but is he here?"

"He is," the professor admitted. "Between ourselves," he added, a white, scared look upon his pale face, "he is spoiling my whole peace of mind. My enjoyment of the comforts which Elizabeth is able to provide for me is interfered with by that man's constant presence. He seldom speaks, and yet he seems always to be watching. I do not trust him, Beatrice. I am a judge of men and I tell you that I do not trust him."

"I wish that Elizabeth would go away," Beatrice said in a low tone. "Of course, I have no right—to say things. Nothing serious has perhaps ever happened. And yet—and yet, for her own sake, I do not think that she should stay here in London with Pritchard close at hand."

The professor raised his glass with shaking fingers.

"Elizabeth knows what is best," he declared, "I am sure that Elizabeth knows what is best, but I, too, am beginning to wish that she would go away. Last night we met him at Walter Crease's."

Once more he turned a little nervously towards Tavernake, who was looking down into the body of the restaurant with immovable face.

"We tried to persuade him then to go away. He is really in rather a dangerous position here. Jimmy Post has sworn that he will not be taken back to New York, and there are one or two others—a pretty desperate crew. We tried last night to reason with Pritchard."

"It was no good?" she whispered.

"No good at all," the professor answered, drily. "Perhaps, if we had not been interrupted, we might have convinced him."

"Tell me about it," she begged.

The professor shook his head. Tavernake still had that air of paying no attention whatever to their conversation.

"It is not for you to know about, my dear," he concluded. "You have chosen very wisely to keep out of these matters. Elizabeth has such wonderful courage. My own nerve, I regret to say, is not quite what it was. Waiter, I will take a liqueur of the old brandy in a large glass."

The brandy was brought, but the professor seemed haunted by memories and his spirits never wholly returned. Not until the lights were turned down and Tavernake had paid the bill, did he partially recover his former manner.

"Dear child," he said, as they stood up together, "I cannot tell you what the pleasure has been of this brief reunion."

She rested her fingers upon his shoulders and looked up into his face.

"Father," she begged, softly, "come to me. I can keep you, if you don't mind for a short time being poor. You shall have all my salary except just enough for my clothes, and anything will do for me to wear. I will try so hard to make you comfortable."

He looked at her with an air of offended dignity.

"My child," he replied, "you must not talk to me like that. If I did not feel that my duty lay with Elizabeth, I should insist upon your coming to me, and under those conditions it would be I who should provide, not you. But for the moment I cannot leave your elder sister altogether. She needs me."

Beatrice turned away a little sadly. They all three descended the stairs.

"I shall leave our young friend, Mr. Tavernake, to escort you to your home," the professor announced. "I myself shall telephone to see if Elizabeth has returned. If she is still away, I shall spend an hour or two, I think, with my friends at the Blue Room Club. Beatrice, this has been a joy to me, a joy soon, I hope, to be repeated."

He took both her hands. She smiled at him with an attempt at cheerfulness.

"Good-night, father!" she said.

"And to you, sir, also, good-night!" the professor added, taking Tavernake's hand and holding it for a minute in his, while he looked impressively in his face. "I will not say too much, but I will say this: so much as I have seen of you, I like. Good-night!"

He turned and strode away. Both Beatrice and Tavernake watched him until he disappeared. Then, with a sigh, she picked up her skirts with her right hand, and took Tavernake's arm.

"Do you mind walking home?" she asked. "My head aches."

Tavernake looked for a moment wistfully across the road toward the Milan Court. Beatrice's hand, however, only held his arm the tighter.

"I am going to make you come with me every step of the way," she declared, "so you can just as well make the best of it. Afterwards—"

"What about afterwards?" he interrupted.

"Afterwards," she continued, with decision, "you are to go straight home!"

CHAPTER XXI. SOME EXCELLENT ADVICE

Tavernake, in response to a somewhat urgent message, walked into his solicitor's office almost as soon as they opened on the following morning. The junior partner of the firm, who took an interest in him, and was anxious, indeed, to invest a small amount in the Marston Rise Building Company, received him cordially but with some concern.

"Look here, Tavernake," he said, "I thought I'd better write a line and ask you to come down. You haven't forgotten, have you, that our option of purchase lasts only three days longer?"

Tavernake nodded.

"Well, what of it?" he asked.

"It's just as well that you should understand the situation," the lawyer continued. "Your old people are hard upon our heels in this matter, and there will be no chance of any extension—not even for an hour. Mr. Dowling has already put in an offer a thousand pounds better than yours; I heard that incidentally yesterday afternoon; so you may be sure that the second your option has legally expired, the thing will be off altogether so far as you're concerned."

"That's all very well," Tavernake remarked, "but what about the plots that already belong to me?"

"They have some sort of scheme for leaving those high and dry," the solicitor explained. "You see, the drainage and lighting will be largely influenced by the purchaser of the whole estate. If Dowling gets it, he means to treat your plots so that they will become practically valueless. It's rather a mean sort of thing, but then he's a mean little man."

Tavernake nodded.

"Well," he announced, "I was coming to see you, anyhow, this morning, to talk to you about the money."

"Your friend isn't backing out?" the lawyer asked, quickly.

"My friend has not said anything about backing out yet," Tavernake replied, "but circumstances have arisen during the last few days which have altered my own views as to the expediency of business relations with this person. I haven't any reason to suppose that the money won't be forthcoming, but if I could get it from any other source, I should prefer it."

The solicitor looked blank.

"Of course," he said, "I'll do what I can, if you like, but I may as well tell you at once that I don't think I should have a ghost of a chance of raising the whole amount."

"I suppose," Tavernake inquired, thoughtfully, "your firm couldn't do anything?"

"We could do something, certainly," the solicitor answered, "on account of our own clients. We might, perhaps, manage up to five thousand pounds. That would still leave us wanting seven, however, and I scarcely see where we could get it."

Tavernake was silent for a few moments.

"You haven't quarreled with your friend, have you?" the solicitor asked.

"No, there has been no quarrel," Tavernake replied. "I have another reason."

"If I were you, I'd try and forget it," his friend advised. "To tell you the truth, I have been feeling rather anxious about this affair. It's a big thing, you know, and the profit is as sure as the dividend on Consols. I should hate to have that little bounder Dowling get in and scoop it up."

"It's a fine investment," admitted Tavernake, "and, as you say, there isn't the slightest risk. That's why I was hoping you might have been able to manage it without my calling upon my friend."

Mr. Martin shook his head.

"It isn't so easy to convince other people. All the same, I don't want to get left. If you'll take my advice, you'll go and call on your friend at once, and see exactly how matters stand. If everything's O.K. and you can induce him to part a few hours before it is absolutely necessary, I must confess that it would take a load off my mind. I don't like these affairs that have to be concluded at the last possible moment."

"Well," Tavernake agreed, "I must try what I can do, then. There is nothing else fresh, I suppose?"

"Nothing," the solicitor answered. "Come back, if you can make any definite arrangement, or telephone. The matter is really bothering me a little. I don't want to have the other people slip in now."...

Tavernake, instead of obeying his first impulse and making his way direct to the Milan Court, walked to the flat in Kingsway, climbed up the stone steps, and asked for Beatrice. She met him at her own door, fully dressed.

"My dear Leonard!" she exclaimed, in surprise. "What an early caller!"

"I want a few words with you," he said. "Can you spare me five minutes?"

"You must walk with me to the theatre," she replied, "I am just off to rehearsal."

They descended the stairs together.

"I have something to tell you," Tavernake began, "something to tell you which you won't like to hear."

"Something which I won't like to hear," she repeated, fearfully. "Go on, Leonard. It can't be worse than it sounds."

"I don't know why I've come to tell you," he went on. "I never meant to. It came into my mind all of a sudden and I felt that I must. It has to do with your sister and the Marston Rise affair."

"My sister and the Marston Rise affair!" Beatrice exclaimed, incredulously.

Then a sudden light broke in upon her. She stopped short and clutched at his hand.

"You don't mean that it was Elizabeth who was going to find you the money?" she cried.

"I do," he answered. "She offered it of her own accord. I do not know why I talked to her of my own affairs, but she led me on to speak of them. Your sister is a wonderful person," he continued, dropping his voice. "I don't know why, but she made me talk as no one else has ever made me talk before. I simply had to tell her things. Then, when I had finished, she showed me her bankbooks and suggested that she should invest some of her money in the Rise."

"But do you mean to tell me," Beatrice persisted, "that it is her money upon which you are relying for this purchase?"

Tavernake nodded.

"You see," he explained, "Mr. Dowling dropped upon us before I was prepared. As soon as he found out, he went to the owners of the estate and made them a bid for it. The consequence was that they shortened my option and gave me very little chance indeed to find the money. When your sister offered it, it certainly seemed a wonderful stroke of fortune. I could give her eight or ten per cent, whereas she would only get four anywhere else, and I should make a profit for myself of over ten thousand pounds, which I cannot do unless I find the money to buy the estate."

"But you mustn't touch that money, you mustn't have anything to do with it!" Beatrice exclaimed, walking very fast and looking straight ahead. "You don't understand. How should you?"

"Do you mean that the money was stolen?" Tavernake asked, after a moment's pause.

"No, not stolen," Beatrice replied, "but it comes—oh! I can't tell you, only Elizabeth has no right to it. My own sister! It is all too awful!"

"Do you think that she has come by this money dishonestly?"

"I am not sure," Beatrice murmured. "There are worse things, more terrible things even than theft."

The practical side of Tavernake's nature was very much to the fore that morning. He began to wonder whether women, after all, strange and fascinating creatures though they were, possessed judgment which could be relied upon—whether they were not swayed too much by sentiment.

"Beatrice," he said, "you must understand this. I have no time to raise the money elsewhere. If I don't get it from your sister, supposing she is still willing to let me have it, my chance has gone. I shall have to take a situation in some one else's office as a clerk—probably not so good a place as I held at Dowling & Spence's. On the other hand, the use of that money for a very short time would be the start of my career. All that you say is so vague. Why need I know anything about it? I met your sister in the ordinary way of business and she has made an ordinary business proposition to me, one by which she will be, incidentally, very greatly benefited. I never thought of telling you this at all, but when the time came I hated to go and draw that money from your sister without having said anything to you. So I came this morning, but I want you, if you possibly can, to look at the matter from my point of view."

She was silent for several moments. Then she glanced at him curiously.

"Why on earth," she asked, "should my sister make this offer to you? She isn't a fool. She doesn't usually trust strangers."

"She trusted me, apparently," Tavernake answered.

"Can you understand why?" Beatrice demanded.

"I think that I can," he replied. "If one can rely upon one's perception, she is surrounded by people whom she might find agreeable companions but whom she is scarcely likely to have much confidence in. Perhaps she realized that I wasn't like them."

"And you want very much to take this money?" she said, half to herself.

"I want to very much indeed," Tavernake admitted. "I was on my way to see her this morning and to ask her to let me have it a day or two before the time, but I felt, somehow, that there seemed to be a certain amount of deceit in going to her and taking it without saying a word to you. I felt that I had to come here first. But Beatrice, don't ask me to give it up. It means such a long time before I can move again. It's the first step that's so difficult, and I must—I must make a start. It's such a chance, this. I have spent so many hours thinking about it. I have planned and worked and sketched it all out as no one else could do. I must have that money."

They walked on in silence until they reached the stage door. Beatrice was thinking of her companion as she had seen him so often, poring over his plans, busy with ruler and india-rubber, absolutely absorbed in the interest of his task. She remembered the first time he had talked about this scheme of his, how his whole face had changed, the almost passionate interest with which he had worked the thing out even to its smallest details. She realized how great a part of his life the thing had become, what a terrible blow it would be to him to have to abandon it. She turned and faced him.

"Leonard," she said, "perhaps, after all, you are right. Perhaps I give way too much to what, after all, is only a sentimental feeling. I am thankful that you came and told me; I shall always be thankful for that. Take the money, but pay it back as soon as you can."

"I shall do that," he answered. "I shall do that you may rely upon it."

She laid her hand upon his arm.

"Leonard," she begged, "I know that Elizabeth is very beautiful and very fascinating, and I don't wonder that you like to go and see her, but I want to ask you to promise me one thing."

He felt as though he were suddenly turned into stone. It was not possible—it could not be possible that she had guessed his secret!

"Well?" he demanded.

"Don't let her introduce you to her friends; don't spend too much time there," she continued. "Elizabeth is my sister and I don't—really I don't want to say anything that doesn't sound kind, but her friends are not fit people for you to know, and Elizabeth—well she hasn't very much heart."

He was silent for several moments.

"How did you know I liked going to see your sister?" he asked, abruptly.

She smiled.

"My dear Leonard," she said, "you are not very clever at hiding your feelings. When you came to see me the other day, do you imagine I believed for a single moment that you asked me to marry you simply because you cared? I think, Leonard, that it was because you were afraid, you were afraid of something coming into your life so big, so terrifying, that you were ready to clutch at the easiest chance of safety."

"Beatrice, this is absurd!" he exclaimed.

She shook her head.

"No, it isn't that," she declared. "Do you know, my dear Leonard, what there was about you from the very first which attracted me?"

"No," he answered.

"It was your honesty," she continued. "You remember that night upon the roof at Blenheim House? You were going to tell a lie for me, and I know how you hated it. You love the truth, you are truthful naturally; I would rely upon you wherever I was. I know that you would keep your word, I know that you would be honest. A woman loves to feel that about a man—she loves it—and I don't want you to be brought near the people who sneer at honesty and all good things. I don't want you to hear their point of view. You may be simple and commonplace in some respects; I want you to stay just as you are. Do you understand?"

"I understand," Tavernake replied gravely.

A call boy shouted her name down the stone passage. She patted him on the shoulder and turned away.

"Run along now and get the money," she said. "Come and see me when it's all over."

Tavernake left her with a long breath of relief and made his way towards the Strand. At the corner of Wellington Street he came face to face with Pritchard. They stopped at once. There seemed to be something embarrassing about this meeting. Pritchard patted him familiarly on the shoulder.

"How goes it, old man?" he asked.

"I am all right," Tavernake answered, somewhat awkwardly. "How are you?"

"I guess I'd be the better for a drink," Pritchard declared. "Come along. Pretty well done up the other night, weren't we? We'll step into the American Bar here and try a gin fizz."

They found themselves presently perched upon two high stools in a deserted corner of the bar to which Pritchard had led the way. Tavernake sipped his drink tentatively.

"I should like," he said, "to ask you a question or two about Wednesday night."

Pritchard nodded.

"Go right ahead," he invited.

"You seem to take the whole affair as a sort of joke," Tavernake remarked.

"Well, isn't that what it was?" the detective asked, smiling.

Tavernake shrugged his shoulders.

"There didn't seem to me to be much joke about it!" he exclaimed.

Pritchard laughed gayly.

"You are not used to Americans, my young friend," he said. "Over on this side you are all so fearfully literal. You are not seriously supposing that they meant to dose me with that stuff the other night, eh?"

"I never thought that there was any doubt about it at all," Tavernake declared deliberately.

Pritchard stroked his moustache meditatively.

"Well," he remarked, "you are certainly green, and yet I don't know why you shouldn't be. Americans are always up to games of that sort. I am not saying that they didn't mean to give me a scare, if they could, or that they wouldn't have been glad to get a few words of information out of me, or a paper or two that I keep pretty safely locked up. It would have been a better joke on me then. But as for the rest, as for really trying to make me take that stuff, of course, that was all bunkum."

Tavernake sat quite still in his chair for several minutes.

"Will you take another gin fizz, Mr. Pritchard?" he asked.

"Why not?"

Tavernake gave the order. He sat on his stool whistling softly to himself.

"Then I suppose," he said at last, "I must have looked a pretty sort of an ass coming through the wall like a madman."

Pritchard shook his head.

"You looked just about what you were," he answered, "a d——d good sort. I'm not playing up to you that it was all pretense. You can never trust that gang. The blackguard outside was in earnest, anyway. After all, you know, they wouldn't miss me if I were to drop quietly out. There 's no one else they 're quite so much afraid of. There 's no one else knows quite as much about them."

"Well, we'll let it go at that," Tavernake declared. "You know so much of all these people, though, that I rather wish you 'd tell me something I want very much to know."

"It's by telling nothing," the detective replied quickly, "that I know as much as I do. Just one cocktail, eh?"

Tavernake shook his head.

"I drank my first cocktail last night," he remarked. "I had supper with the professor and his daughter."

"Not Elizabeth?" Pritchard asked swiftly.

Tavernake shook his head.

"With Miss Beatrice," he answered.

Pritchard set down his glass.

"Say, Tavernake," he inquired, "you are friendly with that young lady, Miss Beatrice, aren't you?"

"I certainly am," Tavernake answered. "I have a very great regard for her."

"Then I can tell you how to do her a good turn," Pritchard continued, earnestly. "Keep her away from that old blackguard. Keep her away from all the gang. Believe me, she is looking for trouble by even speaking to them."

"But the man's her father," Tavernake objected, "and he seems fond of her."

"Don't you believe it," Pritchard went on. "He's fond of nothing and nobody but himself and easy living. He's soft, mind you, he's got plenty of sentiment, he 'll squeeze a tear out of his eye, and all that sort of thing, but he'd sell his soul, or his daughter's soul, for a little extra comfort. Now Elizabeth doesn't know exactly where her sister is, and she daren't seem anxious, or go around making inquiries. Beatrice has her chance to keep away, and I can tell you it will be a thundering sight better for her if she does."

"Well, I don't understand it at all," Tavernake declared. "I hate mysteries."

Pritchard set down his empty glass.

"Look here," he remarked, "this affair is too serious, after all, for us to talk round like a couple of gossips. I have given you your warning, and if you're wise you 'll remember it."

"Tell me this one thing," Tavernake persisted. "Tell me what is the cause of the quarrel between the two? Can't something be done to bring them together again?"

Pritchard shook his head.

"Nothing," he answered. "As things are at present, they are better apart. Coming my way?"

Tavernake followed him out of the place. Pritchard took his arm as he turned down toward the Strand.

"My young friend," he said, "here is a word of advice for you. The Scriptures say that you cannot serve God and mammon. Paraphrase that to the present situation and remember that you cannot serve Elizabeth and Beatrice."

"What then?" Tavernake demanded.

The detective waited until he had lit the long black cigar between his teeth.

"I guess you'd better confine your attentions to Beatrice," he concluded.

CHAPTER XXII. DINNER WITH ELIZABETH

The rest of that day was for Tavernake a period of feverish anxieties. He received two telegrams from Mr. Martin, his solicitor, and he himself was more uneasy than he cared to admit. At three o'clock in the afternoon, at eight in the evening, and again at eleven o'clock at night, he presented himself at the Milan Court, always with the same inquiry. On the last occasion, the hall porter had cheering news for him.

"Mrs. Wenham Gardner returned from the country an hour ago, sir," he announced. "I can send your name up now, if you wish to see her."

Tavernake was conscious of a sense of immense relief. Of course, he had known that she had not really gone away for good, but all the same her absence, especially after the event of the night before last, was a little disquieting.

"My name is Tavernake," he said. "I do not wish to intrude at such an hour, but if she could see me for a moment, I should be glad."

He sat down and waited patiently. Soon a message came that Mr. Tavernake was to go up. He ascended in the lift and knocked at the door of her suite. Her maid opened it grudgingly. She scarcely took the pains to conceal her disapproval of this young man—so ordinary, so gauche. Why Madame should waste her time upon such a one, she could not imagine!

"Mrs. Gardner will see you directly," she told him. "Madame is dressing now to go out for supper. She will be able to spare you only a few seconds."

Tavernake remained alone in the luxurious little sitting-room for nearly ten minutes. Then the door of the inner room was opened and Elizabeth appeared. Tavernake, rising slowly to his feet, looked at her for a moment in reluctant but wondering admiration. She was wearing an ivory satin gown, without trimming or lace of any sort, a gown the fit of which seemed to him almost a miracle. Her only jewelry was a long rope of pearls and a small tiara. Tavernake had never been brought into close contact with any one quite like this.

She was putting on her gloves as she entered and she gave him her left hand.

"What an extraordinary person you are, Mr. Tavernake!" she exclaimed. "You really do seem to turn up at the most astonishing times."

"I am very sorry to have intruded upon you to-night," he said. "As regards the last occasion, however, upon which I made an unexpected appearance, I make no apologies whatever," he added coolly.

She laughed softly. She was looking full into his eyes and yet he could not tell whether she was angry with him or only amused.

"You were by way of being a little melodramatic, were you not?" she remarked. "Still, you were very much in earnest, and one forgives a great deal to any one who is really in earnest. What do you want with me now? I am just going downstairs to supper."

"It is a matter of business," Tavernake replied. "I have a friend who is a partner with me in the Marston Rise building speculation, and he is worried because there is some one else in the field wanting to buy the property, and the day after to-morrow is our last chance of paying over the money."

She looked at him as though puzzled.

"What money?"

"The money which you agreed to lend me, or rather to invest in our building company," he reminded her.

She nodded.

"Of course! Why, I had forgotten all about it for the moment. You are going to give me ten per cent interest or something splendid, aren't you? Well, what about it? You don't want to take it away with you now, I suppose?"

"No," he answered, "it isn't that. To be honest with you,

I came to make sure that you hadn't changed your mind."

"And why should I change my mind?"

"You might be angry with me," he said, "for interfering in your concerns the night before last."

"Perhaps I am," she remarked, indifferently.

"Do you wish to withdraw from your promise?" he asked.

"I really haven't thought much about it," she replied, carelessly. "By-the-bye, have you seen Beatrice lately?"

"We agreed, I think," he reminded her, "that we would not talk about your sister."

She looked at him over her shoulder.

"I do not remember that I agreed to anything of the sort," she declared. "I think it was you who laid down the law about that. As a matter of fact, I think that your silence about her is very unkind. I suppose you have seen her?"

"Yes, I have seen her," Tavernake admitted.

"She continues to be tragic," Elizabeth asked, "whenever my name is mentioned?"

"I should not call it tragic," Tavernake answered, reluctantly. "One gathers, however, that something transpired between you before she left, of a serious nature."

She looked at him earnestly.

"Really," she said, "you are a strange, stolid young man. I wonder," she went on, smiling into his face, "are you in love with my sister?"

Tavernake made no immediate response, only something flashed for a moment in his eyes which puzzled her.

"Why do you look at me like that?" she demanded. "You are not angry with me for asking?"

"No, I am not angry," he replied. "It isn't that. But you must know—you must see!"

Then she indeed did see that he was laboring under a very great emotion. She leaned towards him, laughing softly.

"Now you are really becoming interesting," she murmured. "Tell me—tell me all about it."

"I don't know what love is!" Tavernake declared fiercely. "I don't know what it means to be in love!"

Again she laughed in his face.

"Are you so sure?" she whispered.

She saw the veins stand out upon his temples, watched the passion which kept him at first tongue-tied.

"Sure!" he muttered. "Who can be sure when you look like that!"

He held out his arms. With a swift little backward movement she flitted away and leaned against the table.

"What a brother-in-law you would make!" she laughed. "So steady, so respectable, alas! so serious! Dear Mr. Tavernake, I wish you joy. As a matter of fact, you and Beatrice are very well suited for one another."

The telephone bell rang. She moved over and held the receiver to her ear. Her face changed. After the first few words to which she listened, it grew dark with anger.

"You mean to say that Professor Franklin has not been in since lunch-time?" she exclaimed. "I left word particularly that I should require him to-night. Is Major Post there, then? No? Mr. Crease—no? Nor Mr. Faulkes? Not one of them! Very well, ring me up directly the professor comes in, or any of them."

She replaced the receiver with a gesture of annoyance. Tavernake was astonished at the alteration in her expression. The smile had gone, and with its passing away lines had come under her eyes and about her mouth. Without a word to him she strode away into her bedroom. Tavernake was just wondering whether he should retire, when she came back.

"Listen, Mr. Tavernake," she said, "how far away are your rooms?"

"Down at Chelsea," he answered, "about two miles and a half."

"Take a taxi and drive there," she commanded, "or stop. You will find my car outside. I will telephone down to say that you are to use it. Change into your evening clothes and come back for me. I want you to take me out to supper."

He looked at her in amazement. She stamped her foot.

"Don't stand there hesitating!" she ordered. "Do as I say! You don't expect I am going to help you to buy your wretched property if you refuse me the simplest of favors? Hurry, I say! Hurry!"

"I am really very sorry," Tavernake interposed, "but I do not possess a dress suit. I would go, with pleasure, but I haven't got such a thing."

She looked at him for a moment incredulously. Then she broke into a fit of uncontrollable laughter. She sat down upon the edge of a couch and wiped the tears from her eyes.

"Oh, you strange, you wonderful person!" she exclaimed. "You want to buy an estate and you want to borrow twelve thousand pounds, and you know where Beatrice is and you won't tell me, and you are fully convinced, because you burst into a house through the wall, that you saved poor Pritchard from being poisoned, and you don't possess a dress suit! Never mind, as it happens it doesn't matter about the dress suit. You shall take me out as you are."

Tavernake felt in his pockets and remembered that he had only thirty shillings with him.

"Here, carry my purse," she said carelessly. "We are going downstairs to the smaller restaurant. I have been traveling since six o'clock, and I am starving."

"But how about my clothes?" Tavernake objected. "Will they be all right?"

"It doesn't matter where we are going," she answered. "You look very well as you are. Come and let me put your tie straight."

She came close to him and her fingers played for a

moment with his tie. She was very near to him and she laughed deliberately into his face. Tavernake held himself quite stiff and felt foolish. He also felt absurdly happy.

"There," she remarked, when she had arranged it to her satisfaction, "you look all right now. I wonder," she added, half to herself, "what you do look like. Something Colonial and forceful, I think. Never mind, help me on with my cloak and come along. You are a most respectable-looking escort, and a very useful one."

Although Tavernake was nominally the host, it was Elizabeth who selected the table and ordered the supper. There were very few other guests in the room, the majority being down in the larger restaurant, but among these few Tavernake noticed two of the girls from the chorus at the Atlas. Elizabeth had chosen a table from which she had a view of the door, and she took the seat facing it. From the first Tavernake felt certain that she was watching for some one.

"Talk to me now, please, about this speculation," she insisted. "I should like to know all about it, and whether you are sure that I shall get ten per cent for my money."

Tavernake was in no way reluctant. It was a safe topic for conversation, and one concerning which he had plenty to say. But after a time she stopped him.

"Well," she said, "I have discovered at any rate one subject on which you can be fluent. Now I have had enough of building properties, please, and house building. I should like to hear a little about Beatrice."

Tavernake was dumb.

"I do not wish to talk about Beatrice," he declared, "until I understand the cause of this estrangement between you."

Her eyes flashed angrily and her laugh sounded forced.

"Not even talk of her! My dear friend," she protested, "you scarcely repay the confidence I am placing in you!"

"You mean the money?"

"Precisely," she continued. "I trust you, why I do not know—I suppose because I am something of a physiognomist—with twelve thousand pounds of my hard-earned savings. You refuse to trust me with even a few simple particulars about the life of my own sister. Come, I don't think that things are quite as they should be between us."

"Do you know where I first met your sister?" Tavernake asked.

She shook her head pettishly.

"How should I? You told me nothing."

"She was staying in a boarding-house where I lived," Tavernake went on. "I think I told you that but nothing else. It was a cheap boarding-house but she had not enough money to pay for her meals. She was tired of life. She was in a desperate state altogether."

"Are you trying to tell me, or rather trying not to tell me, that Beatrice was mad enough to think of committing suicide?" Elizabeth inquired.

"She was in the frame of mind when such a step was possible," he answered, gravely. "You remember that night when I first saw you in the chemist's shop across the street? She had been very ill that evening, very ill indeed. You could see for yourself the effect meeting you had upon her."

Elizabeth nodded, and crumbled a little piece of roll between her fingers. Then she leaned over the table towards Tavernake.

"She seemed terrified, didn't she? She hurried you away—she seemed afraid."

"It was very noticeable," he admitted. "She was terrified. She dragged me out of the place. A few minutes later she fainted in the cab."

Elizabeth smiled.

"Beatrice was always over-sensitive," she remarked. "Any sudden shock unnerved her altogether. Are you terrified of me, too, Mr. Tavernake?"

"I don't know," he answered, frankly. "Sometimes I think that I am."

She laughed softly.

"Why?" she whispered.

He looked into her eyes and he felt abject. How was it possible to sit within a few feet of her and remain sane!

"You are so wonderful," he said, in a low tone, "so different from any one else in the world!"

"You are glad that you met me, then—that you are here?" she asked.

He raised his eyes once more.

"I don't know," he answered simply. "If I really believed —if you were always kind like this—but, you see, you make two men of me. When I am with you I am a fool, your fool, to do as you will with. When I am away, some glimmerings of common sense come back, and I know."

"You know what?" she murmured.

"That you are not honest," he added.

"Mr. Tavernake!" she exclaimed, lifting her head a little.

"Oh, I don t mean dishonest in the ordinary way!" he protested, eagerly. "What I mean is that you look things which you don't feel, that you are willing for any one who can't help admiring you very much to believe for a moment that you, too, feel more kindly than you really do. This is so clumsy," he broke off, despairingly, "but you understand what I mean!"

"You have an adorable way of making yourself understood," she laughed. "Come, do let us talk sense for a minute or two. You say that when you are with me you are my slave. Then why is it that you do not bring Beatrice here when I beg you to?"

"I am your slave," he answered, "in everything that has to do with myself and my own actions. In that other matter it is for your sister to decide."

She shrugged her shoulders.

"Well," she said, "I suppose I shall be able to endure life without her. At any rate, we will talk of something else. Tell me, are you not curious to know why I insisted upon bringing you here?"

"Yes," he admitted, "I am."

"Spoken with your usual candor, my dear Briton!" she exclaimed. "Well, I will gratify your curiosity. This, as you see, is not a popular supping place. A few people come in—mostly those who for some reason or other don't feel smart enough for the big restaurants. The people from the theatres come in here who have not time to change their clothes. As you perceive; the place has a distinctly Bohemian flavor."

Tavernake looked around.

"They seem to come in all sorts of clothes," he remarked. "I am glad."

"There is a man now in London," Elizabeth continued, "whom I am just as anxious to see as I am to find my sister. I believe that this is the most likely place to find him. That is why I have come. My father was to have been here to take me, but as you heard he has gone out somewhere and not returned. None of my other friends were available. You happened to come in just in time."

"And this man whom you want to see," Tavernake asked, "is he here?"

"Not yet," she answered.

There were, indeed, only a few scattered groups in the place, and most of these were obviously theatrical. But even at that moment a man came in alone through the circular doors, and stood just inside, looking around him. He was a man of medium height, thin, and of undistinguished appearance. His hair was light-colored and plastered a little in front over his forehead. His face was thin and he walked with a slight stoop. Something about his clothes and his manner of wearing them stamped him as an American. Tavernake glanced at his companion, wondering whether this, perhaps, might not be the person for whom she was watching. His first glance was careless enough, then he felt his heart thump against his ribs. A tragedy had come into the room! The woman at his side sat as though turned to stone. There was a look in her face as of one who sees Death. The small patch of rouge, invisible before, was now a staring daub of color in an oasis of ashen white. Her eyes were as hard as stones; her lips were twitching as though, indeed, she had been stricken with some disease. No longer was he sitting with this most beautiful lady at whose coming all heads were turned in admiration. It was as though an image of Death sat there, a frozen presentment of horror itself!

CHAPTER XXIII. ON AN ERRAND OF CHIVALRY

The seconds passed; the woman beside him showed no sign of life. Tavernake felt a fear run cold in his blood, such as in all his days he had never known. This, indeed, was something belonging to a world of which he knew nothing. What was it? Illness? Pain? Surprise? There was only his instinct to tell him. It was terror, the terror of one who looks beyond the grave.

"Mrs. Gardner!" he exclaimed. "Elizabeth!"

The sound of his voice seemed to break the spell. A half-choked sob came through her teeth; the struggle for composure commenced.

"I am ill," she murmured. "Give me my glass. Give it to me."

Her fingers were feeling for it but it seemed as though she dared not move her head. He filled it with wine and placed the stem in her hand. Even then she spilled some of it upon the tablecloth. As she raised it to her lips, the man who stood still upon the threshold of the restaurant looked into her face. Slowly, as though his quest were over, he came down the room.

"Go away," she said to Tavernake. "Go away, please. He is coming to speak to me. I want to be alone with him."

Strangely enough, at that moment Tavernake saw nothing out of the common in her request. He rose at once, without any formal leave-taking, and made his way toward the other end of the cafe. As he turned the corner towards the smoking-room, he glanced once behind. The man had approached quite close to Elizabeth; he was standing before her table, they seemed to be exchanging greetings.

Tavernake went on into the smoking-room and threw himself into an easy-chair. He had been there perhaps for ten minutes when Pritchard entered. Certainly it was a night of surprises! Even Pritchard, cool, deliberate, slow in his movements and speech, seemed temporarily flurried. He came into the room walking quickly. As the door swung back, he turned round as though to assure himself that he was not being followed. He did not at first see Tavernake. He sat on the arm of an easy-chair, his hands in his pockets, his eternal cigar in the corner of his mouth, his eyes fixed upon the doors through which he had issued. Without a doubt, something had disturbed him. He had the look of a man who had received a blow, a surprise of some sort over which he was still ruminating. Then he glanced around the room and saw Tavernake.

"Hullo, young man!" he exclaimed. "So this is the way you follow my advice!"

"I never promised to follow it," Tavernake reminded him.

Pritchard wheeled an easy-chair across the room and called to the waiter.

"Come," he said, "you shall stand me a drink. Two whiskies and sodas, Tim. And now, Mr. Leonard Tavernake, you are going to answer me a question."

"Am I?" Tavernake muttered.

"You came down in the lift with Mrs. Wenham Gardner half an hour ago, you went into the restaurant and ordered supper. She is there still and you are here. Have you quarreled?"

"No, we did not quarrel," Tavernake answered. "She explained that she was supping in the cafe only for the sake of meeting one man. She wanted an escort. I filled that post until the man came."

"He is there now?" Pritchard asked.

"He is there now," Tavernake assented.

Pritchard withdrew the cigar from his mouth and watched it for a moment.

"Say, Tavernake," he went on, "is that man who is now having supper with Mrs. Wenham Gardner the man whom she expected?"

"I imagine so," Tavernake replied.

"Didn't she seem in any way scared or disturbed when he first turned up?"

"She looked as I have seen no one else on earth look before," Tavernake admitted. "She seemed simply terrified to death. I do not know why—she didn't explain—but that is how she looked."

"Yet she sent you away!"

"She sent me away. She didn't care what became of me. She was watching the door all the time before he came. Who is he, Pritchard?"

"That sounds a simple question," Pritchard answered gravely, "but it means a good deal. There's mischief afoot to-night, Tavernake."

"You seem to thrive on it," Tavernake retorted, drily. "Any more bunkum?"

Pritchard smiled.

"Come," he said, "you're a sensible chap. Take these things for what they're worth. Believe me when I tell you now that there is a great deal more in the coming of this man than Mrs. Wenham Gardner ever bargained for."

"I wish you'd tell me who he is," Tavernake begged. "All this mystery about Beatrice and her sister, and that lazy old hulk of a father, is most irritating."

Pritchard nodded sympathetically.

"You'll have to put up with it a little longer, I'm afraid, my young friend," he declared. "You've done me a good turn; I'll do you one. I'll give you some good advice. Keep out of this place so long as the old man and his daughter are hanging out here. The girl 's clever—oh, she's as clever as they make them—but she's gone wrong from the start. They ain't your sort, Tavernake. You don't fit in anywhere. Take my advice and hook it altogether."

Tavernake shook his head.

"I can't do that just now," he said. "Good-night! I'm off for the present, at any rate."

Pritchard, too, rose to his feet. He passed his arm through

Tavernake's.

"Young man," he remarked, "there are not many in this country whom I can trust. You're one of them. There's a sort of solidity about you that I rather admire. You are not likely to break out and do silly things. Do you care for adventures?"

"I detest them," Tavernake answered, "especially the sort I tumbled into the other night."

Pritchard laughed softly. They had left the room now and were walking along the open space at the end of the restaurant, leading to the main exit.

"That's the difference between us," he declared thoughtfully. "Now adventures to me are the salt of my life. I hang about here and watch these few respectable-looking men and women, and there doesn't seem to be much in it to an outsider, but, gee whiz! there's sometimes things underneath which you fellows don't tumble to. A man asks another in there to have a drink. They make a cheerful appointment to meet for lunch, to motor to Brighton. It all sounds so harmless, and yet there are the seeds of a conspiracy already sown. They hate me here, but they know very well that wherever they went I should be around. I suppose some day they'll get rid of me."

"More bunkum!" Tavernake muttered.

They stood in front of the door and passed through into the courtyard. On their right, the interior of the smaller restaurant was shielded from view by a lattice-work, covered with flowers and shrubs. Pritchard came to a standstill at a certain point, and stooping down looked through. He remained there without moving for what seemed to Tavernake an extraordinarily long time. When he stood up again, there was a distinct change in his face. He was looking more serious than Tavernake had ever seen him. But for the improbability of the thing, Tavernake would have thought that he had turned pale.

"My young friend," he said, "you've got to see me through this. You 've a sort of fancy for Mrs. Wenham Gardner, I know. To-night you shall be on her side."

"I don't want any more mysteries," Tavernake protested. "I'd rather go home."

"It can't be done," Pritchard declared, taking his arm once more. "You've got to see me through this. Come up to my rooms for a minute."

They entered the Court and ascended to the eighth floor. Pritchard turned on the lights in his room, a plainly furnished and somewhat bare apartment. From a cupboard he took out a pair of rubber-soled shoes and threw them to Tavernake.

"Put those on," he directed.

"What are we going to do?" Tavernake asked.

"You are going to help me," Pritchard answered. "Take my word for it, Tavernake, it's all right. I could tackle the job alone, but I'd rather not. Now drink this whiskey and soda and light a cigarette. I shall be ready in five minutes."

"But where are we going?" Tavernake demanded.

"You are going," Pritchard replied, "on an errand of chivalry. You are going to become once more a rescuer of woman in distress. You are going to save the life of your beautiful friend Elizabeth."

CHAPTER XXIV. CLOSE TO TRAGEDY

The actual words of greeting which passed between Elizabeth and the man whose advent had caused her so much emotion were unimpressive. The newcomer, with the tips of his fingers resting upon the tablecloth, leaned slightly towards her. At close quarters, he was even more unattractive than when Tavernake had first seen him. He was faultily shaped; there was something a little decadent about his deep-set eyes and receding forehead. Neither was his expression prepossessing. He looked at her as a man looks upon the thing he hates.

"So, Elizabeth," he said, "this pleasure has come at last!"

"I heard that you were back in England," she replied. "Pray sit down."

Even then her eyes never left his. All the time they seemed to be fiercely questioning, seeking for something in his features which eluded them. It was terrible to see the change which the last few minutes had wrought in her. Her smooth, girlish face had lost its comeliness. Her eyes, always a little narrow, seemed to have receded. It was such a change, this, as comes to a brave man who, in the prime of life, feels fear for the first time.

"I am glad to find you at supper," he declared, taking up the menu. "I am hungry. You can bring me some grilled cutlets at once," he added to the waiter who stood by his side, "and some brandy. Nothing else."

The waiter bowed and hurried off. The woman played with her fan but her fingers were shaking.

"I fear," he remarked, "that my coming is rather a shock to you. I am sorry to see you looking so distressed."

"It is not that," she answered with some show of courage. "You know me too well to believe me capable of seeking a meeting which I feared. It is the strange thing which has happened to you during these last few months—this last year. Do you know—has any one told you—that you seem to have become even more like—the image of—"

He nodded understandingly.

"Of poor Wenham! Many people have told me that. Of course, you know that we were always appallingly alike, and they always said that we should become more so in middle-age. After all, there is only a year between us. We might have been twins."

"It is the most terrible thing in likenesses I have ever seen," the woman continued slowly. "When you entered the room a few seconds ago, it seemed to me that a miracle had happened. It seemed to me that the dead had come to life."

"It must have been a shock," the man murmured, with his eyes upon the tablecloth.

"It was," she agreed, hoarsely. "Can't you see it in my face? I do not always look like a woman of forty. Can't you see the gray shadows that are there? You see, I admit it frankly. I was terrified—I am terrified!"

"And why?" he asked.

"Why?" she repeated, looking at him wonderingly. "Doesn't it seem to you a terrible thing to think of the dead coming back to life?"

He tapped lightly upon the tablecloth for a minute with the fingers of one hand. Then he looked at her again.

"It depends," he said, "upon the manner of their death."

An executioner of the Middle Ages could not have played with his victim more skillfully. The woman was shivering now, preserving some outward appearance of calm only by the most fierce and unnatural effort.

"What do you mean by that, Jerry?" she asked. "I was not even with—Wenham, when he was lost. You know all about it, I suppose,—how it happened?"

The man nodded thoughtfully.

"I have heard many stories," he admitted. "Before we leave the subject for ever, I should like to hear it from you, from your own lips."

There was a bottle of champagne upon the table, ordered at the commencement of the meal. She touched her glass; the waiter filled it. She raised it to her lips and set it down empty. Her fingers were clutching the tablecloth.

"You ask me a hard thing, Jerry," she said. "It is not easy to talk of anything so painful. From the moment we left New York, Wenham was strange. He drank a good deal upon the steamer. He used to talk sometimes in the most wild way. We came to London. He had an attack of delirium tremens. I nursed him through it and took him into the country, down into Cornwall. We took a small cottage on the outskirts of a fishing village—St. Catherine's, the place was called. There we lived quietly for a time. Sometimes he was better, sometimes worse. The doctor in the village was very kind and came often to see him. He brought a friend from the neighboring town and they agreed that with complete rest Wenham would soon be better. All the time my life was a miserable one. He was not fit to be alone and yet he was a terrible companion. I did my best. I was with him half of every day, sometimes longer. I was with him till my own health began to suffer. At last I could stand the solitude no longer. I sent for my father. He came and lived with us."

"The professor," her listener murmured.

She nodded.

"It was a little better then for me," she went on, "except that poor Wenham seemed to take such a dislike to my father. However, he hated every one in turn, even the doctors, who always did their best for him. One day, I admit, I lost my temper. We quarreled; I could not help it—life was becoming insupportable. He rushed out of the house—it was about three o'clock in the afternoon. I have never seen him since."

The man was looking at her, looking at her closely although he was blinking all the time.

"What do you think became of him?" he asked. "What do people think?"

She shook her head.

"The only thing he cared to do was swim," she said. "His clothes and hat were found down in the little cove near where we had a tent."

"You think, then, that he was drowned?" the man asked.

She nodded. Speech seemed to be becoming too painful.

"Drowning," her companion continued, helping himself to brandy, "is not a pleasant death. Once I was nearly drowned myself. One struggles for a short time and one thinks—yes, one thinks!" he added.

He raised his glass to his lips and set it down.

"It is an easy death, though," he went on, "quite an easy death. By the way, were those clothes that were found of poor Wenham's identified as the clothes he wore when he left the house?"

She shook her head.

"One could not say for certain," she answered. "I never noticed how he was dressed. He wore nearly always the same sort of things, but he had an endless variety."

"And this was seven months ago—seven months."

She assented.

"Poor Wenham," he murmured. "I suppose he is dead. What are you going to do, Elizabeth?"

"I do not know," she replied. "Soon I must go to the lawyers and ask for advice. I have very little more money left. I have written several times to New York to you, to his friends, but I have had no answer. After all, Jerry, I am his wife. No one liked my marrying him, but I am his wife. I have a right to a share of his property if he is dead. If he has deserted me, surely I shall be allowed something. I do not even know how rich he was."

The man at her side smiled.

"Much better off than I ever was," he declared. "But, Elizabeth!"

"Well?"

"There were rumors that, before you left New York, Wenham converted very large sums of money into letters of credit and bonds, very large sums indeed." She shook her head. "He had a letter of credit for about a thousand pounds, I think," she said. "There is very little left of the money he had with him."

"And you find living here expensive, I dare say?"

"Very expensive indeed," she agreed, with a sigh. "I have been looking forward to seeing you, Jerry. I thought, perhaps, for the sake of old times you might advise me."

"Of old times," he repeated to himself softly. "Elizabeth, do you think of them sometimes?"

She was becoming more herself. This was a game she was used to playing. Of old times, indeed! It seemed only yesterday that these two brothers, who had the reputation in those days of being the richest young men in New York, were both at her feet. So far, she had scarcely been fortunate. There was still a chance, however. She looked up. It seemed to her that he was losing his composure. Yes, there was something of the old gleam in his eyes! Once he had been madly enough in love with her. It ought not to be impossible!

"Jerry," she said, "I have told you these things. It has been so very, very painful for me. Won't you try now and be kind? Remember that I am all alone and it is all very difficult for me. I have been looking forward to your coming. I have thought so often of those times we spent together in New York. Won't you be my friend again? Won't you help me through these dark days?"

Her hand touched his. For a moment he snatched his away as though stung. Then he caught her fingers in his and held them as though in a vice. She smiled, the smile of conscious power. The flush of beauty was streaming once more into her face. Poor fellow, he was still in love, then! The fingers which had closed upon hers were burning. What a pity that he was not a little more presentable!

"Yes," he muttered, "we must be friends, Elizabeth. Wenham had all the luck at first. Perhaps it's going to be my turn now, eh?"

He bent towards her. She laughed into his face for a moment and then was once more suddenly colorless, the smile frozen upon her lips. She began to shiver.

"What is it?" he asked. "What is it, Elizabeth?"

"Nothing," she faltered, "only I wish—I do wish that you were not so much like Wenham. Sometimes a trick of your voice, the way you hold your head—it terrifies me!"

He laughed oddly.

"You must get used to that, Elizabeth," he declared. "I can't help being like him, you know. We were great friends always until you came. I wonder why you preferred Wenham."

"Don't ask me—please don't ask me that," she begged. "Really, I think he happened to be there just at the moment I felt like making a clean sweep of everything, of leaving New York and every one and starting life again, and I thought Wenham meant it. I thought I should be able to keep him from drinking and to help him start a new life altogether over here or on the Continent."

"Poor little woman," he said, "you have been disappointed, I am afraid."

She sighed.

"I am only human, you know," she went on. "Every one told me that Wenham was a millionaire, too. See how much I have benefited by it. I am almost penniless, I do not know whether he is dead or alive, I do not know what to do to get some money. Was Wenham very rich, Jerry?"

The man laughed.

"Oh, he was very rich indeed!" he assured her. "It is terrible that you should be left like this. We will talk about it together presently, you and I. In the meantime, you must let me be your banker."

"Dear Jerry," she whispered, "you were always generous."

"You have not spoken of the little prude—dear Miss Beatrice," he reminded her suddenly.

Elizabeth sighed.

"Beatrice was a great trial from the first," she declared. "You know how she disliked you both—she was scarcely even civil to Wenham, and she would never have come to Europe with us if father hadn't insisted upon it. We took her down to Cornwall with us and there she became absolutely insupportable. She was always interfering between Wenham and me and imagining the most absurd things. One day she left us without a word of warning. I have never seen her since."

The man stared gloomily into his plate.

"She was a queer little thing," he muttered. "She was good, and she seemed to like being good."

Elizabeth laughed, not quite pleasantly.

"You speak as though the rest of us," she remarked, "were qualified to take orders in wickedness."

He helped himself to more brandy.

"Think back," he said. "Think of those days in New York, the life we led, the wild things we did week after week, month after month, the same eternal round of turning night into day, of struggling everywhere to find new pleasures, pulling vice to pieces like children trying to find the inside of their playthings."

"I don't like your mood in the least," she interrupted.

He drummed for a moment upon the tablecloth with his fingers.

"We were talking of Beatrice. You don't even know where she is now, then?"

"I have no idea," Elizabeth declared.

"She was with you for long in Cornwall?" he asked.

Elizabeth toyed with her wineglass for a minute.

"She was there about a month," she admitted.

"And she didn't approve of the way you and Wenham behaved?" he demanded.

"Apparently not. She left us, anyway. She didn't understand Wenham in the least. I shouldn't be surprised," Elizabeth went on, "to hear that she was a hospital nurse, or learning typing, or a clerk in an office. She was a young woman of gloomy ideas, although she was my sister."

He came a little closer towards her.

"Elizabeth," he said, "we will not talk any more about Beatrice. We will not talk any more about anything except our two selves."

"Are you really glad to see me again, Jerry?" she asked softly.

"You must know it, dear," he whispered. "You must know that I loved you always, that I adored you. Oh, you knew it! Don't tell me you didn't. You knew it, Elizabeth!"

She looked down at the tablecloth.

"Yes, I knew it," she admitted, softly.

"Can't you guess what it is to me to see you again like this?" he continued.

She sighed.

"It is something for me, too, to feel that I have a friend close at hand."

"Come," he said, "they are turning out the lights here. You want to know about Wenham's property. Let me come upstairs with you for a little time and I will tell you as much as I can from memory."

He paid the bill, helped her on with her cloak. His fingers seemed like burning spots upon her flesh. They went up in the lift. In the corridors he drew her to him and she began to tremble.

"What is there strange about you, Jerry?" she faltered,

looking into his face. "You terrify me!"

"You are glad to see me? Say you are glad to see me?"

"Yes, I am glad," she whispered.

Outside the door of her rooms, she hesitated.

"Perhaps," she suggested, faintly,—"wouldn't it be better if you came to-morrow morning?"

Once more his fingers touched her and again that extraordinary sense of fear seemed to turn her blood cold.

"No," he replied, "I have been put off long enough! You must let me in, you must talk with me for half an hour. I will go then, I promise. Half an hour! Elizabeth, haven't I waited an eternity for it?"

He took the keys from her fingers and opened the door, closing it again behind them. She led the way into the sitting-room. The whole place was in darkness but she turned on the electric light. The cloak slipped from her shoulders. He took her hands and looked at her.

"Jerry," she whispered, "you mustn't look at me like that. You terrify me! Let me go!"

She wrenched herself free with an effort. She stepped back to the corner of the room, as far as she could get from him. Her heart was beating fiercely. Somehow or other, neither of these two young men, over whose lives she had certainly brought to bear a very wonderful influence, had ever before stirred her pulses like this. What was it, she wondered? What was the meaning of it? Why didn't he speak? He did nothing but look, and there were unutterable things in his eyes. Was he angry with her because she had married Wenham, or was he blaming her because Wenham had gone? There was passion in his face, but such passion! Desire, perhaps, but what else? She caught up a telegram which lay upon her writing desk, and tore it open. It was an escape for a moment. She read the words, stared, and read them aloud incredulously. It was from her father.

"Jerry Gardner sailed for New York to-day."

She looked up at the man, and as she looked her face grew gray and the thin sheet went quivering from her lifeless fingers to the floor. Then he began to laugh, and she knew.

"Wenham!" she shrieked. "Wenham!"

There was murder in his face, murder almost in his laugh.

"Your loving husband!" he answered.

She sprang for the door but even as she moved she heard the click of the bolt shot back. He touched the electric switch and the room was suddenly in darkness. She heard him coming towards her, she felt his hot breath upon her cheek.

"My loving wife!" he whispered. "At last!"

CHAPTER XXV. THE MADMAN TALKS

Tavernake turned on the light. Pritchard, with a quick leap forward, seized Wenham around the waist and dragged him away. Elizabeth had fainted; she lay upon the floor, her face the color of marble.

"Get some water and throw over her," Pritchard ordered.

Tavernake obeyed. He threw open the window and let in a current of air. In a moment or two the woman stirred and raised her head.

"Look after her for a minute," Pritchard said. "I Il lock this fierce little person up in the bathroom."

Pritchard carried his prisoner out. Tavernake leaned over the woman who was slowly coming back to consciousness.

"Tell me about it," she asked, hoarsely. "Where is he?"

"Locked up in the bathroom," Tavernake answered. "Pritchard is taking care of him. He won't be able to get out."

"You know who it was?" she faltered.

"I do not," Tavernake replied. "It isn't my business. I'm only here because Pritchard begged me to come. He thought he might want help."

She held his fingers tightly.

"Where were you?" she asked.

"In the bathroom when you arrived. Then he bolted the door behind and we had to come round through your bedroom."

"How did Pritchard find out?"

"I know nothing about it," Tavernake replied. "I only know that he peered through the latticework and saw you sitting there at supper."

She smiled weakly.

"It must have been rather a shock to him," she said. "He has been convinced for the last six months that I murdered Wenham, or got rid of him by some means or other. Help me up."

She staggered to her feet. Tavernake assisted her to an easy chair. Then Pritchard came in.

"He is quite safe," he announced, "sitting on the edge of the bath playing with a doll."

She shivered.

"What is he doing with it?" she asked.

"Showing me exactly, with a shawl pin, where he meant to have stabbed you," Pritchard answered, drily. "Now, my dear lady," he continued, "it seems to me that I have done you one injustice, at any rate. I certainly thought you'd helped to relieve the world of that young person. Where did he come from? Perhaps you can tell me that."

She shrugged her shoulders.

"I suppose I may as well," she said. "Listen, you have seen what he was like to-night, but you don't know what it was to live with him. It was Hell!"—she sobbed—"absolute Hell! He drank, he took drugs, it was all his servant could do to force him even to make his toilet. It was impossible. It was crushing the life out of me."

"Go on," Pritchard directed.

"There isn't much more to tell," she continued. "I found an old farmhouse—the loneliest spot in Cornwall. We moved there and I left him—with Mathers. I promised Mathers that he should have twenty pounds a week for every week he kept his master away from me. He has kept him away for seven months."

"What about that story of yours—about his having gone in swimming?" Pritchard asked.

"I wanted people to believe that he was dead," she declared defiantly. "I was afraid that if you or his relations found him, I should have to live with him or give up the money."

Pritchard nodded.

"And to-night you thought—"

"I thought he was his brother Jerry," she went on. "The likeness was always amazing, you know that. I was told that Jerry was in town. I felt nervous, somehow, and wired to

Mathers. I had his reply only last night. He wired that Wenham was quite safe and contented, not even restless."

"That telegram was sent by Wenham himself," Pritchard remarked. "I think you had better hear what he has to say."

She shrank back.

"No. I couldn't bear the sight of him again!"

"I think you had better," Pritchard insisted. "I can assure you that he is quite harmless. I will guarantee that."

He left the room. Soon he returned, his arm locked in the arm of Wenham Gardner. The latter had the look of a spoilt child who is in disgrace. He sat sullenly upon a chair and glared at every one. Then he produced a small crumpled doll, with a thread of black cotton around its neck, and began swinging it in front of him, laughing at Elizabeth all the time.

"Tell us," Pritchard asked, "what has become of Mathers?"

He stopped swinging the doll, shivered for a moment, and then laughed.

"I don't mind," he declared. "I guess I don't mind telling. You see, whatever I was when I did it, I am mad now—quite mad. My friend Pritchard here says I am mad. I must have been mad or I shouldn't have tried to hurt that dear beautiful lady over there."

He leered at Elizabeth, who shrank back.

"She ran away from me some time ago," he went on, "sick to death of me she was. She thought she'd got all my money. She hadn't. There's plenty more, plenty more. She ran away and left me with Mathers. She was paying him so much a week to keep me quiet, not to let me go anywhere where I should talk, to keep me away from her so that she could live up here and see all her friends and spend my money. And at first I didn't mind, and then I did mind, and I got angry with Mathers, and Mathers wouldn't let me come away, and three nights ago I killed Mathers."

There was a little thrill of horror. He looked from one to

the other. By degrees their fear seemed to become communicated to him.

"What do you mean by looking like that, all of you?" he exclaimed. "What does it matter? He was only my man-servant. I am Wenham Gardner, millionaire. No one will put me in prison for that. Besides, he shouldn't have tried to keep me away from my wife. Anyway, it don't matter. I am quite mad. Mad people can do what they like. They have to stop in an asylum for six months, and then they're quite cured and they start again. I don't mind being mad for six months. Elizabeth," he whined, "come and be mad, too. You haven't been kind to me. There's plenty more money—plenty more. Come back for a little time and I'll show you."

"How did you kill Mathers?" Pritchard asked.

"I stabbed him when he was stooping down," Wenham Gardner explained. "You see, when I left college my father thought it would be good for me to do something. I dare say it would have been but I didn't want to. I studied surgery for six months. The only thing I remember was just where to kill a man behind the left shoulder. I remembered that. Mathers was a fat man, and he stooped so that his coat almost burst. I just leaned over, picked out the exact spot, and he crumpled all up. I expect," he went on, "you'll find him there still. No one comes near the place for days and days. Mathers used to leave me locked up and do all the shopping himself. I expect he's lying there now. Some one ought to go and see."

Elizabeth was sobbing quietly to herself. Tavernake felt the perspiration break out upon his forehead. There was something appalling in the way this young man talked.

"I don't understand why you all look so serious," he continued. "No one is going to hurt me for this. I am quite mad now. You see, I am playing with this doll. Sane men don't play with dolls. I hope they'll try me in New York, though. I am well-known in New York. I know all the lawyers and the jurymen.

Oh, they're up to all sorts of tricks in New York! Say, you don't suppose they'll try me over here?" he broke off suddenly, turning to Pritchard. "I shouldn't feel so much at home here."

"Take him away," Elizabeth begged. "Take him away." Pritchard nodded.

"I thought you'd better hear," he said. "I am going to take him away now. I shall send a telegram to the police-station at St. Catherine's. They had better go up and see what's happened."

Pritchard took his captive once more by the arm. The young man struggled violently.

"I don't like you, Pritchard," he shrieked. "I don't want to go with you. I want to stay with Elizabeth. I am not really afraid of her. She'd like to kill me, I know, but she's too clever—oh, she's too clever! I'd like to stay with her."

Pritchard led him away.

"We'll see about it later on," he said. "You'd better come with me just now."

The door closed behind them. Tavernake staggered up.

"I must go," he declared. "I must go, too."

Elizabeth was sobbing quietly to herself. She seemed scarcely to hear him. On the threshold Tavernake turned back.

"That money," he asked, "the money you were going to lend me—was that his?"

She looked up and nodded. Tavernake went slowly out.

CHAPTER XXVI. A CRISIS

Pritchard was the first visitor who had ever found his way into Tavernake's lodgings. It was barely eight o'clock on the same morning. Tavernake, hollow-eyed and bewildered, sat up upon the sofa and gazed across the room.

"Pritchard!" he exclaimed. "Why, what do you want?"

Pritchard laid his hat and gloves upon the table. Already his first swift glance had taken in the details of the little apartment. The overcoat and hat which Tavernake had worn the night before lay by his side. The table was still arranged for some meal of the previous day. Apart from these things, a single glance assured him that Tavernake had not been to bed.

Pritchard drew up an easy-chair and seated himself deliberately.

"My young friend," he announced, "I have come to the conclusion that you need some more advice."

Tavernake rose to his feet. His own reflection in the looking-glass startled him. His hair was crumpled, his tie undone, the marks of his night of agony were all too apparent. He felt himself at a disadvantage.

"How did you find me out?" he asked. "I never gave you my address."

Pritchard smiled.

"Even in this country, with a little help," he said, "those things are easy enough. I made up my mind that this morning would be to some extent a crisis with you. You know, Tavernake, I am not a man who says much, but you are the right sort. You've been in with me twice when I should have missed you if you hadn't been there."

Tavernake seemed to have lost the power of speech. He had relapsed again into his place upon the sofa. He simply waited.

"How in the name of mischief," Pritchard continued, impressively, "you came to be mixed up in the lives of this amiable trio, I cannot imagine! I am not saying a word against Miss Beatrice, mind. All that surprises me is that you and she should ever have come together, or, having come together, that you should ever have exchanged a word. You see, I am here to speak plain truths. You are, I take it, a good sample of the hard, stubborn, middle-class Briton. These three people of whom I have spoken, belong—Miss Beatrice, perhaps, by force of circumstances—but still they do belong to the land of Bohemia. However, when one has got over the surprise of finding you on intimate terms with Miss Beatrice, there comes a more amazing thing. You, with hard common sense written everywhere in your face, have been prepared at any moment, for all I know are prepared now, to make an utter and complete idiot of yourself over Elizabeth Gardner."

Still Tavernake did not speak. Pritchard looked at him curiously.

"Say," he went on, "I have come here to do you a service, if I can. So far as I know at present, this very wonderful young lady has kept on the right side of the law. But see here, Tavernake, she's been on the wrong side of everything that's decent and straight all her days. She married that poor creature for his money, and set herself deliberately to drive him off his head. Last night's tragedy was her doing, not his, though he, poor devil, will have to end his days in an asylum, and the lady will have his money to make herself more beautiful than ever with. Now I am going to let you behind the scenes, my young friend."

Then Tavernake rose to his feet. In the shabby little room he seemed to have grown suddenly taller. He struck the crazy table with his clenched fist so that the crockery upon it rattled. Pritchard was used to seeing men—strong men, too—moved by various passions, but in Tavernake's face he seemed to see new things.

"Pritchard," Tavernake exclaimed, "I don't want to hear

another word!"

Pritchard smiled.

"Look here," he said, "what I am going to tell you is the truth. What I am going to tell you I'd as soon say in the presence of the lady as here."

Tavernake took a step forward and Pritchard suddenly realized the man who had thrown himself through that little opening in the wall, one against three, without a thought of danger.

"If you say a single word more against her," Tavernake shouted hoarsely, "I shall throw you out of the room!"

Pritchard stared at him. There was something amazing about this young man's attitude, something which he could not wholly grasp. He could see, too, that Tavernake's words were so few simply because he was trembling under the influence of an immense passion.

"If you won't listen," Pritchard declared, slowly, "I can't talk. Still, you've got common sense, I take it. You've the ordinary powers of judging between right and wrong, and knowing when a man or a woman's honest. I want to save you —"

"Silence!" Tavernake exclaimed. "Look here, Pritchard," he went on, breathing a little more naturally now, "you came here meaning to do the right thing—I know that. You're all right, only you don't understand. You don't understand the sort of person I am. I am twenty-four years old, I have worked for my own living up here in London since I was twelve. I was a man, so far as work and independence went, at fifteen. Since then I have had my shoulder to the wheel; I have lived on nothing; I have made a little money where it didn't seem possible. I have worried my way into posts which it seemed that no one could think of giving me, but all the time I have lived in a little corner of the world—like that."

His finger suddenly described a circle in the air.

"You don't understand—you can't," he went on, "but there it is. I never spoke to a woman until I spoke to Beatrice. Chance made me her friend. I began to understand the outside of some of those things which I had never even dreamed of before. She set me right in many ways. I began to read, think, absorb little bits of the real world. It was all wonderful. Then Elizabeth came. I met her, too, by accident—she came to my office for a house—Elizabeth!"

Pritchard found something almost pathetic in the sudden dropping of Tavernake's voice, the softening of his face.

"I don't know how to talk about these things," Tavernake said, simply. "There's a literature that's reached from before the Bible to now, full of nothing else. It's all as old as the hills. I suppose I am about the only sane man in this city who knew nothing of it; but I did know nothing of it, and she was the first woman. Now you understand. I can't hear a word against her—I won't! She may be what you say. If so, she's got to tell me so herself!"

"You mean that you are going to believe any story she likes to put up?"

"I mean that I am going to her," Tavernake answered, "and I have no idea in the world what will happen—whether I shall believe her or not. I can see what you think of me," he went on, becoming a little more himself as the stress of unaccustomed speech passed him by. "I will tell you something that will show you that I realize a good deal. I know the difference between Beatrice and Elizabeth. Less than a week ago, I asked Beatrice to marry me. It was the only way I could think of, the only way I could kill the fever."

"And Beatrice?" Pritchard asked, curiously.

"She wouldn't," Tavernake replied. "After all, why should she? I have my way to make yet. I can't expect others to believe in me as I believe in myself. She was kind but she wouldn't."

Pritchard lit a cigar.

"Look here, Tavernake," he said, "you are a young man, you've got your life before you and life's a biggish thing. Empty out those romantic thoughts of yours, roll up your shirt sleeves and get at it. You are not one of these weaklings that need a woman's whispers in their ears to spur them on. You can work without that. It's only a chapter in your life—the passing of these three people. A few months ago, you knew nothing of them. Let them go. Get back to where you were."

Then Tavernake for the first time laughed—a laugh that sounded even natural.

"Have you ever found a man who could do that?" he asked. "The candle gives a good light sometimes, but you'll never think it the finest illumination in the world when you've seen the sun. Never mind me, Pritchard. I'm going to do my best still, but there's one thing that nothing will alter. I am going to make that woman tell me her story, I am going to listen to the way she tells it to me. You think that where women are concerned I am a fool. I am, but there is one great boon which has been vouchsafed to fools—they can tell the true from the false. Some sort of instinct, I suppose. Elizabeth shall tell me her story and I shall know, when she tells it, whether she is what you say or what she has seemed to me."

Pritchard held out his hand.

"You're a queer sort, Tavernake," he declared. "You take life plaguy seriously. I only hope you 'll get all out of it you expect to. So long!"

Tavernake opened the window after his visitor had gone, and leaned out for some few minutes, letting the fresh air into the close, stifling room. Then he went upstairs, bathed and changed his clothes, made some pretense at breakfast, went through his letters with methodical exactness. At eleven o'clock he set out upon his pilgrimage.

CHAPTER XXVII. TAVERNAKE CHOOSES

Tavernake was kept waiting in the hall of the Milan Court for at least half an hour before Elizabeth was prepared to see him. He wandered aimlessly about watching the people come and go, looking out into the flower-hung courtyard, curiously unconscious of himself and of his errand, unable to concentrate his thoughts for a moment, yet filled all the time with the dull and uneasy sensation of one who moves in a dream. Every now and then he heard scraps of conversation from the servants and passers-by, referring to the last night's incident. He picked up a paper but threw it down after only a casual glance at the paragraph. He saw enough to convince him that for the present, at any rate, Elizabeth seemed assured of a certain amount of sympathy. The career of poor Wenham Gardner was set down in black and white, with little extenuation, little mercy. His misdeeds in Paris, his career in New York, spoke for themselves. He was quoted as a type, a decadent of the most debauched instincts, to whom crime was a relaxation and vice a habit. Tavernake would read no more. He might have been all these things, and yet she had become his wife!

At last came the message for which he was waiting. As usual, her maid met him at the door of her suite and ushered him in. Elizabeth was dressed for the part very simply, with a suggestion even of mourning in her gray gown. She welcomed him with a pathetic smile.

"Once more, my dear friend," she said, "I have to thank you."

Her fingers closed upon his and she smiled into his face. Tavernake found himself curiously unresponsive. It was the same smile, and he knew very well that he himself had not changed, yet it seemed as though life itself were in a state of suspense for him.

"You, too, are looking grave this morning, my friend," she continued. "Oh, how horrible it has all been! Within the last two hours I have had at least five reporters, a gentleman from Scotland Yard, another from the American Ambassador to see me. It is too terrible, of course," she went on. "Wenham's people are doing all they can to make it worse. They want to know why we were not together, why he was living in the country and I in town. They are trying to show that he was under restraint there, as if such a thing were possible! Mathers was his own servant— poor Mathers!"

She sighed and wiped her eyes. Still Tavernake said nothing. She looked at him, a little surprised.

"You are not very sympathetic," she observed. "Please come and sit down by my side and I will show you something."

He moved towards her but he did not sit down. She stretched out her hand and picked something up from the table, holding it towards him. Tavernake took it mechanically and held it in his fingers. It was a cheque for twelve thousand pounds.

"You see," she said, "I have not forgotten. This is the day, isn't it? If you like, you can stay and have lunch with me up here and we will drink to the success of our speculation."

Tavernake held the cheque in his fingers; he made no motion to put it in his pocket. She looked at him with a puzzled frown upon her face.

"Do talk or say something, please!" she exclaimed. "You look at me like some grim figure. Say something. Sit down and be natural."

"May I ask you some questions?"

"Of course you may," she replied. "You may do anything sooner than stand there looking so grim and unbending. What is it you want to know?"

"Did you understand that Wenham Gardner was this sort of man when you married him?"

She shrugged her shoulders slightly.

"I suppose I did," she admitted.

"You married him, then, only because he was rich?"

She smiled.

"What else do women marry for, my dear moralist?" she demanded. "It isn't my fault if it doesn't sound pretty. One must have money!"

Tavernake inclined his head gravely; he made no sign of dissent.

"You two came over to England," he went on, "with Beatrice and your father. Beatrice left you because she disapproved of certain things."

Elizabeth nodded.

"You may as well know the truth," she said. "Beatrice has the most absurd ideas. After a week with Wenham, I knew that he was not a person with whom any woman could possibly live. His valet was really only his keeper; he was subject to such mad fits that he needed some one always with him. I was obliged to leave him in Cornwall. I can't tell you everything, but it was absolutely impossible for me to go on living with him."

"Beatrice," Tavernake remarked, "thought otherwise."

Elizabeth looked at him quickly from below her eyelids. It was hard, however, to gather anything from his face.

"Beatrice thought otherwise," Elizabeth admitted. "She thought that I ought to nurse him, put up with him, give up all my friends, and try and keep him alive. Why, it would have been absolute martyrdom, misery for me," she declared. "How could I be expected to do such a thing?"

Tavernake nodded gravely.

"And the money?" he asked.

"Well, perhaps there I was a trifle calculating," she confessed. "But you," she added, nodding at the cheque in his hand, "shouldn't grumble at that. I knew when we were married that I should have trouble. His people hated me, and I knew that in the event of anything happening like this thing which has happened, they would try to get as little as possible allowed me. So before we left New York, I got Wenham to turn as much as ever he could into cash. That we brought away with us."

"And who took care of it?"

Elizabeth smiled.

"I did," she answered, "naturally."

"Tell me about last night," Tavernake said. "I suppose I am stupid but I don't quite understand."

"How should you?" she answered. "Listen, then. Wenham, I suppose got tired of being shut up with Mathers, although I am sure I don't see what else was possible. So he waited for his opportunity, and when the man wasn't looking—well, you know what happened," she added, with a shiver. "He got up to London somehow and made his way to Dover Street."

"Why Dover Street?"

"I suppose you know," Elizabeth explained, "that Wenham has a brother—Jerry—who is exactly like him. These two had rooms in Dover Street always, where they kept some English clothes and a servant. Jerry Gardner was over in London. I knew that, and was expecting to see him every day. Wenham found his way to the rooms, dressed himself in his brother's clothes, even wore his ring and some of his jewelry, which he knew I should recognize, and came here. I believed—yes, I believed all the time," she went on, her voice trembling, "that it was Jerry who was sitting with me. Once or twice I had a sort of terrible shiver. Then I remembered how much they were alike and it seemed to me ridiculous to be afraid. It was not till we got upstairs, till the door was closed behind me, that he turned round and I knew!"

Her head fell suddenly into her hands. It was almost the first sign of emotion. Tavernake analyzed it mercilessly. He knew very well that it was fear, the coward's fear of that terrible moment.

"And now?"

"Now," she went on, more cheerfully, "no one will venture to deny that Wenham is mad. He will be placed under restraint, of course, and the courts will make me an allowance. One thing is absolutely certain, and that is that he will not live a year."

Tavernake half closed his eyes. Was there no sign of his suffering, no warning note of the things which were passing out of his life! The woman who smiled upon him seemed to see nothing. The twitching of his fingers, the slight quivering of his face, she thought was because of his fear for her.

"And now," she declared, in a suddenly altered tone, "this is all over and done with. Now you know everything. There are no more mysteries," she added, smiling at him delightfully. "It is all very terrible, of course, but I feel as though a great weight had passed away. You and I are going to be friends, are we not?"

She rose slowly to her feet and came towards him. His eyes watched her slow, graceful movements as though fascinated. He remembered on that first visit of his how wonderful he had thought her walk. She was still smiling up at him; her fingers fell upon his shoulders.

"You are such a strange person," she murmured. "You aren't a little bit like any of the men I've ever known, any of the men I have ever cared to have as friends. There is something about you altogether different. I suppose that is why I rather like you. Are you glad?"

For a single wild moment Tavernake hesitated. She was so close to him that her hair touched his forehead, the breath from her upturned lips fell upon his cheeks. Her blue eyes were half pleading, half inviting.

"You are going to be my very dear friend, are you not— Leonard?" she whispered. "I do feel that I need some one strong like you to help me through these days."

Tavernake suddenly seized the hands that were upon his shoulders, and forced them back. She felt herself gripped as though by a vice, and a sudden terror seized her. He lifted her up and she caught a glimpse of his wild, set face. Then the breath came through his teeth. He shook all over but the fit had passed. He simply thrust her away from him.

"No," he said, "we cannot be friends! You are a woman without a heart, you are a murderess!"

He tore her cheque calmly in pieces and flung them scornfully away. She stood looking at him, breathing quickly, white to the lips though the murder had gone from his eyes.

"Beatrice warned me," he went on; "Pritchard warned me. Some things I saw for myself, but I suppose I was mad. Now I know!"

He turned away. Her eyes followed him wonderingly.

"Leonard," she cried out, "you are not going like this? You don't mean it!"

Ever afterwards his restraint amazed him. He did not reply. He closed both doors firmly behind him and walked to the lift. She came even to the outside door and called down the corridor.

"Leonard, come back for one moment!"

He turned his head and looked at her, looked at her from the corner of the corridor, steadfastly and without speech. Her fingers dropped from the handle of the door. She went back into her room with shaking knees, and began to cry softly. Afterwards she wondered at herself. It was the first time she had cried for many years.

Tavernake walked to the city and in less than half an hour's time found himself in Mr. Martin's office. The lawyer welcomed him warmly.

"I'm jolly glad to see you, Tavernake," he declared. "I hope you've got the money. Sit down."

Tavernake did not sit down; he had forgotten, indeed, to take of his hat.

"Martin," he said, "I am sorry for you. I have been fooled and you have to pay as well as I have. I can't take up the option on the property. I haven't a penny toward it except my own money, and you know how much that is. You can sell my plots, if you like, and call the money your costs. I've finished."

The lawyer looked at him with wide-open mouth.

"What on earth are you talking about, Tavernake?" he exclaimed. "Are you drunk, by any chance?"

"No, I am quite sober," Tavernake answered. "I have made one or two bad mistakes, that's all. You have a power of attorney for me. You can do what you like with my land, make any terms you please. Good-day!"

"But, Tavernake, look here!" the lawyer protested, springing to his feet. "I say, Tavernake!" he called out.

But Tavernake heard nothing, or, if he heard, he took no notice. He walked out into the street and was lost among the hurrying throngs upon the pavements.

BOOK TWO

CHAPTER I. NEW HORIZONS

Towards the sky-line, across the level country, stumbling and crawling over the deep-hewn dikes, wading sometimes through the mud-oozing swamp, Tavernake, who had left the small railway terminus on foot, made his way that night steadily seawards, as one pursued by some relentless and indefatigable enemy. Twilight had fallen like a mantle around him, fallen over that great flat region of fens and pastureland and bog. Little patches of mist, harbingers of the coming obscurity, were being drawn now into the gradual darkness. Lights twinkled out from the far-scattered homesteads. Here and there a dog barked, some lonely bird seeking shelter called to its mate, but of human beings there seemed to be no one in sight save the solitary traveler.

Tavernake was in grievous straits. His clothes were caked with mud, his hair tossed with the wind, his cheeks pale, his eyes set with the despair of that fierce upheaval through which he had passed. For many hours the torture which had driven him back towards his birthplace had triumphed over his physical exhaustion. Now came the time, however, when the latter asserted itself. With a half-stifled moan he collapsed. Sheer fatigue induced a brief but merciful spell of uneasy slumber. He lay upon his back near one of the broader dikes, his arms outstretched, his unseeing eyes turned toward the sky. The darkness deepened and passed away again before the light of the moon. When at last he sat up, it was a new world upon which he looked, a strange land, moonlit in places, yet full of shadowy somberness. He gazed wonderingly around—for the moment he had forgotten. Then memory came, and with memory once more the stab at his heart. He rose to his feet and went resolutely on his way.

Almost until the dawn he walked, keeping as near as he could to that long monotonous line of telegraph posts, yet avoiding the road as much as possible. With the rising of the sun, he crept into a wayside hovel and lay there hidden for hours. Hunger and thirst seemed like things which had passed him by. It was sleep only which he craved, sleep and forgetfulness.

Dusk was falling again before he found himself upon his feet, starting out once more upon this strangely thought-of pilgrimage. This time he kept to the road, plodding along with tired, dejected footsteps, which had in them still something of that restless haste which drove him ceaselessly onward as though he were indeed possessed of some unquiet spirit. He was recovering now, however, a little of his natural common sense. He remembered that he must have food and drink, and he sought them from the wayside public-house like an ordinary traveler, conquering without any apparent effort that first invincible repugnance of his toward the face of any human being. Then on again across this strange land of windmills and spreading plains, until the darkness forced him to take shelter once more. That night he slept like a child. With the morning, the fever had passed from his blood. A great wind blew in his face even as he opened his eyes, touched to wakefulness by the morning sun, a wind that came booming over the level places, salt with the touch of the ocean and fragrant with the perfume of many marsh plants. He was coming toward the sea now, and within a very short distance from where he had spent the night, he found a broad, shining river stealing into the land. With eager fingers he stripped himself and plunged in, diving again and again below the surface, swimming with long, lazy strokes backwards and forwards. Afterwards he lay down in the warm, dry grass, dressed himself slowly, and went on his way. The wind, which had increased now since the early morning, came thundering across the level land, bending the tops of the few scattered trees, sending the sails of the windmills spinning, bringing on its bosom now stronger than ever the flavor of the sea itself, salt and stimulating. Tavernake told himself that this was a new world into which he was coming. He would pass into its embrace and life would become a new thing.

Towards evening with many a thrill of reminiscence, he descended a steep hill and walked into a queer time-forgotten village, whose scattered red-tiled cottages were built around an arm of the sea. Boldly enough now he entered the one inn which flaunted its sign upon the cobbled street, and, taking a seat in the stone-floored kitchen, ate and drank and bespoke a bed. Later on, he strolled down to the quay and made friends with the few fishermen who were loitering there. They answered his questions readily, although he found it hard at first to pick up again the dialect of which he himself had once made use. The little place was scarcely changed. All progress, indeed, seemed to have passed it by. There were a handful of fishermen, a boat-builder and a fish-curer in the village. There was no other industry save a couple of small farmhouses on the outskirts of the place, no railway within twelve miles. Tourists came seldom, excursionists never. In the half contented, half animal-like expression which seemed common to all the inhabitants, Tavernake read easily enough the history of their uneventful days. It was such a shelter as this, indeed, for which he had been searching.

On the second night after his arrival, he walked with the boatbuilder upon the wooden quay. The boatbuilder's name was Nicholls, and he was a man of some means, deacon of the chapel, with a fair connection as a jobbing carpenter, and possessor of the only horse and cart in the place.

"Nicholls," Tavernake said, "you don't remember me, do you?"

The boat-builder shook his head slowly and ponderously.

"There was Richard Tavernake who farmed the low fields," he remarked, reminiscently. "Maybe you're a son of his. Now I come to think of it, he had a boy apprenticed to the carpentering."

"I was the boy," Tavernake answered. "I soon had enough of it and went to London."

"You'm grown out of all knowledge," Nicholls declared, "but I mind you now. So you've been in London all these years?"

"I've been in London," Tavernake admitted, "and I think, of the two, that Sprey-by-the-Sea is the better place."

"Sprey is well enough," the boat-builder confessed, "well enough for a man who isn't set on change."

"Change," Tavernake asserted, grimly, "is an overrated joy. I have had too much of it in my life. I think that I should like to stay here for some time."

The boat-builder was surprised, but he was a man of heavy and deliberate turn of mind and he did not commit himself to speech. Tavernake continued.

"I used to know something of carpentering in my younger days," he said, "and I don't think that I have forgotten it all. I wonder if I could find anything to do down here?"

Matthew Nicholls stroked his beard thoughtfully.

"The folk round about are not over partial to strangers," he observed, "and you'm been away so long I reckon there's not many as'd recollect you. And as for carpentering jobs, there's Tom Lake over at Lesser Blakeney and his brother down at Brancaster, besides me on the spot, as you might say. It's a poor sort of opening there'd be, if you ask my opinion, especially for one like yourself, as 'as got education."

"I should be satisfied with very little," Tavernake persisted. "I want to work with my hands. I should like to forget for a time that I have had any education at all."

"That do seem mightily queer to me," Nicholls remarked, thoughtfully.

Tavernake smiled.

"Come," he said, "it isn't altogether unnatural. I want to make something with my hands. I think that I could build boats. Why do you not take me into your yard? I could do no harm and I should not want much pay."

Matthew Nicholls stroked his beard once more and this time he counted fifty, as was his custom when confronted with a difficult matter. He had no need to do anything of the sort, for nothing in the world would have induced him to make up his mind on the spot as to so weighty a proposal.

"It's not likely that you're serious," he objected. "You are a young man and strong-limbed, I should imagine, but you've education—one can tell it by the way you pronounce your words. It's but a poor living, after all, to be made here."

"I like the place," Tavernake declared doggedly. "I am a man of small needs. I want to work all through the day, work till I am tired enough to sleep at night, work till my bones ache and my arms are sore. I suppose you could give me enough to live on in a humble way?"

"Take a bite of supper with me," Nicholls answered. "In these serious affairs, my daughter has always her say. We will put the matter before her and see what she thinks of it."

They lingered about the quay until the light from Wells Lighthouse flashed across the sea, and until in the distance they could hear the moaning of the incoming tide as it rippled over the bar and began to fill the tidal way which stretched to the wooden pier itself. Then the two men made their way along the village street, through a field, and into the little yard over which stood the sign of "Matthew Nicholls, Boat-Builder." At one corner of the yard was the cottage in which he lived.

"You'll come right in, Mr. Tavernake," he said, the instincts of hospitality stirring within him as soon as they had passed through the gate. "We will talk of this matter together, you and me and the daughter."

Tavernake seemed, on his introduction to the household, like a man unused to feminine society. Perhaps he did not expect to find such a type of her sex as Ruth Nicholls in such a remote neighborhood. She was thin, and her cheeks were paler than those of any of the other young women whom he had seen about the village. Her eyes, too, were darker, and her speech different. There was nothing about her which reminded him in the least of the child with whom he had played. Tavernake watched her intently. Presently the idea came to him that she, too, was seeking shelter.

Supper was a simple meal, but it was well and deftly served. The girl had the gift of moving noiselessly. She was quick without giving the impression of haste. To their guest she was courteous, but her recollection of him appeared to be slight, and his coming but a matter of slight interest. After she had cleared the cloth, however, and produced a jar of tobacco, her father bade her sit down with them.

"Mr. Tavernake," he began, ponderously, "is thinking some of settling down in these parts, Ruth."

She inclined her head gravely.

"It appears," her father continued, "that he is sick and tired of the city and of head-work. He is wishful to come into the yard with me, if so be that we could find enough work for two."

The girl looked at their visitor, and for the first time there was a measure of curiosity in her earnest gaze. Tavernake was, in his way, good enough to look upon. He was well-built, his shoulders and physique all spoke of strength. His features were firmly cut, although his general expression was gloomy. But for a certain moroseness, an uncouthness which he seemed to cultivate, he might even have been deemed good-looking.

"Mr. Tavernake would make a great mistake," she said, hesitatingly. "It is not well for those who have brains to work with their hands. It is not a place for those to live who have been out in the world. At most seasons of the year it is but a wilderness. Sometimes there is little enough to do, even for father."

"I am not ambitious for over-much work or for over-much money, Miss Nicholls," Tavernake replied. "I will be frank with you both. Things out in the world there went ill with me; it was not my fault, but they went ill with me. What ambitions I had are finished—for the present, at any rate. I want to rest, I want to work with my hands, to grow my muscles again, to feel my strength, to believe that there is something effective in the world I can do. I have had a shock, a disappointment,—call it what you like."

The old man Nicholls nodded deliberately.

"Well," he pronounced, "it's a big change to make. I never thought of help in the yard before. When there's been more than I could do, I've just let it go. Come for a week on trial, Leonard Tavernake. If we are of any use to one another, we shall soon know of it."

The girl, who had been looking out into the night, came back.

"You are making a mistake, Mr. Tavernake," she said. "You are too young and strong to have finished your battle."

He looked at her steadily and sighed. It was only too obvious that hers had been fought and lost.

"Perhaps," he replied softly, "you are right. Perhaps it is only the rest I want. We shall see."

CHAPTER II. THE SIMPLE LIFE

So Tavernake became a boat-builder. Summer passed into winter and this hamlet by the sea seemed, indeed, as though it might have been one of the forgotten spots upon the earth. Save for that handful of cottages, the two farmhouses a few hundred yards inland, and the deserted Hall half-hidden in its grove of pine trees, there was no dwelling-place nor any sign of human habitation for many miles. For eight hours a day Tavernake worked, mostly out of doors, in the little yard which hung over the beach. Sometimes he rested from his labors and looked seaward, looked around him as though rejoicing in that unbroken solitude, the emptiness of the gray ocean, the loneliness of the land behind. What things there were which lay back in the cells of his memory, no person there knew, for he spoke of his past to no one, not even to Ruth. He was a good workman, and he lived the simple life of those others without complaint or weariness. There was nothing in his manner to denote that he had been used to anything else. The village had accepted him without question. It was only Ruth who still, gravely but kindly enough, disapproved of his presence.

One day she came and sat with him as he smoked his after-dinner pipe, leaning against an overturned boat, with his eyes fixed upon that line of gray breakers.

"You spend a good deal of your time thinking, Mr. Tavernake," she remarked quietly.

"Too much," he admitted at once, "too much, Miss Nicholls. I should be better employed planing down that mast there."

"You know that I did not mean that," she said, reprovingly, "only sometimes you make me—shall I confess it? —almost angry with you."

He took his pipe from his mouth and knocked out the ashes. As they fell on the ground so he looked at them.

"All thought is wasted time," he declared, grimly, "all

thought of the past. The past is like those ashes; it is dead and finished."

She shook her head.

"Not always," she replied. "Sometimes the past comes to life again. Sometimes the bravest of us quit the fight too soon."

He looked at her questioningly, almost fiercely. Her words, however, seemed spoken without intent.

"So far as mine is concerned," he pronounced, "it is finished. There is a memorial stone laid upon it, and no resurrection is possible."

"You cannot tell," she answered. "No one can tell."

He turned back to his work almost rudely, but she stayed by his side.

"Once," she remarked, reflectively, "I, too, went a little way into the world. I was a school-teacher at Norwich. I was very fond of some one there; we were engaged. Then my mother died and I had to come back to look after father."

He nodded.

"Well?"

"We are a long way from Norwich," she continued, quietly. "Soon after I left, the man whom I was fond of grew lonely. He found some one else."

"You have forgotten him?" Tavernake asked, quickly.

"I shall never forget him," she replied. "That part of life is finished, but if ever my father can spare me, I shall go back to my work again. Sometimes those work the best and accomplish the most who carry the scars of a great wound."

She turned away to the house, and after that it seemed to him that she avoided him for a time. At any rate, she made no further attempt to win his confidence. Propinquity, however, was too much for both of them. He was a lodger under her father's roof. It was scarcely possible for them to keep apart. Saturdays and Sundays they walked sometimes for miles across the frost-bound marshes, in the quickening atmosphere of the darkening afternoons, when the red sun sank early behind the hills, and the twilight grew shorter every day. They watched the sea-birds together and saw the wild duck come down to the pools; felt the glow of exercise burn their cheeks; felt, too, that common and nameless exultation engendered by their loneliness in the solitude of these beautiful empty places. In the evenings they often read together, for Nicholls, although no drinker, never missed his hour or so at the village inn. Tavernake, in time, began to find a sort of comfort in her calm, sexless companionship. He knew very well that he was to her as she was to him, something human, something that filled an empty place, yet something without direct personality. Little by little he felt the bitterness in his heart grow less. Then a late spring—late, at any rate, in this quaint corner of the world—stole like some wonderful enchantment across the face of the moors and the marshes. Yellow gorse starred with golden clumps the brown hillside; wild lavender gleamed in patches across the silver-streaked marshes; the dead hedges came blossoming into life. Crocuses, long lines of yellow and purple crocuses, broke from waxy buds into starlike blossoms along the front of Matthew Nicholls's garden. And with the coming o spring, Tavernake found himself suddenly able to thin of the past. It was a new phase of life. He could sit down and think of those things that had happened to him, without fearing to be wrecked by the storm. Often he sat out looking seaward, thinking of the days when he had first met Beatrice, of those early days of pleasant companionship, of the marvelous avidity with which he had learned from her. Only when Elizabeth's face stole into the foreground did he spring from his place and turn back to his work.

One day Tavernake sat poring over the weekly local paper, reading it more out of curiosity than from any real interest. Suddenly a familiar name caught his eye. His heart seemed to stop beating for a moment, and the page swam before his eyes. Quickly he recovered himself and read:

THE QUEEN'S HALL, UNTHANK ROAD,
NORWICH

TWICE DAILY.
PROFESSOR FRANKLIN
assisted by his daughter,
MISS BEATRICE FRANKLIN,
will give his REFINED and MARVELOUS
ENTERTAINMENT, comprising HYPNOTISM, feats
Of SECOND SIGHT never before attempted on
any stage, THOUGHT-READING, and a BRIEF
LECTURE upon the connection between ANCIENT
SUPERSTITIONS and the EXTRAORDINARY
DEVELOPMENTS OF THE NEW SCIENCE.

PROFESSOR FRANKLIN Can be CONSULTED
PRIVATELY,
by letter or by appointment. Address for this
week—The Golden Cow, Bell's Lane, Norwich.

Twice Tavernake read the announcement. Then he went
out and found Ruth.

"Ruth," he told her, "there is something calling me back,
perhaps for good."

For the first time she gave him her hand.

"Now you are talking like a man once more," she
declared. "Go and seek it. Comeback and say good-bye to us, if
you will, but throw your tools into the sea."

Tavernake laughed and looked across at his workshop.

"I don't believe," he said, "that you've any confidence in
my boat."

"I'm not sure that I would sail with you," she answered,
"even if you ever finished it. A laborer's work for a laborer's
hand. You must go back to the other things."

CHAPTER III. OLD FRIENDS MEET

The professor set down his tumbler upon the zinc-rimmed counter. He was very little changed except that he had grown a shade stouter, and there was perhaps more color in his cheeks. He carried himself, too, like a man who believes in himself. In the small public-house he was, without doubt, an impressive figure.

"My friends," he remarked, "our host's whiskey is good. At the same time, I must not forget—"

"You'll have one with me, Professor," a youth at his elbow interrupted. "Two special whiskies, miss, if you please."

The professor shrugged his shoulders—it was a gesture which he wished every one to understand. He was suffering now the penalty for a popularity which would not be denied!

"You are very kind, sir," he said, "very kind, indeed. As I was about to say, I must not forget that in less than half an hour I am due upon the stage. It does not do to disappoint one's audience, sir. It is a poor place, this music-hall, but it is full, they tell me packed from floor to ceiling. At eight-thirty I must show myself."

"A marvelous turn, too, Professor," declared one of the young men by whom he was surrounded.

"I thank you, sir," the professor replied, turning towards the speaker, glass in hand. "There have been others who have paid me a similar compliment; others, I may say, not unconnected with the aristocracy of your country—not unconnected either, I might add," he went on, "with the very highest in the land, those who from their exalted position have never failed to shower favors upon the more fortunate sons of our profession. The science of which I am to some extent the pioneer—not a drop more, my young friend. Say, I'm in dead earnest this time! No more, indeed."

The young man in knickerbockers who had just come in banged the head of his cane upon the counter.

"You'll never refuse me, Professor," he asserted, confidently. "I'm an old supporter, I am. I've seen you in Blackburn and Manchester, and twice here. Just as wonderful as ever! And that young lady of yours, Professor, begging your pardon if she is your daughter, as no doubt she is, why, she's a nut and no mistake."

The professor sighed. He was in his element but he was getting uneasy at the flight of time.

"My young friend," he said, "your face is not familiar to me but I cannot refuse your kindly offer. It must be the last, however, absolutely the last."

Then Tavernake, directed here from the music-hall, pushed open the swing door and entered. The professor set down his glass untasted. Tavernake came slowly across the room.

"You haven't forgotten me, then, Professor?" he remarked, holding out his hand.

The professor welcomed him a little limply; something of the bombast had gone out of his manner. Tavernake's arrival had reminded him of things which he had only too easily forgotten.

"This is very surprising," he faltered, "very surprising indeed. Do you live in these parts?"

"Not far away," Tavernake answered. "I saw your announcement in the papers."

The professor nodded.

"Yes," he said, "I am on the war-path again. I tried resting but I got fat and lazy, and the people wouldn't have it, sir," he continued, recovering very quickly something of his former manner. "The number of offers I got through my agents by every post was simply astounding—astounding!"

"I am looking forward to seeing your performance this evening," Tavernake said politely. "In the meantime—"

"I know what you are thinking of," the professor interrupted. "Well, well, give me your arm and we will walk down to the hall together. My friends," the professor added, turning round, "I wish you all a good-night!"

Then the door was pushed half-way open and Tavernake's heart gave a jump. It was Beatrice who stood there, very pale, very tired, and much thinner even than the Beatrice of the boardinghouse, but still Beatrice.

"Father," she exclaimed, "do you know that it is nearly
—"

Then she saw Tavernake and said no more. She seemed to sway a little, and Tavernake, taking a quick step forward, grasped her by the hands.

"Dear sister," he cried, "you have been ill!"

She was herself again almost in a moment.

"Ill? Never in my life," she replied. "Only I have been hurrying—we are late already for the performance—and seeing you there, well, it was quite a shock, you know. Walk down with us and tell me all about it. Tell us what you are doing here—or rather, don't talk for a moment! It is all so amazing."

They turned down the narrow cobbled street, the professor walking in the middle of the roadway, swinging his cane, a very imposing and wonderful figure, with the tails of his frock-coat streaming in the wind, his long hair only half-hidden by his hat. He hummed a tune to himself and affected not to take any notice of the other two. Then Tavernake suddenly realized that he had done a cowardly action in leaving her without a word.

"There is so much to ask," she began at last, "but you have come back."

She looked at his workman's clothes.

"What have you been doing?" she asked, sharply.

"Working," Tavernake answered, "good work, too. I am the better for it. Don't mind my clothes, Beatrice. I have been mad for a time, but after all it has been a healthy madness."

"It was a strange thing that you did," she said,—"you disappeared."

He nodded.

"Some day," he told her, "I may, perhaps, be able to make you understand. Just now I don't think that I could."

"It was Elizabeth?" she whispered, softly.

"It was Elizabeth," he admitted.

They said no more then till they reached the hall. She stopped at the door and put out her hand timidly.

"I shall see you afterwards?" she ventured.

"Do you mind my coming to the performance?" he asked.

She hesitated.

"A few moments ago," she remarked, smiling, "I was dreading your coming. Now I think that you had better. It will be all over at ten o'clock, and I shall look for you outside. You are living in Norwich?"

"I shall be here for to-night, at any rate," he answered.

"Very well, then," she said, "afterwards we will have a talk."

Tavernake passed through the scattered knot of loiterers at the door and bought a seat for himself in the little music-hall, which, notwithstanding the professor's boast, was none too well filled. It was a place of the old-fashioned sort, with small tables in the front, and waiters hurrying about serving drinks. The people were of the lowest order, and the atmosphere of the room was thick with tobacco smoke. A young woman in a flaxen wig and boy's clothes was singing a popular ditty, marching up and down the stage, and interspersing the words o f her song with grimaces and appropriate action. Tavernake sat down with a barely-smothered groan. He was beginning to realize the tragedy upon which he had stumbled. A comic singer followed, who in a dress suit several sizes too large for him gave an imitation of a popular Irish comedian. Then the curtain went up and the professor was seen, standing in front of the curtain and bowing solemnly to a somewhat unresponsive audience. A minute later

Beatrice came quietly in and sat by his side. There was nothing new about the show. Tavernake had seen the same thing before, with the exception that the professor was perhaps a little behind the majority of his fellow-craftsmen. The performance was finished in dead silence, and after it was over, Beatrice came to the front and sang. She was a very unusual figure in such a place, in a plain black evening gown, with black gloves and no jewelry, but they encored her heartily, and she sang a song from the musical comedy in which Tavernake had first seen her. A sudden wave of reminiscence stirred within him. His thoughts seemed to go back to the night when he had waited for her outside the theatre and they had had supper at Imano's, to the day when he had left the boarding-house and entered upon his new life. It was more like a dream than ever now.

He rose and quitted the place immediately she had finished, waiting in the street until she appeared. She came out in a few minutes.

"Father is going to a supper," she announced, "at the inn where he has a room for receiving people. Will you come home with me for an hour? Then we can go round and fetch him."

"I should like to," Tavernake answered.

Her lodgings were only a few steps away—a strange little house in a narrow street. She opened the front door and ushered him in.

"You understand, of course," she said, smiling, "that we have abandoned the haunts of luxury altogether."

He looked around at the tiny room with its struggling fire and horsehair sofa, linoleum for carpet, oleographs for pictures, and he shivered, not for his own sake but for hers. On the sideboard were some bread and cheese and a bottle of ginger beer.

"Please imagine," she begged, taking the pins from her hat, "that you are in those dear comfortable rooms of ours down at Chelsea. Draw that easy-chair up to what there is of the fire, and listen. You smoke still?"

"I have taken to a pipe," he admitted.

"Then light it and listen," she went on, smoothing her hair for a minute in front of the looking-glass. "You want to know about Elizabeth, of course."

"Yes," he said, "I want to know."

"Elizabeth, on the whole," Beatrice continued, "got out of all her troubles very well. Her husband's people were wild with her, but Elizabeth was very clever. They were never able to prove that she had exercised more than proper control over poor Wenham. He died two months after they took him to the asylum. They offered Elizabeth a lump sum to waive all claims to his estate, and she accepted it. I think that she is now somewhere on the Continent."

"And you?" he asked. "Why did you leave the theatre?"

"It was a matter of looking after my father," she explained. "You see, while he was there with Elizabeth he had too much money and nothing to do. The consequence was that he was always—well, I suppose I had better say it—drinking too much, and he was losing all his desire for work. I made him promise that if I could get some engagements he would come away with me, so I went to an agent and we have been touring like this for quite a long time."

"But what a life for you!" Tavernake exclaimed. "Couldn't you have stayed on at the theatre and found him something in London?"

She shook her head.

"In London," she said, "he would never have got out of his old habits. And then," she went on, hesitatingly, "you understand that the public want something else besides the hypnotism—"

Tavernake interrupted her ruthlessly.

"Of course I understand," he declared, "I was there to-night. I understood at once why you were not very anxious for me to go. The people cared nothing at all about your father's performance. They simply waited for you. You would get the same money if you went round without him."

She nodded, a trifle shamefacedly.

"I am so afraid some one will tell him," she confessed. "They nearly always ask me to leave out his part of the performance. They have even offered me more money if I would come alone. But you see how it is. He believes in himself, he thinks he is very clever and he believes that the public like his show. It is the only thing which helps him to keep a little self-respect. He thinks that my singing is almost unnecessary."

Tavernake looked into that faint glimmer of miserable fire. He was conscious of a curious feeling in his throat. How little he knew of life! The pathos of what she had told him, the thought of her bravely traveling the country and singing at third-rate music-halls, never taking any credit to herself, simply that her father might still believe himself a man of talent, appealed to him irresistibly. He suddenly held out his hand.

"Poor little Beatrice!" he exclaimed. "Dear little sister!"

The hand he gripped was cold, she avoided his eyes.

"You—you mustn't," she murmured. "Please don't!"

He held out his other hand and half rose, but her lips suddenly ceased to quiver and she waved him back.

"No, Leonard," she begged, "please don't do or say anything foolish. Since we do meet again, though, like this, I am going to ask you one question. What made you come to me and ask me to marry you that day?"

He looked away; something in her eyes accused him.

"Beatrice," he confessed, "I was a thick-headed ignorant fool, without understanding. I came to you for safety. I was afraid of Elizabeth, I was afraid of what I felt for her. I wanted to escape from it."

She smiled piteously.

"It wasn't a very brave thing to do, was it?" she faltered.

"It was mean," he admitted. "It was worse than that. But, Beatrice," he went on, "I was missing you horribly. You did leave a big empty place when you went away. I am not going to excuse myself about Elizabeth. I lived through a time of the strangest, most marvelous emotions one could dream of. Then the thing came to an end and I felt as though the bottom had gone out of life. I suppose—I loved her," he continued hesitatingly. "I don't know. I only know that she filled every thought of my brain, that she lived in every beat of my heart, that I would have gone down into Hell to help her. And then I understood. That morning she told me something of the truth about herself, not meaning to—unconsciously—justifying herself all the time, not realizing that every word she said was damnable. And then there didn't seem to be anything else left, and I had only one desire. I turned my back upon everything and I went back to the place where I was born, a little fishing village. For the last thirty miles I walked. I shall never forget it. When I got there, what I wanted was work, work with my hands. I wanted to build something, to create anything that I could labor upon. I became a boat builder—I have been a boatbuilder ever since."

"And now?" she asked.

"Beatrice!"

She turned and faced him. She looked into his eyes very searchingly, very wistfully.

"Beatrice," he said, "I ask you once more, only differently. Will you marry me now? I'll find some work, I'll make enough money for us. Do you remember," he went on, "how I used to talk, how I used to feel that I had only to put forth my strength and I could win anything? I'll feel like that again, Beatrice, if you'll come to me."

She shook her head slowly. She looked away from him with a sigh. She had the air of one who has sought for something which she has failed to find.

"You mustn't think of that again, Leonard," she told him. "It would be quite impossible. This is the only way I can save my father. We have a tour that will take us the best part of another year."

"But you are sacrificing yourself!" he declared. "I will keep your father."

"It isn't that only," she replied. "For one thing, I couldn't let you; and for another, it isn't only the money, it's the work. As long as he's made to think that the public expect him every night, he keeps off drinking too much. There is nothing else in the whole world which would keep him steady. Don't look as though you didn't understand, Leonard. He is my father, you know, and there isn't anything more terrible than to see any one who has a claim on us give way to anything like that. You mayn't quite approve, but please believe that I am doing what I feel to be right."

The little fire had gone out. Beatrice glanced at the clock and put on her jacket again.

"I am sorry, Leonard," she said, "but I think I must go and fetch father now. You can walk with me there, if you will. It has been very good to see you again. For the rest I don't know what to say to you. Do you think that it is quite what you were meant for—to build boats?"

"I don't seem to have any other ambition," he answered, wearily. "When I read in the paper this morning that you and your father were here, things seemed suddenly different. I came at once. I didn't know what I wanted until I saw you, but I know now, and it isn't any good."

"No good at all," she declared cheerfully. "It won't be very long, Leonard, before something else comes along to stir you. I don't think you were meant to build boats all your life."

He rose and took up his hat. She was waiting for him at the door. Again they passed down the narrow street.

"Tell, me, Beatrice," he begged, "is it because you don't

like me well enough that you won't listen to what I ask?"

For a moment she half closed her eyes as though in pain. Then she laughed, not perhaps very naturally. They were standing now by the door of the public house.

"Leonard," she said, "you are very young in years but you are a baby in experience. Mind, there are other reasons why I could not—would not dream of marrying you, other reasons which are absolutely sufficient, but—do you know that you have asked me twice and you have never once said that you cared, that you have never once looked as though you cared? No, don't, please," she interrupted, "don't explain anything. You see, a woman always knows—too well, sometimes."

She nodded, and passed in through the swinging-doors. Standing out there in the narrow, crooked street, Tavernake heard the clapping and applause which greeted her entrance, he heard her father's voice. Some one struck a note at the piano— she was going to sing. Very slowly he turned away and walked down the cobbled hill.

CHAPTER IV. PRITCHARD'S GOOD NEWS

Late in the afternoon of the following day, Ruth came home from the village and found Tavernake hard at work on his boat. She put down her basket and stopped by his side.

"So you are back again," she remarked.

"Yes, I am back again."

"And nothing has happened?"

"Nothing has happened," he assented, wearily. "Nothing ever will happen now."

She smiled.

"You mean that you will stay here and build boats all your life?"

"That is what I mean to do," he announced.

She laid her hand upon his shoulder.

"Don't believe it, Leonard," she said. "There is other work for you in the world somewhere, just as there is for me."

He shook his head and she picked up her basket again, smiling.

"Your time will come as it comes to the rest of us," she declared, cheerfully. "You won't want to sit here and bury your talents in the sands all your days. Have you heard what is going to happen to me?"

"No! Something good, I hope."

"My father's favorite niece is coming to live with us— there are seven of them altogether, and farming doesn't pay like it used to, so Margaret is coming here. Father says that if she is as handy as she used to be I may go back to the schools almost at once."

Tavernake was silent for a moment. Then he got up and threw down his tools.

"Great Heavens!" he exclaimed. "If I am not becoming the most selfish brute that ever breathed! Do you know, the first thought I had was that I should miss you? You are right, young woman, I must get out of this."

She disappeared into the house, smiling, and Tavernake called out to Nicholls, who was sitting on the wall.

"Mr. Nicholls," he asked, "how much notice do you want?"

Matthew Nicholls removed his pipe from his mouth.

"Why, I don't know that I'm particular," he replied, "being as you want to go. Between you and me, I'm gettin' fat and lazy since you came. There ain't enough work for two, and that's all there is to it, and being as you're young and active, why, I've left it to you, and look at my arms."

He held them up.

"Used to be all muscle, now they're nothin' but bloomin' pap. And no' but two glasses of beer a day extra have I drunk, just to pass the time. You can stay if you will, young man, but you can go out fishin' and leave me the work, and I'll pay you just the same, for I'm not saying that I don't like your company. Or you can go when you please, and that's the end of it."

Matthew Nicholls spat upon the stones and replaced his pipe in his mouth. Tavernake came in and sat down by his side.

"Look here," he said, "I believe you are right. I'll stay another week but I'll take things easy. You get on with the boat now. I'll sit here and have a smoke."

Nicholls grunted but obeyed, and for the next few days Tavernake loafed. On his return one afternoon from a long walk, he saw a familiar figure sitting upon the sea wall in front of the workshop, a familiar figure but a strange one in these parts. It was Mr. Pritchard, in an American felt hat, and smoking a very black cigar. He leaned over and nodded to Tavernake, who was staring at him aghast.

"Hallo, old man!" he called out. "Run you to earth, you see!"

"Yes, I see!" Tavernake exclaimed.

"Come right along up here and let's talk," Pritchard continued.

Tavernake obeyed. Pritchard looked him over approvingly. Tavernake was roughly dressed in those days, but as a man he had certainly developed.

"Say, you're looking fine," his visitor remarked. "What wouldn't I give for that color and those shoulders!"

"It is a healthy life," Tavernake admitted. "Do you mean that you've come down here to see me?"

"That's so," Pritchard announced; "down here to see you, and for no other reason. Not but that the scenery isn't all it should be, and that sort of thing," he went on, "but I am not putting up any bluff about it. It's you I am here to talk to. Are you ready? Shall I go straight ahead?"

"If you please," Tavernake said, slowly filling his pipe.

"You dropped out of things pretty sudden," Pritchard continued. "It didn't take me much guessing to reckon up why. Between you and me, you are not the first man who's been up against it on account of that young woman. Don't stop me," he begged. "I know how you've been feeling. It was a right good idea of yours to come here. Others before you have tried the shady side of New York and Paris, and it's the wrong treatment. It's Hell, that's what it is, for them. Now that young woman—we got to speak of her—is about the most beautiful and the most fascinating of her sex—I'll grant that to start with—but she isn't worth the life of a snail, much less the life of a strong man."

"You are, quite right," Tavernake confessed, shortly. "I know I was a fool—a fool! If I could think of any adjective that would meet the case, I'd use it, but there it is. I chucked things and I came here. You haven't come down to tell me your opinion of me, I suppose?"

"Not by any manner of means," Pritchard admitted. "I came down first to tell you that you were a fool, if it was necessary. Since you know it, it isn't. We'll pass on to the next stage, and that is, what are you going to do about it?"

"It is in my mind at the present moment," Tavernake

announced, "to leave here. The only trouble is, I am not very keen about London."

Pritchard nodded thoughtfully.

"That's all right," he agreed. "London's no place for a man, anyway. You don't want to learn the usual tricks of money-making. Money that's made in the cities is mostly made with stained fingers. I have a different sort of proposal to make."

"Go ahead," Tavernake said. "What is it?"

"A new country," Pritchard declared, altering the angle of his cigar, "a virgin land, mountains and valleys, great rivers to be crossed, all sorts of cold and heat to be borne with, a land rich with minerals—some say gold, but never mind that. There is oil in parts, there's tin, there's coal, and there's thousands and thousands of miles of forest. You're a surveyor?"

"Passed all my exams," Tavernake agreed tersely.

"You are the man for out yonder," Pritchard insisted. "I've two years' vacation—dead sick of this city life I am—and I am going to put you on the track of it. You don't know much about prospecting yet, I reckon?"

"Nothing at all!"

"You soon shall," Pritchard went on. "We'll start from Winnipeg. A few horses, some guides, and a couple of tents. We'll spend twenty weeks, my friend, without seeing a town. What do you think of that?"

"Gorgeous!" Tavernake muttered.

"Twenty weeks we'll strike westward. I know the way to set about the whole job. I know one or two of the capitalists, too, and if we don't map out some of the grandest estates in British Columbia, why, my name ain't Pritchard."

"But I haven't a penny in the world," Tavernake objected.

"That's where you're lying," Pritchard remarked, pulling a newspaper from his pocket. "See the advertisement for yourself: 'Leonard Tavernake, something to his advantage.' Well, down I went to those lawyers—your old lawyer it was—Martin.

I told him I was on your track, and he said—'For Heaven's sake, send the fellow along!' Say, Tavernake, he made me laugh the way he described your bursting in upon him and telling him to take your land for his costs, and walking out of the room like something almighty. Why, he worked that thing so that they had to buy your land, and they took him into partnership. He's made a pot of money, and needs no costs from you, and there's the money for your land and what he had of yours besides, waiting for you."

Tavernake smoked stolidly at his pipe. His eyes were out seaward, but his heart was beating to a new and splendid music. To start life again, a man's life, out in the solitudes, out in the great open spaces! It was gorgeous, this! He turned round and grasped Pritchard by the shoulder.

"I say," he exclaimed, "why are you doing all this for me, Pritchard?"

Pritchard laughed.

"You did me a good turn," he said, "and you're a man. You've the pluck—that's what I like. You knew nothing, you were as green and ignorant as a young man from behind the counter of a country shop, but, my God! you'd got the right stuff, and I meant getting even with you if I could. You'll leave here with me to-morrow, and in three weeks we sail."

Ruth came smiling out from the house.

"Won't you bring your friend in to supper, Mr. Tavernake?" she begged. "It's good news, I hope?" she added, lowering her voice a little.

"It's the best," Tavernake declared, "the best!"

CHAPTER V. BEATRICE REFUSES

A week later Tavernake was in London. A visit to his friend Mr. Martin had easily proved the truth of Pritchard's words, and he found himself in possession of a sum of money at least twice as great as he had anticipated. He stayed at a cheap hotel in the Strand and made purchases under Pritchard's supervision. For the first few days he was too busy for reflection. Then Pritchard let him alone while he ran over to Paris, and Tavernake suddenly realized that he was in the city to which he had thought never to return. He passed the back of the theatre where he had waited for Beatrice, he looked up at the entrance of the Milan Court; he lunched alone, and with a curious mixture of feelings, at the little restaurant where he had supped with Beatrice. It was over, that part of his life, over and finished. Yet, with his natural truthfulness, he never attempted to disguise from himself the pain at his heart. Three times in one day he found himself, under some pretext or another, in Imano's Restaurant. Once, in the middle of the street, he burst into a fit of laughter. It was while Pritchard was in London, and he asked him a question.

"Pritchard," he remarked, "you area man of experience. Did any one ever care for two women at the same time?"

Pritchard removed his cigar from his teeth and stared at his companion.

"Why, my young friend," he replied, "I've found no trouble myself in being fond of a dozen."

Tavernake smiled and said no more. Pritchard was one of the good fellows of the world, but there were things which were hidden from him. Yet Tavernake, who had fallen into a habit, during his solitude, of analyzing his sensations, was puzzled by this one circumstance, that when he thought of Elizabeth, though his heart never failed to beat more quickly, the sense of shame generally stole over him; and when he thought of Beatrice, a curious loneliness, a loneliness that brought with it a pain, seemed suddenly to make the hours drag and his pleasures flavorless. For two days he was puzzled. Then his habit of taking long walks helped him toward a solution. In a small outlying music-hall in the east-end of London, he saw the same announcement that he had noticed in the Norfolk newspaper, —"Professor Franklin" in large type, and "Miss Beatrice Franklin" in small.

That night he attended the music-hall. The scene was practically a repetition of the one in Norwich, only with additions. The professor's bombastic performance met with scarcely any applause. Its termination was, indeed, interrupted by catcalls and whistles from the gallery. Beatrice's songs, on the other hand, were applauded more vociferously than ever. She had hard work to avoid a third encore.

At the end of the performance, Tavernake made his way to the stage-door and waited. The neighborhood was an unsavory one, and the building itself seemed crowded in among a row of shops of the worst order, fish stalls, and a glaring gin palace. Long before Beatrice came out, Tavernake could hear the professor's voice down the covered passage, the professor's voice apparently raised in anger.

"Undutiful behavior, that's what I call it—undutiful!"

They emerged into the street, the professor very much the same as usual; Beatrice paler, with a pathetic droop about her mouth. Tavernake came eagerly forward.

"Beatrice!" he cried, holding out his hand.

The professor drew back. Beatrice stood still,—for a moment it seemed as though she were about to faint. Tavernake grasped her hands.

"I am so sorry!" he exclaimed, clumsily. "I ought not to have come up like that."

She smiled a little wan smile.

"I am quite all right," she replied, "only the heat inside was rather trying, and even out here the atmosphere isn't too good, is it? How did you find us out?"

"By chance again," Tavernake answered. "I have news. May I walk with you a few steps?"

She glanced timidly toward her father. The professor was holding aloof in dignified silence.

"Perhaps," Tavernake said quickly, "you would take supper with me? I am going abroad, and I should like to say good-bye properly. A bottle of champagne and some supper. What do you say, Professor?"

The professor suffered his features to relax.

"A very admirable idea," he declared. "Where shall we go?"

"Is it too late to get to Imano's?" Tavernake suggested.

The professor hesitated.

"A taxicab," he remarked, "would do it, if—"

He paused, and Tavernake smiled.

"A taxicab it shall be," he decided. "I am in funds just for the moment. Come along, both of you, and I'll tell you all about it."

He made her take his arm, although her fingers did no more than touch his coat sleeve.

"Pritchard came and dug me out," he continued. "I am going abroad with him. It's sort of prospecting in some new country at the back of British Columbia. We see what we can find and then go to a financier's and start companies, mining companies and oil fields—anything. I am off in a week."

Beatrice half closed her eyes. They had hailed a passing cab and she sank back among the cushions with a sigh of relief.

"Dear Leonard," she murmured, "I am so glad, so very happy for your sake. This is the sort of thing which I hoped would happen."

"And now tell me about yourselves," he went on.

There was a sudden silence. Tavernake was conscious that Beatrice's clothes were distinctly shabbier, that the professor's hat was shiny. The professor cleared his throat.

"I do not wish," he said, "to intrude our private matters upon one who, although I will not call him a stranger, is assuredly not one of our old friends. At the same time, I admit that a little trouble has arisen between Beatrice and myself, and we were discussing it at the moment you arrived. I shall appeal to you now. As an unprejudiced member of the audience to-night, Mr. Tavernake, you will give me your honest opinion?"

"Certainly," Tavernake promised, with a sinking premonition of what was to come.

"What I complain of," the professor began, speaking with elaborate and impressive slowness, "is that my performance is hurried over and that too long a time is taken up by Beatrice's songs. The management remark upon the applause which her efforts occasionally ensure, but, as I would point out to you, sir," he continued, "a performance such as mine makes too deep an impression for the audience to show their appreciation of it by such vulgar methods as hand-clapping and whistling. You follow me, I trust, Mr. Tavernake?"

"Why, yes, of course," Tavernake admitted.

"I take a sincere and earnest interest in my work," the professor declared, "and I feel that when it has to be scamped that my daughter may sing a music-hall ditty, the result is, to say the least of it, undignified. For some reason or other, I have been unable to induce the management to see entirely with me, but my point is that Beatrice should sing one song only, and that the additional ten minutes should be occupied by me in either a further exposition of my extraordinary powers as a hypnotist, or in a little address to the audience upon the hidden sciences. Now I appeal to you, Mr. Tavernake, as a young man of common sense. What is your opinion?"

Tavernake, much too honest to be capable in a general way of duplicity, was on the point of giving it, but he caught Beatrice's imploring gaze. Her lips were moving. He hesitated.

"Of course," he began, slowly, "you have to try and put yourself into the position of the major part of the audience, who are exceedingly uneducated people. It is very hard to give an opinion, Professor. I must say that your entertainment this evening was listened to with rapt interest."

The professor turned solemnly towards his daughter.

"You hear that, Beatrice?" he said severely. "You hear what Mr. Tavernake says? 'With rapt interest!'"

"At the same time," Tavernake went on, "without a doubt Miss Beatrice's songs were also extremely popular. It is rather a pity that the management could not give you a little more time."

"Failing that, sir," the professor declared, "my point is, as I explained before, that Beatrice should give up one of her songs. What you have said this evening more than ever confirms me in my view."

Beatrice smiled thankfully at Tavernake.

"Well," she suggested, "at any rate we will leave it for the present. Sometimes I think, though, father, that you frighten them with some of your work, and you must remember that they come to be amused."

"That," the professor admitted, "is the most sensible remark you have made, Beatrice. There is indeed something terrifying in some of my manifestations, terrifying even to myself, who understand so thoroughly my subject. However, as you say, we will dismiss the matter for the present. The thought of this supper party is a pleasant one. Do you remember, Mr. Tavernake, the night when you and I met in the balcony at Imano's?"

"Perfectly well," Tavernake answered.

"Now I shall test your memory," the professor continued, with a knowing smile. "Can you remember, sir, the brand of champagne which I was then drinking, and which I declared, if you recollect, was the one which best agreed with me, the one brand worth drinking?"

"I am afraid I don't remember that," Tavernake confessed. "Restaurant life is a thing I know so little of, and I have only drunk champagne once or twice in my life."

"Dear, dear me!" the professor exclaimed. "You do astonish me, sir. Well, that brand was Veuve Clicquot, and you may take my word for it, Mr. Tavernake, and you may find this knowledge useful to you when you have made a fortune in America and have become a man of pleasure; there is no wine equal to it. Veuve Clicquot, sir, if possible of the year 1899, though the year 1900 is quite drinkable."

"Veuve Clicquot," Tavernake repeated. "I'll remember it for this evening."

The professor beamed.

"My dear," he said to Beatrice, "Mr. Tavernake will think that I had a purpose in testing his memory."

Beatrice smiled.

"And hadn't you, father?" she asked.

They all laughed together.

"Well, it is pleasant," the professor admitted, "to have one's weaknesses ministered to, especially when one is getting on in life," he added, with a ponderous sigh. "Never mind, we will think only of pleasant subjects this evening. It will be quite interesting, Mr. Tavernake, to hear you order the supper."

"I sha'n't attempt it," Tavernake answered. "I shall pass it on to you."

"This reminds me," the professor declared, "of the old days. I feel sure that this is going to be a thoroughly enjoyable evening. We shall think of it often, Mr. Tavernake, when you lie sleeping under the stars. Why, what a wonderful thing these taxicabs are! You see, we have arrived."

They secured a small table in a corner at Imano's, and Tavernake found himself curiously moved as he watched Beatrice take off her worn and much mended gloves and look around uneasily at the other guests. Her clothes were indeed shabby, and there were hollows now in her cheeks.

Again he felt that pain, a pain for which he could not account. Suddenly America seemed so far away, the loneliness of the great continent became an actual and appreciable thing. The professor was very much occupied ordering the supper. Tavernake leaned across the table.

"Do you remember our first supper here, Beatrice?" he asked.

She nodded, with an attempt at brightness which was a little pitiful.

"Yes," she replied, "I remember it quite well. And now, please, Leonard, don't talk to me again until I have had a glass of wine. I am tired and worn out, that is all."

Even Tavernake knew that she was struggling against the tears which already dimmed her eyes. He filled her glass himself. The professor set his own down empty with the satisfied smile of a connoisseur.

"I think," he said, "that you will agree with me about this vintage. Beatrice, this is what will bring color into your cheeks. My little girl," he continued, turning to Tavernake, "will soon need a holiday. I am hoping presently to be able to arrange a short tour by myself, and if so, I shall send her to the seaside. Now I want you particularly to try the fish salad—the second dish there. Beatrice, let me help you."

Presently the orchestra began to play. The warmth of the room, the wine and the food—Tavernake had a horrible idea once that she had eaten nothing that day—brought back some of the color to Beatrice's cheeks and a little of the light to her eyes. She began to talk something in the old fashion. She avoided, however, any mention of that other supper they had had together. As time went on, the professor, who had drunk the best part of two bottles of wine and was talking now to a friend, became almost negligible. Tavernake leaned across the table.

"Beatrice," he whispered, "you are not looking well. I am

afraid that life is getting harder with you."

She shook her head.

"I am doing what I must," she answered. "Please don't sympathize with me. I am hysterical, I think, tonight. It will pass off."

"But, Beatrice," he ventured, timidly, "could one do nothing for you? I don't like these performances, and between you and me, we know they won't stand your father's show much longer. It will certainly come to an end soon. Why don't you try and get back your place at the theatre? You could still earn enough to keep him."

"Already I have tried," she replied, sorrowfully. "My place is filled up. You see," she added, with a forced laugh, "I have lost some of my looks, Leonard. I am thinner, too. Of course, I shall be all right presently, but it's rather against me at these west-end places."

Again he felt that pain at his heart. He was sure now that he was beginning to understand!

"Beatrice," he whispered, "give it up—marry me I will take care of him."

The flush of color faded from her cheeks. She shivered a little and looked at him piteously.

"Leonard," she pleaded, "you mustn't. I really am not very strong just now. We have finished with all that—it distresses me."

"But I mean it," he begged. "Somehow, I have felt all sorts of things since we came in here. I think of that night, and I believe—I do believe that what came to me before was madness. It was not the same."

She was trembling now.

"Leonard," she implored, "if you care for me at all, be quiet. Father will turn round directly and I can't bear it. I shall be your very faithful friend; I shall think of you through the long days before we meet again, but don't—don't spoil this last evening."

The professor turned round, his face mottled, his eyes moist, a great good-humor apparent in his tone.

"Well, I must say," he declared, "that this has been a most delightful evening. I feel immensely better, and you, too, I hope, Beatrice?"

She nodded, smiling.

"I trust that when Mr. Tavernake returns," the professor continued, "he will give us the opportunity of entertaining him in much the same manner. It will give me very much pleasure, also Beatrice. And if, sir," he proceeded, "during your stay in New York you will mention my name at the Goat's Club, or the Mosquito Club, you will, I think, find yourself received with a hospitality which will surprise you."

Tavernake thanked him and paid the bill. They walked slowly down the room, and Tavernake was curiously reluctant to release the little hand which clasped his.

"I have kept this to the last," Beatrice said, in a low tone. "Elizabeth is in London."

He was curiously unmoved.

"Yes?" he murmured.

"I should like you—I think it would be well for you to go and see her," she went on. "You know, Leonard, you were such a strange person in those days. You may imagine things. You may not realize where you are. I think that you ought to go and see her now, now that you have lived through some suffering, now that you understand things better. Will you?"

"Yes, I will go," Tavernake promised.

Beatrice glanced round towards where her father was standing.

"I don't want him to know," she whispered. "I don't want either him or myself to be tempted to take any of her money. She is living at Claridge's Hotel. Go there and see her before you leave for your new life."

He stood at the door and watched them go down the Strand, the professor, flamboyant, walking erect with flying coat-tails, and his big cigar held firmly between his teeth; Beatrice, a wan figure in her black clothes, clinging to his arm. Tavernake watched them until they disappeared, conscious of a curious excitement, a strange pain, a sense of revelation. When at last they were out of sight and he turned back for his coat and hat, his feet were suddenly leaden. The band was playing the last selection—it was the air which Beatrice had sung only that night at the east-end music-hall. With a sudden overpowering impulse he turned and strode down the Strand in the direction where they had vanished. It was too late. There was no sign of them.

CHAPTER VI. UNDERSTANDING COMES TOO LATE

Tavernake's first impression of Elizabeth was that he had never, even in his wildest thoughts, done her justice. He had never imagined her so wonderfully, so alluringly beautiful. She had received him, after a very long delay, in her sitting-room at Claridge's Hotel—a large apartment furnished more like a drawing-room. She was standing, when he entered, almost in the center of the room, dressed in a long lace cloak and a hat with a drooping black feather. She looked at him, as the door opened, as though for a moment half puzzled. Then she laughed softly and held out her hands.

"Why, of course I remember you!" she exclaimed. "And to think that when I had your card I couldn't imagine where I had heard the name before! You are my dear estate agent's clerk, who wouldn't take my money, and who was so wretchedly rude to me twelve months ago."

Tavernake was quite cool. He found himself wondering whether this was a pose, or whether she had indeed forgotten. He decided that it was a pose.

"I was also," he reminded her, "one night in your rooms at the Milan Court when your husband—"

She stopped him with an imperative gesture.

"Spare me, please," she begged. "Those were such terrible days—so dull, too! I remember that you were quite one of the brightest spots. You were absolutely different from every one I had ever met before, and you interested me immensely."

She looked at him and slowly shook her head.

"You look very nice," she said. "Your clothes fit you and you are most becomingly tanned, but you don't look half so awkward and so adorable."

"I am sorry," he replied, shortly.

"And you came to see me!" she went on. "That was really nice of you. You were quite fond of me, once, you know. Tell me, has it lasted?"

"That is exactly what I came to find out," he answered deliberately. "So far, I am inclined to think that it has not lasted."

She made a little wry face and drew his arm through hers.

"Come and sit down and tell me why," she insisted. "Be honest, now. Is it because you think I am looking older?"

"I have thought of you for many hours a day for months," Tavernake said, slowly, "and I never imagined you so beautiful as you seem now."

She clapped her hands.

"And you mean it, too!" she exclaimed. "There is just the same delightfully convincing note in your tone. I am sure that you mean it. Please go on adoring me, Mr. Tavernake. I have no one who interests me at all just now. There is an Italian Count who wants to marry me, but he is terribly poor; and a young Australian, who follows me everywhere, but I am not sure about him. There is an English boy, too, who is going to commit suicide if I don't say 'yes' to him this week. On the whole, I think I am rather sorry that people know I am a widow. Tell me, Mr. Tavernake, are you going to adore me, too?"

"I don't think so," Tavernake answered. "I rather believe that I am cured."

She shrugged her shoulders and laughed musically.

"But you say that you still think I am beautiful," she went on, "and I am sure my clothes are perfect—they came straight from Paris. I hope you appreciate this lace," she added, drawing it through her fingers. "My figure is just as good, too, isn't it?"

She stood up and turned slowly round. Then she sat down suddenly, taking his hand in hers.

"Please don't say that you think I have grown less attractive," she begged.

"As regards your personal attractions," Tavernake replied, "I imagine that they are at least as great as ever. If you want the truth, I think that the reason I do not adore you any longer is because I saw your sister last night."

"Saw Beatrice!" she exclaimed. "Where?"

"She was singing at a miserable east-end music-hall so that her father might find some sort of employment," Tavernake said. "The people only forbore to hiss her father's turn for her sake. She goes about the country with him. Heaven knows what they earn, but it must be little enough! Beatrice is shabby and thin and pale. She is devoting the best years of her life to what she imagines to be her duty."

"And how does this affect me?" Elizabeth asked, coldly.

"Only in this way," Tavernake answered. "You asked me how it was that I could find you as beautiful as ever and adore you no longer. The reason is because I know you to be wretchedly selfish. I believed in you before. Everything that you did seemed right. That was because I was a fool, because you had filled my brain with impossible fancies, because I saw you and everything that you did through a distorted mirror."

"Have you come here to be rude?" she asked him.

"Not in the least," he replied. "I came here to see whether I was cured."

She began to laugh, very softly at first, but soon she threw herself back among the cushions and laid her hand caressingly upon his shoulder.

"Oh, you are just the same!" she cried. "Just the same dear, truthful bundle of honesty and awkwardness and ignorance. So you are going to be victim of Beatrice's bow and spear, after all."

"I have asked your sister to marry me," Tavernake admitted. "She will not."

"She was very wise," Elizabeth declared, wiping the tears from her eyes. "As an experience you are delightful. As a husband you would be terribly impossible. Are you going to stay and take me out to dinner this evening? I'm sure you have a dress suit now."

Tavernake shook his head.

"I am sorry," he said. "I have already an engagement."

She looked at him curiously. Was it really true that he had become indifferent? She was not used to men who escaped.

"Tell me," she asked, abruptly, "why did you come? I don't understand. You are here, and you pass your time being rude to me. I ask you to take me to dinner and you refuse. Do you know that scarcely a man in London would not have jumped at such a chance?"

"Very likely," Tavernake answered. "I have no experience in such matters. I only know that I am going to do something else."

"Something you want to do very much?" she whispered.

"I am going down to a little music-hall in Whitechapel," Tavernake said, "and I am going to meet your sister and I am going to put her in a cab and take her to have some supper, and I am going to worry her until she promises to be my wife."

"You are certainly a devoted admirer of the family," she laughed. "Perhaps you were in love with her all the time."

"Perhaps I was," he admitted.

She shook her head.

"I don't believe it," she said. "I think you were quite fond of me once. You have such absurdly old-fashioned ideas or I think that you would be fond of me now."

Tavernake rose to his feet.

"I am going," he declared. "This will be good-bye. To-morrow I am going to British Columbia."

The laughter faded for a moment from her face. She was suddenly serious.

"Don't go," she begged. "Listen. I know I am not good like Beatrice, but I do like you—I always did. I suppose it is that wonderful truthfulness of yours. You are a different type from the men one meets. I am rather a reckless person. It is such a comfort sometimes to meet any one like you. You seem such an anchorage. Stay and talk to me for a little time. Take me out to-night. You asked me to go with you once, you know, and I would not. To-night it is I who ask you."

He shook his head slowly.

"This is good-bye!" he said, firmly. "I suppose, after all, you were not unkind to me in those days, but you taught me a very bitter lesson. I came to you to-day in fear and trembling. I was afraid, perhaps, that the worst was not over, that there was more yet to come. Now I know that I am free."

She stamped her foot.

"You shall not go away like that," she declared.

He smiled.

"Do you think I do not understand?" he continued. "It is only because I am able to go, because the touch of your fingers, that look in your eyes, do not drive me half mad now, that you want me to stay. You would like to try your powers once more. I think not. I am satisfied that I am cured indeed, but perhaps it is safer to risk nothing."

She pointed to the door.

"Very well, then," she ordered, "you can go."

He bowed, and already his fingers were on the handle. Suddenly she called to him.

"Leonard! Leonard!"

He turned round. She was coming towards him with her arms outstretched, her eyes were full of tears, there were sobs in her voice.

"I am so lonely," she begged. "I have thought of you so much. Don't go away unkindly. Stay with me for this evening, at any rate. You can see Beatrice at any time. It is I who need you most now."

He looked around at the splendid apartment; he looked at the woman whose fingers, glittering with jewels, rested upon his shoulders. Then he thought of Beatrice in her shabby black gown and wan little face, and very gently he removed her hands.

"No," he said, "I do not think that you need me any more than I need you. This is a caprice of yours. You know it and I know it. Is it worth while to play with one another?"

Her hands fell to her sides. She turned half away but she said nothing. Tavernake, with a sudden impulse which had in it nothing of passion—very little, indeed, of affection—lifted her fingers to his lips and passed out of the room. He descended the stairs, filled with a wonderful sense of elation, a buoyancy of spirit which he could not understand. As he walked blithely to his hotel, however, he began to realize how much he had dreaded this interview. He was a free man, after all. The spell was broken. He could think of her now as she deserved to be thought of, as a consummate woman of the world, selfish, heartless, conscienceless. He was well out of her toils. It was nothing to him if even he had known that at that moment she was lying upon the sofa to which she had staggered as he left the room, weeping bitterly.

For over an hour Tavernake endured the smells and the bad atmosphere of that miserable little music-hall, watching eagerly each time the numbers were changed. Then at last, towards the end of the program, the manager appeared in front.

"Ladies and gentlemen," he announced, "I regret very much to inform you that owing to the indisposition of the young lady, Miss Beatrice Franklin and her father are unable to appear to-night. I have pleasure in announcing an extra turn, namely the Sisters De Vere in their wonderful burlesque act."

There was a murmur of disapprobation mingled with some cheering. Tavernake left his place and walked around to the back of the hall. Presently the manager came out to him.

"I am sorry to trouble you, sir," Tavernake said, "but I heard your announcement just now from the front. Can you give me the address of Professor Franklin? I am a friend, and I should like to go and see them."

The manager pointed to the stage-doorkeeper.

"This man will give it you," he announced, shortly. "It's quite close. I shall look in myself after the show to know how the young lady is."

Tavernake procured the address and set out in the taxicab which he had kept waiting. The driver listened to the direction doubtfully.

"It's a poor sort of neighborhood, sir," he remarked.

"We've got to go there," Tavernake told him.

They reached it in a few minutes, a miserable street indeed. Tavernake knocked at the door of the house to which he was directed, with sinking heart. A man, collarless and half dressed, in carpet slippers, opened the door after a few moments' waiting.

"Well, what is it?" he asked, gruffly.

"Is Professor Franklin here?" Tavernake inquired.

The man seemed as though he were about to slam the door, but thought better of it.

"If you're a friend of the professor's, as he calls himself," he said, "and you've any money to shell out, why, you're welcome, but if you're only asking out of curiosity, let me tell you that he used to lodge here but he's gone, and if I'd had my way he'd have gone a week ago, him and his daughter, too."

"I don't understand," Tavernake protested. "I thought the young lady was ill."

"She may be ill or she may not," the man replied, sulkily. "All I know is that they couldn't pay their rent, couldn't pay their food bill, couldn't pay for the drinks the old man was always sending out for. So tonight I spoke up and they've gone."

"At least you know where to!" Tavernake exclaimed.

"I ain't no sort of an idea," the man declared. "Take my word for it straight, guvnor, I know no more about where they went to than the man in the moon, except that I'm well shut of them, and there's a matter of eighteen and sixpence, if you care to pay it."

"I'll give you a sovereign," Tavernake promised, "if you will tell me where they are now."

"What's the good of making silly conditions like that!" the man grumbled. "If I knew where they were, I'd earn the quid soon enough, but I don't, and that's the long and the short of it! And if you ain't going to pay the eighteen and six, well, I've answered all the questions I feel inclined to."

"I'll make it two pounds," Tavernake promised. "I'm going to sail for America to-morrow morning early, and I must see them first."

The man leaned forward.

"Look here," he said, "if I knew where they was, a quid would be quite good enough for me, but I don't, and that's straight. If you want to look for them, I should try one of the doss houses. As likely there as anywhere."

He slammed the door and Tavernake turned away. A sudden despair had seized him. He looked up and down the street, he looked away beyond and thought of the miles and miles of streets, the myriads of chimneys, the huge branches of the great city stretching far and wide. At eight o'clock the next morning, he must leave for Southampton. Was it too late, after all, that he had discovered the truth?

CHAPTER VII. IN A VIRGIN COUNTRY

One night Tavernake began to laugh. He had grown a long brown beard and the hair was over his ears. He was wearing a gray flannel shirt, a handkerchief tied around his neck, and a pair of worn riding breeches held up by a belt. He had kicked his boots off at the end of a long day, and was lying in the moonlight before a fire of pine logs, whose smoke went straight to the star-hung sky. No word had been spoken for the last hour. Tavernake's fit of mirth came with as little apparent reason as the puffs of wind which every now and then stole down from the mountain side and made faint music in the virgin forests.

Pritchard turned over on his side and looked at him. Cigars had for many weeks been an unknown thing, and he was smoking a corn-cob pipe full of coarse tobacco.

"Stumbled across a joke anywhere?" he asked.

"I'm afraid no one but myself would see the humor of it," Tavernake answered. "I was thinking of those days in London; I was thinking of Beatrice's horror when she discovered that I was wearing ready-made clothes, and the amazement of Elizabeth when she found that I hadn't a dress suit. It's odd how cramped life gets back there."

Pritchard nodded, pressing the tobacco down into the bowl of his pipe with his forefinger.

"You're right, Tavernake," he agreed. "One loses one's sense of proportion. Men in the cities are all alike. They go about in disguise."

"I should like," Tavernake said, inconsequently, "to have Mr. Dowling out here."

"Amusing fellow?" Pritchard inquired.

Tavernake shook his head, smiling.

"Not in the least," he answered, "only he was a very small man. Out here it is difficult to keep small. Don't you feel it, Pritchard? These mountains make our hills at home seem like dust-heaps. The skies seem loftier. Look down into that valley.

It's gigantic, immense."

Pritchard yawned.

"There's a little place in the Bowery," he began,—

"Oh, I don't want to know any more about New York," Tavernake interrupted. "Lean back and close your eyes, smell the cinnamon trees, listen to that night bird calling every now and then across the ravine. There's blackness, if you like; there's depth. It's like a cloak of velvet to look into. But you can't see the bottom—no, not in the daytime. Listen!"

Pritchard sat up. For a few moments neither spoke. A dozen yards or so off, a scattered group—the rest of the party— were playing cards around a fire. The green wood crackled, an occasional murmur of voices, a laugh or an exclamation, came to their ears, but for the rest, an immense, a wonderful silence, a silence which seemed to spread far away over that weird, half-invisible world! Tavernake listened reverently.

"Isn't it marvelous!" he exclaimed. "We haven't seen a human being except our own party, for three days. There probably isn't one within hearing of us now. Very likely no living person has ever set foot in this precise spot."

"Oh, it's big," Pritchard admitted, "it's big and it's restful, but it isn't satisfying. It does for you for a time because you started life wrong and you needed a reaction. But for me—ah, well!" he added, "I hear the call right across these thousands of miles of forests and valley and swamp. I hear the electric cars and the clash of the overhead railway, I see the flaring lights of Broadway and I hear the babel of tongues. I am going back to it, Tavernake. There's plenty to go on with. We've done more than carry out our program."

"Back to New York!" Tavernake muttered, disconsolately.

"So you're not ready yet?" Pritchard demanded.

"Heavens, no!" Tavernake answered. "Who would be? What is there in New York to make up for this?"

Pritchard was silent for a moment.

"Well," he said, "one of us must be getting back near civilization. The syndicate will be expecting to hear from us. Besides, we've reports enough already. It's time something was decided about that oil country. We've done some grand work there, Tavernake."

Tavernake nodded. He was lying on his side and his eyes were fixed wistfully southward, over the glimmering moonlit valley, over the great wilderness of virgin pine woods which hung from the mountains on the other side, away through the cleft in the hills to the plains beyond, chaotic, a world unseen.

"If you like to go on for a bit," Pritchard suggested, slowly, "there's no reason why you shouldn't take McCleod and Richardson with you, and Pete and half the horses, and strike for the tin country on the other side of the Yolite Hills. So long as we are here, it's quite worth it, if you can stick it out."

Tavernake drew a long breath.

"I'd like to go," he admitted, simply. "I know McCleod is keen about prospecting further south. You see, most of our finds so far have been among the oil fields."

"Settled," Pritchard declared. "To-morrow, then, we part. I'm for the valley, and I reckon I'll strike the railway to Chicago in a week. Gee whiz! New York will seem good!"

"You think that the syndicate will be satisfied with what we have done so far?" Tavernake asked.

His companion smiled.

"If they aren't, they'll be fools. I reckon there's enough oil fields here for seven companies. There'll be a bit for us, too, Tavernake, I guess. Don't you want to come back to New York and spend it?"

Tavernake laughed once more, but this time his laugh was not wholly natural.

"Spend it!" he repeated. "What is there to spend it on? Uncomfortable clothes, false plays, drinks that are bad for you, food that's half poisoned, atmosphere that stifles. My God, Pritchard, is there anything in the world like this! Stretch out your arms, man. Lie on your back, look up at the stars, let that wind blow over your face. Listen."

They listened, and again they heard nothing, yet again there seemed to be that peculiar quality about the silence which spoke of the vastness of space.

Pritchard rose to his feet.

"New York and the fleshpots for me," he declared. "Keep in touch, and good luck old man!"

Next day at dawn they parted, and Tavernake, with his three companions, set his face towards an almost undiscovered tract of land. Their progress was slow, for they were all the time in a country rich with possibilities. For weeks they climbed, climbed till they reached the snows and the wind stung their faces and they shivered in their rugs at night. They came to a land of sparser vegetation, of fewer and wilder animals, where they heard the baying of wolves at night, and saw the eyes of strange animals glisten through the thicket as the flames of their evening fire shot up toward the sky. Then the long descent began, the long descent to the great plain. Now their faces were bronzed with a sun ever hotter, ever more powerful. No longer the snow flakes beat their cheeks. They came slowly down into a land which seemed to Tavernake like the biblical land of Canaan. Three times in ten days they had to halt and make a camp, while Tavernake prepared a geographical survey of likely-looking land.

McCleod came up to Tavernake one day with a dull-looking lump in his hand, glistening in places.

"Copper," he announced, shortly. "It's what I've been looking for all the time. No end to it. There's something bigger than oil here."

They spent a month in the locality, and every day McCleod became more enthusiastic. After that it was hard work to keep him from heading homeward at once.

"I tell you, sir," he explained to Tavernake, "there's millions there, millions between those four stakes of yours. What's the good of more prospecting? There's enough there in a square acre to pay the expenses of our expedition a thousand times over. Let's get back and make reports. We can strike the railway in ten days from here—perhaps sooner."

"You go," Tavernake said. "Leave me Pete and two of the horses."

The man stared at him in surprise.

"What's the good of going on alone?" he asked. "You're not a mining expert or an oil man. You can't go prospecting by yourself."

"I can't help it," Tavernake answered. "It's something in my blood, I suppose. I am going on. Think! You'll strike that railway and in a month you will be back in New York. Don't you imagine, when you're there, when you hear the clatter and turmoil of it, when you see the pale crowds chivvying one another about to pick the dollars from each other's pockets,— don't you believe you'll long for these solitudes, the big empty places, great possibilities, the silence? Think of it, man. What is there beyond those mountains, I wonder?"

McCleod sighed.

"You're right," he said. "One may never get so far out again. Our fortunes will keep, I suppose, and anyhow we ought to strike a telegraph station in about a fortnight. We'll go right ahead, then."

In ten days they dropped ten thousand feet. They came to a land where their throats were always dry, where the trees and shrubs seemed like property affairs from a theatre, where they plunged their heads into every pool that came to wash their noses and mouths from the red dust that seemed to choke them up. They found tin and oil and more copper. Then, by slow stages, they passed on to a land of great grassy plains, of blue grass, miles and miles of it, and suddenly one day they came to the telegraph posts, rough pine trees unstripped of their bark, with a few sagging wires. Tavernake looked at them as Robinson Crusoe might have looked at Man Friday's footsteps. It was the first sign of human life which they had seen for months.

"It's a real world we are in, after all!" he sighed. "Somehow or other, I thought—I thought we'd escaped."

CHAPTER VIII. BACK TO CIVILIZATION

Pritchard, trim and neat, a New Yorker from the careful arrangement of his tie to the tips of his patent boots, gazed with something like amazement at the man whom he had come to meet at the Grand Central Station. Tavernake looked, indeed, like some splendid bushman whose life has been spent in the kingdom of the winds and the sun and the rain. He was inches broader round the chest, and carried himself with a new freedom. His face was bronzed right down to the neck. His beard was fullgrown, his clothes travel-stained and worn. He seemed like a breath of real life in the great New York depot, surrounded by streams of black-coated, pale-cheeked men.

Pritchard laughed softly as he passed his arm through his friend's.

"Come, my Briton," he said, "my primitive man, I have rooms for you in a hotel close here. A bath and a mint julep, then I'll take you to a tailor's. What about the big country? It's better than your salt marshes, eh? Better than your little fishing village? Better than building boats?"

"You know it," Tavernake answered. "I feel as though I'd been drawing in life for month after month. Have I got to wear boots like yours—patent?"

"Got to be done," Pritchard declared.

"And the hat—oh, my Heavens!" Tavernake groaned. "I'll never become civilized again."

"We'll see," Pritchard laughed. "Say, Tavernake, it was a great trip of ours. Everything's turning out marvelously. The oil and the copper are big, man—big, I tell you. I reckon your five thousand dollars will be well on the way to half a million. I'm pretty near there myself."

It was not until later on, when he was alone, that Tavernake realized with how little interest he listened to his companion's talk of their success. It was so short a time ago since the building up of a fortune had been the one aim upon which every nerve of his body was centered. Curiously enough, now he seemed to take it as a matter of course.

"On second thoughts, I'll send a tailor round to the hotel," Pritchard declared. "I've rooms myself next yours. We can go out and buy boots and the other things afterwards."

By nightfall, Tavernake's wardrobe was complete. Even Pritchard regarded him with a certain surprise. He seemed, somehow, to have gained a new dignity.

"Say, but you look great!" he exclaimed. "They won't believe it at the meeting to-morrow that you are the man who crossed the Yolite Mountains and swam the Peraneek River. That's a wonderful country you were in, Tavernake, after you left the tracks."

They were in Broadway, with the roar of the city in their ears, and Tavernake, lifting his face starwards, suddenly seemed to feel the silence once more, the perfume of the pine woods, the scent of nature herself, freed through all these generations of any presence of man.

"I'll never keep away from it," he said, softly. "I'll have to go back."

Pritchard smiled.

"When your report's in shape and the dollars are being scooped in, they'll send you back fast enough—that is, if you still want to go," he remarked. "I tell you, Leonard Tavernake, our city men here are out for the dollars. Over on your side, a man makes a million or so and he's had enough. One fortune here only seems to whet the appetite of a New Yorker. By the way," he added, after a moment's hesitation, "does it interest you to know that an old friend of yours is in New York?"

Tavernake's head went round swiftly.

"Who is it?" he asked.

"Mrs. Wenham Gardner."

Tavernake set his teeth.

"No," he said, slowly, "I don't know that that interests

308

me."

"Glad of it," Pritchard went on. "I can tell you I don't think things have been going extra well with the lady. She's spent most of what she got from the Gardner family, and she doesn't seem to have had the best of luck with it, either. I came across her by accident. She is staying at a flashy hotel, but it's in the wrong quarter—second-rate—quite second-rate."

"I wonder whether we shall see anything of her," Tavernake remarked.

"Do you want to?" Pritchard asked. "She'll probably be at Martin's for lunch, at the Plaza for tea, and Rector's for supper. She's not exactly the lady to remain hidden, you know."

"We'll avoid those places, then, if you are taking me around," Tavernake said.

"You're cured, are you?" Pritchard inquired.

"Yes, I am cured," Tavernake answered, "cured of that and a great many other things, thanks to you. You found me the right tonic."

"Tonic," Pritchard repeated, meditatively. "That reminds me. This way for the best cocktail in New York."...

The night was not to pass, however, without its own especial thrill for Tavernake. The two men dined together at Delmonico's and went afterwards to a roof garden, a new form of entertainment for Tavernake, and one which interested him vastly. They secured one of the outside tables near the parapets, and below them New York stretched, a flaming phantasmagoria of lights and crude buildings. Down the broad avenues with their towering blocks, their street cars striking fire all the time like toys below, the people streamed like insects away to the Hudson, where the great ferry boats, ablaze with lights, went screaming across the dark waters. Tavernake leaned over and forgot. There was so much that was amazing in this marvelous city for a man who had only just begun to find himself.

The orchestra, stationed within a few yards of him,

commenced to play a popular waltz, and Pritchard to talk. Tavernake turned his fascinated eyes from the prospect below.

"My young friend," Pritchard said, "you are up against it to-night. Take a drink of your wine and then brace yourself."

Tavernake did as he was told.

"What is this danger?" he asked. "What's wrong, anyway?"

Pritchard had no need to answer. As Tavernake set his glass down, his eyes fell upon the little party who had just taken the table almost next to theirs. There were Walter Crease, Major Post, two men whom he had never seen before in his life—heavy of cheek, both, dull-eyed, but dressed with a rigid observance of the fashion of the city, in short dinner coats and black ties. And between them was Elizabeth. Tavernake gripped the sides of his chair and looked. Yes, she had altered. Her eyebrows were a trifle made up, there was a tinge in her hair which he did not recognize, a touch of color in her cheeks which he doubted. Yet her figure and her wonderful presence remained, that art of wearing her clothes as no other woman could. She was easily the most noticeable-looking of her sex among all the people there. Tavernake heard the sound of her voice and once more the thrill came and passed. She was the same Elizabeth. Thank God, he thought, that he was not the same Tavernake!

"Do you wish to go?" Pritchard asked.

Tavernake shook his head.

"Not I!" he answered. "This place is far too fascinating. Can't we have some more wine? This is my treat. And, Pritchard, why do you look at me like that? You are not supposing for a moment that I am capable of making an ass of myself again?"

Pritchard smiled in a relieved fashion.

"My young friend," he said, "I have lived in the world so long and seen so many strange things, especially between men and women, that I am never surprised at anything. I thought you'd shed your follies as your grip upon life had tightened, but one is never sure."

Tavernake sighed.

"Oh, I have shed the worst of my follies!" he answered. "I only wish—"

He never finished his sentence. Elizabeth had suddenly seen him. For a moment she leaned forward as though to assure herself that she was not mistaken. Then she half sprang to her feet and sat down again. Her lips were parted—she was once more bewilderingly beautiful.

"Mr. Tavernake," she cried, "come and speak to me at once."

Tavernake rose without hesitation, and walked firmly across the few yards which separated them. She held out both her hands.

"This is wonderful!" she exclaimed. "You in New York! And I have wondered so often what became of you."

Tavernake smiled.

"It is my first night here," he said. "For two years I have been prospecting in the far west."

"Then I saw your name in the papers," she declared. "It was for the Manhattan Syndicate, wasn't it?"

Tavernake nodded, and one of the men of the party leaned forward with interest.

"You're going to make millions and millions," she assured him. "You always knew you would, didn't you?"

"I am afraid that I was almost too confident," he answered. "But certainly we have been quite fortunate."

One of Elizabeth's companions intervened—he was the one who had pricked up his ears at the mention of the Manhattan Syndicate.

"Say, Elizabeth," he remarked, "I'd like to meet your friend."

Elizabeth, with a frown, performed the introduction.

"Mr. Anthony Cruxhall—Mr. Tavernake!"

Mr. Cruxhall held out a fat white hand, on the little finger of which glittered a big diamond ring.

"Say, are you the Mr. Tavernake that was surveyor to the prospecting party sent out by the Manhattan Syndicate?" he inquired.

"I was," Tavernake admitted, briefly. "I still am, I hope."

"Then you're just the man I was hoping to meet," Mr. Cruxhall declared. "Won't you sit down with us right here? I'd like to talk some about that trip. I'm interested in the Syndicate."

Tavernake shook his head.

"I've had enough of work for a time," he said. "Besides, I couldn't talk about it till after my report to the meeting to-morrow."

"Just a few words," Mr. Cruxhall persisted. "We'll have a bottle of champagne, eh?"

"You will excuse me, I am sure," Tavernake replied, "when I tell you that it would not be correct on my part to discuss my trip until after I have handed in my report to the company. I am very glad to have seen you again, Mrs. Gardner."

"But you are not going!" she exclaimed, in dismay.

"I have left Mr. Pritchard alone," Tavernake answered.

Elizabeth smiled, and waved her hand to the solitary figure.

"Our friend Mr. Pritchard again," she remarked. "Well, it is really a curious meeting, isn't it? I wonder,"—she lifted her head to his and her eyes called him closer to hers—"have you forgotten everything?"

He pointed over the roofs of the houses. His back was to the river and he pointed westward.

"I have been in a country where one forgets," he answered. "I think that I have thrown the knapsack of my follies away. I think that it is buried. There are some things which I do not forget, but they are scarcely to be spoken of."

"You are a strange young man," she said. "Was I wrong, or were you not once in love with me?"

"I was terribly in love with you," Tavernake confessed.

"Yet you tore up my cheque and flung yourself away when you found out that my standard of morals was not quite what you had expected," she murmured. "Haven't you got over that quixoticism a little, Leonard?"

He drew a deep sigh.

"I am thankful to say," he declared, earnestly, "that I have not got over it, that, if anything, my prejudices are stronger than ever."

She sat for a moment quite still, and her face had become hard and expressionless. She was looking past him, past the line of lights, out into the blue darkness.

"Somehow," she said, softly, "I always prayed that you might remember. You were the one true thing I had ever met, you were in earnest. It is past, then?"

"It is past," Tavernake answered, bravely.

The music of a Hungarian waltz came floating down to them. She half closed her eyes. Her head moved slowly with the melody. Tavernake looked away.

"Will you come and see me just once?" she asked, suddenly. "I am staying at the Delvedere, in Forty-Second Street."

"Thank you very much," Tavernake replied. "I do not know how long I shall be in New York. If I am here for a few days, I shall take my chance at finding you at home."

He bowed, and returned to Pritchard, who welcomed him with a quiet smile.

"You're wise, Tavernake," he said, softly. "I could hear no words, but I know that you have been wise. Between you and me," he added, in a lower tone, "she is going downhill. She is in with the wrong lot here. She can't seem to keep away from them. They are on the very fringe of Bohemia, a great deal nearer the arm of the law than makes for respectable society. The man to whom I saw you introduced is a millionaire one day and a thief the next. They're none of them any good. Did you notice, too, that she is wearing sham jewelry? That always looks bad."

"No, I didn't notice," Tavernake answered.

He was silent for a moment. Then he leaned a little forward.

"I wonder," he asked, "do you know anything about her sister?"

Pritchard finished his wine and knocked the ash from his cigar.

"Not much," he replied. "I believe she had a very hard time. She took on the father, you know, the old professor, and did her best to keep him straight. He died about a year ago and Miss Beatrice tried to get back into the theatre, but she'd missed her chance. Theatrical business has been shocking in London. I heard she'd come out here. Wherever she is, she keeps right away from that sort of set," he wound up, moving his head towards Elizabeth's friends.

"I wonder if she is in New York," Tavernake said, with a strange thrill at his heart.

Pritchard made no reply. His eyes were fixed upon the little group at the next table. Elizabeth was leaning back in her chair. She seemed to have abandoned the conversation. Her eyes were always seeking Tavernake's. Pritchard rose to his feet abruptly.

"It's time we were in bed," he declared. "Remember the meeting to-morrow."

Tavernake rose to his feet. As they passed the next table, Elizabeth leaned over to him. Her eyes pleaded with his almost passionately.

"Dear Leonard," she whispered, "you must—you must come and see me. I shall stay in between four and six every evening this week. The Delvedere, remember."

"Thank you very much," Tavernake answered. "I shall not forget."

CHAPTER IX. FOR ALWAYS

Once again it seemed to Beatrice that history was repeating itself. The dingy, oblong dining-room, with its mosquito netting, stained tablecloth, and hard cane chairs, expanded until she fancied herself in the drawing-room of Blenheim House. Between the landladies there was little enough to choose. Mrs. Raithby Lawrence, notwithstanding her caustic tongue and suspicious nature, had at least made some pretense at gentility. The woman who faced her now—hard-featured, with narrow, suspicious eyes and a mass of florid hair—was unmistakably and brutally vulgar.

"What's the good of your keeping on saying you hope to get an engagement next week?" she demanded, with a sneer. "Who's likely to engage you? Why, you've lost your color and your looks and your weight since you came to stay here. They don't want such as you in the chorus. And for the rest, you're too high and mighty, that's my opinion of you. Take what you can get, and how you can get it, and be thankful,—that's my motto. Day after day you tramp about the streets with your head in the air, and won't take this and won't take that, and meanwhile my bill gets bigger and bigger. Now where have you been to this morning, I should like to know?"

Beatrice, who was faint and tired, shaking in every limb, tried to pass out of the room, but her questioner barred the way.

"I have been up town," she answered, nervously.

"Hear of anything?"

Beatrice shook her head.

"Not yet. Please let me go upstairs and lie down. I am tired and I need to rest."

"And I need my money," Mrs. Selina P. Watkins declared, without quitting her position, "and it's no good your going up to your room because the door's locked."

"What do you mean?" Beatrice faltered.

"I mean that I've done with you," the lodging-house

keeper announced. "Your room's locked up and the key's in my pocket, and the sooner you get out of this, the better I shall be pleased."

"But my box—my clothes," Beatrice cried.

"I'll keep 'em a week for you," the woman answered. "Bring me the money by then and you shall have them. If I don't hear anything of you, they'll go to the auction mart."

Something of her old spirit fired the girl for a moment. She was angry, and she forgot that her knees were trembling with fatigue, that she was weak and aching with hunger.

"How dare you talk like that!" she exclaimed. "You shall have your money shortly, but I must have my clothes. I cannot go anywhere without them."

The woman laughed harshly.

"Look here, my young lady," she said, "you'll see your box again when I see the color of your money, and not before. And now out you go, please,—out you go! If you're going to make any trouble, Solly will have to show you the way down the steps."

The woman had opened the door, and a colored servant, half dressed, with a broom in her hand, came slouching down the passage. Beatrice turned and fled out of the greasy, noisome atmosphere, down the wooden, uneven steps, out into the ugly street. She turned toward the nearest elevated as though by instinct, but when she came to the bottom of the stairs she stopped short with a little groan. She knew very well that she had not a nickel to pay the fare. Her pockets were empty. All day she had eaten nothing, and her last coin had gone for the car which had brought her back from Broadway. And here she was on the other side of New York, in the region of low-class lodging houses, with the Bowery between her and Broadway. She had neither the strength nor the courage to walk. With a half-stifled sob she took off her one remaining ornament, a cheap enameled brooch, and entered a pawnbroker's shop close to where she had been standing.

"Will you give me something on this, please?" she asked, desperately.

A man who seemed to be sorting a pile of ready-made coats, paused in his task for a moment, took the ornament into his hand, and threw it contemptuously upon the counter.

"Not worth anything," he answered.

"But it must be worth something," Beatrice protested. "I only want a very little."

Something in her voice compelled the man's attention. He looked at her white face.

"What's the trouble?" he inquired.

"I must get up to Fifth Avenue somehow," she declared. "I can't walk and I haven't a nickel."

He pushed the brooch back to her and threw a dime upon the counter.

"Well," he said, "you don't look fit to walk, and that's a fact, but the brooch isn't worth entering up. There's a dime for you. Now git, please, I'm busy."

Beatrice clutched the coin and, almost forgetting to thank him, found her way up the iron stairs on to the platform of the elevated. Soon she was seated in the train, rattling and shaking on its way through the slums into the heart of the wonderful city. There was only one thing left for her to try, a thing which she had had in her mind for days. Yet she found herself, even now she was committed to it, thinking of what lay before her with something like black horror. It was her last resource, indeed. Strong though she was, she knew by many small signs that her strength was almost at an end. The days and weeks of disappointments, the long fruitless trudges from office to office, the heart-sickness of constant refusals, poor food, the long fasts, had all told their tale. She was attractive enough still. Her pallor seemed to have given her a wonderful delicacy. The curve of her lips and the soft light in her gray eyes, were still as potent as ever.

When she thought, though, what a poor asset her appearance had been, the color flamed in her cheeks.

In Broadway she made her way to a very magnificent block of buildings, and passing inside took the lift to the seventh floor. Here she got out and knocked timidly at a glass-paneled door, on which was inscribed the name of Mr. Anthony Cruxhall. A very superior young man bade her enter and inquired her business.

"I wish to see Mr. Cruxhall for a moment, privately," she said. "I shall not detain him for more than a minute. My name is Franklin—Miss Beatrice Franklin."

The young man's lips seemed about to shape themselves into a whistle, but something in the girl's face made him change his mind.

"I guess the boss is in," he admitted. "He's just got back from a big meeting, but I am not sure about his seeing any one to-day. However, I'll tell him that you're here."

He disappeared into an inner room. Presently he came out again and held the door open.

"Will you walk right in, Miss Franklin?" he invited.

Beatrice went in bravely enough, but her knees began to tremble when she found herself in the presence of the man she had come to visit. Mr. Anthony Cruxhall was not a pleasant-looking person. His cheeks were fat and puffy, he wore a diamond ring upon the finger of his too-white hand, and a diamond pin in his somewhat flashily arranged necktie. He was smoking a black cigar, which he omitted to remove from between his teeth as he welcomed his visitor.

"So you've come to see me at last, little Miss Beatrice!" he said, with a particularly unpleasant smile. "Come and sit down here by the side of me. That's right, eh? Now what can I do for you?"

Beatrice was trembling all over. The man's eyes were hateful, his smile was hideous.

"I have not a cent in the world, Mr. Cruxhall," she faltered, "I cannot get an engagement, I have been turned out of my rooms, and I am hungry. My father always told me that you would be a friend if at any time it happened that I needed help. I am very sorry to have to come and beg, yet that is what I am doing. Will you lend or give me ten or twenty dollars, so that I can go on for a little longer? Or will you help me to get a place among some of your theatrical people?"

Mr. Cruxhall puffed steadily at his cigar for a moment, and leaning back in his chair thrust his hand into his trousers' pocket.

"So bad as that, is it?" he remarked. "So bad as that, eh?"

"It is very bad indeed," she answered, looking at him quietly, "or you know that I should not have come to you."

Mr. Cruxhall smiled.

"I remember the last time we talked together," he said, "we didn't get on very well. Too high and mighty in those days, weren't you, Miss Beatrice? Wouldn't have anything to say to a bad lot like Anthony Cruxhall. You're having to come to it, eh?"

She began to tremble again, but she held herself in.

"I must live," she murmured. "Give me a little money and let me go away."

He laughed.

"Oh, I'll do better than that for you," he answered, thrusting his hand into his waistcoat pocket and drawing out a pile of dollar bills. "Let's look at you. Gee whiz! Yes, you're shabby, aren't you? Take this," he went on, slamming some notes down before her. "Go and get yourself a new frock and a hat fit to wear, and meet me at the Madison Square roof garden at eight o'clock. We'll have some dinner and I guess we can fix matters up."

Then he smiled at her again, and Beatrice, whose hand was already upon the bills, suddenly felt her knees shake. A great black horror was upon her. She turned and fled out of the room, past the astonished clerk, into the lift, and was downstairs on the main floor before she remembered where she was, what she had done. The clerk, after gazing at her retreating form, hurried into the inner office.

"Young woman hasn't bolted with anything, eh?" he asked.

Mr. Cruxhall smiled wickedly.

"Why, no," he replied, "I guess she'll come back!"

Tavernake left the meeting on that same afternoon with his future practically assured for life. He had been appointed surveyor to the company at a salary of ten thousand dollars a year, and the mine in which his savings were invested was likely to return him his small capital a hundredfold. Very kind things had been said of him and to him.

Pritchard and he had left the place together. When they had reached the street, they paused for a moment.

"I am going to make a call near here," Pritchard said. "Don't forget that we are dining together, unless you find something better to do, and in the meantime"—he took a card from his pocket and handed it to Tavernake—"I don't know whether I am a fool or not to give you this," he added. "However, there it is. Do as you choose about it."

He walked away a little abruptly. Tavernake glanced at the address upon the card: 1134, East Third Street. For a moment he was puzzled. Then the light broke in upon him suddenly. His heart gave a leap. He turned back into the place to ask for some directions and once more stopped short. Down the stone corridor, like one who flies from some hideous fate, came a slim black figure, with white face and set, horrified stare. Tavernake held out his hands and she came to him with a great wondering sob.

"Leonard!" she cried. "Leonard!"

"There's no doubt about me," he answered, quickly. "Am I such a very terrifying object?"

She stood quite still and struggled hard. By and by the giddiness passed.

"Leonard," she murmured, "I am ill."

Then she began to smile.

"It is too absurd," she faltered, "but you've got to do it all over again."'

"What do you mean?" he asked.

"Get me something to eat at once," she begged. "I am starving. Somewhere where it's cool. Leonard, how wonderful! I never even knew that you were in New York."

He called a carriage and took her off to a roof garden. There, as it was early, they got a seat near the parapet. Tavernake talked clumsily about himself most of the time. There was a lump in his throat. He felt all the while that tragedy was very near. By degrees, though, as she ate and drank, the color came back to her cheeks, the fear of a breakdown seemed to pass away. She became even cheerful.

"We are really the most amazing people, Leonard," she declared. "You stumbled into my life once before when I was on the point of being turned out of my rooms. You've come into it again and you find me once more homeless. Don't spend too much money upon our dinner, for I warn you that I am going to borrow from you."

He laughed.

"That's good news," he remarked, "but I'm not sure that I'm going to lend anything."

He leaned across the table. Their dinner had taken long in preparing and the dusk was falling now. Over them were the stars, the band was playing soft music, the hubbub of the streets lay far below. Almost they were in a little world by themselves.

"Dear Beatrice," he said, "three times I asked you to marry me and you would not, and I asked you because I was a selfish brute, and because I knew that it was good for me and that it would save me from things of which I was afraid. And now I am asking you the same thing again, but I have a bigger reason, Beatrice. I have been alone most of the last two years, I have lived the sort of life which brings a man face to face with the truth, helps him to know himself and others, and I have found out something."

"Yes?" she faltered. "Tell me, Leonard."

"I found out that it was you I cared for always," he continued, "and that is why I am asking you to marry me now, Beatrice, only this time I ask you because I love you, and because no one else in the world could ever take your place or be anything at all to me."

"Leonard!" she murmured.

"You are not sorry that I have said this?" he begged.

She opened her eyes again.

"I always prayed that I might hear you say it," she answered, "but it seems—oh, it seems so one-sided! Here am I starving and penniless, and you—you, I suppose, are well on the way towards the success you worshiped."

"I am well on the way," he said, earnestly, "towards something greater, Beatrice. I am well on the way towards understanding what success really is, what things count and what don't. I have even found out," he whispered, "the thing which counts for more than anything else in the world, and now that I have found it out, I shall never let it go again."

He pressed her hand and she looked across the table at him with swimming eyes. The waiter, who had been approaching, turned discreetly away. The band started to play a fresh tune. From down in the streets came the clanging of the cars. A curious, cosmopolitan murmur of sounds, but between those two there was the wonderful silence.

Lightning Source UK Ltd.
Milton Keynes UK
UKHW042213071019
351185UK00004B/133/P